TOP 10 HITS

A pop culture novel

Peter Travers

To fuck

*love
Peter
x x*

PETER TRAVERS PUBLISHING
www.petertravers.co.uk

TOP 10 HITS
A pop culture novel

Peter Travers was born in Bristol in 1972. He's a British journalist and author who writes for many reputable publications including *The Sunday Times*, BBC magazines and other best-selling titles. Although Peter only got an 'E' in his English GSCE exam, he's been working full-time on magazines since 1996. He lives in Bristol, and really likes it there. *TOP 10 HITS* is his first novel. He hopes you enjoy reading it.

More details at **www.petertravers.co.uk**

Praise for *TOP 10 HITS*

'It rocks and shocks!'
Stephen Lawson, Editor, *Total Guitar* magazine

'There's murder on the dance floor in this poptastic page-turner!'
Jeff Maysh, Senior Staff Writer, *Loaded*

'Well, well, well, somebody wants to murder his Top 10 most-hated pop stars. Could be Spinal Tap goes weird or it just could be true. One thing is for sure – I'm glad I'm not on the Hit List!'
Suzi Quatro, BBC Radio 2

'Breathless entertainment'
Joe Spurgeon, Editor, *Venue* magazine

'A thumping great read set to be a No.1 hit'
Adam Portingale, Publisher, *iDJ* magazine

'I'm in it so it's bound to be good'
Roy D Hacksaw, from Hacksaw, the second worst punk band in the West Country

For Verity, the No.1 in my life

No. 10

It's the final countdown
Europe

As far back as you can remember you always wanted to be a rock star.

It wasn't because you liked the idea of the fame and fortune, it wasn't because you wanted to have a long poodle perm and wear stone-washed denim, it wasn't because you wanted the glamour and girls, it wasn't because you'd written in your little yellow All About Me exercise book aged nine-years-old that 'one day I want to become a rock 'n' rolling star', and it wasn't because you wanted to play to thousands of adoring fans: it was simply because you loved rock music. Really loved it.

It was great bands like Led Zep, AC/DC and Guns N' Roses that lit a red-hot fire inside until... well, you'll get to that later... you just loved the hook of the huge monster riffs, the lull of the verse, the rise of the chorus that made everyone want to sing-along, and you really loved the solos that made you want to pick up a guitar and play it perfectly until each and every one of your fingers bled.

You struggled to play the guitar initially so you'd paid for some after school guitar lessons with your paper round money. For the first few months you could barely string a series of notes together and you got picked on at school for carrying your guitar bag on your back. But you stuck at it. Your tenacity and focus were strong even then. You remember your fingers ached as you held them in those funny positions as old Mr Parry drilled the basic chords into your head as you strummed and strummed your beloved guitar. Another year of school and extra lessons passed and finally you were slowly, painfully slowly, getting somewhere.

And then it clicked. You remember vividly because you'd been listening to *Sweet Child O' Mine* on your double cassette deck and you were somehow able to mimic Slash's riffs on your Les Paul. After only a few more listens you'd even nailed most of the chorus. The solo took another week, and copying Axel's primal screams took a little longer, but eventually, gloriously, you got it.

When you left school and formed your band, The Good, The Bad, and The Ugly, you loved jamming with Jim and Steveo, trying to play your songs you'd spent days and nights dreaming up and writing down. You eventually got to play your first gig in a dirty local pub. You can still vaguely recall the smell of smoke in the air and stale booze on the floor, but you'll never forget your songs rocking out of the pub's knackered old speakers, and the sound of the clapping and cheering at the end of that night.

You were finally starting to feel like a rock star.

*　　*

I don't really want to be here.

It's March and it's been a bitter, typical winter's day in Wales. Yet here, stood by the side of the stage in Cardiff's International Arena, I'm almost unbearably hot. It's a sell out Wednesday afternoon gig for the youth audience, but I'm sure the manager has let a bunch more in on the door to up his takings. I look back at the expectant faces as they all jostle for position in futile attempts to get a glimpse of the stage. Every now and then the cheers and screams get louder as they eagerly encourage the grand entrance of their so-called idols. I look at my watch. It's 3:40pm, still twenty minutes to go. We've already endured the solo 'celebrity' support act, Jimmy Fink, a sub-standard singer who's only claim to fame was coming third in *Pop Factory*. But the main act keep the crowd waiting. Probably because West Side need to preen their pretty boy faces and designer hairdos a few more times.

I'm glad I'm this side of the crowd as the hysteria steadily grows. There's nothing more damaging for your eardrums than piercing prepubescent screams. Actually, there is something worse, and that's the pop pap about to be sincerely – always sincerely – sung by the talent-free wonders due on stage.

As I said, I'm not exactly thrilled to be here.

I'm stood in the safety of the press area at the front of the stage along with a few other journalists and photographers milling about. I'm here reluctantly as my editor, Gary, felt it would be a good idea if I reported on West Side's Welsh gig for the next issue of our esteemed publication, *TOP 10 HITS*. He's getting his own back after I wrote that a prominent pop star called Princess is, in fact, a prince. My reliable source was Dan from *Guitar World* who works on the same floor as us at Good Publishing Network. He told me she'd had a sex change ten years ago. I later found out he was just winding me up and we had to print a full page retraction and apology. We were told she especially didn't like the *'Princess and the Penis'* headline. I thought it was inspired.

So now Gary gives all the boy band and girl band live reviews to me. I normally try and get more of the indie and rock gigs to write up, as long as the song or album has made it up somewhere near the top ten. A task that can be difficult for any proper and passionate musical-instrument-playing bands. The top ten seems to get filled up with painfully wet soulless soul, lame rock-lite groups, R&B (ironic that it's called that these days, when there's no rhythm or blues in the modern R&B, only disjointed drum beats and good looking guys and girls rapping and posing), regurgitated and mindless dance tunes, and the recent flop idol or pop 'talent' show winners/losers.

The crowd continues to cheer and jeer not-so-patiently for the four bum boys to make an entrance. At least it gives me the chance to scan the press pit for Sophie, a pretty pop photographer I met a couple of weeks ago. I have a good look around but instead I can only see Fat Pat grinning as he comes towards me.

"Alright Hardy, how's it hanging my son?" says Fat Pat as he smacks me on the shoulder. Fat Pat is a freelance writer for various tabloids, he's also a good friend and we go way back. Sweat's trying to escape from every one of his pores.

"Pat you twat." I say, genuinely surprised to see his fat, friendly face over in Wales. "What are you doing this side of the Severn Bridge!?"

"About to ask you same facking question Hardy," he says, London accent still intact. He's wearing a Sex Pistols T-shirt that hugs his generous belly tightly.

"Yeah, I got the short straw again as Gary's still pissed off with me," I say.

"Because of that Princess and her penis story fiasco?" laughs Fat Pat.

"Yep."

"Oh well. So how is *TOP 10* going these days?" asks Fat Pat.

TOP 10 HITS is a fun little, fortnightly 'music' magazine aimed squarely at the teen girl and boy demographic, reacting as quickly as possible to the latest musical fad or scene that's being listened to in playgrounds – even though our editor thinks forty per cent of our readers are older university students. Bless the poor, deluded fool. But Good Publishing Network is based in Bath, not London like all the big mags and daily papers, and that has it's good and bad sides.

3

What can I say? It's a job. It keeps me mostly out of mischief.

"It's top," I say flatly. "Mag sales could be a lot better."

"When're you going to become a journalist on a real music mag in the capital then Hardy?" says Fat Pat. This is one of the bad sides, the London lot think we're a farmyard outfit working out of barns in the countryside. But our readers don't care where we're based, as long as we keep banging out the same brightly coloured covers with photos of cute pop stars or starlets, they keep on buying our silly little magazine.

"Yeah, yeah, I'm working on it. *Q* and *Mojo* have my CV. Just waiting for the right reviews or features ed job to crop up," I say.

"Haven't heard anything back recently then?" asks Fat Pat.

"No, bugger all." Probably as I haven't actually sent them my CV.

"You should move up to London anyway. It's where it's at," says Fat Pat.

"I like the West Country. I like Bath, and Bristol's only next door."

"Too scared to join the rat race are you?"

"If you win the race, Pat, you're still a rat," I say.

We both turn to survey the crowd. A podgy teen girl with pink streaks in her hair and even pinker cheeks faints at the front. A burly security guard stretches over the barrier and picks her up not-all-that-delicately out of the crowd and carries her off to the first aid area. A gaggle of smiling mums and a few bored dads are in the background while infants through to teens bop about. I'm sure some of the kids are too tiny to be at a gig like this. It's like a school disco times fifty.

"That reminds me, I've got a question for you," says Fat Pat.

We look away from the kindergarten.

"How many five year olds do you reckon you could take on in a fight?" asks Fat Pat.

"Eh?"

"How many five year olds do you think you could beat up in an organised fight?"

"Good one. I like it," I say rubbing my chin.

"There are rules. They'll all be up for proper fighting even though they're only five years old, and they'll only come at you one at a time. But once you've entered combat with one, the following one can join in, and so on. You fight until either they're unconscious or you are," explains Pat.

"Cool, I see. There won't be hundreds of them piling on top of me then," I confirm.

"No. It's more like that old chop-socky arcade game where they only come at you after you've started scrapping," Fat Pat says. "The kids are motivated enough not to get scared regardless of the bloodshed and every little bugger will give it his/her best shot to take you down. The kids will be split 50/50 boy/girl. No weapons for them or you."

"Okay."

"So, how many could you beat in a scrap?"

"Erm, I feel pretty confident against those little blighters," I answer, glancing at a couple of what-I-think-are five year olds in the crowd. They look so small. "I could just continually, casually kick them in their faces. So I reckon around seventy or eighty."

"Not bad at all. That's a good bunch of unconscious five year olds," laughs Pat.

"What about picking one of the unconscious ones up by the legs and whacking the others with them?" I ask.

"Hadn't thought of that. Kiddie baseball. Nice," he says.

"That could get me up to one-fifty or so I reckon."

"You're probably right."

"So what's everyone else said?"

"Jez," Fat Pat points out a tall, goofy looking student journalist across the other side of the stage, "said about ten or fifteen. He's a soft twat though."

"Lame," I say.

"But Mikaela..."

"...the freelance photographer for the weekend magazines?"

"Yeah, that's her. She's over there." He points to a bright-faced girl who seems to be demonstrating some bizarre new dance routine that looks like a cross between karate and skipping. "She's got two little boys herself, and she said 'about 500 of the little bastards on a good day.'" Pat laughs his fat head off at this.

"Christ, I'd pay to see that fight," I say, scanning all the other snappers.

"Yeah. Don't mess with a nutty yummy mummy, eh?"

"And what about you, how many five year olds could you beat up in one go?"

"One more than you," says Fat Pat as he smiles smugly.

"You arsehole," I say.

I give up on Fat Pat and look around the press pit. I finally spot Sophie. She's got a red cap on, but I spy the unmistakable pony tail of brunette hair peaking out through the back of her hat. Her mane shines as it flickers in the spotlights.

I feel myself stirring downstairs. No, I don't mean I physically feel myself down my trousers. Or that I'm downstairs stirring some soup on the boil. More that I *sense* myself rousing from a slumber. I smile, and my throat goes dry. Sophie did that to me last time.

She's stood away from the other photographers, off to the left of the stage, intent on getting a different shot to the others probably.

I make my excuses with Fat Pat and move around the press pit so I can still see the stage, while being able to sneak a side profile view of Sophie. Her strong feminine cheekbones glow under the stage lights. She tucks a few strands of hair behind her ears as she plays with her camera lens. She's got a tight little black Foo Fighters T-shirt on that shows off her breasts while a pair of fitted jeans hug her arse for all they're worth. Lucky Diesels.

I almost forget we're waiting for those pretty little posers to come on stage until the sweaty, young crowd go into another screaming-as-loud-as-they-can phase. God, how late is fashionably late these days anyway? Is it even fashionable to be late anymore?

And, more importantly, what excuse shall I use to talk to Sophie?

*   *

As you jog along the side of the River Taff you smile to yourself. It's nice to be jogging for a purpose rather than jogging for ten miles from point-to-point with a 30kg Burgan on your back and a compass in your hand. You cross the river and pick up your pace a little from Castle Street down to the High Street. Welsh patriotism hangs in shop windows in the shape of flags and red dragon emblems. You watch the aimless, gormless shoppers wandering from window to window like a human railway line, shuffling from shop to shop, regardless of what's for sale. You continue jogging into St Mary Street, then turn left on to Caroline Street. You're breathing deeply and as you exhale a stream of vapour appears in the cold afternoon air. But you're not out of breath. You want to act the part and look like a real jogger, a slightly unfit one as you'd decided. You take a sip of water from the tube poking out from your CamelBak on your back then cross the junction to Bridge Street, and on to Mary Ann Street and destination X.

You trot down Mary Ann Street to find a few stragglers hanging around the side of the Cardiff International Arena. A lone tout is attempting to flog his last handful of black-market tickets. You wipe the sweat from your brow and, at the same time, surreptitiously check your black haired wig is still in place. It hasn't moved since you carefully glued it in place two hours ago. It felt weird when you first tried it on and looked in the mirror. The straight hair tickled your ears unlike your closely cropped crew cut, but anybody who meets you today wouldn't know you any different, and when you'd done a quick trial run down the local shops you didn't get any funny looks. That gave you extra confidence.

As you round the corner to find the Arena's main entrance, you clock a handful of small, medium and overweight security guards. Just as you'd predicted. You continue past them and jog around the back to the fire exit. You'd disabled the alarm on the door the night before with a simple bit of rewiring, plus you already know there's no CCTV covering this door. Even so, you lean against a wall and do a few mock jogger stretches. After checking nobody from security's followed you around the back, you use the metal ruler from your CamelBak to slide between the lock to ease the door open, and slip quietly inside. You check your watch. It's 3:40pm. Bang on schedule. The support act will be clear of the stage by now and you have twenty minutes to get in, setup before the boy band hits the stage, and get out.

You can hear the screams of the anticipation from the crowd as you saunter down a long, empty corridor. You quickly find the cleaning cupboard you're after and nip inside. The smell of cleaning products inside the cupboard is almost overwhelming. You slide the CamelBak off your back, get out the black security guard shirt and ID badge you've had knocking around the flat and adapted the night before, and swap it with your white jogging top. You keep your black jogging bottoms and black trainers on. With the security shirt on you're reminded of those long, teeth-grindingly boring hours spent staring at ranks of CCTV screens through the night in a tiny office in a basement. Those tedious rounds of the empty office floors without seeing a soul the whole night. It won't be that boring today. Using a cloth you've brought, you carefully put a small, homemade black box in your pocket without getting your fingerprints over it. You stash the CamelBak behind some floor cleaner and get yourself into security mode as you head into the corridor and towards backstage.

The temperature rises the closer you get to the stage. Riggers and roadies are hanging around corridors looking busy but nobody gives you a second glance as you stride past to stand by the side of the stage. You'd already checked the roadies working today would be a mixture of local labourers as well as the touring party – otherwise a close-knit crew might spot you as an impostor. Security men wander around with the same black shirt and ID badge as yours. You're proud of your attention to detail. You move along by the side of the stage. You're almost in position now.

For the last four months you've been meticulously planning this moment. You've started taking less security shifts and bodyguard work to dedicate time to your little pop project. You're dipping into the money you'd saved when you did your long and enjoyable tour of duty in The Gulf. You were going to use it to buy a house one day, but you've decided this is a much more worthy cause. You think back to Christmas when all around you people were at parties, getting boozed up and fat on turkey, and swapping presents, while you were indoors, planning and setting up your Top 10.

Your Top 10 Hit List.

You smirk when you remember how those two blokes back in the pub in Liverpool last November inspired your killer idea.

Killer idea, indeed.

*   *

You were sat in your local on the outskirts of Liverpool, with one ear on the pub's stereo and the other eavesdropping on a couple of young men chatting on the table opposite.

"The real problem is there's no proper rock stars anymore," said the spiky haired one.

It had been over twenty years since you first played the old classic *Sweet Child O' Mine* all the way through, and over ten years since you'd picked up your guitar. It was a dull November evening and rain trickled down the outside of the pub's windows as inside the bass-heavy stereo pumped out *The Bends*. You sipped on your Jack Daniels and coke and listened in on the two men while you continued to read your book.

"It's all about banal, over produced pop crap and manufactured music these days," said the one with the trimmed goatie.

"Yeah, yeah, I know what you mean mate," said his spiky haired friend.

"What's pop about it? It's not popular with me that's for sure," said goatie beard.

"The charts and music scene are just shite these days," said Spiky flatly.

They were both in their mid-to-late twenties, dressed in bright T-shirts, baggy, low-slung jeans and trendy trainers. You were sat at a table in the corner of the pub while punters chatted over drinks and cigarettes at the bar. Wafts of tobacco smoke slowly wandered in your direction as you quietly read your book and enjoyed your Jack Daniels. You were dressed down in an old, dark blue T-shirt and your favourite pair of faded Levi's. Only your sturdy footwear hinted at your past. You turned the page of your book but found yourself being drawn back to their conversation. You felt exactly the same about today's sodding music scene.

"The Brit indie scene has been getting progressively better but the pop music crap still outnumbers the good," said Beardy.

"I can never listen to the radio for long. You might get one good song, then it's the same tosh over and over again," said Spiky.

"It's so frustrating. I used to really love the charts. Used to buy *Smash Hits* magazine and watch *Top Of The Pops* religiously every week when I was a kid. I even used to tape the Top 40 on Radio 1 on a Sunday night with Simon Mayo!" said Beardy excitedly.

You smiled. When you used to tape the Top 40 you even used to pause the recording when Mayo was rabbiting on or if he cut to the news. But you liked to record all of the Top 10 count down before Mayo announced that week's No.1. You remembered sitting in your bedroom anticipating the new No.1, with the hairs standing up on the back of your neck. But you hadn't felt like that for a long time.

"But now *Smash Hits* has closed and *Top Of The Pops* has been axed. Ironic, really, considering there's tons more cheesy pop fodder for them these days," said Spiky.

You couldn't remember the last time you heard a song in the charts you felt compelled to buy. You couldn't remember the last time you saw the chart countdown on TV. Was it even still on terrestrial or on one of the cable channels? Your mouth went dry at the thought. You took a long glug on your drink, playing with an ice cube in your mouth until it melted.

"I don't think it's just cos we've gotten older either. The radio and telly was never full of this many chancers who couldn't play instruments or write their own songs," said Spiky. "What's happened to the real music by honest musicians who could hold a tune?"

"Exactly, mate. What the hell is that latest horseshit from West Side for starters?" Beardy said slurring slightly. "They're just churning out another naff old cover version while sat on some stools."

"It sucks that these pretty boys have made it while real musicians get left in the wilderness. It doesn't matter if they sound amazing, it's not enough anymore," said Spiky.

You didn't look up from your book but you stopped reading. This was what drove you insane when you were in The Good, The Bad, and The Ugly. You were a talented bunch, Steveo on bass, Jim on drums, you on lead guitar and vocals. You had some bloody good songs too. You had to practice all the time, and there were many late nights perfecting the lyrics and guitar licks, but you played pretty tight most of the time. You went down well on the local circuit and you half filled nearly all the venues on your mini tour of the UK. Your EP did okay and sold a few thousand through independent record shops, and your first and only single, *Hot Dog*, even got played on John Peel's Radio 2 show when he was still around. An *Enemy* magazine live review described your band as: *'Outdated grungy guitarists who need to drag themselves away from the '80s cock rock band influences and lame Led Zeppelin pretences – a better looking frontman wouldn't hurt either'*. You weren't happy about the last bit or the idea that you tried to mimic Plant and Page's lot, yet as first reviews go you were pretty chuffed.

But after years of hard graft trying to progress beyond the pub scene, you were told bluntly by your record label that you simply didn't look the part. They dropped you and your band like a stone, and your rock star dreams ended right there.

It still hurts whenever you think about it.

"What really gets me is all the TV talent shows encouraging the fame-hungry halfwits and talent-less wannabes to saturate the TV and radio..." said Beardy.

"Yeah! That wonky toothed winner..." said Beardy.

"Loser!" said Spiky.

"Yeah, that loser's rendition of Elvis's *Suspicious Minds* was so bad it was insulting. Must've had The King turning in his grave."

"There's nothing worse than bloody *Pop Factory*."

"Yeah there is... *American Pop Factory!*"

You casually glanced up at the men laughing before returning to your book. The scream of a custom exhaust outside was followed closely by a siren and flashing blue and white. You loved living back home after working away and being based in Hereford for so long. Now you'd take any excuse to get out again.

"I saw an interview last week with Hoodwink on MTV. God damn boy bands. They were so cocky and confident," said Spiky. "Playing up to the camera and posing around. They had nothing interesting to say and it was insulting how bad their song was."

They should've tried working for them. You'd been a bodyguard and security for boy bands like them. You'd got to witness their egos and arrogance growing firsthand. You'd thought about kicking their heads in more than once.

"They're all just a bunch of karaoke singers aren't they? And they're murdering the songs too," spat Spiky. He was getting angry.

"Murdering, yeah..." repeated Beardy, laughing a little. "What we need is a murderer! Someone to purge the pop charts."

Your ears perked up. They were talking your language. You peered across at Beardy and Spiky. Sod it. You decided you'd join them. You folded down the corner of the page and closed your old copy of Hugh Laurie's *The Gun Seller* – it was funny as you'd hoped, and funnier still when the main character was tortured. You finished your drink and walked over to their table as Thom Yorke started singing about some fake plastic trees on the stereo.

"Sorry lads, don't mean to eavesdrop," you said casually in your Scouse dialect, "but I couldn't help overhearing."

Spiky eyed you up and down cautiously. Beardy just grinned at you. You thought he liked the idea he'd had an audience.

10

"I couldn't agree more," you said in your friendliest manner. "The bloody music scene has been frustrating me for years."

"Good man!" said Beardy.

Spiky eased up and let out a smile of sorts.

"What are you drinking?" you said pointing at their nearly empty glasses. "I'm off up to the bar anyway."

"Stella!" They said in unison.

"He seems a nice bloke," you thought you heard Beardy say as you were stood at the bar. From the corner of your eye you saw Spiky glance up at you.

"Big bugger ain't he, though. Did you see his forearms?"

"Yeah. Cool old school tattoos 'n' all. He's an old rocker I reckon," said Beardy.

You placed each pint down in front of Spiky and Beardy and pulled up a chair.

"What's your name, mate?" asked Spiky.

"Rob," you lied instinctively. No need to use your real name.

You chatted away, breaking the ice by talking about great albums. "Especially classics like this one of Radiohead's," you said, pointing up to the pub's speakers. "Has to be good albums though, stuff from The Stone Roses, Led Zep, Nirvana, G 'n' R or something."

Beardy and Spiky nodded in agreement as they eagerly swigged at their fresh pints. Soon enough you were all laughing and joking as you compared theories on the artificial pop singers that were churning up the charts.

As the slender, understated tones of *Street Spirit* started to seep of out the stereo, you felt it was time to change the conversation back to what had really interested you.

"So, how do you think we should knock off all these celebrity-seeking singers and bloody boy bands then?" you said, drinking deeply on your JD.

The pair of them cracked up. They loved this. But you couldn't understand why.

You were being serious.

*   *

As you stand by the stage, you wonder if Spiky and Beardy would recognise you if they saw you now. Doubt it, if they weren't pissed when you'd met them, they were when you'd finished with them. Besides, today's trusty disguise solves that problem. You stroke your wig and pad down a strand of hair by your ear as if it was your own.

From the left-hand side of the stage you take in its sheer size as the lights flash around and out and over the crowd. The kids' cheering goes loud to quiet as you peer around the corner to check them out. So that's what a proper-sized crowd looks like from a proper-sized stage. You didn't get that sort of crowd when The Good, The Bad, and The Ugly played down the local juicer. You nearly let yourself dwell in the moment but you're quick to stay focused.

You look across the stage. Roadies stroll back and forth, a couple of them carry out final sound checks. As they're finishing up you check your watch. 3:53pm. You realise it's now or never.

*   *

Like the kindergarten crowd, even I'm getting restless now. These little pop tarts better get on stage soon or I will just piss off to the pub and write my review from there. It'll be the same songs and the same show with the same 'fabulous' light display as every other gig West Side's played throughout the UK so far. The crowd show their boredom too as the rise and fall of their cheers get further apart.

To be honest, the only reason I've stuck around is because of Sophie. She is still diligently taking aim, ready to fire off a few rounds as soon as the band take to the stage. I think of what I'm going to say to her. But, after mulling over some lame chat-up lines, I decide I'm not going to walk over and reel off any pre-planned spiel. No, Sophie deserves better than that. I'm just going to go over and have a quick chat. Just say hello. Just be myself.

"Hello," I say when I reach Sophie's side. After feeling like a nervy school boy, I feel strangely relaxed.

"Hi," says Sophie. She looks up briefly, before returning to carefully cleaning the lens of her camera.

"We met at the West Side gig in Birmingham, I'm Hardy," I say, "from *TOP 10 HITS* magazine."

"I know, I remember you," says Sophie. "You were very drunk." She doesn't take her eyes off her camera.

"There was a big free bar, and I was very bored," I say a little sheepishly.

"Know how you feel. I've been bloody commissioned to photograph every bloody West Side gig for their official UK bloody tour book. I've been bored for weeks."

"Christ!" I say, "and I thought I had it bad being sent to review three of their UK gigs."

"Think yourself lucky, Hardy." She looks up at me for the first time, peering underneath the peak of her cap, smiling as she says my name. I notice her dark brown eyes as the stage lights flicker overhead. I also notice how tall she is. She must be around 5ft 8in as she still has to look up at me. I like her height. It's a nice height. A very nice height. Not too short, not too tall.

"I guess I am lucky if you look at it like that," I say, "That's twenty-odd gigs isn't it?"

"Twenty bloody four," she says.

I melt when she says 'bloody' in her clipped, oh-so English accent.

Suddenly the lights change colour as rays of white, orange and green shoot down and around the stage. West Side's intro music booms from the stage speakers. The crowd are quick to react and release a tidal wave of cheers and screams. It's deafening. This means Sophie and I have to do that lovely, intimate act people do at concerts of getting closer to talk in each other's ears.

"Well, you look like you're enjoying yourself, I've seen how thorough you are at setting up your shots," I say into her pretty little ear. I can smell a sweet concoction of perfume and shampoo.

"I like to be professional whoever I'm shooting," she shouts in my ear, the heat from her breath warming the inside. It feels lovely. I'm glad I slapped on some Boss aftershave this morning now.

"But doesn't the music do your nut in after a while?" I shout in her ear.

"It did my brain in before the first gig. I bloody hate the shite West Side are churning out," she laughs loudly, putting her hand on my shoulder to get closer. I think I almost feel her nose brush up on my neck and behind my ear. Is she *smelling* me?

"So what music *do* you like then?" I shout in her shell-like.

She thrusts her bust out to proudly show off her Foo Fighters T-shirt, pointing at her chest just in case I didn't gather that she's a fan of Dave Grohl's rock lot.

Then Sophie does something to make me fall in love with her.

To emphasize her music of choice Sophie lets her camera hang around her neck and does a full-on air guitar solo. Screwing her face up and contorting her body. Oh shit. I'm in trouble now. Even her air guitar turns me on.

"I like rock music, of course!" she shouts, unleashing a gleaming smile.

*　　　*

You look across the stage now dowsed in coloured light and a surge of adrenalin rushes through your veins. You take a deep breath and stroll nonchalantly up on stage. You head to the mixer junction station at the rear of the stage where it's dark, and swiftly unplug the middle mic's cable and plug it into the little black box you had in your pocket, plugging the other end of your box into the junction station. You're careful not to leave fingerprints on the box, holding it with the cloth from your pocket.

You learned a lot about electrics from setting up your own PA systems for countless gigs back in the day. Your little box of tricks switches the wiring so the earth of the microphone is actually connected to the live socket on the mixer. It also disconnects the real live wire and neutral to avoid blowing the circuit. The roadies are too wrapped up in their own role or ogling the crowd to care what you're doing. You quickly get off stage, but as you look towards the press pit, a female photographer in a red cap takes a picture of the stage. You think about quickly knocking her out and nicking her camera... but then you realise she's just testing the light and composing shots before the boy band come on stage. You keep your cool and slip into the darkness backstage, into a corner away from everyone else.

A voice on the PA says, "Ladies and gentlemen, mums and dads, boys and girls, please give it up... for West Side!" The crowd goes hysterical.

Mums? Boys? Girls? This is why these fuckwits are able to sell records. It's the under-developed, under-educated ears of the youngsters and housewives who know no better than to buy it.

From where you're standing you get a rear view of five boys in bright blue suits bouncing on stage. The two on the outside grab their microphones and start shouting, "Come on Cardiff, come on Cardiff!" as some mindless dance beat booms from the giant speakers. All five jump straight into an energetic dance routine. Just when you think the crowd can't scream any louder, they go nuclear. You can't believe the entire first 'song' has no lyrics, just a load of dancers prancing about. Jesus Christ. They're not even natural dancers, they look like a bunch of fat kids at a youth club party.

You've already justified why you've created a Top 10 Hit List. The music scene and pop charts need purging. And there's no better example of manufactured music than West Side and their formulaic ballads and constant crappy cover versions – that are *never* an improvement on the originals. Not one of the five arse bandits in the 'band' can write a song, read music or play an instrument. It's glorified, glossy karaoke.

For them, it's not about making music, it's about making money.

You've singled out Dazza because he's the celebrity-obsessed, gobby, egotistical, deluded wanker who thinks he's some kind of modern-day, British Sinatra. He's not got an ounce of talent compared to Ole Blue Eyes. So when they come on stage and just shuffle and jump about, you justify to yourself what's going to happen a little bit more.

West Side stop dancing.

The music stops.

The lights go down.

The crowd go mental.

In the darkness five roadies quickly line up five stools and five mics in a row and sprint off stage. A spotlight is switched on to the central mic and stool. Dazza, the slightly overweight one with the ridiculous spiky hair, walks in to the light. As his face moves into the spotlight, he sweeps his hair back from his glistening face and releases a cocky smile for the crowd. Still breathing hard from dance routine, he leans into the mic and wraps both of his sweaty hands around it, theatrically preparing to begin one of their big ballads. Thankfully he doesn't get that far. He doesn't even get to sing a note: 240 volts raging through his blue-suited body put a stop to that.

You've seen someone get electrocuted by direct current when you were in the Gulf so you know the whole body goes into spasm, and all their muscles contract making it impossible to let go of whatever they've inadvertently grabbed hold of. Yet it's actually the amps that are bad for the body, not all those volts. So you were careful to make sure your little black box pushes 250 milliamps through the cable, enough to shock an elephant. The live current is making Dazza vibrate on the spot.

It certainly gives a new meaning to appearing 'Live On Stage'.

The crowd love it. They think Dazza's jerking around on purpose. They think he's still *dancing*. As demented body popping goes it's pretty impressive. His band mates aren't quite so happy to see their mate violently convulsing and a couple of them shout at roadies to shut the power down.

A skinny roadie rushes past you to the main mixing desk and shuts down the power to the mics. Dazza finally lets go of the mic and drops to the floor in an awkward, podgy heap. One of his arms flops out with his hand facing the ceiling. You can just make out the electrical burn marks on his palm. As he lies motionless, the crowd's screams of joy slowly but surely transform into screams of terror as one by one they realise what's happened. Chaos spreads through the crowd. They don't know whether to run, or stand and stare. Some mums drag their kids away, others shield their own eyes. Roadies dash from one side of the stage to the other, while the four remaining band members are dragged off stage, presumably for their own safety. Amazingly the spotlight stays on Dazza.

Security starts ushering the shocked crowd out and eventually a paramedic runs on stage and gets to his knees to check for a pulse. He rolls Dazza over on his side, clears his air way, then rolls him on his back and starts carrying out CPR. After five futile minutes he stops. A small collection of roadies circle around Dazza and the paramedic. You move closer to the stage to see the paramedic's reaction. He looks up to a man, West Side's manager probably, wearing a white shirt and black tie. The paramedic looks apologetic as he shakes his head. Cardiac arrest. A shudder runs down your spine and you ease backwards.

As you slip off towards the corridor, you see the red-capped photographer in the press pit again. She looks uneasy and unsure whether to take a picture of dead Dazza. Business-sense takes over and she quickly fires off a succession of shots before being escorted out of the press pit. That's it girl. You wouldn't want your first hit, your No.10, not to make it into the media.

While the chaos continues, and the crowds frenetically disperse among panicking roadies and security, you take the opportunity to slip unnoticed back to the corridor and cleaning cupboard. You quickly change back into the jogger's outfit, stash the security stuff into your CamelBak, and you're back out the fire exit and into the late afternoon sun in less than two minutes.

After the intense heat by the stage, the cold air feels freezing as you inhale a lungful, but as you casually break into a jog and leave the shocked crowds coming out and looking lost in the street, you can't stop grinning. "You've done it," you say quietly under your breath. "You've fucking done it."

Your Top 10 countdown has begun. One hit down, nine to go.

*   *

I was standing next to Sophie when the pop tarts took to the stage, and I was still next to her when Dazza lined up to launch into song. I remember because I'd taken my eyes off her in the press pit to see what Dazza was going to sing first up on stage. I remember staring up at him almost interested to see if he was going to sing their latest 'hit' or something new. I say almost because really I was dreading his weasel-like voice ringing throughout the stadium for the next hour or so.

But, when he didn't even manage to squeeze out a note before being electrocuted, it was almost comical, and almost a relief. I know this sounds bad, disrespectful even, but I nearly started giggling when he was spazzing out still grappling the microphone. It was just so... well, entertaining. Ironic, really, as when they're singing and performing I find West Side anything but.

Suddenly everybody, journalists and photographers included, are being ushered outside by security staff. The lights go on and the crowds pour out the main doors and fire exits while a Welsh voice over the PA asks everyone to remain calm as they leave the building. A paramedic appears on stage as roadies gather around the body. All the other journalists and photographers have been dragged away, but Sophie and I have been overlooked as we're on the side of the press pit. I stick around to see what's happened to Dazza, while Sophie takes a bunch of photos.

It finally takes some roadies to manhandle Sophie and me towards the exit before we leave. But we don't reach the exit. Two smarter looking security guards in shirts and ties grab us and ask us to follow them through a side door. Sophie looks scared and holds her camera close to her chest, but smiles when she realises I'm by her side. I want to hug her, reassure her everything will be alright.

In a small, windowless office we're greeted by a smartly dressed, greasy faced man who introduces himself as the "Cardiff International Arena Manager." He has a short, uniformed policeman with a moustache by his side. The moustache isn't by his side, it's on the policeman's top lip. The policeman's helmet is tucked under his right arm, a notepad in his left hand. The police act fast around here it seems. Must've been on site already. Perhaps the police like West Side's music.

"We won't keep you a minute," says the cop politely. He takes down our names, job details and work addresses, then says, "We just want to ask if you saw anything suspicious when you were in the press area before West Side came on stage."

Sophie and I look at each other, then shake our heads.

"Not that I can remember," I say.

"No, I don't recall anything out of the ordinary," says Sophie, her voice slightly shaky.

"What sort of thing are you looking for then?" I ask.

The manager glares at me. He doesn't like me asking questions. Hey, I'm a journalist, it's my job.

"We're not at liberty to say just yet, sir," says the cop.

"So you don't think it was just an accident?" I ask.

The manager glares at me again, the cop smiles without giving me an answer.

"Did you see anyone hanging around on stage that looked out of place?" asks the cop.

"Not really. Roadies were going back and forth doing roadie things – aren't they always? – but nobody really stood out," I say.

"Same here," says Sophie. Her sweet face looks so worried.

"Are you sure you didn't see anyone looking suspicious? Or anything suspicious?" asks the cop with slightly more authority in his Welsh accent.

Ever since a local cop gave me a rough time for throwing crab apples at Mr 'Grumpy' Gregory's windows when I was fourteen, I've not been a big fan of the police (not counting Sting's lot). And when I was twenty five I was walking down Park Street in Bristol as a bunch of blokes fell out of a pub and started scrapping. I stopped to watch, it was good value viewing, but when the cops arrived they only aggravated matters. At one point it was hard to spot who were the scrappers and who were the coppers, and then they started arresting anyone in the vicinity, me included. So I spent a night in cells with a group of bruised brawlers drunk on Blackthorn. Not had much respect for cops since really.

And now, as much as I'd like this cop to catch whoever did whatever it is they think they did, I'm enjoying the fact I can't help them.

"Sorry, but as I'm sure you're aware, Sophie and I are a little shocked – no pun intended – after what's happened." I'm lying. I don't feel shocked at all, I'm feeling quite excited to be honest, but they're both beginning to get on my tits, and Sophie is clearly uncomfortable so I think it's time we got out. "If that's all we would like to get some fresh air now please."

The manager turns crimson but before he can explode the cop, realising he has no right to detain us any longer, simply opens the door allowing us to leave.

"Thank you for your time," he says.

It's still light outside as the March sun pokes its head above the office blocks and high rise car park across the road. I squint into the sunshine. I always find it hard to adjust to daylight when I've been indoors in the dark. Like when I've been to an afternoon matinee at the cinema, it always confuses me heading outside to be greeted by daylight.

Parents console children in the streets, while others from the youth audience wander around aimlessly. Sophie and I slip our jackets on, she throws a scarf around her neck, and we walk away from the Arena.

"Thanks for that," she says, still clutching her camera tight to herself.

"Eh?" I say.

"Thanks. Y'know, for getting us out of there so quickly," she says quietly. I think she's being a bit shy.

"That's alright. You looked like you needed to get out. You okay?" I say softly. She's obviously upset after seeing Dazza's body popping act on stage.

"Yeah, I'm okay," she says sweetly.

"Are you a bit upset after seeing what happened to Dazza?" I ask.

"Nah, not at all!" she says suddenly brightening up. "I was just shitting myself they were going to want me to hand over my camera and memory cards that's all."

I laugh out loud, partly relieved that she's okay and partly surprised that she wasn't upset after all. There's more to this pretty girl than meets the eye.

"I've got shots of Dazza before, during and after, you see. I don't think the other photographers got anything from where they were standing, plus they were too stunned and got dragged away by security from what I saw. These photos could be worth a whack if I'm clever," she says holding up a Compact Flash card she'd hidden in the front pocket of her jeans.

"You little beauty," I say, letting a little affection slip out. "I can't believe the cop didn't ask if you might've captured something on camera."

"Yeah, what a pair of idiots. That manager was such a greasy little git." She's laughing now. "I don't know about you, but I could really do with a pint."

She drinks pints. I love slim, sexy girls who drink pints. Oh no. Be cool, Hardy, be cool. "A pint sounds great," I say as casually as I can.

We cross the road and walk straight into one of Cardiff's fine public houses.

"But I think we should listen to *The Colour And The Shape*. I love *Monkey Wrench*, and *Everlong* near the end is awesome," she says.

"But there's not much substance in between. Nope, his first album was his best, so much more upbeat and punk than his more recent slant towards stadium rock. I'm putting that on," I say. I slip the CD into the player.

But after the chorus of *This Is A Call* she ejects Dave Grohl's fine debut album. "Let's put on something we *both* fancy listening to," she suggests.

"Okay," I say giving in.

We're in my red, slightly grubby, slightly worse for wear Golf GTI heading down the M4 back towards the Severn Bridge, and England. The day has given way to night. I've convinced Sophie that it would be a good idea for me to drop her home in Bristol on my way back to Bath. We only had three pints of Guinness each in Cardiff – 1 loved the way she gulped down pints of the black stuff – so our logic said I'm good to drive now it's dark. Plus I've only been sipping (surreptitiously, of course, I'm driving!) on one of the four-pack of beers we bought in the off licence for the drive home. Sophie's cracking into her second can.

"So…" she says smiling and flicking through my CD wallet I keep in the car, "…we've got Maximo Park, Elastica, Brendan Benson, Moby, Rage Against The Machine, Nina Simone, Public Enemy…"

I know my CD wallet off by heart. For instance, I could tell her I've got Queens Of The Stone Age, Portishead, Coldplay, Dean Martin, Radiohead, AC/DC, The Killers, Arctic Monkeys, Stone Temple Pilots, The Beatles, Franz Ferdinand, the *Grosse Pointe Blank* soundtrack, and more, and even more again with my colossal collection on my iPod that I rig up to the stereo, but I let Sophie enjoy flicking through the CDs for now.

"…The Pixies, Stone Roses, Norah Jones, Jimi Hendrix, The Beach Boys, Athlete. Quite a cool, eclectic mix you've got here Hardy…"

"Never know what mood I'm going to be when driving. I like to be prepared for every eventuality," I say. I like the fact she likes my music. That used to be one of my main criteria when searching for girls, trying to find one with the same music tastes. Perhaps that's why I've got such a varied music collection. Different music for different girls. I hope I look for more important things in the fairer sex now.

"…oooh, oooh, you've got Jimmy Eat World's *Bleed American*. Ace! Can we listen to this? Pleeease?" Her clipped accent is getting huskier after drinking, but she still sounds so sweet. How can I refuse? Besides, it's one of my favourite CDs.

"Sure thing," I say.

The title track *Bleed American* kicks off nicely. As we pass Newport, and Jimmy Eat World tear into *Praise Chorus*, I decide to blurt out what's been on my mind since we left Cardiff.

"So, Dazza then. Sorry if this sounds harsh. But he's not exactly a great loss to the music industry is he?" I say. I put my foot down and the Golf accelerates hard as I pull into the outside lane.

Sophie stares out of the window for a while, staring at the cars pouring back down the other side of the motorway. She sips her beer. It's a while before she replies.

"I was going to take the moral high ground and say 'How can you say that? Somebody's just died' and all that crap. But, oddly enough, that's not how I feel at all," she says. "You're right, the charts won't be missing anything now he's gone, and I'm not gutted I won't have to tour the rest of UK trying to take interesting shots of the same show every day either."

"That's the spirit. Let's hope the others disappear into oblivion now, and don't try and continue touring on the back of everyone's misguided grief," I say.

"God, yeah, that would be rubbish," says Sophie, pausing briefly. "This might sound weird, but were you excited when Dazza was freaking out on stage?"

"Yeah, totally. It was like we were witnessing musical history or something," I say.

"I felt such a rush when it was happening, I couldn't resist clicking away with my camera," says Sophie.

"I haven't experienced that mixture of feeling both excited and disturbed since I saw Bjork take a dump on stage mid-song when she was still with the Sugarcubes."

"Nice." Sophie laughs, a real guttural, heart felt bellow. "I remember reading about the little Inuit princess doing that!"

Jimmy Eat World's *Authority Song* bounds out of the car stereo as we cruise over the 'new' bridge and across the murky Severn estuary churning about way below.

"Do you think somebody could be behind Dazza's involuntary electric boogaloo then?" asks Sophie quietly, her tone slightly more serious.

"I don't know. I'm not sure. Accidents can happen. But it's possible someone could've rigged up the mic to electrocute Dazza, I guess." I pause to look at Sophie, she's taken off her red cap and is stroking her long, deep brown ringlets, twirling a few of them around her finger. The shine on her locks is stunning. I can't help myself. "Your hair looks really nice when you wear it down," I say.

"Thank you," she says quietly. I could be wrong, but when some passing headlights highlight her face, I think her cheeks have turned slightly rouge.

That's what always amazes me about women. They're the most complicated and confusing thing known to man, and yet offer them a simple compliment, and they can be deeply touched. I must remember to give compliments more often. It's nice to be nice. Sophie turns her head slightly and skilfully hides her face with a curtain of hair.

"Yeah, it's possible somebody could've tampered with the mic," she says softly.

"Yet one thing's for sure. If somebody did do it, I wish I could meet them," I say.

"You want to be careful what you wish for Hardy Matthews," she says.

We continue the rest of drive back on the M4 in a comfortable silence, only discussing whether to listen to GWR or Radio 1 or something else. News of Dazza's death hasn't reached the radio stations yet. All the stations seem to be playing the same pop plop so I put another CD on. As we're heading up to the M32 junction for Bristol, Sophie turns down the stereo a little.

"It's been a weird day and I don't know about you, but I don't want to go home and be on my own in my flat just yet," she says.

21

"Shall I come back to Bath with you for a couple more drinks? Would that be okay?"

"Of course," I say, slightly higher pitched than I would've liked. I cough, regaining my usual slightly deeper tone, and say casually, "That would be cool. I could do with another drink and some company this evening."

I accelerate steadily as we pass the Bristol junction and continue up the M4 to the Bath turn off. Today just keeps getting better and better. I try not to smile too brightly. But inside I'm fucking beaming.

No. 9

Try to see it my way, only time will tell if I am right or I am wrong
We Can Work It Out, The Beatles

Back in Bath *Back in Black* ramps out of the car stereo. I park up close-ish – three streets away – to my flat in Camden Crescent but Sophie and I both happily wait until Brian Johnson's wailing vocals and *that* Angus Young guitar riff tail off before I turn the stereo off and we get out of the car. It seems rude to leave before they've finished.

In my flat I freshen up in the bathroom, and throw on a slightly cleaner T-shirt. As an after thought I wet my hands and run my wet fingers through my excuse of a hairstyle. It's dark brown, middle-ish length, and does me just fine.

Sophie takes the time to download her photos via a digital card reader to my Apple Mac, and uses my broadband connection to upload her pictures of 'Dying Dazza on stage' and 'Dead Dazza on stage' to her photo agency's website. She gives her agency a quick call and puts the digital card back in her pocket. Takes her all of fifteen minutes. At the same time I call my editor quickly and tell him the bad news (Dazza is dead) and good news (I was there to see it) in case it's not made it on to this evening's news. It hasn't. Gary's unable to contain his shock and excitement but I tell him I'll speak to him in the morning in detail about us running a big exclusive story. I hang up and then Sophie and I are out the door and back into the night.

"I haven't been out much in Bath," says Sophie as we walk under the streetlights.

"Well, I'd better show you a mixture of grotty pubs and posh bars then," I say.

"Ideal."

We start with pints in the Farmhouse, my local little dive around the corner, followed by the plush Grappa bar further down Lansdown Road for reassuringly expensive cocktails. Then we fall down the hill into town to take in some locally-brewed ale in the old wooden charm of the Star Inn. From there we shuffle down the steps off the Paragon to The Bell on Walcot Street to see a fun folk band and have a fruity beer I'm still not sure the name of (think it might've been Strange Brew, but I could be getting confused with the Cream song).

Perched on a bench facing the singing, bearded band, Sophie turns to me and asks, "Where exactly are you from? Your accent is…"

"A little village outside Bristol. I'm a West Country Boy, that side of my accent will be the local schooling, although the parents are from London so that's why I'm not so much 'Yer, babber, where that rough zider too? Cheers, ta, cocker etc' I guess."

"Babber? Cocker?" she laughs.

"Aaaaargh, that's roight!" I say in my bestest Bristolian. "Plus working in Baaath waters down the old aaaaacccccent, like. And what about you, my luver?"

"Grew up on the outskirts of Oxford, hence the slightly posh, slightly proper English accent I'm stuck with," says Sophie.

"And are you, posh and proper?" I ask.

"Am I fuck," she says smiling her pretty little head off.

It's nice to chat about this and that and forget about Cardiff. It's nice to have a good drink too. I've had lots of practice sessions as a journalist so I'm still in my sober-ish zone. Sophie seems to coping like a true booze hound too. I take us to Ha Ha! Bar next but it's too packed full of Bath's prettiest and pretentious, and not even very funny, so we have a vodka and coke to be polite, and quickly move on the more down to earth Pig & Fiddle.

"I'm sure I should be wasted by now," says Sophie over another pint. "Must be the adrenalin pumping from the day's excitement that's keeping me lucid."

"We're doing ourselves and our livers proud," I say.

The drink makes us go all serious and we end up having some sensible adult conversations.

"Who'd win a fight, a silverback gorilla or Mike Tyson?" asks Sophie.

"Instead of Ali's 'Thriller in Manilla' it would be the 'Thriller with the gorilla'."

"Very clever, yes, but who'd win?"

"There's not much difference between them. Tyson, by an ear."

"Which fruit's sexiest: a strawberry or a banana?" asks Sophie.

"Have you looked at a strawberry cut in half recently? Remind you of anything does it? Strawberries are easily sexier. And tastier. Banana's too obviously phallic," I say looking her straight in the eye.

"What would you prefer: to sleep with *all* of The Corrs or *none* of the Corrs?" she asks with a big smile.

"Now there's a dilemma. All of them, or none of them?"

"That's it. What would you do?"

"Crikey. I dunno," I say. "I think I'd go for it and shag 'em all, but leave a gap – say, thirty years – before doing Jim Corr last."

"Don't think that's allowed. All in one night or not at all."

"Arse," I say. That gives me an idea. "Then I'd shag 'em all up the Wembley Way, and hope I get to the hairy arse last."

"Hardy!" Sophie sounds offended, but the glint in her eye tells me otherwise. "You bummer," she says laughing.

The conversation continues at this high brow level and we end up discussing other such matters of national importance. It all feels so natural. No pressure, no first date nerves – this isn't a date anyway, is it? Just a boy and a girl getting on, and getting steadily drunk. We chat about everything and nothing, people watching, piss taking. Sophie seems to be laughing at my jokes a lot too. Perhaps she's doing that girl thing of letting me know she likes me, laughing at my stories, flattering my ego, even if I'm not that funny. Yet I feel like the funniest man in town. But the best thing is Sophie's just letting me be myself. My silly, chatty, slightly charming, slightly cheeky self.

We stay at the Pig and over another pint Sophie playfully tells stories, chuckling about "this bloody kid from this band was all of sixteen, he still had spots for Christ's sake, yet was telling me how to photograph him, what angle to take the shot from, and he tried it on with me after. Freaking cheek…" As I watch her I notice she seems so happy and comfortable in herself. I've met girls before where you could almost see two heavy fistfuls of emotional baggage dragging them down. She appears not to have a care in the world.

I'm fairly happy with my lot too. I know I'm no Brad Pitt, but I'm no Shane MacGowan either. I'm comfortable with my inoffensive features and semi-athletic build, and I like who I am. The *TOP 10 HITS* mag job's not my dream career but it pays the bills, I get to listen to lots of music and see lots of live bands. I have a laugh and it'll do for now. I feel fairly confident in most situations, I'm happy chatting to anyone, and I'm happy to listen to Sophie chat away tonight.

"…then there was this really heavily made-up boy band singer who just couldn't pose naturally in front of the camera. He just kept pouting, it was making him look so camp…" says Sophie giggling.

I find myself staring her. She's everything I look for in a girl: nice proportions, nice shapes. Not that any of that matters these days, for me it's all about the eyes. When I was twelve years old it was whether a girl could run fast and climb trees like me. When I was eighteen it was big, beautiful boobs. By my early twenties I was a goner if I saw a girl in a Pearl Jam T-shirt. Personalities came into it somewhere along the way. It took me a while to realise it's the girl's eyes that you should look out for. A window to the soul and all that. So now it's the eyes I look into first. Looking into Sophie's big brown, inviting puppy dog eyes I could see a kindness, an intelligence, but there was an all-important sparkle too, a twinkle of mischief. As I'm swimming in her deep brown pool-like eyes, she catches me off guard.

"You've got really nice blue eyes Hardy," she says smiling at me.

Damn it. That was my line. I say nothing. It would be too corny to give the same compliment now. So I just smile.

Near the end of the evening I treat us to a late night curry. On the way to the Eastern Eye, Sophie seems to be holding on to my arm a lot and she even holds my hand at one point. Her skin feels soft, her touch is gentle. We share a moment when, over the poppadoms and mango chutney, she holds my gaze for a little longer than standard procedure and hits me with her smiling eyes. She looks like the pussy cat who's got the cream, although I don't really know why. I figure she's just drunk. My brain's now certainly full of beer.

After my Tikka Massala, her Dansak, and our Kingfisher lagers, Sophie's body seems to switch off and she leans on me all the way up Lansdown Road and back to my flat on Camden. I've got a wobble on too, but we make it back with only minor scrapes against various parked cars. In my front room, with a view peering down over Bath's city lights, I expertly make a couple of white rum 'n' cokes to perk us up.

"You're quite a classy bloke really, Hardy, aren't you," says Sophie gratefully accepting the rum.

"Am I? Never really thought much about it," I say, purposely slurping the rum loudly through my straw. "Do you want to play one of my favourite games?"

"Oooh, games. Go on then. Which one?"

"Hide the sausage?"

Sophie rolls her eyes. She doesn't roll them across the floor like a pair of dice – now that would be a great party trick – she rolls them towards the ceiling.

"Sorry. I meant the CD game." I explain the rules. "We take it in turns to play one song each on the hi-fi. We have to be strict, only one song at a time. It's harder than you think when you really love an album and are almost singing the next song before the other's closing bars have finished."

"Cool," says Sophie.

Her big drunken eyes come back to life and she animatedly picks her tunes. I lead with *Black Dog*, Sophie boozely bops about when she plays *Holiday In Cambodia*, we both sing along when I put on *Love Spreads*, and we both battle with our air guitars when she plays *I Hate To Say I Told You So* and I put on *Richard III*. At around 3am or 4am or whatever, after we've finished our third or fifth rum, Sophie stands up, and simply, sweetly, asks if she can borrow a T-shirt to sleep in.

And then we go to bed.

It might sound odd, but as we lay in my bed, me on my back, Sophie resting her head on my naked chest, I didn't feel the need to make a move. Not one kiss. I even keep my pants on. Don't get me wrong, I wanted to kiss Sophie's inviting pink lips, but there's a bigger part of me that didn't want to blow it with her. She's worth more than a one-night stand. I want something more than that. Of course, there is also a smaller, randy part of me that did feel like a shag: a really desperate, passionate, leg-trembling tumble. Death does that to you sometimes, they say, makes you want to procreate as soon as possible to replace the deceased. But I don't want to spoil it by pouncing on her. And, besides, it isn't like Dazza was family or a friend. I'm content just stroking Sophie's hair and holding her. *Moon Safari* plays out on the CD player in the bedroom. I'd popped it on for the ultimately relaxing opening track, *La Femme D'Argent*, but now the simple and sublime *All I Need* is soothing our bones.

All I need is a little time...

I glance over at my book folded open on the bedside table. I'm halfway through Colin Bateman's *Shooting Sean*. I usually read in bed before going to sleep. I love the chance to read anything other than music mags, but with Sophie breathing deeply in my arms it reminds me how much I've missed falling asleep with someone.

Sophie rubs her nose, and then she catches me off guard again.

"I like you Hardy Matthews," she says. Sophie raises her head off my chest to look up, with one eye half open, and smiles at me briefly. She pauses in that drunken way when you don't even realise you've paused at all, flopping her head back down onto my chest, then says, "You have a good looking personality."

I'm not sure if she thinks I'm good looking, or if she thinks I have a good personality, or if she means both. But I don't care. She likes me. *She* likes me. She *likes* me. She likes *me*.

I kiss her softly on the forehead and she returns the favour by softly snoring.

In the morning my head's fuzzy and the weather outside's foggy. Sophie's already up and dressed and is sat on the end of bed. Judging by the bright grin on her face she's not suffering nearly as much as me.

"Today," she proudly announces, "I'm the most popular photographer in the land."

She's already popped out to the newsagents to buy up all the tabloids and broadsheets. She spreads them out on the bed. Each and every British paper has used either her 'Dazza Dying' or 'Dead Dazza' photo on their front page. She's not lying: she is the most popular photographer in the country.

"My agency's even managed to flog my photos to a bunch of overseas papers as well," she says. Perhaps the most popular in the world, even.

I read the various headlines. The broadsheets have gone with *'West Side Star Dies On Stage'* and *'Pop Star Electrocuted Live On Stage'* whereas the tabloids have used *'Dazza Is Dead'* and the moving *'West Side Gory'*.

It's quite a lot to take in first thing. I get out of bed and pull on a T-shirt and jeans, stretching and scratching as I pad around the bedroom.

"I'm also probably the most profitable photographer in the country today as well. I just spoke to my agency and they told me how much I'll be getting paid for the photos," she says. "It's thanks to you that I managed to sneak the shots and my camera out under that cop's nose. So, please, take this." Sophie hands me a cheque. "It's only fair you get half of what I've made."

"Don't be silly. I can't take this." I look at the cheque. "Cocking hell! How much did your agency charge!?"

"Top dollar. They were exclusive shots of a celebrity dying on stage. I got between seven and ten grand per newspaper. There's enough for both of us and some. It's only fair you get half. Please. I insist. I won't accept no for an answer."

I could certainly do with the money. Magazines don't pay as much as people think. "Well, if you insist," I say. "I can't remember the last time I've been so much in credit," I say.

"Me neither," she says.

Sophie stays for an early morning cuppa but her mobile refuses to stop ringing – lots of press people eager to get more pictures of dead Dazza, a certain Welsh policeman wondering if he could have a word, as well as her boss asking where the hell she is.

"I'd better get a taxi to the train station and make my way back to the Bristol office to deal with all the attention," she says.

"Guess you should, yep."

"Thanks for yesterday, and a fun time last night. You're a real gent Hardy Matthews," says Sophie. She hands me her business card. "Call me."

A quick peck on the cheek, a squeeze on my arm, a bright eyed smile, and Sophie's gone.

My flat feels empty as soon as she closes the front door. What's that all about?

I leave my mobile switched off for now. I think I need a day off. I use my landline to call Gary in the office. We discuss the big story and cover options for *TOP 10 HITS* and I tell him I need some time out to grieve.

"You take today to get your head together Hardy. It's not every day you see a pop star die on stage," he says. He sounds almost sympathetic.

Dazza wasn't a pop star. Poor Gary and his pop ideals.

"We'll see you bright and breezy in the morning and we'll plan some big mag pieces," he says.

"Okay," I say suitably sadly. I don't need to time to grieve at all. I just fancy bunking off work.

As it turns out I don't get much peace on my day off as my mobile doesn't stop ringing as soon as I switch it on mid-morning. I'm forced to field calls the rest of the morning and most of the afternoon as news spreads about Dazza in Cardiff. Apart from friends and media mates calling, I give quotes to a few broadsheet and tabloids, as well as for *Q* magazine and *Enemy* magazine. As much as I've grown out of every student's favourite indie rag, I like the *Enemy* story angle their writer is going for: slightly respectful about Dazza's death, slightly disrespectful about West Side's music, and how it'll leave more room for singer-songwriters and real musicians to possibly elbow their way onto the music scene.

TV stations run newsflashes throughout the day and I can't turn the radio on without it cutting to the news to talk about Dazza's electric shock death and West Side still being in shock. I know Dazza dying on stage is big news but even in our current celebrity obsessed culture I didn't think everyone would be going so barmy over it.

By early evening I need a drink. I take myself around to the Farmhouse and swap stories and jokes with the regulars over a few pints sat at the bar. They don't really understand what I do for a living so it makes a nice change talking rugby and giving opinions on the new bar opened up down the road, rather than the Cardiff episode and front page headlines. I pop a few quid into the jukebox. The soothing guitars and vocals of *Gimme Shelter* warm up the pub and I'm able to put Dazza to the back of my mind. By the time

Brown Sugar is rocking out of the jukebox I almost forget that yesterday I saw a pop pretender get electrocuted live on stage.

*   *

The doorbell rings. Well, it plays a tune. It's meant to be the *Smoke On The Water* guitar riff. The Interlink delivery man looks confused rather than amused as the digitized song crackles out of the tiny speaker at your front door below.

"Hello?" you say through the intercom.

"Parcel for Mr G Harrison."

"I'll buzz you in. Leave it in the hallway."

You smile to yourself at the false name you gave the web site. You decided from now on you'd use false names to cover your tracks. You also used a fake credit card you've obtained though one of your fellow bodyguard's dodgy contacts in Manchester. As long as you don't spend obscene amounts of money and keep individual purchases to below £250 it'll be very difficult for the fraud squad to trace.

You watch out the window from your first floor flat as the delivery man walks back to his van and drives off. You wait another two minutes before jumping down the stairs to get your parcel. No point showing your face if you don't need to.

Back up in your flat you carefully cut the polythene courier bag and slide the box out. Inside the box is a Paul McCartney mask. Not your cheap, plastic 99p joke shop crap with skinny elastic hanging limply from it, this is a professionally-made rubber number with 'McCartney's' face on the front and 'real' mop top hair on the top, back and sides. As you try it on for size, pulling the whole thing over your head, smelling the rubbery newness, you're pleasantly impressed with the funny latex creation. From McNamara to McCartney in one move. Nobody will actually think you're the fresh-faced Scouse mop top in his hey day, but people will recognise who you're *trying* to be.

You press the 'random play' button on your stereo. *A Hard Day's Night* starts up. You see this as a sign. A good sign. Keeping the Macca mask on, you sing along while looking at your reflection in the long mirror hanging on your bedroom wall.

And you have been working like a dog. In fact, since your little pop project took off you've never been busier. Planning this here, setting up that there, buying this, doing that, running around like MC Hammer (but not in silly baggy gold trousers). And yet you've never had so much energy. You're sleeping less but, apart from a few late night security shifts, you've dedicated all your time to your project.

You've spent a lot of time on your Top 10 Hit List too of course. It was very important to you that the people on your list deserved it, nobody could just slip in easily. You started with a long list of all the untalented chancers who are filling up the music industry with their manufactured music and gradually, painfully, you reduced it down to those who you feel have earned it. Those true wannabes who have no musical talent of their own and are nothing more than glamorised karaoke singers. Those fame-seekers who just want to get their over-tanned faces on TV or in the papers. Your shortlist contains those: who just want to be famous for being famous; who are more interested in their clothes, their pretty faces and their hairstyles than their music; who don't give a damn about the music, just about making money. But it's those 'talent' show winners who seem to be multiplying every other month, they're the ones that really make you want to puke. Those that can't play an instrument, those that have never written a song on a guitar or piano, or those that have never written heart-felt lyrics. These are the ones that have made it on to your original hit list.

But to be rewarded with a place on your Top 10 Hit List, you've narrowed it down to the truly deluded, arrogant, conceited, egotistical dickheads who think they're god's gift to pop music.

After a final check, you're satisfied with your final Top 10 Hit List. You smile as you strike through Dazza's name at No.10 with a red pen. You fold the piece of paper up and slip it in your wallet.

You pull the Macca mask off and pull on the black wig you used in Cardiff, making sure it's all lined up and neat. You drive in your beat up, white Astra to a small internet café towards the centre of Liverpool. In the café you make sure nobody can see your screen, and set up a free Googlemail address as 'top10hitlist@gmail.com' with the username 'Hitman'. Nobody will be able to trace you from here.

It's time to tell the media world and general public about your little pop project. Just a quick teaser. You type a short but succinct email. You read it through. Satisfied, you type in the five email addresses you'd jotted down. You double-check the addresses. Two broadsheets, two tabloids, and *TOP 10 HITS* magazine. You smile then press the send button.

You log out and shut down the computer, pay your two pounds for using the PC, and drive back home. You're starting to get a good feeling about your little project. The Cardiff mission had been successful, and today you're buzzing with anticipation. The press coverage on TV and in the papers on dead Dazza has only reassured you that you're doing the right thing. You're glad that, apart from his band mates and manager, nobody else has started the whole 'his death will be a great loss to music' nonsense.

Back in your flat you put the Macca mask on again and stand in front of the mirror in your bedroom. You stare at your reflection, and start singing to yourself.

*   *

After my day off skiving I reluctantly return to the office on Friday morning. Around 10am I trudge down into the Good Publishing Network offices in central Bath. After a few tracks from The Vines, The Subways and Brendan Benson on my iPod I feel awake and in a positive frame of mind. I love the way music can change your mood. The sun even breaks through the clouds to join me in my good spirits. As soon as I walk into the hustle and bustle of our cosy offices on Trim Street that all changes.

"Hardy, can I have a word?" says Gary, waving me towards one of our funky little meeting rooms.

I've barely got my coat off and sat down at my desk. I hate it when he does this. Everybody here is always in a hurry. Deadlines for everything, rushing from one to the next. I don't like being rushed. Why do I work on magazines again?

"Sure thing," I say, grimacing. My editor has this way of being super polite to you on the shop floor, then a little bastard behind closed doors. He's wearing a stripy pink, red and white shirt and his Elvis Costello-style glasses. Dressing smart usually means today he's going to be all business. Jane and Robin, our deputy editor and art editor, smile supportively over the top of their Apple Mac screens as I head to meet Gary.

In the meeting room Gary makes a quick internal call. Within two minutes we're joined by our publisher, Andrew, and MD John, who makes a point of avoiding the chairs, choosing to sit sideways on the table instead. I wonder briefly if MD John would sit side saddle if he climbed aboard a horse. MD John is forty-plus and wearing a brown suede shirt tucked into an ironed pair of Wranglers. It's not helping to stop my cowboy imagery. In complete contrast, late thirties Andrew is trying too hard to keep up with the kids with an über fashionable, ripped-for-effect, double-layered T-shirt and highly styled, yet in-denial-cos-he's-going-slightly-thin-on-top spiky mullet.

"Quite an eventful day in Cardiff then?" says MD John, swinging his legs playfully under the desk.

Easy cowboy. I think about replying but he's being rhetorical.

"I won't ask you to explain what it was like to see Dazza die on stage, Hardy." MD John pauses for effect. "I imagine it was terrible to watch. But I thank you for coming back into work so quickly. You're a true professional."

32

I know he doesn't mean it. I've never really been a true professional.

"But now is not the time to grieve. Now is the time to be proactive and not reactive," says MD John. "We all know chart interest is flagging and with our rival magazine closing and the seminal *Top Of The Pops* being axed..."

"Rest in peace *TOTP*," I mutter under my breath.

"...we now have to work even harder to increase the sales of *TOP 10 HITS*. The public now just watch the TV talent shows like *Pop Factory* or whatever's playing on cable music channels or listen to whatever's on the radio... or just download what everyone else is listening to on their iPods. But what punters need is to be reminded of the importance of the Top 10 charts and the excitement of what's going to be the new No.1," says MD John shaking his clenched fist. "Well, people, Dazza dying on stage could well be what we need to kick start *TOP 10 HITS* sales once again. On the back of Hardy's exclusive Dazza tributes we can use it as a launch pad to shout out and tell readers what they're missing. We can give them what they can't get anywhere else: comprehensive coverage of the Top 10 charts. We can give them exclusive insider information they won't even be able to get online, thanks to Hardy's dogged and front-line journalism."

"So you want to capitalise on Dazza's death?" I say unenthusiastically.

Gary glares at me. Andrew joins him. MD John puts his clenched fist away and squirms.

"Capitalise is such an ugly word. We're publishing a pop music magazine. In-depth coverage of Dazza's death is what our readers would want, and how we attract new readers," says MD John.

"It's what Dazza would want as well," says Gary.

"Exactly," says Andrew.

I don't say anything and just let the three amigos get on with it.

"So let's throw some ideas up in the air and see how they land, huh?" says MD John.

How about we throw you three out of the window and see how you all land?

"We need to cover all the angles and we need to get our dedicated edition to Dazza and West Side out on the shelves as soon as possible," says Gary taking over. "Stories on Dazza's grieving band mates, the fan's shock. We can talk to readers to get quotes in the mag. Let's do a little piece on conspiracy theories and the possibility of murder, then the big piece on Hardy's eyewitness account."

"What about the cover image?" asks Andrew.

"Do you know who took the photos that ran on all the front pages of papers?" MD John asks me.

I nearly laugh out loud. "I should be able to find out and source something," I say as I scribble down a note to call Sophie. I find myself drawing doodles around her name in my red pen.

"Where next for West Side? What about the remainder of the tour...?" Gary continues. I stop listening and ignore Gary writing enthusiastically on the white board in different coloured pens. Little chief Gary is sucking up to the big powerful white men. At one point Gary is trying to shove his nose so far up MD John's arse I think he's actually going to get his whole head up there, glasses and all. The only thing I do catch is that Gary wants me to write up three of the stories by lunchtime, including a new section called The Insider, so we can rush a special issue on to the shelves for early next week. Normally I'd have at least two days not two hours to rattle off features like this. Do they not get it? I don't *like* being rushed.

"Don't cock this story up, Hardy," says Gary. He's still mad at me for the Pop Princess story. "The future of *TOP 10 HITS* is in the balance right now."

"I'll see what I can do," I say before excusing myself. I blink a few times for dramatic effect. "These past couple of days have been quite traumatising."

But not nearly as traumatising as all this 'blue sky brain storming' bollocks in this meeting room. All three nod sympathetically as I head back to my desk.

I spend the next hour chatting to Jane and Robin, and most of the floor who drop by, about what I saw in Cardiff. I don't mind the gossiping, it's being called Harvey by people who don't know me that pisses me off. Afterwards I get a moment to trawl through my email. I've got 156 new emails. Everybody wants to know if I'm okay, but they're really asking what it was like seeing Dazza die on stage. I fire off a few personal replies to workmates based on different floors and different offices dotted around Bath, as well as to mates in London, Bristol and Manchester, then compile a stock answer for everyone else and begin cutting and pasting a reply.

Even Mum has emailed me, bless her. She'd called on Wednesday evening but I was too busy having fun with Sophie to call *anyone* back. I still haven't managed to call her back. A quick email will do for now. I email her telling her about 'a nice, pretty photographer called Sophie' and how great she is. That'll keep her quietly excited for a while.

I shut down my email – I never get any bloody work done if it's open – and fire up Word and get typing.

Two hours later I've done myself and *TOP 10 HITS* magazine proud. I've hammered out the 'eyewitness account' for The Insider and two other stories Gary wanted by the 1pm deadline. We might have to get a magazine out to press every two weeks but thankfully our little music mag doesn't have the high word counts of other music mags. *TOP 10 HITS* is all about instantly accessible features and tabloid mag style design – 'more pictures than words please' demand the kids – so it isn't hard to hit the word counts. Even so I suck up the praise Gary lays on me when I file my copy.

"You've done a great job considering how upset you are," he says. No point putting him straight.

I sit back and look around the office. We share our floor with other music-type magazines; specialist guitar and drumming mags, digital music mags, and a thrash metal mag in the far corner. The latter never lets us down and all of them dress in black five days a week, complete with moody mops and neatly shaven facial hair. Upstairs is computer and photography mag geekdom, downstairs are mountain bike, sci-fi and car mags. Good Publishing Network does a fine line in specialist magazines, tapping into the male obsession with hobbies and exploiting them very successfully.

It's organised chaos. Piles of magazines fill every spare surface on desks and shelves. There are lines of magazine covers stuck on the walls, Post-It notes stuck on them with each issue's sales figures. The hum of top spec Macs is overshadowed by the buzz of human activity. Test eds pluck the strings of guitars and try out new amps, while reviews eds listen to the latest CD to land on their desks, everyone else typing away on their keyboards. A few writers are listening to the radio, some band's new single probably. Designers play with images in Photoshop on their screens, mugs of tea and coffee and biscuits are passed around while others scoff sandwiches at their desks. Every so often there's a rise of laughter or a gathering around someone's Mac to check out the latest gross, humorous or smutty email attachment doing the rounds.

I decide to call Sophie. I need to get her photos of Dazza for the mag's cover but it's also an excuse to say hello. I call the mobile number on her business card. She answers after four rings.

"Hi, Sophie speaking."

"Hey, it's Hardy."

"Hey you. How are you?" She emphasises the 'you' nicely. I picture her smiling face.

"I'm fine. Back at work. Everyone's hyped up about the Dazza thing, of course. How's you?"

"I'm cool. But it's mental around here as well. The agency's chuffed I've brought in the Dazza pics, we're still selling loads of images everyday, but the police weren't so impressed that I'd taken the shots in the first place."

"F-f-fuck, f-fuck, f-fuck the police." My NWA impression needs some work.

"Was that your attempt at rapping, Hardy?"

"Yo check my bad self. Or something," I say. "Anyway, speaking of your photos, we need a great image. Can you sort us out?"

"Of course, I'd love to. I've got a couple of better, subtle angles that might be a bit more suitable for your kiddy readers."

"Kiddy fiddlers?"

"Readers. I said kiddy r-e-a-d-e-r-s." She spells it out for me.

"Oh. Yes. Of course. Great."

"I'll get the photo agency to put them in a folder on our FTP site for you."

"Cheers. Okay, best crack on. Speak to you soon."

"Oh," she says. I think she's sad I'm hanging up already. "Okay, speak soon."

I thought about asking her out there and then. But, for once in my life, I thought I'd try and play it cool. It won't last. I'm shit at playing anything cool. I'm certainly no Fonz, put it that way. Although I wouldn't want to have a greased up quiff or wear a leather jacket these days anyway.

I pass on Sophie's photo agency's site details to Robin so he can download her images, then I reopen my email to find another new stack. Most are replies to my reply, so I'm almost glad when Dan from *Guitar World* appears by my side. Almost. Dan's personal hygiene has a lot to be desired. Although when I say a lot to be desired, I mean there is no desire for his personal hygiene whatsoever. His greasy tresses, shiny skin, BO soaked black wool jumper and grubby black-now-faded-grey jeans are invading my personal space. I still haven't forgiven him for the Princess who's not a prince wind up.

"Alright Hardly," says Dan. He likes to call me that. "How's it hanging?"

"All the better for smelling you, Danny boy," I say breezily.

"Smelling you?" he says, genuinely hurt.

"No, I said seeing. All the better for *seeing* you," I say quickly, moving my chair back to be out of the full whiff zone.

Dan tugs at his hair, then scratches his crotch through his jeans.

"Crabs, Dan?"

"Eh?"

I point where he's scratching.

"Oh." He looks down. He scratches some more, then stops.

"So…" I'm about to tell him I'm dead busy what with dead Dazza and deadlines – that's a lot of dead – but he gets in first.

"Today, Hardly, I decided I'd count my farts," says Dan proudly. Oh Jesus bloody hell.

"I had seven pints of Bath Ales' lovely Gem last night, then went for a spicy curry in the Bengal Brasserie, so I'm more than pumped up to parp."

For God's sake. Why me? I don't know what to say.

"The full English breakfast with extra baked beans has been helping me out immensely too," he chuckles.

Oh Christ. Seriously, why?

"Wow," I say flatly.

"Loud, quiet, long, short, wet, dry, they all count my friend." Dan says as he pats his belly.

"I'm sure they do."

"Yep! I've been creating some very interesting new noises."

"That's so wrong."

"How many do you think I'm up to since I woke up this morning?" he asks as his eyes grow with anticipation. Mine nearly close with disinterest. "Go on. Guess!"

"Dunno. Fifteen?" I offer.

"Nope!" He's laughing now. "So far, since I woke up, I've farted eighty seven times."

"Eighty bloody seven? Already? Well don't make it eighty eight near me, shit brain."

"I won't, don't worry, I've got it all under control. My arse is like a tap. I can open and close it at will," he says.

"Lovely. Well, good luck with that," I turn back to my desk and start typing an email reply. He doesn't take the hint. Dan never does. He's still loitering, hopefully not to leave me a stinky present behind from his, well, behind. Luckily my phone rings. "Best get this Dan. Speak to you later, let me know if you make it to the magic one hundred." I give him the thumbs up. I want to give him the 'clear off' sign instead.

"Oh I will my friend. I'll hit TWO hundred before the day's out. I'm off for chilli and chips and two pints of Guinness for lunch at The Hob Goblin. That should do the trick," he says. I'm sure the dirty bastard counts out eighty-eight, eighty-nine, ninety as he waddles off.

I pick up the phone. It's Fat Pat on the other end.

"Well, that was the best West Side gig I've ever facking been to." He's got a point.

We compare notes on what happened and what we both saw. I don't let on I know about Sophie's photos or our little episode with the police afterwards just yet. I want to hear what he knows first.

"People are saying it might not have been an accident," he says.

He may be a wide load and a wide boy but Fat Pat's London contacts are usually pretty safe, and since I saved his fat arse and his job he's been filtering any information down my way. I found him semi-conscious in the toilets in Brixton Academy last year after he'd snorted one line too many and he and his blubbery body had a heart attack. I slapped him awake, called an ambulance and dragged him quietly out the fire exit so he could be rescued without the glare of the media who were inside at the gig. He survived, so did his freelance career on the tabloids, and ever since he's been a goldmine of gossip.

"That was my gut feeling too. I figured as much. Accidents like that don't happen anymore. It's not the seventies with all that crap roadie wiring and rigging. There's too much red tape and QA standards to meet these days," I say.

"My source tells me the electrics could've been tampered with," says Fat Pat.

"So it could be murder?"

Fat Pat doesn't say anything to confirm my conclusion jumping.

Then I do something I wouldn't normally do. I never ask Fat Pat about his sources: out of respect, professional integrity, as well as compromising the source's position. But this is different. It's not about some pop starlet's coke habit or other sordid secret. Somebody has died.

"So who told you?" I ask plainly.

"Hardy, mate, you know better than that. I can't reveal me sources me old china. It's not been confirmed yet anyway," he says, still friendly but I can tell he's not happy.

"Sorry Pat, had to ask," I say.

"Another call's coming in. Gotta go, speak later Hardy," says Fat Pat. He hangs up.

I did have to ask. I want to know whether it's true or not. Had somebody fried Dazza? I check the web and online news wires for any updates on Dazza's death. There are pages of grief-induced sympathy, with a few quotes from teary, shocked kids who were at Cardiff Arena, and on *The Guardian* site I find a quote from the outspoken Adam McWright, boss of the independent Scottish record company, McGoo Music. The bit I like says: *'It's not like we'll miss West Side's music now Dazza's gone. Plus there's already three cloned boy bands sitting smartly in the wings eager to step up on the big stage. But at least this means there's one less manufactured band on the scene for now. With any luck West Side will now disappear – hopefully the remaining members won't feel encouraged to continue playing in Dazza's memory – and leave the charts to the real musicians.'* I've always admired McWright.

On the Reuters website the official line is *'It was an unfortunate accident'* but the more I think it over, the more I think it was setup. But why Dazza? Why someone like him?

I mull this over while I thumb through my post. There's the usual handful of demos and preview CDs of the latest pop sensations the record companies want us to listen to, a few press releases about gigs coming up, and some reader's letters. I tear them open and scan them before filing the potentials for our letters pages in the mag, filing the rejects in the bin.

My email continues to ping. I check it again to find rows of new mails. Some more replies, some more press releases, some MP3s of new singles. But one email does catch my eye.

It's from 'Hitman' with a Googlemail address and it's titled 'Top 10 Hit List'. I open it.

I scan the email but don't take it in. I read it again but I still can't believe what it says.

I try to read it again but I just find myself staring at it. Hang on. It could be another bloody wind up. I look around the corner to see if Dan's concealing a smile. He's not, he's plucking an electric guitar with his headphones on. I hit reply and type 'Who the hell are you?' and send it. I read the email over again. It could be real. After five fruitless minutes of staring, looking up, then staring again, I print off the email, and pull my coat on. I put the print out in my pocket and walk out the office.

I need a pint.

I head to the Salamander. It's one of Bath's typical little gems tidied away down a back street. It has traditional wooden decor and smells of sweet tobacco. I order a pint of Bath Ales' Spa and a pint of Guinness. I swig the easy drinking Spa down in three gulps, all before the barman's had a chance to let Guinness settle and top up the remaining third like all good barmen should.

"Thirsty?" he asks as he places the Guinness down in front of me.

"You could say that." I pay him and find a table, sitting with my back to the wall so nobody can read over my shoulder. I glug down a third of my Guinness then take out the printed email from my pocket. Now I'm ready. I read it once more and finally take it all in.

It says:

```
Subject: Top 10 Hit List
From: Hitman <top10hitlist@gmail.com>
To: Hardy Matthews <hardy@top10hits.co.uk>
Cc: The Times, The Guardian, The Sun, The Daily Mail
```

The celebrity-obsessed, money-hungry music industry and TV talent shows are about to get a wake-up call…

For too long the music scene has been overflowing with manufactured pop artists, fame-hungry fuckwits and pop star wannabes who wouldn't know how to write a song or play an instrument if their life depended on it.

Well, now their life does depend on it.

I've got a Top 10 Hit List and I've got murder on my mind.

I aim to purge the pop charts strictly in accordance with my Top 10 Hit List. No pop star chancer is safe; boy bands who sing ballads, pretty vacant girl bands, three-piece rock clones, R&B divas, posh boys posing as punks and TV talent show losers… they could all be next on my Hit List.

I aim to clean up the music industry, leaving the path free for the real musicians, the real talent, the real songwriters.

Obviously I can't divulge all the juicy details just yet, that would spoil the fun for all of us, but as you probably know by now, I was in Cardiff on Wednesday for the West Side gig. Dazza was No.10, the first on my Top 10 Hit List. He'd had it coming for a long time that fat, fame-seeking Frank Sinatra wannabe. But he was nothing more than a stylised karaoke singer.

You will find out who will be No.9 on my Top 10 Hit List by the end of the weekend.

All the best.

Why the fuck has someone – some psycho – sent this email to me!?
    What the hell is this 'Top 10 Hit List' stuff all about?
    Part of me feels it's from a crank. Someone attention seeking. Who else would call themselves Hitman? But the way it's written, what they're saying, they gain nothing from telling me and the

media. There is no ransom, no requests. Just a bold, bonkers statement about a Top 10 Hit List. That's why the other part of me believes this could be the man – it has to be a man, doesn't it? – who knocked off Dazza. This is an email from a murderer. The Musician Murderer. Although that's not accurate – I'm a journalist and I need to get my facts right – because he hasn't technically killed a musician. As the email says, Dazza was just a karaoke singer. Karry-no-key singer.

If he hadn't already copied in the press I would think of selling it to them. One of the bigger papers would pay me handsomely for the scoop.

I read the email again. It has quite a nice tone really. Must be a fairly jolly sort of killer. I drain my pint, smile and feel myself relax. I order another Guinness, and a fat ham sandwich and a side portion of fat chips. I sip slowly on my pint this time. The sun pours through the window as shoppers and workers walk past outside. A grey bearded man sat on a tall stool at the bar meticulously smokes his pipe. The smell of flavoured tobacco swirls around the pub before making its way out the open window.

My sandwich arrives and I tuck in. I don't know why I was so panicked when I first read the email. I'm not in danger. It's only confirmed what I'm thinking anyway about Dazza being killed to death. Everything's cool.

But then why do I find myself repeating the end of the email again?

You will find out who will be No.9 on my Top 10 Hit List by the end of the weekend.

He's already killed once. I'm going to call them a 'he' for now. Wonder who No.9 is going to be on his Hit List then? Another boy band member? Someone from a girl band, a solo singer? Or maybe a whole band will get the chop? No, that would just be sick. My mind starts buzzing. I'd be lying if I said I wasn't finding the whole situation bloody exciting.

I try to think of any big gigs lined up this weekend, just in case he is planning to attack someone in public again. But I can't think who else is playing or what other potential bands are on tour or in the charts. Oh well. Not to worry. I'll find out after the weekend whether the crank is full of shit or not. I sip on my pint.

Everything's cool.

I almost float the short walk down the cobble stones of Queen Street back to the office. Sat at my desk it's nice to feel so relaxed on a fine Friday afternoon. While looking busy I start looking forward to the weekend, having a few beers, mooching about, not thinking about work. Trying not to think about psycho pop killers. Ignoring

41

thoughts of Hit Lists. Maybe I'll go and watch a dirty little punk rock band. I might even call Sophie.

Yes. It's going to be a good weekend.

*   *

You walk confidently down Abbey Road breathing in the surprisingly fresh London winter air as you take in your surroundings. Four students with bright scarves amble past you. Three businessmen with black suits, black trench coats and shiny shoes walk purposefully in front of you. It's late afternoon but it's already getting dark. Passing cars have their lights on.

Although you carried out your hit in Cardiff first, you had planned for Hit No.9 right from the start. You know exactly what you want to achieve today.

For this late Saturday afternoon mission you're dressed in an unassuming black woollen jumper over a grey T-shirt, with a pair of dark grey chinos, some fitted leather gloves and a grey canvas satchel over your shoulder. You smile as a pretty little French tourist glances your way as she walks past. You can tell she's French by the overtly colourful coat, the skirt and tights combination, and the tone of her skin.

You find what you're looking for and wait for the traffic to stop. A blue BMW comes to a halt, and you stroll over *that* zebra crossing. You can't stop yourself from smiling. Instead of bare hippy feet like the Fab Four you're wearing your trusty black Timberlands. You reach the front entrance of Abbey Road Studios, but walk straight around the back. Without breaking stride you deftly shimmy over the ten foot high perimeter wall using a tree's branches as leverage, and drop down inside the studio car park. An Aston Martin, Lotus, Porsche, two BMWs and three Mercedes are all lined up, but there's nobody around. Still, you cautiously hide behind the Lotus before taking out the rubber mask from your satchel and pulling it over your head.

Without wasting any time you run up to the studio building and get the screwdriver, pliers and metal ruler out from your satchel. While avoiding the CCTV camera's eye, you find the security alarm box on the wall, and quickly remove the cover. You cut the green wire (it's not always red like in the movies) and replace the cover. You slide the ruler through the gap in the fire exit door to undo the bar lock. You're inside in two minutes and twenty seconds just as you'd planned.

You march along the empty corridor. You've thoughtfully sanded down the soles on your boots so there's no tread to trace from your footprints on the damp paving slabs outside or on the red carpets inside. You squeeze your fingers inside the leather gloves. You won't be leaving any sign of your presence from either feet or fingers. There are seven doors off the corridor, low level lighting leads the way. Framed photos of bands who have recorded here line the walls. The Beatles take up most of the photo slots. There's a large black and white shot of a young Paul McCartney on his own. With your mask on, it's like staring into a mirror.

A framed red and white Les Paul guitar signed by Jon Squire from the Stone Roses hangs on the wall. The guitar brings memories flooding back. You picture your own first red and white guitar – a tiny, plastic, battery-operated one – and how you played and played with it, dreaming of becoming a rock star. You remember your first electric guitar, a Les Paul that took months of paper rounds to save up for. Years later when you'd formed The Good, The Bad, and The Ugly, you loved playing little gigs in local pubs. Becoming a rock star didn't feel impossible anymore. You were in a rock band, it was only the star quality that needed some work.

There's no lack of star quality at Abbey Road Studios. However, the security on this place is a doddle. From your experience when your band recorded in studios, and the basic security guarding you've done in them, most studio security is lax. There's nothing to steal. Any decent instruments come and go with the bands, and apart from a few exclusive recordings which normally go in the safe or home with the band manager, there's nothing of value – unless you fancy trying to shift an entire mixing desk or old rock star memorabilia that's imminently traceable. Even if Abbey Road does have some of the best recording equipment in the country there's no need for Bank Of England-like security.

You check nobody can see you as you take a sleeping gas canister out of your satchel and hold it in your left hand. You quickly weave your way around the series of corridors carefully ducking under the windows on doors. Not even the faint sound of singing can be heard through the sound proof walls and doors. You find Studio 3 and pause for thought, carefully checking nobody can see you or that you can't see anyone.

No.9 on your Hit List is the irritating and contrived three-piece boy band called Hoodwink.

You know the three little gits are here because one of the tabloids had written a story about them recording their new album here this month. They call it 'their album' but you know damn well none of the pretty little boys has written a lyric or song between them, even if they did claim with oversized egos to have written all of the last album and much of this new one in an interview in *TOP 10 HITS*

43

magazine. Although you can see why people would think three kids had written the drivel they feel so compelled to share with the pop world. Self obsessed songs like *Me, Myself & Me* and *Mirror, Mirror On The Wall* is only half of the puke-inducing pop Hoodwink continue to bring to the charts each month. Their latest ring-tone friendly single, *1-2-3 Are We* – that is, implausibly, high up the charts – is what helped them make it on to your Top 10 Hit List. Self-absorbed lyrics, a nauseating synthesized drum loop running from start to finish, and cheeky, chirpy vocals.

You can't believe a boy band like Hoodwink are recording at Abbey Road. They don't deserve it. You and your band did, but you never got the chance. It bothers you deeply that a boy band gets to waste such high-quality studio time on such low-quality music.

It's enough to drive anyone to murder.

You look through the little window in the door and peer inside to see the backs of the producer and manager, and mixing desk engineer all hunkered over the mixing desk. You quietly start off the sleeping gas canister, open the studio door, and ignoring the cries of "what the hell?", you quickly throw the weeping canister on the floor inside. With your right hand you immediately twist the lock on the recording booth door inside to keep the band locked up, before closing the studio door behind you. You easily hold the door closed from the corridor as the manager, then producer, then engineer attempt to open the door. Studio 3 fills with smoke and after 45 seconds of crying, shouting and thumping on the door, all of which you or anyone else can't hear because of the excellent sound-proofing, the three men drop one by one to the floor. You relax your grip on the door handle, nip inside the studio, and lock the door behind you.

The gaseous fumes are still strong but thanks to a small oxygen capsule you've fixed inside your Macca mask you can breathe quite happily. You stop the canister weeping by picking it up in your gloved hand and simply switching it off. Visibility is minimal but you're able to see the producer, manager and engineer all slumped on the floor. You still check none of them are faking it by opening each man's left eyelid. They're not. You promptly pull out a handful of zip-ties from your satchel and individually tie up their wrists behind their backs. Even though you quite miss physical confrontations, you're glad you didn't have to resort to that today – it just wouldn't have felt right while you're dressed up as Mr Nice Guy Himself, Sir Paul McCartney.

The air begins to clear as you look up to see the three scared but angry faces of Hoodwink staring back at you through the thick glass window separating the sizeable recording booth. As you'd calculated, the fumes didn't reach inside their sound proofed booth. The sleeping gas on your side of the studio is quick to disperse through the air vents. You check your watch, then remove the oxygen capsule. You sit yourself down in front of the mixing desk and switch on the interconnecting mic and speaker.

"Alright boys?" you say in an exaggerated version of your Liverpudlian accent.

All three boys are still wearing oversized headphones, but while two of them keep still and look frightened, the taller of the three's lost none of his lip as he shouts at you via his mic hanging from the ceiling. "Who the hell are you wearing a Paul McCartney mask? Why the fuck have you locked us in here? And what have you done to Dan, Neal and Justin!?"

"Calm down, calm down," you say, and think of going all super scouse with some hand movements as well as the voice, but you resist. "They'll be fine." A slight pause. "You three are the ones who should be worried."

"What the hell is that supposed to mean?" says the tall guy, all cocky again, tugging on his spiky hair. Even now he uses the faint reflection in the window to check his hair. You look him in the eye through your mask. He has one those faces you love to hate; slightly gormless features, dead eyed stare, all hidden behind some freaky, fancy haircut. The other two no-brainers just stare at you with their mouths open. It's going to be your pleasure to get rid of them. You're doing them a favour really.

"The industry doesn't need manufactured music like Hoodwink anymore," you say matter of factly.

"Eh?" says tall guy, still fiddling with his spikes.

"I think it's about time you boys learned a valuable lesson about music."

"What the hell are you going on about? You, you... you bitch!"

Still so lippy. Where do they get these egos from? Have they always been that way or did they grow them in pop school? You pull out a CD case from your satchel and, slowly removing the CD, you put it into the player connected to the mixing desk. You also take out a selection of electrical screwdrivers, and your homemade volume boosting amp from your satchel. When you were in your band you used to get into trouble at pub gigs for using your secret booster. Landlords would try and turn the volume down remotely when glasses started vibrating off tables, but you could control it from the stage to give the locals a real blast of rock.

You turn off the desk's power and quickly remove a control panel on the mixing desk with the tools. You quickly plug in your home-made box of tricks and turn it all back on again. You take out some earplugs and carefully poke them deep down into your ears.

You smile as you enjoy how each boy's reacting to being locked inside the booth. One of them has taken to hopelessly barging into the door with his shoulder, the tall guy is still mouthing off and screaming obscenities at you, while the smaller of the three seems to be sulking in the corner, preoccupied with his mullet.

"Are you sitting comfortably?" you say into the microphone. "Then I'll begin. This is what you sound like after your producer and mixing man has kindly improved your vocals."

You press play on the CD player. *Me, Myself & Me* blasts out of the speakers in the booth, although you're careful to keep the volume down to setting number one for now. The boys have removed their headphones and actually start singing along. The quieter of the three even breaks into a dance routine. You think they'd be bored of 'their own' song by now: you are, and you've only listened to it three times. It smacks of a classically overproduced pop song. Once it's been through the mixing desk the engineer enhances every part of their pathetic voices, boosting the depth by duplicating layer after layer to give the vocals that synthesised and powerful edge that they'd never be able to achieve with their own weak voice boxes.

"However," you say, still with your OTT scouse accent, "this is what you sound like without any computerised help."

You skip to track two. What crawls out of the speakers this time is a painful mix of out of tune vocals, two of the boys singing in the wrong key, while the other sings too high and out of time. At one point the lead singer keeps tripping over the words – because they're not his words. You're glad you've got earplugs in.

"Anything you'd like to say now boys?" you ask.

"Bollocks!" says mouth all mighty. "We don't sound like that."

They believe they sound like the finished article and don't need any producing or remixing. You like this, it helps you justify what you're about to do even more.

You switch the microphone off and the speakers on your side so you can't hear the gobby one swearing. He's boring you now. You switch to track three and turn the volume up to two. The Beatles – who else? – and their delightful *A Day In The Life* begins to play into their booth. Judging by their reactions you're guessing the boys have never heard the song before – they probably grew up on a diet of Radio 1 and cable TV dance music channels.

You turn the volume up to three, from your calculations it's now at around 90 decibels, just as Lennon sings *'He blew his mind out in a car'*. One of the boys puts his hands over his ears. After Lennon sings *'I love to turn you on'* you wind the volume up to four, then five as the orchestra rises into the crescendo. It's up to around 110 decibels now. The high frequency sound of the horns seems to be doing the trick. All three cover their ears. Just before the song switches to the piano and McCartney's soothing lines about waking up and getting out of bed, your skilful mixing cuts straight to the Fab Four's *Revolution*. The rawness of the opening guitar rages through the speakers into the studio as you turn it up to six, and then seven. That's 130 decibels. According to your research, 120 decibels is the point at which humans will start to feel pain. The effect is doubled in a small enclose space such as, say, a recording studio. The boys show their appreciation of the music by hopping about while grimacing and covering their ears tightly with their hands. It's a strange dance but it has a certain charm under the circumstances.

You really love this track and your feet start tapping along. The boys are bending over unsure what to do with themselves. You start to sweat lightly in the mask and gloves, but you're really getting into this mission and would never compromise yourself by removing either.

As the guitar and piano solo booms into the speakers you turn it up to eight. 140 decibels. One of the boys keels over. Even you can feel the thundering bass vibrating through the mixing desk now.

The two remaining boys are bouncing around the booth, one of them takes a long run up to try and kick the door down. Like you, the door doesn't even flinch. The mouthy, tall one comes up to the booth's window and starts hammering on the two-inch thick glass screaming something at you. You point to your ears, and shake your head explaining you can't hear. You nudge it up to nine, and 150 decibels. That's the usual peak of rock music in a wide-open arena: the same volume reaching the compact little recording booth is now lethal.

It's then you see a tell-tale trickle of blood seeping out of the tall one's ears. Even on your side of the glass and with earplugs the music's ruthlessly loud. You pull on some headphones over your already protected ears and then turn the volume up to the maximum of ten. Thanks to your booster that's around 160 decibels. The smaller boy starts shaking before dropping to the floor. As Lennon starts screaming 'Alright, alright…' the tall guy finally falls to the floor too. You're glad you didn't need a Spinal Tap-esque amp that went up to 11 to finish the job properly.

Some think it's the eardrums shattering and internal bleeding that kills people, but if the human body is exposed to abnormally high volumes of sound, especially inside an enclosed space, it's the vibrations and pressure that eventually shake the body to death. You remember laughing when you'd read about some petrol head who'd killed himself after proudly and loudly playing his amped up car stereo inside his little bad boy hatchback. Natural selection works in beautiful ways sometimes.

47

You press stop on the CD player, eject the disc and place it quickly back in its case.

You'd thought long and hard about which songs you'd play today. *Good Vibrations* has sprung to mind, but it was always going to be a Beatles' track. Narrowing it down had been the tricky bit. At one point you'd even thought of going with Wing's *Live And Let Die*, maybe even with the Gun N' Roses cover version for a laugh, but you're at Abbey Road and it didn't feel right. *A Day In The Life* followed by *Revolution* did feel right, though, with its balance of educational listening for the boys backed up with some great guitar and apt lyrics.

You remove the headphones and earplugs and stuff them quickly back in your satchel. You check the three wise men behind you are still unconscious. They're still out for the count. You unplug your volume booster and put it back in your satchel, then unlock the recording booth door and check on your boys. Two of them are face down after collapsing, while the tall guy is strangely curled up like a cat. You check all three's pulses on their necks. Not a blip from either one.

Mission accomplished. Hit No.9 on your Top 10 Hit List.

Keeping the mask and gloves on you let yourself out of Studio 3, carefully checking nobody's along the corridor. It's empty. You love the efficiency of these high-tech recording studios. Nobody's heard your deadly little DJ slot, least of all the security guards 75 metres and a series of sound-proof doors away on the front desk. As you retrace your steps back down the corridor and around the corner you notice a CCTV camera hanging from the ceiling. You didn't it notice before. It annoys you and you find yourself briefly looking straight at it. A red light flashes above the camera lens. Never mind. Security didn't spot you on the way in from it, and it's too late now, even if they are looking straight back at you in your mask. You make straight for the fire exit, ease the door open and check there's nobody in the car park. It's empty too.

As you'd planned it's night-time now – you like escaping under the cover of darkness. You jog through the car park, avoiding the CCTV and glare of the streetlights just the other side of the perimeter wall, and in one swift motion you vault on to the top of the wall where you'd entered earlier. A few cars roll past on the road below, and a businessman talking on his mobile phone walks past on the pavement across the road. You wait until it's clear, and remove your mask and shove it into your satchel, before dropping down to the pavement.

You walk nonchalantly into the London night. It's a freezing evening. Ice starts to form on the pavement under foot, but with every stride you feel yourself glowing with pride and a real sense of achievement. You start singing under your breath.

"You say you want a revolution, weeeell yoou know, we all want to change the world."

Well you know, you're already beginning to change the pop world.

Two down, eight to go.

No. 8

Don't stop me now, I'm having such a good time
Queen

Saturdays. Sundays. I love the weekends. I don't mean I *live* for the weekends. I make sure I entertain myself on school nights too. I mess about whenever I can these days.

I wake up early and hangover-free on Saturday morning after leaving the pub and workmates reasonably early last night. I cook up some bacon and eggs then potter into town to buy some music. I walk down Milsom Street and, avoiding the open top tourist buses and lines of Italian school children, walk into Waterstones. I browse for twenty minutes then buy a large photo-heavy book on John Lennon and John Buchcan's *39 Steps* – the original espionage novel, or so they say. I've always had a fascination with spying. I guess every boy does when they're younger, and every man who ever walked the earth wants to be James Bond. The desire to track someone down, to follow someone, to be stealthy and secretive, to use high-tech weaponry, to be silent but deadly, to search and destroy, and to sleep with painfully attractive, exotic women.

I read my new novel in the posh coffee shop around the corner. A good book always gives me goose bumps and over a latté I happily escape for three chapters more than planned. I slope off and walk down the high street. I pass a T-shirt stall on the way that's already selling 'Dazza is Dead' T-shirts with an image of Dazza's face underneath. He's meant to look like he's singing but the artist's drawing is so bad it makes him look he's in shock. Which is ironic.

From there I nip to Fopp. This place is dangerous. I never leave with less than three CDs or two DVDs. It's always cheaper than everywhere else and it always has a 3-for-2 or similar cut-price deal to suck me in. I buy a bag of CDs, a couple of classics, a couple of new releases, and *The Best Of RUN DMC* by the till, and leave before my wallet's empty.

Then a quick trip to HMV for the singles chart to see if I've missed anything that should be in our magazine. I haven't. On *TOP 10 HITS* magazine we know what's going to be released into the charts months before they're on sale, via emailed release dates and trade magazines, even before the radio starts playing the singles, which is usually four to six weeks too early so listeners are bored of it before the single has hit the shelves. The only thing we don't know is what position they'll reach in the charts. It always has and always will be a lottery. Like now, the three-piece boy band Hoodwink have a song just outside the coveted top ten spot. It's possibly the most irritating song I've heard for a decade, and yet it's here, at No. 11. People, well, kids, are lapping up Hoodwink's artificial brand of pop. I wonder if catchy – like an unwanted virus – songs like this didn't exist maybe the kids would buy songs by real musicians.

I leave HMV empty handed and go out of my way to walk around the back through Abbey Square and past the Roman Baths and Bath Abbey. I chuck some coins to a reasonable Jamaican busker. I don't mean he's only reasonably Jamaican. He's from Jamaica all right, his luminous yellow outfit, the flag on his guitar case, his guitar plucking technique and unmistakable accent are evidence enough. I mean his busking is reasonable. Even, so a touristy crowd and people passing have stopped to listen to his freestyle never-ending version of *No Woman, No Cry*.

I don't get Marley's lyrics. Does he mean, 'if you don't have a woman, you won't have the need to cry'? Or does he mean, while possibly consoling a lady, 'hey, little woman, there's no need to cry like that'? Who knows? Who cares? Probably not Bob Marley.

I keep walking, crossing the road past Parade Gardens and up to Pulteney Weir. I stop to breathe in the view spreading out and up into the hills and watch the weir below as water gushes beneath the bridge and down the pretty tiered waterfall. A pair of swans circle in the water and seagulls swoop down to gobble up scraps of bread floating on the river. I can hear the ooohs, ahhs and cheers emanating from The Rec across the river as Bath's brick shit houses and Gloucester's thick necked farmers knock lumps out of each other on the rugby field. The sun's in my eyes but it's warming my face nicely. The local limestone architecture behind me somehow seems friendlier with the sky's bright blue backdrop. Bath's a truly beautiful city that really comes to life on sunny wintry days like this.

I wonder what Sophie is doing today.

My mobile beeps and vibrates in my pocket. It's a text from Richie. He's with JP in the pub. I walk across Pulteney Bridge and down

Great Pulteney Street to the Pulteney Arms, a city centre pub with a local feel full of drinkers and smokers enjoying the unfussy and unpolished pub atmosphere. I join Richie and JP at their table and find there's a pint already waiting for me.

"Gentlemen," I say as I sit down.

"Hardy," says Richie and nods.

"Matthews," says JP and smiles.

Richie and JP are old workmates from a different publishing house. These days we usually meet to drink, watch sport, and drink. Richie is sort of stocky, sort of Mancunian and all sorts of ginger. JP has a French-sounding name but is, in fact, a Devon boy. He's stockier than Richie, but his closely cropped hair is less ginger and more grey. After a couple more pints we each order a giant Yorkshire pudding filled with meat, veg and gravy. A handful of pints later and there's been a solid victory for Bath against Glos. We'd kept one eye on Sky Sports on the box, although the smiling fans in blue and white flooding through the pub doors helpfully confirm the win. We three kings have more pints to celebrate.

"Musical trends," says Richie all of a sudden.

"Musical friends?" asks JP.

"No. Not friends. Trends. Musical trends. Have you ever noticed that they go in circles?" says Richie.

"What, like how we've had seventies influenced-music in the nineties, and eighties influences in 2000," I say. I'm still not sure if I should I call this decade the noughties.

"Exactly. There is no new music. It's all regurgitated," says Richie.

He's got a point. But I'm not thinking too much about music or anything else today. I haven't thought about next week's deadlines all day, and that email from the Hitman is starting to fade from the forefront of my mind. I'm still not sure whether to believe or dismiss its contents. Either way, I tell myself it's still nothing to worry about.

It's dark and I'm drunk by the time we fall out of the pub. I hug Richie and JP goodbye – one at a time, I'm not a slag – then stumble back up Great Pulteney Street and up to Camden and home. Confusingly it's only early evening, and as I get a march on up Lansdown Road it seems a good time as any to call Sophie on my mobile. I've programmed her number in under Sexy Sophie.

"Hey Hardy, it's Sophie!" I say as she answers her mobile. I'm slightly out of breath trying to walk and talk up the hill. Mixed with the pints, I'm not sure what I've just said.

"Eh? I'm Sophie. You're Hardy, silly," she says. Luckily she's laughing. "You sound out of breath. Are you okay?"

I stop walking and take a deep breath.

"Yeah. I'm fine. I'm fine." I don't know why I said it twice. To reassure us both? "What are you up to this evening?"

"I'm meant to be going out with a few girls from my Yoga class for a healthy veggie meal at someone's house over here in Clifton," she says. I get the feeling she's not in the mood for vegetarians tonight.

"Will you be sitting properly, eating butter squash nut with correct postures and poses?" I say. Is it butter squash nut or butter nut squash?

"Almost certainly. Poses and everything. It's butter nut squash by the way."

Can she hear my thoughts? "Butter nut squash?"

"Yes."

"Is that like the game 'paper scissors rock' for vegetarians?"

Sexy Sophie laughs.

"You don't fancy coming to see a dirty little punk rock band with me and some mates over in Bath then?" I say casually.

"What time shall I come over?" says Sophie.

The Porter Butt on London Road is a great, grubby little venue for the UK circuit of punk bands. Oddly enough the tiny right-hand bar has folk music jams where bizarre bearded men in cords play even more bizarre instruments and chords. The left-hand bar is for locals and pool players. But it's out back where the action is: in a window-less function room about the size of a tennis court.

It's heaving inside. The smattering of tables are full and most of the standing room is being stood in by old-school punks with mohicans, underage emo kids, greasy-haired students and middle-aged men with middle-aged spreads who are old enough to know better. Condensation drips from the brick walls that are painted white and covered in large posters and graffiti. Somebody's setting up a drum kit on the stage at the far end. I think it's Black Rebel Motorcycle Club that's creeping out of the speakers hanging high up in the darkened corners.

"Makes a refreshing change to those giant, sterile pop venues I've been stuck in recently," says Sophie as she soaks up the surroundings. She looks gorgeous. She's wearing her hair down tonight, and as she slips off her denim jacket she reveals a worn out, white Iggy Pop T-shirt that says 'I Wanna Be Your Dog'. I only just resist the temptation to start barking.

I've sort of sobered up since my afternoon session – the home-made pizzas Sophie and I ate before we came out have helped. But I'm sure more evening beers will see that my sobriety doesn't last.

I spot my gig mates Susan and Ollie at the bar. Their rosy cheeks could be to do with the heat, although I think it's more to do with the cider. Ollie has the best spiky black hair in a traditional punk sense. He's the nicest, smiliest punk you'll ever meet. He's wearing tight blue jeans, old skool Converse boots, a rare black Dead Kennedy's T-shirt, and white and black sweat bands on his wrists. Scottish Susan is a cute blonde who enjoys walking and biking in the country by day and drinking and dancing to punk rock by night. She's got her usual blue jeans and fitted black top combo on. I do the introductions and get a round in. We chat about this, that and the other, Susan and Ollie avoid asking both of us about the Cardiff gig. They're cool like that.

A few drinks later and Kinesis, the warm act, bound on stage. They start well with a rocked up version of the A-Team theme music, and then tear into a quick-fire set of ska punk stuff I'm not so sure about. What's with all the trumpet playing where there should be crafty guitar licks? Ollie and I hang at the back and chat while Sophie and Susan kick their heels up at the front. Susan's swaying in time while Sophie's making a good fist of bopping in time with the band's pacey tempo. Somehow she even makes bopping look sexy.

"Women. They love to dance," I say.

"They sure do. It's like they've been cut free from their strings and responsibilities," says Ollie.

"Free to express themselves," I say.

"And it gives us a moment to express the way we feel about their bouncy bits," says Ollie.

He has a point. And so do Sophie and Susan. Two nicely rounded points each, in fact. We stand in silence for a while and admire the show. Too bad Kinesis keep getting in the way. After their last song the band slip off stage and the girls slip through the crowd back to me and Ollie and their drinks. Sophie's lightly sweating and heavily smiling as she slides next to me. I hand her G 'n' T over and she sucks greedily on her straw. She keeps looking at me as she sucks on her straw while we all give our verdict of the first band.

"Seven out of ten. Good fun but not much else," says Susan.

"Six out of ten. Punky but too poppy," says Ollie.

"Four out of ten. Can't bloody stick that horn and trumpet rubbish," I say.

"Harsh. If I had ten I'd give 'em one. Especially the lead singer. He was slightly handsome," says Sophie with a twinkle in her eye.

"And almost out of school," I say.

We all giggle like we're in a double period English lesson.

Sophie starts toying with the ice in her glass with a straw. I have an overwhelming urge to rip off her T-shirt and bra, slip an ice

55

cube out of her glass, and start rubbing it over her nipples. But instead I just smile at her.

"It was so nice to have a bop up and down," says Sophie.

Has she caught me staring at her boobs?

"You were both bouncing up and down very well," says Ollie. It's not just me then. Only I detect his sarcasm. Hopefully nobody's detected my erection. I'm glad it's so dark in here.

Ollie gets a round in before the main act, Hacksaw, take to the little stage. Hacksaw are a local two-piece punk rock band like no other. They're a bit like other two-piece punk rockers, The White Stripes or The Black Keys, that consist of a guitarist/lead singer and drummer/back-up singer. But where The White Stripes enjoy a punk influence with swamp blues and acoustic folk thrown into the melting pot, The Black Keys exude filth with dirty blues all the way back to Mississippi. Both guitarists have a stupid amount of talent, and I've had the pleasure of seeing both boys up close when they've played live at different UK venues. Jack White brilliantly bashes his guitar like he's battling with inner demons and sings like a banshee with a sore head, but it's Dan Auerbach from The Black Keys who's able to just make his guitar... sing. To the point that when I was watching them at the Fleece & Firkin in Bristol, I couldn't work out if the amazing sounds were coming from him or his guitar.

Don't get me wrong, nobody has and ever will match Hendrix's power and natural raw talent for roaring rock and such heart-felt blues, but Auerbach came damn close. And Auerbach's gruff vocals are the perfect accompaniment to his fret board frenzies and beautifully coarse bluesy rock guitar. That night I saw them in Bristol they blew me sideways.

But The Black Keys aren't a tenth as entertaining as Hacksaw. For a start, the bulldog-faced Roy D Hacksaw does all his lead singing from behind his drum kit, while he's ably backed up by his competent sidekick and guitarist, George McSaw. Their songs aren't littered with Mississippi blues references either. They're rocket-fuelled punk all the way back to Dunkerton, just south of Bath. And these old punks are born entertainers: they're funny and they know how to work a crowd. They rock from the moment when Roy, in his stripy red and black Dennis The Menace jumper, sits behind the drums, scrunches his face into a comedy punk pose, and crashes through the first of a stream of mucky two-minute thrashes. They even try to instigate a mini riot by throwing countless toilet rolls into the crowd, goading everyone to throw them back with gusto. But not after any nose blowing or bottom wiping.

By song three the Porter Butt is going nuts. People don't know whether to pogo, laugh or cheer. Sophie and Susan are having a good go at doing all three. Me and Ollie are bouncing up and down hopelessly out of time. Hacksaw ends on a classic of theirs, *Do Not Feed The Geese*.

"Right you 'orrible lot. Our last song involves a bit of audience participation!" shouts Roy over the jovial jeers. "When we sing, 'Do not feed the geese', I need you to shout back 'THEY'RE DEAD!'"

The big laugh he gets would make grown comedians weep. Roy rips into the song, and we all do as we're told and join in with the chorus. We all move to the front for this one. Me and Sophie are arm-in-arm, shouting for all we're worth.

"Do not feed the geese," growls Roy.

"THEY'RE DEAD!" shouts the crowd.

"Do not feed the geese."

"THEY'RE DEAD!"

"Do not feed the geese."

"THEY'RE DEAD!'"

"The geese, the geese, the geese are dead."

What a handsome racket Hacksaw made. The crowd's reaction of heckles and laughs says it all. Hacksaw finish to a monstrous round of applause and cheers. A few stray toilet rolls bounce off the back of Roy's head as he struts off stage. He turns round, glares, grins, and dramatically throws back double V-signs. Such a shame *TOP 10 HITS* doesn't feature local acts like this.

The post-gig silence makes my ears ring as we all gather near the bar.

"They kicked ass. They played so tight yet brilliantly rough around the edges," Sophie says a little breathlessly. I wouldn't mind making her more breathless. "And so bloody funny. I haven't laughed at a rock gig that much since I saw The Darkness live."

Without warning, Sophie reaches up to me on her tiptoes, rests her hands on my chest, and softly kisses me on the lips. A trickle of sweat from her near-perfect top lip touches mine. It's only a quick kiss. So why am I tingling all over?

"Thanks for inviting me," she says.

"Thanks for coming." It's all I can think of to say back.

"Maybe later," she says, winking very obviously.

Then we both laugh. Because it's a crap joke. Because it's funny. Because it's silly. And because we're laughing nervously in anticipation that it might happen later.

Back to my place then you sexy bitch.

"Back to my place then?" I say.

"Sure thing, you sexy bitch," she says.

Christ, is she a mind reader?

We get back to my flat in impressive time considering the steep hills in the way. We say nothing as we walk inside, throw our coats on chairs in the lounge, and turn and smile to each other, enjoying the moment in silence. I feel strangely alert and almost sober. Sophie makes the first move. She comes towards me, standing close enough for our feet to touch. She tilts her head slightly to one side and looks up at me expectantly. I tuck her curly hair behind her right ear. I tuck another stray strand of curliness behind her left. Using my thumb I touch her chin, and softly touch her bottom lip, then her top lip.

"Can I taste these again?" I say in my sexiest voice. She answers by pushing her lips then her whole body on to me. Our mouths open and our tongues probe inside to begin what I like to call Tongue Kung-Fu.

Sophie breaks away. Are we moving too fast? Or too slow?

"Hang on," she says. "Wait here."

So I wait. I guess we won't be moving things to the bedroom.

I hear the tap running in the kitchen. Must be thirsty. I give her a minute.

Sophie comes back into the lounge holding the washing up bowl full of water. She quickly ambles in, and promptly throws the lot over me. As I'm not exactly expecting Sophie to throw a bowl of water over me in my lounge, I don't think about moving out of the way. Instead I get very wet. I stand still, stunned, as water drips off my sopping wet T-shirt and jeans and trickles down to my feet.

"Oh dear," Sophie says with a cheeky grin. "Well, I guess we'd better get you out of these wet clothes then."

I wipe some of the water off my face, and start laughing. Sophie moves in and kisses me softly, then firmly, on my wet lips. She pauses to take off my T-shirt that's sticking to me and undo the buttons on my jeans, then we snog, and shuffle, and snog, and shuffle all the way to the bedroom.

Sunday morning. Ouch. Head hurts a bit. Belly's grumbling a lot. I don't think I've slept for more than four hours. And yet I feel fantastic. Because Sophie's lying by my side. And because of what happened last night.

Sophie lies on her front, with her eyes closed, curly hair hiding half of her face. I prop myself up on my elbow and I stare at her beautiful lashes and lush lips. Her bare, brown shoulders and lightly muscular back are on display as the duvet covers her modesty below. She sounds like she's purring as she breathes slowly in and out. I'm sure she's smiling in her sleep.

I think back to last night and the natural events that unfolded as we snogged like teenagers and passionately moved things to the bedroom. I could go into all the juicy details as we tenderly made love for the first time.

But I won't.

I'm trying to be a gentleman.

A groan, a stretch, a yawn, and Sophie rolls on her side and pushes herself back into me so we make a pair of perfect spoons. I feel her warm nakedness against mine and I can't help myself rise to the occasion.

"You're awake then?" she mumbles. "What's the story, morning glory?"

I kiss the nape of her neck and she moans with delight, reaching around and placing her hand on the back of my head, rubbing my hair, pulling me closer. I kiss her some more, softly, lingering. My hand's on her hip, then I playfully slide it round to her velvet-covered love pie. She matches my move by reaching around behind her to stroke my hot banana. She wriggles and pushes herself back on to me. We're rolling. And rocking. And rolling. I slide my hand up over her breasts. Her nipples are already pointing out like little pink buttons on a stereo. I try tuning in Radio 2. But it's no use. I try Radio 1. No joy. I'm sure I should be able to tune in something. I try once more. Tweak, fondle, tweak. Then I find it. I tune into Radio Hot Sex. There we go. We're rocking. And rolling. And rocking.

We share a shower and make magnificent hot banana love once more, improvising with the sink, and edge of the bath. And the towel rail. And the fluffy bath mat.

We dry off and get dressed.

Sophie makes some poached eggs on toast, I make some fresh pineapple and mango smoothies. We sit in my window seat, Sophie leans on me, and we survey the view from Camden and down across the city of Bath. The sky's a mixture of grey fluffy clouds and sun rays trying to break through.

I put on Radio 2. I'm able to tune it in first time now. Steve Rong's playing a nausea-inducing love song. Even in my deliriously soppy state I can't listen for more than thirty seconds. I don't think I'll ever manage a whole minute of this mouldy old show from the moustached wonder. I change it to Radio 1 just as it cuts to the news. It's 11:00am.

"Today's top stories. Suspicious deaths at Abbey Road Studios, Tory MP exposed on camera in night club, and will Chelsea win at home today?" says the newsreader.

"What the…"

"…fuck!?"

I turn the volume up.

"Three people have died in suspicious circumstances at Abbey Road Studios in London. The police have yet to release official details of exactly who has died, and how they died, but what we do know is that three people are dead, and three people have been taken to hospital with breathing difficulties."

"Shit the bed!" I say.

"Shitting hell!" says Sophie.

"We don't know yet if this is a murder investigation or a terrible, unfortunate accident. The police have said it happened late yesterday afternoon between the hours of four and six pm."

It cuts to a live broadcast at Abbey Road Studios. The roving reporter repeats what the newsreader has already told us, then goes on to describe the world famous studio and atmosphere outside on the street, but without really giving us anymore information. I turn the volume down.

"Weren't those weasels from Hoodwink recording there?" I say.

"Yeah, yeah," says Sophie, her voice noticeably shaky. "Yes, they were. I have a commission to photograph them on Monday."

"Poor you. I interviewed them once. Never met three boys who have such delusions of grandeur with such a lack of talent," I say.

I instinctively reach for my mobile phone and switch it on. As soon as it's powered up it rings with a voicemail message. It's from Fat Pat.

"Hardy, turn your phone on you cock monster. Have you heard the news? Police aren't releasing details to the news agencies yet, but my source says that all three members of Hoodwink have been killed in their recording booth in Abbey Road Studios last night... by Paul facking McCartney! Fack me. What's going on eh!? Give us a call back when you get this message." Fat Pat left his message at 9:12am. Nearly two hours ago.

"Hoodwink have been murdered," I say, struggling to get the words out, "by Paul McCartney!"

"The three people who've been murdered..." she starts.

"...were Hoodwink," I finish.

"And they were murdered by Paul McCartney!?"

"According to Fat Pat, yes."

"No shitting way," says Sophie. "Guess I won't be photographing them on Monday now then. No way. No shitting way."

It's pronounced with perfect eloquence. She sounds so cute when she swears.

"Yes shitting way," I say. "What the hell is going on?"

"Christ knows Hardy!" She's laughing excitedly now.

"Christ knows Sophers!" For some reason I start half running up and down on the spot and half dancing.

"Bloody great isn't it!? Bloody scary, but bloody great!" Sophie joins me by jumping up and down on the sofa.

"What now then?" she says, eyes bright and hopeful.

Then I remember the email. The bloody email. I stop dancing/running. I feel hot under the collar and I'm not even wearing one.

"There's something you need to see," I say quietly.

I go to the hall and fetch the print out from my jacket pocket then slowly hand it over. I'm about to explain what I think about it all, then I wait: I want to hear and see Sophie's reaction. I want to see if she thinks it's real. She reads it quickly then looks up at me.

"Well shag me backwards," she says.

"Maybe later. Do you think it's a hoax?" I say.

"Do you think Hoodwink have been murdered?"

"Seems that way."

"This email seems that way too. I mean, it could be a hoax. Who's this Hitman?"

"I don't know. That's the big question."

"It's worded very flippantly, but it does talk about Dazza in Cardiff accurately. When did you get this?" She waves the print out around in the air.

"Arrived in my inbox on Friday. I haven't told *anyone* or shown anyone – accept you," I say. But by showing it to Sophie I feel a weight lifting off my shoulders. A problem shared is a problem halved. So now we both have half each. Half an apple each. We're the same apple, hanging off a tree. Like two peas in a pod. Is a pea a fruit or vegetable? My booze addled brain isn't thinking straight.

"You idiot! Why didn't you show it to anyone?"

I feel embarrassed now. I feel my cheeks turn a light shade of red. "I guess because I didn't think it was real."

"Or want to believe it's real," she says.

"Mmm. That too," I say barely audibly. I feel an arse. Not hers, not even mine, I just feel *like* one.

"I thought it might be another wind up. I'm very dubious about any sources after the Princess incident," I say

"It doesn't read like a wind up, and it says," Sophie reads from the email. "'You will find out who will be No.9 on my Top 10 Hit List by the end of the weekend.' And true to their word it looks like we have."

"If Hoodwink are actually dead. We don't know that. It could be that three members of GR8 are dead," I say.

"That's wishful thinking."

"I know. I wish the three crap ones from GR8 would bugger off and die," I say. "I can but dream."

"So who the hell's it from?"

"God knows," I say. "I've no idea. I'm not in the habit of hanging out with psycho killers."

"The email's copied to four newspapers too. Why haven't they published it?" asks Sophie.

"Not everything makes it into the papers or on TV, you know that. Sometimes PR agencies, like Max Clifford's, or higher authorities like the police or Scotland Yard, block the papers printing stories. Failing to comply results in them being shutdown. No slapped wrists, no fired editors, no pissing about, your publication will be closed down," I say.

"But this isn't a case of holding it back in case it endangers national security. This is pop news. Exciting bloody news! About a musician murderer!"

"They're not musicians. They're just singers. Manufactured singers."

"Okay, manufactured singers. But that doesn't mean it shouldn't or won't be printed."

"I'm guessing that since Dazza's death the police have been on red alert. They've probably got hold of a copy of this email from one of the papers and don't want them printing it or showing it on TV. Perhaps so they don't give the killer any publicity, possibly fuelling his motivation, and partly because it only highlights their incompetence because they've not caught anyone yet."

Blimey, where'd that all come from?

"You're quite the investigative journalist, Hardy," she says with an ounce of pride.

"I *am* an investigative journalist, Sophie," I say.

"So you've not shown the email to anybody else? Not even the police?"

"Nope. The newspapers can tell them – if they haven't told them already. I don't want to get involved," I say.

"Don't you think you should at least show it to your editor?"

"No. Not yet," I say.

"So what shall we do now, Inch High Private Eye?" she says, eyes shining.

Fifteen minutes later we're in my trusty Golf driving up the M4 to London. We're heading for Abbey Road Studios, and not sparing the horses. In fact, I'm letting the horses under the bonnet positively gallop along as we nudge into the naughty side of the speed limit. We're both fizzing with excitement. It didn't take much to convince each other we should head up to our fair capital to see what's happening. It just seems like the right thing to do. And the fun thing to do. Besides, I'm a journalist, Sophie's a photographer. We're just doing our jobs.

We arrive around the corner from Abbey Road in just under two hours. We try parking closer but the UK's media and nosey public have already set up camp around the studios. We park up on a multi-story's third floor but don't get out. We both want to hear the end of the song on my car stereo. I want to gather my thoughts too. We sit back and enjoy the Kaiser Chiefs singing the chorus and closing verse of *Modern Way*, and then get out and head to the recording studio.

The closer we get to Abbey Road Studios the denser the crowds become. I lead the way as we push our way through to the barriers stopping the public getting through to the studio doors. Uniformed policemen line the barriers, patiently policing. The crowd are a mixture of ages and nationalities, but they're mostly white English teenage girls. Younger girls are screaming, some are crying, some are singing Hoodwink songs together. One or two are wearing red caps with Hoodwink written in white writing on the front. A small tribute of flowers and letters and Hoodwink CDs have piled up against the barrier. Word must've got out. Or they're fearing the worst. I'm fearing nothing. I'm looking forward to the worst. Hoodwink were a jumped up bunch of brats when I had the misfortune of interviewing them for *TOP 10 HITS*. It was like they walked into the room and all three of their egos were visibly glowing around them. Especially the tall lead singer – Andy? Addie? Eddie? Can't remember – who's head seemed to shine with smugness. I won't miss their conceited faces on TV singing self-centred songs.

I'd called Fat Pat on the way up in the car and arranged to meet him here. It turns out either I'd misheard Fat Pat's message on my phone, or he was misinformed, either way by the time we'd reached London we'd found out – cue comedy drum roll, and cymbal clash – Paul McCartney hadn't killed Hoodwink. But someone with a Paul McCartney *mask* on had. Now, I'm no Inspector Morse, I'd probably be more of a bumbling Lewis anyway, but I think there's a difference between the real ex-Beatle and someone with a mask on of said ex-Beatle.

I'd also called Gary. He bounced off the walls with excitement when I told him the Abbey Road news, and was glad I was already up in London to report on it. I said I'd try and get a scoop of sorts. Probably two scoops. Of chocolate. Or maybe one chocolate and one strawberry. All in a crispy cone, with a flake sticking out of the top. I could be a detective journalist whose 'thing' is that he constantly eats ice cream.

Speaking of greedy bastards, I spot Fat Pat and his portly belly. He's standing in between the TV cameras, journalists and presenters milling about. I shout in his general direction, he waves and walks over to where Sophie and I are hanging over the barrier.

"Alright, nob face?" he says cheerily.

"Alright, lard ass?" I say cheerily.

"And I recognise you," he says smiling in Sophie's direction. "You're the photographer who was at the Cardiff Arena for the Dead Dazza Show."

"The very same. Pleased to meet you," she says.

"Fat Pat, this is Sophie. Sophie, Fat Pat," I say.

"Hello Sophie. Please, call me Pat," he says, sweating out some old cockney charm. Today he's wearing a figure-hugging red hoodie, probably XXL, bleached jeans and bright white trainers. He's not exactly blending into the background. "Nice exclusive shots of Dazza, by the way. You must've done well out of that little collection of front page photos."

"Thank you. Yeah, I did okay," Sophie smiles, glancing at me ever so quickly.

Fat Pat shows us round to a gap in the barrier where a thickset uniformed PC asks to see our ID.

"CID?" he asks.

"NUJ." I flash my National Union of Journalists card, Sophie does the same, and he moves aside to let us through. A gaggle of girls try to slip in with us, but the PC moves into their path and stops them.

"It's getting quite exciting all this lark isn't it?" says Fat Pat, indicating to the media hounds and police surrounding us.

"Yeah, first Cardiff and now this. You wait ages for a pop star murder then two come along at once. Typical," I say.

"I'm going to grab what shots I can," says Sophie, holding up her camera. She pulls her hair up into a pony tail and puts on her red cap. As she skips off her pony tail jumps up and down. I sneak a cheeky glance at her arse. It looks so tasty in her jeans.

"So, it wasn't Paul McCartney who's murdered Hoodwink then?" I say to Fat Pat, deadpan.

"I didn't say it was, wise ass. You must've misheard my message. From what the security guards have said to my source, their CCTV caught..."

"...their CCTV caught? Not anything with their own fat stubby fingers?" I interrupt.

"Of course not, they were too busy watching the action down the Arsenal ground on the TV, instead of watching the action down the corridor on the CCTV," says Fat Pat. He starts again. "From what the lazy security bastards have said, the CCTV tapes caught a well-built man wearing a Paul McCartney mask on camera. He was dressed in dark colours and left the building around 5pm. But it wasn't actually until around 6pm, when one of the guards was doing their rounds, that they found Hoodwink's manager, producer and mixing engineer unconscious and tied up on the floor in Studio 3. There was a smell of gas in the studio. Sleeping gas by all accounts."

"Christ," I say.

"My friend said the security guard opened the studio door, then unlocked the recording booth door to find..." Fat Pat goes quieter, "...all three members of Hoodwink lying in a pile on the floor. All three were dead."

"Christ," I say again.

"The security guard said he saw some dried blood in one of the boy's ears."

"Bloody ear holes? What's that all about?" I say.

"This is where it gets interesting. Our karaoke killer – I thought of that name by the way – rigged up the mixing desk so he could pipe extra loud music into the sound proof recording booth. The combination of extreme volume and a confined space meant our three little boy band members suffered death by decibels."

I find myself laughing. Not very respectful I know but I can't help it. "You've got to admire this karaoke killer's style."

"Admire. And fear."

I stop laughing.

"I suppose the other three were lucky to survive," I say.

"You could say that."

"Although, if he could tie them up and put them to sleep, he could've murdered them as well. Perhaps he's only after pop stars," I say. There I go again. When did I suddenly become a detective?

"You could be right."

"What's the line from the cops? Have they any other evidence to go on apart from the CCTV tape? What about fingerprints, things left behind at the scene?" I ask.

"What are you? Columbo all of a sudden or summat?"

"Just thinking, that's all." And I am. It makes a nice change.

"Apparently the place was clean as a whistle, no prints or clues left behind. Whoever's behind this is a real professional."

"And a real psycho too," I say.

There's a succession of screams from one of the larger groups of girls. I look round and spot Sophie in her red cap clicking away, taking various photos of the outside of the studio and of groups of girls singing and crying. She moves gracefully into different positions to get the best angle for each photo.

"Any of the cops hinted that it could be the same guy behind the Dead Dazza episode in Cardiff?" I ask.

"Remember they haven't even officially admitted that Dazza was murdered yet. Let alone admit Hoodwink were murdered, or that the two are linked. They're keeping it all as quiet as possible."

"Probably means they don't know anything or have any leads that's why," I say. I think about telling Fat Pat about the Hitman email, but think better of it. He doesn't need to know. One of his sources will let it slip sooner or later anyway. Plus I like this give and take of information. Pat gives, I take.

"You could be right there, Columbo," he says.

I look nothing like Columbo. Why can't he call me Starsky. Or Hutch. Who was the dark haired one again?

"You heard anything else about Cardiff then?" I ask.

"Not exactly."

"Not exactly what? Just tell me, dear Pat. You were about to tell me on the phone on Friday anyway."

"Okay, okay. But you owe me. Twice now!" he says. It's become our little running joke that I owe him, even though we both know it's Fat Pat who owes me after his coke snorting cock up last year. He speaks quieter now. "Apparently there was some sort of special device found on the lead connected to the mic Dazza was using when he got electrocuted. Something that shouldn't have been there. It altered how the electric current was carried or something."

"So the electrics were definitely fiddled with, and it definitely wasn't an accident just like we'd suspected."

"It weren't no accident, no," says Fat Pat quietly. "Seems we've got a karaoke killer on the loose, Columbo."

I try talking to the cops but they say nothing worth jotting down. Fat Pat's told me more than enough, though, so I think a pint is in order. I leave Sophie to try and get access inside to take pictures, and find a friendly enough, warm enough pub two streets away. Out of respect I have three pints of London beer for three dead boy band members, while I efficiently type up a few pages of notes on my laptop. It's mainly what Fat Pat told me, details about what the security guards found, plus a few official yet empty quotes I got from the cop in charge of the crime scene – although they aren't worth the Word document they are written on. The police didn't have much to go on. Or weren't letting on if they did.

Even though it's Sunday – working on the sacred day? Really! – I quickly write up a kid-friendly news story for the magazine from my notes. I call Gary to tell him I'm emailing it down, tapping into the pub's WiFi web access.

"Great, that's great! Good work Hardy," he says excitedly. "I'll put your story and other teasers up on the *TOP 10 HITS* website for now, but I'll say more exclusive news to follow in the next issue of the mag. Early sales figures for the current issue are looking strong already, by the way."

He doesn't seem overly bothered to learn that Hoodwink were murdered. I know the feeling.

"Great to see you using your initiative. I think you should stay up there. Get a nice hotel room – not too nice! – and stay for a few days, see if you can dig up anything else exciting before next Tuesday's mag deadline okay?"

"Sounds like a plan," I say. I shouldn't drink and drive home now anyway. "I'll see what I can do."

I fire up my web browser and find the best hotel our little publishing house can afford. Gary normally insists on budget hotels when we stay over after gigs or interviews, but as he's said 'get a nice hotel room' I'll take nice to mean stupidly expensive. I find The Royal's telephone number from their website and provisionally book a room. Then I call Sophie.

"Do you fancy staying the night in a really swanky hotel instead of spending hours dredging across London and back home to the West Country?" I say.

"Well, the photography job I had in the morning has been cancelled because the inconsiderate little boy band brats got themselves murderalized in a bizarre recording booth incident, " says Sophie. Seems she's been digging for dirt too.

"You've heard it's definitely Hoodwink, too, then," I say.

"Yep!"

What a detective duo we could make.

"So, wanna stay up in London with me?"

"I'd love to accept your gracious offer."

"Cool,"

"Are you paying then?"

"The mag's paying."

"Cool!"

"Meet me at the end of Abbey Road in five minutes."

I drive us up Park Lane while London's Sunday traffic chugs along. I don't mind the city in small doses but I couldn't handle the constant congestion. Shouldn't everyone be out in the countryside? It's Sunday for lord's sake. The three tributary beers I had earlier don't seem to affect my driving as I pull neatly into the splendour of The Royal Hotel and park around the back. My grubby, old VW stands out nicely against the ranks of polished Jaguars and Porsches shining under the car park lights. We walk around the front and Sophie grins at me as she takes my arm and we climb the steps all the way up to a five star evening of glitz, glamour and posh plonk. We walk past the immaculate doorman and into an atrium as big at the Albert Hall. Gold adorns the vast ceiling that feels so far away I go giddy when I look all the way up.

"One of your finest double en suite rooms please," I say to the smartly dressed receptionist.

Sophie is resting against me. I have my arm around her slim waist. We're acting like newly weds. The receptionist smiles at us. I smile at her, then at Sophie. Sophie smiles at her, then at me. It's probably too much smiling but, sod it, we're about to live the high life so what's not to smile about. I take our key card and we head off to the lift, passing the main bar, the member's bar, and the lounge bar.

We'd only packed bare essentials when we left Bath as we didn't know if we'd stop for the night. There is going to be something liberating about wearing jeans, trainers and scruffy sweatshirts in a palace that's frequented by royalty and rock and pop stars.

As we wait for the lift I look through the large, open lounge bar doors. That's when I spot him. He's enveloped by a sea of blondes. Sean Bates. Used to be in the boy band Red, but has since pursued a solo career. He hasn't done anything of note other than shag his way through six month's worth of Page 3 models, generally appearing on page five the following day. He has the looks and celebrity status to attract pretty vacant groupies, although he's really hiding a very average face and very average talent behind an above average haircut.

One of the blondes pours champagne down his neck straight from the bottle. No class. Some of the drink misses his mouth, dribbling off his chin and bubbling down his neck and over an exposed chest and an expensive-looking shirt barely buttoned up. He throws his head back and laughs loudly like he owns the place. He grabs the bottle and gets his own back by pouring ridiculous amounts of booze into the blonde's mouth. She greedily gulps but it's no use, she looks ready to enter a wet T-shirt competition, and judging by her fake appendages she'd probably win first prize. Sean Bates laughs loudly again then puts his arms around two other gormless blondes, reaching down and aggressively grabbing their ample breasts.

"Before I worked in the music mag industry I thought it would be pretty cool to be a pop star," I say quietly to Sophie as I look over to Sean Bates, "but the more I see the more I realise there are so many pop star cocks like Sean Bates. I'm glad I'm only ever on the outside looking in."

"He's such a dick," Sophie says simply.

We turn away, bored of watching The Sean Show. The lift is taking its time, but then it does have over twenty floors to cover. We stand close to each other and both manage to surreptitiously grope each other's behinds. Great dirty minds think alike. We're giggling like lovers do when the lift arrives.

In our huge, extravagant room up on the eighth floor, we explore the big bathroom, the lounge area and mini bar, and then get down to exploring the king size bed and each other's bodies.

*   *

In contrast to Bob Geldof and his Boomtown Rats, you quite like Mondays. It defines the start of the week. This Monday you've set yourself a mission you're particularly looking forward to accomplishing. You'd thought about putting it off, but no sense waiting until later in the week. No rest for the wicked.

You'd put plans in place for No.8 on your Hit List before Christmas. You'd phoned your bodyguard contacts, pumping them for details, so you could work out the best place to pin down this pop pretender. Carney was the bodyguard who came up with the goods. You made up excuses like talking to him about the good old days when you worked as bodyguards together, pretending you're bodyguarding for such and such now. "Who are you guarding at the mo? Oh yeah, nice. So where you working? Yeah? And where are they staying? Sweet. What name are they using there? Bruce Wayne? Ha ha. Yeah, good one..." until you knew enough to make solid plans.

Your singer of choice this week is staying in London while working and promoting his new single via any radio station or TV programme that'll have him. Thanks to your bodyguard contacts you've managed to track him down to the hotel he's staying in. Once he's secure in the hotel he's safe from the prying public, and the bodyguards will leave him to it. Free to do as he pleases. You'll be free to do as you please as well.

You stroll casually along Park Lane as bright streetlights line the way. One hand is tucked in your trouser pocket, the other's carrying a silver Nokia mobile phone-cum-PDA. You're freshly shaven, wearing aftershave, and dressed in a bespoke black single-breasted suit, pressed white cotton shirt, and neat black leather shoes: they have no tread on the soles already so you didn't need to sand them down to cover your footprints. You pull on your cuffs so your shirt and silver cuff links can be seen poking out under your suit sleeves. You look like a penguin, but feel much more at ease than one out of water, you're used to wearing a suit or uniform. Today you're McNamara the businessman off to a business meal and so you'll act the business too. The medium-length black wig you've glued on and slicked back with a bit of gel is helping you get into your 'greed is good' Gordon Gecko mode too. This week's made-to-measure wig

69

isn't itchy at all and you're becoming more and more comfortable with each disguise.

Although your fake moustache has taken a little getting used to. You're wearing it in tribute to Freddie and today's mission. It's medium length, medium bush. It's not tickling your top lip or nose but you feel like it wants to. You read recently in some magazine that the moustache will never come back in fashion. They don't know what they're on about. It was popular as ever when you were in Hereford, even if you didn't have facial hair then, and if it was good enough for Freddie, it's good enough for you. You had thought about the fake teeth as a full complement for Freddie, but that would be taking the piss. You'd look more Peter Sellers as Inspector Clouseau. And this ain't the movies. This is real. This is serious.

You stroke your moustache and look at your watch. 7:45pm. The target for Hit No.8 should be having his evening drink shortly. You take a deep breath and relax as you walk into the hotel entrance, up the steps, nodding at the doorman, and into The Royal. You pretend to answer a call on your phone and talk as you walk through the expansive reception. You spy a plain-clothed security guard sat on a range of sofas feigning interest in a magazine. His furtive eyes say it all. He's not waiting for someone. He's waiting for *something*. The phone trick isn't because you're concerned you may not fit into the hotel's clientele, it's to keep up the businessman act.

You walk up to reception, end the pretend call, and check into the room you booked on the phone yesterday. You use some fake ID and pay in cash.

"Room 525, Mr O'Nory," says the uniformed receptionist as she hands you a key card.

"Thank you."

You don't go up to your room, instead you casually walk into the lounge bar. You survey your surroundings, careful not to look anyone in the eye, then slide onto a stool around to the right of the large crescent-shaped bar. From here you can see whoever walks in from either entrance and will be able to keep an eye on anyone, wherever they sit in the bar, even if they're behind you thanks to the mirrors above the bar. Not that you're planning to sit around and socialise all night, you've got a job to do. Just as soon as your target arrives.

You order a JD and coke. The rock 'n' roll drink of choice and the drink of choice for your sharply dressed businessman. You keep one eye on the door and the other on the match on the box. The sound's off on the TV as Robbie Williams's *No Regrets* plays quietly on the stereo. There are a handful of tables with a mixture of rich American tourists, you can tell by the caps and expensive clothes, and British businessmen, none of the suits or hairstyles are sharp enough to be European. Two businesswomen in power suits, could be French judging by the way they're handling their cigarettes, are sat on the other side of the bar drinking fine, chilled wine. You wish you had a third eye to watch them as well. You sip on your JD and coke, careful to keep the napkin around the glass to avoid leaving fingerprints.

You hear their drunken laughter before they enter the bar. A man's dirty laugh followed by girly giggles. Sean Bates bundles through the door with a busty blonde on either arm. He flops down on a bar stool in between you and the businesswomen, about twenty feet away, and orders champagne. There aren't any bodyguards looking over him just as you'd calculated. He kisses the nape of the neck of the blonde on his left, while the one on the right is smiling and looking content. You can't see his right hand from where you're sitting. Perhaps he's multi-tasking.

You're on your third JD and coke, when Sean is on his second bottle of champagne, and second neck to nibble. At 10:21pm Sean is joined by five more girls and two boys, all of which look so young you wonder if their parents just dropped them off. You've found a newspaper to pretend to read, but you're enjoying half-watching Sean in action from your vantage point at the bar and checking out the match on TV that's stuck at 1-1. You're not enjoying the fact he's taking advantage of some underage groupies and has moved from busty to pert on the boob stakes – you'd heard he likes them young. And you're not enjoying listening to his inflated ego brag loudly about who he's been rubbing shoulders and singing with recently. You're enjoying it because it'll make your task more enjoyable when you follow him up to his room and kill him.

At 11:13pm Sean Bates takes the hand of a pretty but painfully skinny teenage girl and announces to anyone who's listening that "I'm off to my room to snort some Charlie off her tits." Sean and his groupie head for the lift. It's all so easy for you to follow. Too easy. You double check he hasn't got a bodyguard lurking close by. You're clear. You down your drink, still careful with the napkin, and pay in cash and leave a healthy tip for the barman who's paid you no attention all night – just as you'd wanted. You reach the lift just in time to jump in with Sean and groupie.

They're too busy with each other's lips and propping each other up to notice you. They've already pushed the button for the 12th floor. You select the 13th floor and ignore them as you tuck some strands of hair behind your ears and stroke your moustache. It's only a short lift ride but Sean still manages to whisper a little too loudly – on purpose? – into the girl's ear what he plans to do to her when

71

they get to his room. They fall out of the lift on the 12th floor and drunkenly bounce off the corridor walls to his room. You pull on a pair of thin leather gloves from your pocket, press the 'hold doors' button, check nobody else is on the floor, and step out to see which door Sean's gone in. Once they're inside you walk down to their door. Room 1209.

You walk back to the lift, but walk straight past to find the way to the stairs. There's a staircase next to the lifts. You don't want that one. You walk back past Sean's room to the end of the corridor and find the fire exit staircase you're after. You check the door works and there aren't any cameras. It works, no cameras. You already know these stairs lead to the basement car park and your escape route out of the hotel. You walk back to the lift and ride down to the fifth floor and head to your room. You immediately phone the concierge from the room's telephone by the bed. You don't sit on the bed. You keep your gloves on, no fingerprints will be left behind. You enjoy the feeling of wearing the leather gloves. They help you switch on, get in the mood for murdering.

"Hello Mr O'Nory," says the concierge reading your name from the computer screen no doubt.

"I believe you have a special rocking chair I've ordered and arranged to be delivered to me here. It should've arrived today addressed to Mr O'Nory. My first name's Jack," you say politely.

"Hold please and I'll go and check for you," says the concierge. Your little name joke is lost on him.

You'd arranged for the rocking chair to be delivered to The Royal earlier in the day. It's authentic as rocking chairs go: it's wooden, and it rocked when you'd tried it out in the shop off Covent Garden. You're no expert when it comes to chairs so it could be a piece of crap for all you know, but it'll serve its purpose. You were already in your businessman suit and disguise when you were rocking chair shopping. The shop assistant treated you with a level of respect you don't normally enjoy. You paid for the chair in cash.

"Hello sir? Yes, your rocking chair is here," says the concierge.

"Can you send it up to my room straight away please?"

"That's room 525. Certainly sir. It'll be right with you."

Six minutes later there's a knock on the door. You check the spy hole out of habit. It's room service. Well, rocking chair service. You open the door.

"Your chair, sir," says the bell boy, with a confused smile.

You smile under your moustache and tip him a tenner. You take the chair into the room for as long as it takes the bell boy to disappear to the lifts and back down to reception. Then you drag it back out into the corridor and carry it to the lift. Making sure the lift is empty, you take the chair up to the 12th floor and carry it to Sean's room. You knock on the door. Three quick knocks.

No answer.

Three more knocks, a little harder.

No answer.

You think about kicking the door open, but stick to your plan. You thump the door with the base of your fist this time, three times. Then stand with your hands behind your back, flexing your fists inside the gloves.

The door half opens, and Sean Bates' head peers around it.

"Yeah, what? I didn't order no room service," he says. His pupils are dilating.

"I'm from Blue Moon your security firm Mr Bates. Your rocking chair you ordered is here," you say, and point proudly at the chair.

"Rocking chair? Y'what? I didn't order no rocking chair." He looks puzzled but intrigued. He opens the door fully. He's wearing nothing on his feet or top half, all he has on is a pair of jeans: Versace is written in big letters on one leg. Sean stares at the rocking chair then walks towards you and the chair and reaches out to touch it.

"It's beautiful isn't it? I was just admiring the craftsmanship myself when I was…" You're just talking. It distracts people. It means when you attack they're not expecting it.

You punch Sean firmly in the stomach, putting all your weight behind it.

He groans and holds his guts. You've punched the wind out of him so he can't shout. As he's doubling over in front of the chair, you bend your knees and strike upwards, extending your body fully with a hard upper cut to the chin. He flops back neatly to sit unconscious in the chair. Blood seeps from his jaw that's now slack, lifeless. You push Sean sat in the rocking chair quickly across the carpet, through the open door and into his room.

The girl groupie sits up and looks tense as she stares at you pushing an unconscious Sean inside. She's naked on top of the bed covers and seems to have been already crying before you entered. She looks barely sixteen years old. The TV's on a music channel and hip hop music blares out of the speakers. The only light emanating into the room is coming from the two bedside lamps. You can see several short lines of coke on the bedside cabinet. A rolled up twenty lies next to them.

"What's happened? What's going on? Is Sean okay?" she sniffs, making an attempt to cover herself with the bed sheet.

"I'm from Sean's security firm. I was delivering his rocking chair when he had a funny turn. It happens to him sometimes. You'd better leave now," you say.

She tries to wipe the tears from her eyes, but they keep coming. She's shocked but seems to have believed you. Speak with authority and they all will.

"Are you okay?" you ask. You don't care about her, but as you're posing as security you feel obliged to ask.

"I didn't like it. What he was doing to me. He said he liked it. But I... didn't like it..." she rambles, tears continuing to trickle down her cheeks.

You haven't got time for this. You gather up her clothes strewn across the floor and the sofa and hand them to her.

"Get dressed. Go home," you say.

You turn your back as she slides off the bed, takes her clothes, sniffs, then slowly gets dressed. You keep an eye on Sean. He doesn't move. You use the remote to turn the volume down on the TV. You could easily kill her as well, but she's not on your Hit List. When she's dressed you quickly walk her to the door.

"Go downstairs, get your friends from the bar, and leave the hotel immediately. Stay away from guys like Sean in the future. Celebrities like him think they're above the law. But they're not," you say looking her in the eye.

The young girl nods.

"Don't tell anybody about this. Not for your sake. Or Sean's sake. If you sell a kiss 'n' tell story to the tabloids, I'll find you and I'll hurt you."

"Why would I want to tell the papers about this? I want to forget the whole thing ever happened. He's such a shit," she says, looking over your shoulder at Sean Bates slumped in the chair.

"Good. Now go."

She nods, and gives you a nervous smile. You close the door.

Maybe she won't tell anyone, maybe she will, but it should give you enough time to complete your Hit No.8.

You pull out a bag of long, thick zip ties from your suit jacket pocket and quickly tie Sean's ankles, legs, arms and wrists to the rocking chair. You pull the zip ties tight. You grab a half-full bottle of champagne that's on top of the mini-bar fridge. You push Sean so he starts rocking back and forth. You shake up the bottle, holding it with your gloved hand and gripping it tightly. Keeping your thumb over the end, you slowly release it to spray the bubbly in Sean's face. He coughs, inhales deeply, splutters, blinks, and opens his eyes. His head's lolling around on his shoulders. It hangs down on to his chest, before he lifts it up to try and focus on you. He's looking in your direction but can't see you. You give him a minute and walk through the bedroom to a lounge area that has a balcony. You walk back to Sean and push him on the chair towards the balcony doors. The rocking chair slides easily on the soft carpet. You turn him around, then slap his face, not hard, just to get his attention. It works.

"Get off! What the...?" he says wriggling around in the chair. "Get off. Who are you? Get off me! What's going on? Get off! What do you want?" As rants go it's not bad, it's almost like a rap. Well, crap rap. You hate crap rap. You slap him again just for the hell of it. Blood begins to run steadily from his mouth as he yanks the zip ties holding him securely by the feet and wrists. They don't budge, but he does start rocking back and forth on the chair.

"Do you know how famous I am? What have I done to deserve this shit!?" he whines.

"*Will We Rock You.*"

"Our song?" he shouts, confused.

"No. Not your song. Queen's. You did a cover version. A very bad one."

"W-w-what?" he says. He looks up at you. "Who are you?"

"Consider me as your representative from The Trade Union. I'm having you on the Trade Descriptions Act. Because you sang 'we will rock you'. But didn't. You didn't rock at all. You were rubbish. Instead of power chords and guitar solos and Freddie Mercury's soaring vocals, there were immature voices weeping out over a drum 'n' bass backing track and computerised fake guitar sounds."

"But we rocked!" He spits some blood as he says so.

"Nope. All you did was crucify a fine rock song. You didn't rock at all. You swayed slightly with your other putrid pop ballads, but there was certainly no rocking."

You spin Sean around on the chair, open the doors, and push him out on to the balcony. The cold winter air hits you in the face. It's refreshing. Sean's half naked torso should be shivering but instead his sweat glistens under the moon light. The view from the 12th floor balcony is impressive. You can see Hyde Park across the road, although nobody else is out on their balconies this evening to enjoy it.

"W-what... W-w-what are you doing?"

You don't answer. You simply bend down then lift him and the chair up on to the balcony wall. You turn him around, carefully balancing him on the 18-inches of brickwork, so he's facing you. You make sure he's not rocking. You stroke your moustache playfully. You wonder if Sean's realised the moustache is a tribute to the late, great Freddie.

"W-what are y-y-you putting me up h-h-here for? You're having a f-f-fucking laugh aren't you!?"

"For me, music, and this," you point to the chair balancing precariously on the balcony wall, "is no laughing matter."

Sean stares over the side of the chair and looks down to the ground twelve floors below, then closes his eyes and swallows.

"P-p-please. You cannot be serious," he pleads quietly.

"Is that an impression of John McEnroe?" you say.

"Eh?"

"Never mind. Look, it's for the best. You were in a band that was crap, and now you've gone solo and you're even more crap. You can't play an instrument. You can't write lyrics. You can't read music. You can't write songs."

"So?" It's all he manages.

You start the chair rocking very slowly.

"D-d-don't touch the chair."

"You can barely hold a tune now your band mates have pissed off. Your career is doomed. As a wannabe solo singer you're going nowhere. You're just fodder for paparazzi and the tabloids and celebrity pages in cheap magazines. I'm doing you a favour."

He doesn't say anything. He just swallows.

"I'm being nice. I'm giving you one last chance to rock before you die."

You push the chair some more. It's rocks back and forth.

"Now you're rockin' Sean!" you say.

He doesn't laugh. Obviously doesn't share your sense of humour. Back and forth. Back and forth.

"You rock, Sean! I'm rocking your fucking world, man!" You're shouting now.

Back and forth. Back and forth.

You push the chair a little harder. The rockers on the bottom of the chair slide back slightly on the balcony wall. The chair continues to rock back, and forth, and back.

*   *

It's a lovely winter's evening. Mist is rising from the busy roads of London as the streetlights struggle to break through the murky, winter air. It's our second night in The Royal and we're both slipping into the extravagant lifestyle all too easily. I was sticking around here this evening as ordered, in case anything develops from the Abbey Road Studio massacre and I can get a scoop. Sophie had said it seemed a shame to leave me alone with such a nice big bed. So we spent the day together lounging around the three hotel bars, eating and drinking things we'd never even heard of before, let alone tasted.

She's been great company. It's been effortless. Obviously living the posh life doesn't require much effort from anyone, but I don't think I'll ever get bored of a girl like Sophie.

We treated ourselves to some posh new clothes with the money we had from the Dead Dazza photos. She bought a slinky black dress and slinky black shoes and I bought a classic single-breasted suit and white shirt, with smart black lace-ups. We got dressed up earlier, had a deliciously expensive seafood dinner, then slipped back to our room on the eighth floor to rip each other's clothes off and have a deliciously satisfying shag half on the bed, half on the plush carpeted floor. We're just basking in the post-sex glow, posh towelling dressing gowns on. It's late evening.

I pour Sophie a glass of expensive champagne – when in Rome and all that – then pour myself one. I turn round and hand Sophie her glass just in time to see someone sat in a chair plummet past our balcony window.

Someone sat in a chair just plummeted past our window!?

They were really moving as they screamed past so I'm guessing they weren't flying. I'm not sure what I've just seen.

"DID YOU JUST SEE THAT!?" I say very loudly considering Sophie is barely three feet away from me.

"Why are you shouting?" she says. "See what?"

I point to the window.

She looks at me blankly.

I rush over to the balcony doors and fling them open.

I point once again.

"Yes? It's Hyde Park, Hardy," she says. She thinks I'm pointing way across the road. "Did something just happen over there?"

Maybe I've imagined the whole thing.

"Hardy, are you okay?"

I'm sure someone dropped by. I think it could've been a bare-chested man. They were strapped to a chair. A chair? Am I going nuts? What do they put in this champagne anyway? The bubbles always go right to my head.

I need to know. Not about the champagne. About what I think I saw. I need to know if I've made the whole thing up. I walk out on to our balcony and peer over the edge.

I haven't made it up.

Way down below someone is now pavement pizza. They've made a pretty pattern of blood and guts on the tarmac driveway. What's left of the chair is lying splintered all around them.

"Well fuck a duck," I say. I feel sick and nearly wretch.

Sophie comes to my side and looks over the edge with me.

"What is that!?" she says pointing down, squinting through the darkness and the mist.

"Who is... who *was* that, you mean," I say

"That... mess... is someone?"

77

"Was someone."

"Shitting shit it!"

"Shit. And it."

"What a bloody mess."

"Bloody and messy, yes."

The cold evening mist is moving about in the breeze. Luckily – or unluckily, if I'm honest, I'm not keen on blood and guts, whoever's they are – the mist lifts slightly so we get a clear view all the way to the bloody driveway.

"What do you think happened?" Sophie asks.

We ponder in silence for a while. But it doesn't take long before we realise what we could've just witnessed.

"We may have just witnessed No.8 on The Hit List," I say quietly.

"But... but..."

"Or someone's just had an unfortunate accident while tied to a chair."

"Very unfortunate to fall umpteen flights still sat on a chair."

We continue to stare over the edge looking down at what's left of the body and the chair. Stunned, shocked. It feels like forever but probably isn't even a minute. I can see the doorman in his long coat surveying the scene at floor level. After a while he's joined by what looks like the suited hotel manager. He turns away, then walks to the front lawn and throws up. Other staff run out and run back in again holding their mouths. Only the doorman bothers looking up towards us and wherever the chair fell from. I peer upwards as well but can only see the undersides of balconies, and a black, cloudy sky.

I down my glass of champagne. Sophie does the same.

"What should we do now?" she says.

"Let's get dressed. Get your camera. We're going to get that exclusive after all," I say.

No. 7

No I don't have a gun
Come As You Are, Nirvana

I have a theory. Everything men do is to impress women. Whether
that's driving a flash car or buying a smart new shirt to impress an
attractive girl they fancy. Or whether they're trying to impress their
mothers by chasing careers to the top or providing them with grand
kids. The same goes for rock stars; trying to impress girls with their
pseudo-poetic lyrics, passionate singing, moody looks, gratuitous
guitar playing and flirtatious gyrations on stage. Men try to impress
women by acting macho in all sorts of situations.

This is what I'm thinking about as I'm trying not be sick in front
of Sophie outside the front of The Royal. I've got one eye on her and
one eye on what's left of someone splattered across the tarmac.

I say *someone*, but from the jeans and large chunk of head and
hair still intact among the blood and innards, I know it's our dear
friend, Sean Bates.

I think this means he was No.8 on The Top 10 Hit List.

Sophie instinctively starts taking as many different photographs
from as many different angles as possible before the police arrive.
I try to think about something other than Sean Bates' guts, which
is proving difficult as that's all I can see displayed across the cold
floor. My stomach does a back flip. Then a forward roll. I wretch
slightly, a little bit of sick creeps up, but I manage to keep it down
for now.

Sophie looks up at me. I smile at her, putting on a brave face.
She squats down on one knee to get nearer to the remains of Sean
and the chair. She's wearing her red cap to keep her hair out the
way. I love the way she tucks her locks up into her cap. She twiddles
with her telephoto zoom lens and takes some close ups.

"You close enough there Sophie?" I joke. I'm trying to make light of it, for my sake mainly.

"It's funny," she says, continuing to take photos, "I know it's repulsive... and disgusting... and sad. I know I should be upset. But looking through my camera lens at this mess makes it all seem so unreal. I feel so detached."

I'm glad she's feeling as strong as a house. A detached one at that. It's then I notice she doesn't look at bloody entrails and smashed bones without peering through her camera's viewfinder.

"I know you're press, but don't you think that's enough now you two?" It's the doorman. He's not angry, he says it respectfully.

He's been decent enough, after Sophie had hit him with a sexy smile, to let us get close while the hotel manger had gone inside to call the police, and an ambulance for some reason. Although I think it's possibly too late for the latter judging by how little there is left of Sean. I look at the smashed wood of the chair next to the shattered bone sticking out of Sean's thigh. Some of the pieces of wood look like they were from a rocking chair. Maybe an emergency carpenter should be called on to the scene as well. Nobody else has been allowed near. The doorman hasn't let people out of the hotel, nor anyone into the hotel grounds. He's done a good job.

"Yes. You're right," I say to the doorman while still staring at what's left of Sean Bates. "Thank you. You've been very lenient."

I turn towards our happy snapper. "Sophie. That'll do."

She stops clicking and stays still on one knee, then she drops the camera down. She's probably only two feet away from the mess left of Sean Bates. I can smell what can only be described as gone off meat from where I'm stood twenty feet away. (Is that where the phrase 'dead meat' comes from?) God knows what the stench is like right up close. I feel bad. I shouldn't have suggested to Sophie to get photos of all this. I can produce an exclusive without the need for gory images. She puts her hand over her nose and mouth, stands up and walks towards me. It's then, after her work is done, she starts shaking, and quietly weeping.

I hear the faint sound of sirens coming towards the hotel. I put my arm around Sophie and walk us both back inside and into the lounge bar for one or five stiff drinks.

*   *

From the shadows of the trees and the safety of the dense bushes surrounding the front of The Royal, you watch a smartly dressed man and woman walk back inside the hotel. You think you recognise him, but you definitely recognise her.

There are no streetlights or hotel up lights near where you're crouched down so you know nobody can see you. The darkness of night is your friend. You're breathing lightly, aware your breath is visible as it hits the freezing evening air. The doorman is the only person you can see outside the hotel now. He's standing by the main doors but looking around inside the hotel and towards the main gates, away from your position. He's avoiding looking directly at the bloody carnage, the little pile of flesh and wood outside the hotel entrance. You think about taking a closer look at the remains, but even from where you are it's obvious he won't be singing again. That's all you wanted. That was the mission. You feel satisfied.

You can hear a stream of police sirens, you'd estimate the cars are about a mile away. You flex your fingers in your gloves and think about slipping back through the fire exit door in to the basement car park where you've just made your escape. It wouldn't take you long to get to the girl. You recognised her easily. It was the red cap and camera. But no. She's not part of the plan. Leave her. Don't compromise your little pop project. You know she took pictures of Dazza in Cardiff. You remember her with her cap and camera in the press pit as you'd walked off stage. But those photos didn't do any harm then and her photos of the remains of Sean Bates won't do any harm now. She's not the police. She's press. You don't mind a bit of media coverage. Quite like it, in fact. If she was photographing evidence proving you'd been at the scene, rather than the bleeding obvious, that would be different.

You can hear the police sirens getting closer now. Best be off. You stroke your fake 'tache, check the doorman isn't looking your way, and quietly push your way through the bushes, sliding over the hotel wall and dropping down softly into an alley way. As you walk quickly, quietly away from Park Lane, you remember where you know the man from. It's Matthews. Hardy Matthews. *TOP 10 HITS* magazine. One of your five chosen press gangs. You should really give him a call. Let him know your little project is all on schedule, perhaps give him a teaser about the next three victims on your Top 10 Hit List. You quite liked what he wrote in *TOP 10 HITS* about Cardiff. Reading between the lines, it was polite piss taking and pointing out Dazza won't be a real loss to pop.

You smile to yourself as you continue down the alley. Sean Bates is no great loss to pop either. Another job well done from your Top 10 Hit List.

Three down, seven to go.

You think about treating yourself to a late night Chinese. Might even buy yourself a beer or two while you're there. It always tastes better when you've really earned it.

To make the perfect Cuba Libre a barman needs quality white rum, preferably Havana Club. They should put the ice in the glass first, then the rum, squeeze the juice out of two fresh limes, fill the glass up with full fat coke, pop a slice of lime in for good measure, and finish it off with a straw.

Thankfully The Royal barman knows exactly what he's doing. We're sat at the lounge bar. Sophie is sipping on a large glass of white. I'm drinking quickly and I'm about to get stuck into my second rum when Sophie says she should, "Try it for me first." She then proceeds to keep trying it, trying it some more, until it's all but tried out.

"Why do women do that?" I say.

"What?" she says, all big eyes and innocence.

"Say they don't want something, then take it all anyway. You did it last night too by eating more than half of my spectacular tarte tatin after saying 'No, I'm fine, I don't want any dessert.'"

Sophie just smiles at me, sipping the last of my rum.

"And now you've done it again! You said you didn't want one, then you freaking polish off all my lovely rum."

She leans back on her stool and starts laughing. "It's a woman's prerogative to change her mind."

"Hmm," I say. "Now, I'm about to order *myself* another large rum. Would you like one yourself Sophie or another glass of wine?" I raise an eyebrow, just the one. Roger Moore would be proud of me.

"No thank you," she manages before bursting into laughter.

Better than bursting open, I guess. And better than bursting into tears. I'm glad she's stopped crying now. I'm about to order across the bar when a plain-clothed man walks up to us.

"I'm Detective Chief Inspector Johnson from the Avon and Somerset Constabulary. I'm heading up the investigation of the death of Sean Bates," he says opening his wallet to show us his ID.

Make that a plain-clothed *police*man. He certainly is plain-clothed. A brown pair of trousers and even browner jacket are hanging off a middle-aged man. He's wearing a beige shirt and loosely-tied, loosely-colourful tie. He has a soft face and gentle, preoccupied disposition.

"Sorry to disturb you both, but I was hoping you wouldn't mind answering a few questions?" he says.

I see him eyeing up our drinks, I think he even licks his lips, before showing us to a table in the corner of the bar away from prying ears. Although at the moment there's only the barman and a pair of businesswomen across the bar who are in the place. My watch says it's just past one thirty in the morning.

We sit and DCI Johnson takes down our names, addresses and contact details in his little police pad. He must've spoken to the doorman or hotel manager to know to come and talk to us. I wonder how much he knows.

"Can you tell me what you saw, in your own words, and in your own time?" DCI Johnson looks first at me, then at Sophie.

"I saw someone fall past our balcony window tied to a chair," I say.

"Excellent. Excellent. And which floor were you on?"

"The eighth."

"Excellent." DCI Johnson makes some notes in his police pad.

I'm not sure what's so excellent about seeing a man fall to his death, but I'll go with Johnson's methods for now. Sophie seems content to stay quiet so I continue to do the talking.

"Did you notice anything in particular?"

"About Sean, the chair, or the falling?" I say.

He narrows his eyes on me.

"I think he was tied up. His screams weren't those of joy. He was falling at a fair old rate. That's about it really."

"Excellent," says Johnson, eyes still narrow.

"And then what did you do?"

"We looked over the edge of our balcony because I wasn't sure what I'd seen. I mean, you don't see a man fall past your hotel window every day. Then we both saw what's left of Sean on the tarmac way down below."

"Excellent," he says. "And then you thought you'd come down and have a closer look did you?"

He says it in matter-of-fact manner, but it's an obvious change of tactics.

"It's in our nature. I'm a journalist, Sophie's a photographer. Our inquisitive ways got the better of us. If you must know I regret coming down to have a look."

"I do too. It wasn't very nice. Not very nice at all," says Sophie.

Johnson looks up and trains his gaze on Sophie.

"So you're a photographer. Didn't happen to take a few inquisitive pictures did we Sophie?" says Johnson.

He smiles. It's gentle, but not friendly.

Sophie casually looks over his shoulder at her camera bag still by the bar stools we'd sat on. I see her looking, but Johnson misses it.

"No, I didn't take any photos. Have you seen the mess that's left? It's gross. Why would I want to take any photos of that?" she says, theatrically turning her nose up.

Even I'm convinced she's telling the truth. Johnson seems to swallow it too. The doorman can't have told him about Sophie's close-up camera work.

"So, why are you in London? If you're based in the West Country?" he says.

"We're doing a story on the Abbey Road Hoodwink murders. We heard about it on Sunday morning and drove straight up."

"It wasn't confirmed to the press or public that Hoodwink were murdered at Abbey Road Studios. How do you know that?"

Oops.

"I have my sources," I say, "which I won't be revealing."

"Excellent," he says sarcastically through gritted teeth. "So why are you still here? Why are you staying at The Royal?"

"My editor thought it would be a good idea to stick around to see what develops from the Hoodwink murders. I chose The Royal as I like to take the piss with expenses." Might as well be honest, then I added. "I write the stories, Sophie takes the pictures."

"I see. Excellent. Quite a team you both make," says Johnson.

We sneak a glance and smile at each other. I squeeze her knee under the table, she holds on to my hand.

"Bit of a coincidence you were both up here for the Abbey Road incident and then in the same hotel in which Sean Bates gets pushed off a 12th floor balcony."

There he goes again, being all nice, then all direct. He's like a good cop and bad cop all rolled into one. I'm almost beginning to warm to him.

"Tell us about it," I say. Sophie doesn't say anything.

"We know you were both in Cardiff to witness Darren Cox from East Side dying on stage too," says Johnson.

"West Side," I say.

"Excellent. Yes, West Side." Johnson pauses. "You were in Cardiff as well. Three places, three murders. Multiple murders in the case of Hoodwink."

"So Dazza *was* murdered?" I say, trying to sound surprised.

A flicker of annoyance, then a well practiced smile. "Yes, sadly he was. It would appear someone had meddled with the electrics."

"I'd heard that's what happened," I say, more so Johnson knows I knew already.

"Excellent." He doesn't rise to the bait. "But back to you two. You were in Cardiff and now here in London to witness Sean Bates' death. Which is an interesting coincidence wouldn't you agree?"

"Why, what are you implying Mr Johnson?" I say all too politely. I use Mr rather than DCI as I know it'll wind him up. His gentle face takes an ungentle turn.

"I wouldn't imply anything, Master Matthews." Master? Touché. "But if you knew someone who was in the vicinity for three separate, very serious crimes, wouldn't you be suspicious?"

Of course I would. But I'm not about to agree with him. I know it's immature but I still just don't like the police after they mistook me for a thug and arrested me in my youth.

"We weren't here when Hoodwink were murdered. We were in Bath then," I say weakly.

"Still, two outta three ain't bad, no?" he snaps back quickly.

I stay silent. Sophie stares at Johnson, then down at the table.

"Have you got inside information or something?"

I think of Fat Pat but stay silent.

"Is someone feeding you information?"

No, but someone is feeding Fat Pat something. Burgers and chips, supersized, probably.

"Is there anything you'd like to share with me, Mr Matthews," Johnson looks towards Sophie. "Ms Cooper?"

Sophie shakes her head and continues to give him the silent treatment. I was going to join in on the silent act, but I realise there is something I'd like to share. Something I can share and it doesn't matter who knows anymore. Because everyone knows now. For some reason I've made a habit of keeping it with me. I dig into my pocket and find the email print out.

"There is this. I don't know if it's of any use." I know it isn't, it doesn't tell us anything we don't now know, but it looks like I'm trying to help. I push the Hitman's email across the table.

Johnson unfolds the print out and reads it from top to bottom.

"Thank you." He inhales then exhales slowly, excessively. "We've already seen a copy of this from one of the broadsheets. We're keeping it out of the press for obvious reasons."

"Excellent," I say flatly. Johnson gives me a look. I decide I'll ask a few questions myself. "So can you track this Hitman down from his Googlemail account?"

"We've had our IT team on it," says Johnson, surprisingly openly. "They traced the IP number back to an internet café in Liverpool. People are in and out of those places all day. The owner can't remember who was in the café at the time the email was sent."

"It could've been timed to be sent at a later date anyway," I say.

"Exactly. Plus our IT team tell me it's impossible to trace the Googlemail account back to someone's real name or to an actual home address. Just because it was sent from Liverpool doesn't mean the Hitman lives there. He could be anywhere."

"Do you have anybody in the frame for this then?"

"I'm not at liberty to answer that I'm afraid," says Johnson.

That's a no, then.

"You said you're from the Avon and Somerset Constabulary, what are you doing up in London? Don't the Met police deal with murders up here?"

"Not always. It depends who started on the investigation. As a long standing and experienced DCI," says Johnson modestly, "I was initially sent over from Bristol to investigate the death of Darren Cox from West Side in Cardiff. My team of detectives and I thought Hoodwink's suspicious deaths might be linked so we were continuing investigations up in London, and now Sean Bates has been murdered..."

"Do you think whoever murdered Sean Bates, murdered Dazza, and Hoodwink as well?" It's an obvious question, but as Johnson's in charge, I want to know what he has to say on the subject.

"It's possible. There's the Hitman and his Top 10 Hit List. But we can't be sure. We're looking into all possibilities right now," he says reluctantly.

I get the impression he would rather punch me in the face than answer my questions. I keep ploughing on regardless. "Sean Bates was at No.8 on the Top 10 Hit List. Who do you think will be at No.7?"

Johnson's contemplating an answer when a tall boy in a beige suit walks over to our table. He's about six foot tall, and six inches wide, and looks about fifteen years old.

"Sir, can I have a word?" he says, bending down to our level.

"Yes, Detective Constable. We're all but done here anyway," says Johnson smiling. He turns to us. "Thank you both for your time and co-operation."

He gets up to leave with the Detective Constable, then goes all Columbo. "Just one last thing," he says. "Don't go leaving town okay?"

"But we don't live in 'town'. I live in Bath. Sophie lives in Bristol."

Don't go leaving town? What kind of clichéd Columbo cop is he? Although at least he looks a bit like Columbo in his brown outfit. How did Fat Pat ever think I was trash TV's favourite detective?

"Excellent. Well don't go leaving the UK. It would be helpful if you're contactable in case we need any more assistance with our enquiries," says Johnson, and as an afterthought he adds, "Don't print anything I said about Dazza's murder, or the Hitman and Hit Lists – otherwise I'll shut your little magazine down. Don't sell your exclusive to the press either. If anything ends up in the papers tomorrow I'll know where to come won't I?"

He smiles, not with his eyes, they stay steely.

"No problem, inspector. I always like to the help the police in any way I can."

Sophie snorts a little too loudly, otherwise I think I would've got away with such sincerity. Johnson walks off as the young DC talks into his ear.

"So, do you want a rum now, dahling?" I say brightly.

"Oh go on then, yes please, dahling," purrs Sophie.

We return to our bar stools. Sophie pulls her camera bag close to her feet as she saddles up on her stool. I order our drinks and think about her photos of smashed up Sean Bates.

"Bloody cops blocking our exclusive," I say.

"Spoiling our fun, I dunno..." says Sophie.

"We could've made a killing from the tabloids," I say.

"They would've needed to be very creative if they'd used my photos without breaking all sorts of media laws..."

"I'm sure the tabloids would've got around that problem, teasing readers with suggestive images of what was left of Sean Bates. Like that image of Cobain after he'd blown his head off – you only ever got to see a leg in blue jeans and one white-laced Converse trainer."

We sit silently and I think about what might have been a great scoop. I try not to think about the mashed limbs and blood and instead think about what kind of genius is behind all these well targeted, bizarre, brutal murders, and think about who could be lucky No.7 on the Top 10 Hit List. It's a lot of thinking that will only become clearer with a lot of drinking.

I wake up early on Tuesday morning. The mouth's a bit dry so I down most of a litre of bottled water by the bed. I switch on the news on TV with the remote. It's weird seeing the live coverage of the outside of the hotel while we're safely tucked up inside. The media wagons arrived early in the bleakness of night. They're always quick to show up if a celebrity's been murdered. It makes big news in our celebrity-obsessed country. I briefly glance at the balcony where we were standing last night, stunned, staring down into the darkness.

I keep the volume low so I don't disturb Sophie who's sleeping next to me in our giant bed. I can see the outline of her naked body under the silk sheets. I turn my attention to the TV. The smartly dressed female reporter explains how Sean Bates fell a dozen flights to his death. The TV cameras zoom up to his 12th floor balcony and then zoom out and down to the spot he and his chair met their end outside the front of the hotel. It's all rather dramatic. But then I suppose someone has just died dramatically.

I can't actually see the ground where Sean Bates and the chair turned into mush. The TV footage shows that the police have taped off the area, and a large white tent has been erected as Crime Scene Investigators – so it says on TV – and uniformed and plain-clothed police mill about inside and out. Fans are already gathering, looking sad and laying flowers as close to the spot Sean Bates met his maker. This means they're essentially piling up their bouquets in the middle of The Royal's front car park, which is touching.

The reporter then talks to the camera about Dazza's death and Hoodwink dying mysteriously at Abbey Road. They still don't know they were all murdered. But they do know Sean Bates was murdered. Suicide hasn't even been mentioned. Why – or how for that matter – would he tie himself to a rocking chair, then throw himself off a balcony? The reporter speculates about a pop star killer on the loose. She doesn't actually say Sean and Dazza and Hoodwink were all murdered by the same killer, but it's implied.

But the reporter doesn't mention a Hitman or Top 10 Hit List. If only she knew. If only the UK public knew. If only she was telling the country that there are seven more singers or bands in danger. The general public and pop world as we know it would boil up and up before erupting like a volcano of hysteria and paranoia. Which is more dangerous than a volcano spewing out molten lava.

"The fun has only just begun," I say quietly to the reporter on the screen. I always talk to the TV. "Sean Bates was No.8. We still have seven more to go. And who knows who's going to be No.1."

The reporter introduces Chief Superintendent Bishop, a stocky, light grey haired man with light blue eyes, and DCI Johnson. It says 'Head Of The Investigation' on the screen when Johnson appears. He's still dressed in brown head to toe.

"We'd like to reassure the British public that we're doing all we can in this investigation and we will be putting all our best available man power towards finding out who murdered Sean Bates," says Chief Superintendent Bishop. *"DCI Johnson will be heading up the investigation."*

Bishop stands to one side and Johnson comes into view.

"Do you have any suspects yet, DCI Johnson?" asks the reporter as she pushes the microphone in front of him.

"We have a couple of leads and several enquiries under way, plus we'll be interviewing a few key witnesses. But we can't reveal anything just yet," he smiles softly and the skin cracks around the eyes, *"as I'm sure you understand."*

I notice that he seems comfortable and professional talking on camera. The reporter nods her pretty head. I wonder if Johnson's lying about those leads. More than likely. Unless something cropped up overnight. The reporter thanks Johnson for his time, and that's it. Johnson doesn't mention Hoodwink or Dazza. No mention of the Hitman or his Hit List. That's right, keep it all under wraps. See how long you can keep it from the general public. Until Hit No.7 gets it.

I switch off the TV. I think about waking Sophie for some hot sausage action, but kiss her softly on her neck instead and climb out of bed. I pull some clothes on, and as I'm picking up my laptop bag Sophie rolls over in bed.

"Where you going, hot stuff?" she says. I think that's what she says. Her voice is muffled as her face is stuffed into the plump pillows.

"Breakfast," I say. A leg slides out from under the silk sheets. It's a very nice leg. I think about what's at the top of it and put my laptop bag back down.

"Breakfast in bed?" she asks, rolling on to her back, sighing heavily as she stretches. Her other leg slides out under the sheets, only her torso is now covered by the sheets. I can trace the outline of her breasts through the thin lining of silk. She smiles at me and raises an eyebrow.

"What's on the menu?" I say, doing my best Bond eyebrow raising impression to match hers.

"Sophie," she says sweetly, before laughing and whipping back the sheets to reveal the best English breakfast I've ever seen: Sophie on silk, sunny side up.

After a hearty breakfast I head downstairs for, well, more breakfast. I have worked up an appetite after all. I leave Sophie in our room as she wanted to have a long soak in the bath. Plus I need to write some copy for a magazine piece. I choose a big table at the back of the restaurant away from everyone else and set up my laptop. Smartly suited business men and women are dotted around talking quietly, tapping on laptops and reading papers. A group of casually dressed journalists reporting on Sean Bates's death talk loudly over coffee, occasionally jotting things down on notepads. A few uniformed police share a pot of tea while eating bacon sandwiches. It's a pig eat pig world.

Over a china cup of sweet smelling tea and a plate of croissants, I bang out a suitably kid-friendly article on Sean Bates. I write the story from my point of view – which was a very good view point considering Sean flashed past our eighth floor window to his death. But I'm a good boy, DCI Johnson gets mentioned, but I don't write anything about Dazza, Hoodwink or the Hitman. I just use the facts that have been released. For now.

I log my laptop into the hotel's WiFi and email Gary my words. In the email I explain I have access to some photos although they're probably too gruesome for our little magazine. I don't tell him Sophie took them or that she's here with me. Gary emails straight back. I've barely begun reading his reply before he's calling me on my mobile.

"Hardy! Hardy! Another great story mate. Just reading it now. So great you're getting another inside line on these bonkers musician murders. Nice. Nice." He pauses. I think about saying something, but Gary's off again. "I can't believe it all happened in the hotel you just happened to be staying in."

"Yeah," I say.

"SO MENTAL. BUT SO GREAT!" Gary shouts.

"Yeah, it's mental alright," I say. Why does he have to shout?

"I can't believe you actually saw SEAN BATES fly past your window as well. MENTAL!" he shouts. "John's going to shit himself when he finds out we've got another exclusive!"

I hope MD John doesn't shit himself. Grown men shouldn't behave like that.

"Don't worry about photos, we've got a bunch of Bates posing away on file and there's some photos on the news wire of The Royal and police tent outside. We've got a good mug shot of you we'll run next to it as our 'intrepid eyewitness reporter'. Sorted."

"Sorted," I find myself saying. I never say sorted.

"Alright. Great. I've gotta run. What's your plan, dude? You staying up there, yeah?" He shouts. I'm holding my phone a foot away from my ear. A suited businesswoman looks over at me then returns to reading her newspaper. The gaggle of journalists noisily leave the restaurant.

"I was planning to stop up here today, see what pans out, then get the train to Birmingham later on as I've got that interview with MC Whitey in the morning."

"Great. Yeah. Nice one. Okay, see what pans out, yeah? Be in touch." Before I can reply Gary's hung up. I gladly hang up too. "Gary, you're such a git," I say as I place my mobile on the table.

The businesswoman gives me another funny look. I give her a funny look back. I think about doing 'rabbit's ears' with my hands and sticking out my tongue but stop myself. I'm in a respectable hotel and shall act respectably.

While my laptop's still online I log onto our web server in the office and access my email. There's the usual raft of nosey emails from workmates and distant friends asking about Dazza and Hoodwink, and a couple from mates I'd told I was staying at The Royal asking about Sean Bates. Richie's says:

Subject: Snatch
From: Richard Head <rhead@abacus.co.uk>
To: Hardy Matthews <hardy@top10hits.co.uk>

Hi mate,

RIP Sean Bates. Never liked the arrogant wank stick or his tune-less music myself. Too pretty for his own good. At least there will be some dappy, busty birds for the rest of us now.

Any fit snatch hanging around that swanky hotel then? Any looking like they're mourning and need a shoulder to cry on? I could pop up on the hunt and get my perv on...

Pint soon if not?

Cheers then,
Richie

I reply to Richie, about the pint, not the bird hunt, reply to a few more, and sift through the mails from names and companies I don't recognise. Bloody junk mail. Delete, delete, delete. There's a bunch of press invites to various PR pop junkets and new band gigs in and around London, some bands I've heard of, others I haven't. I delete a few email invites I know I won't bother going to and emails with MP3s of new singles I won't listen to. I get an e-newsletter saying that MySpace is getting lots of tribute sites set up by sad fans of Dazza and Hoodwink. This leaves one email I haven't read. I nearly delete it by mistake until I look closely and realise it's from 'Hitman'.

The Hitman.

The title is 'Top 10 Hit List' again.

Normally a title like that would make me think of pop stars, but these days I think of dead pop stars.

The group of journalists begin to leave. I wait until they're all gone, then I gingerly open the email.

"Holy fuck," I say under my breath. Although not under my breath enough. Businesswoman gives me a black look this time. I give her a funny look again. I don't feel in a black mood just yet.

"Holy fucking fuck," I say quietly. I ignore the black looks and simply smile to myself.

It seems our friendly, neighbourhood pop star killer has decided to get in contact again. Even though I know I won't get a reply, I type 'Do I know you?' and press send. I save the email as a text file to my desktop, print off a copy by linking up remotely to the hotel's printer in reception, and close my laptop. I give the businesswoman a quiet smile and let out a loud fart as I walk past her and out of the restaurant.

I grab the printout from the reception's printer before anyone else can read it. While I'm in reception I see the pair of blonde Page 3 types who were hanging around with Sean Bates the other night in the bar. Their eyes are red-rimmed and teary. I think about giving Richie a tip off, but decide that's perhaps not the best move right now.

I head back up to our big hotel room. When I walk in I find Sophie pleasuring herself. Not like that. She's sitting up on the bed with her wet hair wrapped up in a white towel, wearing a thick towelling dressing gown, and cutting and filing her toenails.

"Hello princess," I say.

"Hi there my handsome prince," she says.

"Do you mean I'm short, have weird facial hair, and sing in a scary high voice?" I ask. I don't want to get confused with the little man of pop.

"No," she says. "You sing in a scary low voice anyway."

"When have you heard me sing?"

"In the shower. In the car."

"Oh. Yeah, you're right. About where I sing. Not how I sing. I'm pitch perfect."

"Whatever you say."

"Anyway, enough of that, check *this* out." I flop my laptop on the bed and flip it open. Flop, flip. I like to do things differently. I show Sophie the email from 'Hitman'. She quickly reads it.

"Well. Now. Sodding. Hell. Now then," she says.

"Well now sodding hell then indeed." I say.

"It seems the psycho pop killer wants to be your friend."

"Friend… Or enemy?"

"I'd say friend judging by what he's saying," she says.

"How do you know it's a 'he'?" I ask.

"It's got to be a man. It says *Hitman* for a start. But a woman wouldn't or couldn't kill in the way he's been killing."

"I've been picturing a man all along. Glad you think that too."

I look down at my laptop and read the email again.

Subject: Top 10 Hit List
From: Hitman <top10hitlist@gmail.com>
To: Hardy Matthews <hardy@top10hits.co.uk>

Hope you're well. Thought I'd keep you up to date with my little pop project. As you're no doubt aware my Top 10 Hit List is proceeding as planned. The brat band Hoodwink were lucky enough to make it inside the Top 10 at No.9 with a deafening tune, and as you probably saw at The Royal, Sean Bates dropped in at No.8.

Of course it would ruin the show if I told you what waste of space artist is going to be next on my Hit List, but rest assured the plan is in motion and you'll soon find out who's going to be at No.7 and No.6.

I was going to copy in the broadsheets and tabloids on this email again but figured there was no point this time. You seem to be fuelling the media nicely. Plus I enjoy your music magazine articles so consider this email your backstage pass to my pop show.

Take care of yourself and your photographer lady friend Sophie.

I'll be in touch.

"He likes you doesn't he?" says Sophie.

"Do you think so?" I say nervously.

"Says he likes your writing. Chose you as his main point of contact."

"I guess so. Well, I'm very likeable," I say puffing out my chest. "If we're clever we could use his backstage pass to our advantage to bag a proper big exclusive."

"Perhaps we should keep this email to ourselves for now."

"Perhaps we should," I say.

I read the email from top to bottom again. "He knows about you as well," I say pointing to the end of the email.

"Yeah, I saw that. 'Photographer friend' eh? Not sure if I should be scared or thankful."

"Scared first, thankful second," I say. "He probably saw us at The Royal before or after Sean fell to his messy death."

"He didn't fall, Hardy, he was pushed. Your email mate pushed him. Deliberately tied Sean to a chair. Then shoved him off his 12th floor balcony," says Sophie, suddenly and seriously.

"Did a good job didn't he?"

"Don't," says Sophie smirking a little.

"What?"

"Don't."

"What!?"

"Don't make a joke out of it," she says with a guilty smile on her face.

"But he did do a good job. He's an efficient worker."

"Worker? It's not a bloody job, Hardy." She can't stop herself smiling.

I'm about to continue making light of something, well, not something, it's murder we're dealing with here, murder of somebody I had very little respect for, but murder nonetheless, and murder is something that doesn't sit too comfortably with me just yet... anyway, I'm about to continue keeping the mood light-hearted, when my mobile rings.

It's Fat Pat. After a quick exchange I hang up.

"He wants to meet up for a chat in The Red Lion on Waverton Street in Mayfair," I say to Sophie. "Fancy some lunch?"

It's a typical London pub on a typical working day and the place is full of office staffers smoking and smiling over pints of lager for lunch. Fat Pat's round body is sat around a round table in the window. He's a regular modern-day Henry VIII, minus the penchant for decapitation. I can see he's nursing a pint. He waves, we wave back. We get a couple of pints of daytime Guinness and join him.

"Hey Pat, nice to see you, to see you nice. How you doing?"

"Shit hot, my friend, shit hot."

"You look just hot, to be honest."

He does look hot. He's sweating even though it's not much above freezing outside. To be fair the roaring log fire nearby is pumping out a lot of heat. Fires do that. Although I think Fat Pat is hot as he hasn't taken off his painfully fashionable, brightly coloured nu-wave retro pseudo-ski jacket.

He catches me checking it out, and proudly asks, "Like the jacket, huh?"

"Where'd you get it?" I say. "1985?"

"Yes, very funny Hardy. Always the clever bastard," says Fat Pat. He looks in Sophie's direction. She's smiling.

"So whadda ya know then, '80s guy?" I say, attempting a nicely nasal American accent.

"Eh?" he says.

"So what do you know?" I say, avoiding the accent.

"Oh. Okay." Fat Pat sips his pint. "Well, Sean Bates didn't commit suicide, he was pushed." He lets it hang in the air for a bit, then laughs. "But we all knew that. Sorry. I never liked the jumped up little prick."

"Me neither," I say.

"Me neither," Sophie says.

"I won't miss him," says Fat Pat.

"Neither will the pop charts," I say flatly.

I don't mean it badly. Nobody deserves to die. But I'd be lying if I said I liked the guy, and my opinion won't suddenly change just because he's dead.

"Okay, seriously," says Fat Pat, "from what my man is saying, the cops haven't got a Scooby who's knocking off all these pop upstarts."

"Your man's reliable is he?"

"Very," says Fat Pat. "Apparently DCI Johnson, who's head of investigations, and his detectives are working around the clock. But the killer's covered his tracks very cleanly."

"Shame. Johnson was so nice when he grilled us at The Royal."

"Ah, so you've had the pleasure," says Fat Pat.

"The pleasure was all ours."

"He's struggling so far with his investigation anyway. Hasn't even found a footprint let alone a fingerprint," says Fat Pat.

"Not even a footprint?" asks Sophie. "What can they tell from footprints?"

"Imprints in carpets, wet footprints on dry tiles, that sort of thing. From what I've heard they can tell a lot. The person's weight, their height – judging by the distance the footsteps are apart – and if one is heavier than the other, that helps build a picture of them. Then what sort of footwear, if the tread's old... They can tell a lot."

"Did you go to footprint college?" asks Sophie.

"Were you a foot solider?" I ask.

"You're a right pair of comedians aren't you?"

We both stifle our giggles by swigging our pints. As the table next to us empties, another group of men in suits and ladies in skirts jump in with two bottles of wine to share. They chink glasses before drinking steadily. The drinking classes. They make London's working world go round.

"So what about witnesses?" I ask.

"There were a few from the hotel; the doorman, the barman, the bell boy delivering the rocking chair..." says Fat Pat.

"A rocking chair?" says Sophie.

"I thought I'd seen something in the wreckage..." I say.

"Yep, a rocking chair. Not sure why they used a chair like that..." says Fat Pat.

"Perhaps someone has a fondness for fine woodwork," I say.

"Anyway, quotes from the witnesses range from 'A stocky-ish, well dressed man with slick hair and a dodgy moustache' to someone who was 'Polite and a big tipper'. The same description goes for the shop assistant who sold him the rocking chair, they said 'He seemed a nice geezer in a nice suit.'"

"You're inside man knows a lot doesn't he. Does he know anything about the hotel's security?" I say.

"They like to keep it discreet at The Royal. There was a plain-clothed security guard hanging around reception. He remembers seeing 'a moustached man' arrive. But he didn't see him leave. They think he must've used the fire escape after leaving Sean's room."

"Was anyone up in Sean's room with him?" I ask.

"He was surrounded by bimbos when we saw him," says Sophie.

"My man says a young groupie went up with him but nobody saw her come back down, and she's not been seen since. The cops are trying to pin her down for questioning but she's disappeared."

"Do you think she killed Sean?" I say, then quickly answer my own question. "No way. A young girl wouldn't be able to overpower him, tie him up and push him off the balcony."

"Quite," says Fat Pat. Sophie nods.

"Maybe the young girl was knocked off and buried or something?" I say.

"It's not his style," says Sophie. "He's only interested in wannabe pop stars."

"How'd you know that?" I say.

"He didn't kill Hoodwink's producer and manager did he?"

"Good point, well made."

Is Sophie becoming Miss Marple? No, that's not right. She's too sexy to be Miss Marple. Although Sophie would look sexy even in one of Marple's flowery Victorian dress numbers.

"Your girl's right," says Fat Pat.

"Groupie girl probably ran scared after meeting Mr Murderer..." says Sophie.

"...and after possibly witnessing Sean's death she's run into hiding," says Fat Pat.

"I'd leg it too, if I'd been that close to a murderer," I add.

They both look at me. I'm not a coward, I'm just not ready to die yet. "So does your man know who's in the frame for this yet?" I say quickly.

"That's the thing, the cops had a few suspects. Disgruntled ex-band managers, a few obsessive fans, but all have had solid alibis at the times of the murders or were aggressive, angry sorts, but just weren't murderers."

"Your man really is well informed," says Sophie.

"Sure is. Because he knows I won't blab his name around," says Fat Pat.

There's a surge of laughter from a group of suits on a table behind us. I check over my shoulder they're out of earshot as I figure it's time to see if Fat Pat knows what we know. "I take it you've heard all about the Hitman and his Top 10 Hit List?"

"Top ten what mate?"

"The Hitman's Top 10 Hit List?"

"A Hitman? A Hit List? With ten facking hits on it?" says Fat Pat, eyes wide.

I find myself laughing out loud. Fat Pat's man on the inside knows all about footprints and fire exit escape routes, but nothing about the crucial Top 10 Hit List. It feels good to know we know something he doesn't. Sophie's laughing too although she's much more sneaky than me.

"You joking?"

"No." I show him the original email print out, and the second email I printed out at the hotel.

Fat Pat quietly and carefully reads each email.

"Strike me down," he whispers.

He takes a long drink of his pint.

"You showed the cops these?"

"They've seen the first email, I only got the second one a couple of hours ago," I say. "It doesn't tell us who he intends to kill next though."

"But it does say he is intending to kill next. To keep this mental Top 10 going," says Fat Pat looking at the printout.

"What sort of person would have such a disciplined Hit List?"

"I don't know mate," says Fat Pat looking up. "But they're professional whoever they are."

"Professional enough to nail Hit No.7 on his Top 10," I say.

"Whoever that's going to be," says Sophie.

*   *

MC Whitey is, for all intents and purposes, and for want of a better, more acceptable expression, a Wigga. If only his whiter than white complexion wasn't so pale. I'm having the pleasure of interviewing the hip hop gangster, sorry, 'gangsta' for the mag. The kids love MC Whitey and his twenty eight strong Nuff Respect Crew, so it goes into the mag even if he is a total wannabe.

It's Friday afternoon and three weeks after the weekend of murder and mayhem in London. I'm sat with MC Whitey in a brightly-lit bar in the centre of Birmingham. A few of his crew are loitering around in the background. We're both supping on a couple of cold beers. Well, I'm drinking beer. MC Whitey is drinking a lemon flavoured alcopop. He has no taste in clothes either as his baggy, pink shell suit bottoms and Burberry shirt and sun visor combo prove to anyone within one hundred yards. Chavs. I hate interviewing chavs, especially chav gangsta wannabes. But I'm a professional journalist and will act accordingly.

"How are you White Boy?"

"It's MC Whitey, yo."

"How are you Whitey?"

"I'm safe, man. Safe as fuck," he says, looking shifty, playing with the rim of his visor.

"Quite," I say. I look at my notepad on my lap. I haven't bothered preparing any questions. I'm actually looking at a food shopping list. I write down eggs on the bottom of it. "So what's new in the Nuff Respect Crew?" I ask.

"Hey, yo, we gots mad props for what we do, yeah?" MC Whitey's never shy to big himself up. He's painfully aware of my voice recorder sitting on the table. He even moves in closer to make sure it's picking up everything he says. I'm not really sure what he's saying, though, to be honest.

"What?" I say.

"You feel me, G? We is big on da UK hip hop scene and many bros be givin' us mad props. Even some bros on da Stateside be givin' us mad props yeah? You knows it. Mad props."

"Crazy scaffolding props? Mad costume props? Angry rugby prop forwards?" I say.

I know props means respect, but I hate it when anyone talks like they're some kind of hardcore black rapper from the Bronx, especially a skinny white boy from the Midlands.

"Props. Yeah? Respeck. R-E-S-P-E-C-K." He rubs his spotty adolescent chin and nods to himself. "Nuff Respeck, yeah?"

Yeah? No. Whatever.

"So how long have you been into crap music?" I say. It's childish, I know.

"Say what?"

"How long have you been into rap music?"

"Oh, right, I thoughts yo wuz sayin'..." MC Whitey trails off, then says, "I loved hip hop from way back when I was 'bout ten. My older bro was booming out da old skool in his room and dats got me hooked. Check it."

"Check what?"

"It! Check it! C'mon, man, get wid it." MC Whitey says while playing with one of two gold necklaces hanging around his neck.

"Right, good. So how long have you been crapping?" I say. I have no plans to grow up today.

"Crapping?" he says.

"What?" I say.

"Eh?"

"You said crapping, homes."

"Get wid it, man," I say sounding more Regent Street than 'street'. "How long have you be RAPPING?"

"Oh. Yeah, sorry G, me ears is shot from all da loud shows we be playin' yo. I bin rappin' all my life, yeah? Since I could talk I bin rappin'. Writin' some mad lyrics and dat. All straight from da heart." He pats himself with his fist on his chest, and nods.

"Good," I say. I don't think he detects my sarcasm.

"Why did you start a hip hop band?"

MC Whitey can't stop himself. "For the money, cars and bitches," he brags.

"Nice. No, really... why did you..."

"Yo, for real, yeah? For the money, cars and bitches!" he shouts, and nods. "And the bling, the fly clothes, a top mobile phone, the best trainers..."

"So you're quite materialistic?"

"I ain't materialising nothin', homes."

I don't correct him. On with the questions. "So where did you grow up?"

"On da streets. Yo get me? Da streets, G. Yeah? They be well rough out dere."

"Out dere? Where, in Kidderminster? That is where you grew up isn't it?"

"Yeah, but I was hangin' out in Brum, and there is some rough areas round dere. Big time."

"Big time. Quite."

It's funny. The more ridiculous he sounds, the more English I sound, like I'm counteracting his 'gangsta' language.

"But it's not exactly Compton is it?"

"It's just as rough, G. Just as dangerous. Yo need to learn how to survive on dem streets, yo get me?"

"Of course. My mistake. And is that why you speak in such a strange way, like you're from the streets of LA, and shit?" I say, playing along with the lingo.

"And shit!?" he says surprised.

"Yes. And shit."

"I donts know, man. I jus' talks da way I talks. Yeah?"

"Such a wonderful use of the English language." There I go again, all plummy.

"I likes usin' words. But in a street poetry stylee wid my raps. Yo get me?"

"Not really." I don't. It's best to be honest with chavs.

"So, you write the lyrics, and DJ Spin comes up with the beats and music?"

"Yeah! Spin! He's my boy, yo. My boy!" he shouts. He waves his hands up and down like they're bouncing on air. You could call it dancing. Although he's sat down, and I don't want to encourage the little prick. I want to wind him up.

"Your boyfriend?" I say.

MC Whitey's face drops so quickly it's like it's made out of liquid. From shouting to silence in less than a millisecond.

"Say what!? Boyfriend!? Yo fuckin' wid me, man?" says MC Whitey. His chav mates start looking over.

"No, I am not. It was just a question," I say firmly. "You said he was your boy. I wondered if that was short for boyfriend. It's okay if you're gay."

"Get da fuck outta here."

"Sorry?"

"You heard, player," he snarls.

"So you and Spin aren't together?"

"Nah, man. Nah, man. We ain't no homos. We ain't goin' out like dat."

"How are you going out then? Do you go out, but not in public?"

"We ain't goin' out AT ALL. We ain't goin' out like dat. I mean, we ain't rollin' like that." Then as if I need reassuring he adds, "We ain't no batty boys."

"Batty boy," I repeat slowly. I haven't heard that since *The Ali G Show*. How refreshing. I write it down on my notepad, even though the recorder is getting all this.

"Tell me about your new single, *Bullets On Broad Street*."

"Cool. Yeah, right, it's, like, about representin' yo hood. It's, yeah, like, about lookin' out for yo crew on da streets. And if it comes to poppin' a cap in some ass, that's what yo gots to do, yo get me?"

"And have you?" I say, looking up from my notes, "Popped one up some ass?" I love playing with words.

"Nah man, I not popped one up no asses. I ain't tellin' yo if I popped a cap in anyone either, yo get me?" He stares at me. For a chav it's quite a good attempt at scary. But's he's a chav, and they're not scary – they're silly.

"I'll take that as a no, then. What about DJ Spin? Does he like shooting?" I'm just messing about now.

"Yo'd 'ave to asks Spin 'bout dat, rude bwoy."

He's right. I am a rude boy. My manners have been severely lacking this afternoon. There I go again, all proper Queen's English.

"That's a no as well then," I say.

"I didn't say that. We gets our shit together when we needs to, yeah?" says MC Whitey. It's a weak attempt at trying to build up his rep.

"Well, thank you Nigel. I think that's all I need," I say. I love calling him Nigel. It feels so right to call him by his real name. Feels so right, and sounds so white – just like him.

"It's MC Whitey, man. I donts go by dat name no more."

"What, White Boy *Nigel*?" I say, emphasising the Nigel. I can't stop a smile creeping up on my face. "You don't like being called *Nigel*? But *Nigel* is your real name?"

"MC Whitey," he says. He kicks back his chair and huffs off to join his chav mates by the bar.

Twenty seconds later he's back. He walks up to the table acting all tough, looks at me, then swipes his half finished bottle of alcopops in his scrawny fingers and heads back to the bar, sipping as he walks. Always a chav, never one to waste a free drink. I'm so intimidated I nearly stop laughing.

"Cheers Nigel," I say holding up my beer.

*   *

You tickle Sadie on her neck and stroke her back. She sticks her tongue out, and smiles up at you with her big brown eyes. You love it when she does that. You pick up the leather collar and jangle it around. She loves it when you do that. Sadie jumps down from the bed and starts running around the bedroom. You briefly think of the bondage aspects of what you're about to do, then realise that's daft. You fix the collar around her neck, then she rolls over on her back and you rub the white fur on her tummy.

"C'mon Sadie, let's go for a walk," you say. "It's killing time."

"Bark, bark," says Sadie in Labrador language. You think she's saying 'hooray, hooray' as she frantically wags her tail.

You've made an extra effort for today's outfit. It's mostly thanks to the web. You can buy anything online. You've died your hair with the professionally-made grey colouring, your 'real human hair' fake beard has been died the complementary grey along with your eyebrows too. You're wearing a pair of brown cords, comfortable black ankle boots and a tweed sports jacket over a round necked, grey wool jumper. The look's topped off with a flat cap. As you take one final look in the mirror on your way out you almost don't recognise yourself. You don't look a day under 55 years old. Perfect.

You try to hunch your shoulders and amble rather than stride out the door to the car as you hold on to Sadie's lead. McNamara, the old man and his dog.

You thought about taking the normal route down south from Liverpool, the M62 and M6, but an old man wouldn't like driving on the motorway if possible. Especially on a Saturday. So to help you keep in character you potter down the A557 in your Astra, then the A533 cross country instead, picking up the M6 much further down. You stop at Stafford services, have a piss, walk Sadie around on the grass to do the same, then sit in your car sipping on tea from your flask and eating a sandwich you've made. An old man would probably call it 'elevenses'. You continue down the M6, turning off to Sutton Coldfield before you reach central Birmingham.

You drive to Sutton Park then park about a mile away in a lay-by. You found the location after phoning the record label's production co-ordinator pretending to be security for the band. You say band, they say crew, all twenty-eight of the bastards. You look in the rear view mirror and adjust your flat cap and stroke your beard. This facial hair's becoming something of a habit. You take Sadie out the back of your car and head into the park in search of No.7 on your Hit List. As you amble across the fields Sadie excitedly wags her tail. You know how she feels.

The dew hasn't lifted as you walk across another field, opening and closing the gate like a good dog walker. The midday sun keeps breaking through the overhanging cloud, but even when it does you can still feel a fresh breeze on your face. It feels good to walk, it's warming you up underneath your wool and tweed disguise. You only pass a couple of ramblers on your way to the location. They pat Sadie and don't pay you any attention. Just like you predicted.

You can hear the music before you find what you're looking for. The droning bass line resonates across the fields. When you get closer you recognise the DJ's samples and nasal rapping playing loudly. You climb slowly, old man-like, over a gate that's chained shut – Sadie slips underneath it – and walk slowly towards the noise.

It's an impressive set, you have to give them that. A series of floodlights are illuminating an old warehouse that's seen better days. Its roof is half missing along with most of its windows. Several cameras hang off miniature cranes and one larger camera has two people sat behind it. You squint to see 'Director' and 'Director of Photography' emblazoned on the back of their chairs. A bunch of teenagers, dressed in what looks mostly like basketball clothing, are hanging around together by the edge of the warehouse. When you get closer you realise they're not all teenagers and the basketball tops are accompanied by caps and baggy jeans and bright white trainers.

The Nuff Respect Crew. You're quick to count only twenty six of them. Two missing. A line of lorries and caravans are scattered around the outskirts of the set, crowds of people just seem to be hanging around on the periphery, some drinking tea from plastic cups. All the film crew are dressed in black.

A large security guard squints in your direction and walks towards you. You walk to meet him, keeping your shoulders hunched like an old man.

"Alright lad, so they filming a movie then is it?" you say brightly. You're in character – you know they're shooting a music video. You never got to shoot a video when you were in The Good, The Bad, and The Ugly. The amateur junk your bass player's girlfriend filmed on her camcorder doesn't count.

The security guard stops and looks you up and down. He folds his arms across his chest and says, "You shouldn't be walking around here old man."

Old man? Good, good.

You casually loosen your grip on Sadie's lead to let her jump up on his thighs. She eagerly wags her tail.

"I've been walking my dog 'round here for ten years, sunshine. Just because the circus comes to town doesn't mean I'll be changing my daily routine."

"Right, well..."

"Don't worry." You deftly change tact from grouchy to polite. "I won't get in the way. I'm just interested in what's going on is all."

Sadie is still jumping up on him impatiently. You make no attempt to stop her. He finally unfolds his arms and manages to stroke Sadie's head.

"Okay, well, stand over by the caravans then. But no closer alright?" he says.

You nod and smile. As he walks back to the set, you walk towards the caravans, taking in your surroundings as you go. Nobody's watching you, the film crew are all focused on the warehouse set. A few teenagers in caps and brightly coloured shell suits are hanging around, swigging from cans of Stella and joking around. Hangers on, wannabes of the wannabe hip hop crew. You tie Sadie's lead to one of the caravan's tow-bars and pat her back. She obediently sits down.

You amble off to find the caravan that's dummying as a dressing room. You soon find it: it's the one bigger than the others, and the one with a 'Dressing Room' sign on it. You check for any security or film crew, then nip inside the caravan. You find your two missing crew members. Both are wearing identical white caps, white basketball vests, baggy black jeans and big, brand new, spotless white trainers. MC Rock has a big gold 'MC' pendant hanging around his neck, DJ Spin has 'DJ' hanging around his. They're having what looks like the final touches of make-up applied by a short girl wearing a short skirt.

"Can I help you?" she says.

"Who the hell are you old man time?" Snarls the skinny, dumb looking MC Rock. You notice the anger in his eyes. A dumber-looking, dead-eyed DJ Spin laughs.

"Looking for the toilets," you lie.

"The blue caravan at the end," says the girl pointing out of the caravan door.

"Sorry. Thank you," you say.

"Old twat," says MC Rock. DJ Spin laughs again.

You bite your tongue, pretend you didn't hear and back out of the caravan. You won't blow your cover just to beat them senseless. Teach them to respect their elders. You head towards the toilets but take a detour, carefully avoiding the security guard and anyone else's gaze. You walk around the back of some lorries until – Bingo! – you find the van with two film crewmen playing with two guns. You know they're real guns just by glancing at them – a pair of silver Glocks – but you also know they won't have real bullets in them. The two men are holding one gun each, feeling their weight. You can see a box of blanks sat in the van. You keep your distance and act like you're looking in the opposite direction towards the warehouse set.

Suddenly the floodlights flash from dim to dazzling. Hip hop blasts out of the speakers hanging off the four pillars in the warehouse, and you hear somebody – must be the Director – shout "ACTION!" You move around the back of a lorry so you're out of view but can still see the filming. A skinny lad, in a red basketball top with 'Lucky No.7' on it, a white golfing visor and huge jeans hanging half way down his arse, starts prancing around inside the remains of the warehouse. He's rapping away to the music, his hands bouncing around, moving his gaze from camera to camera, glaring into one, then another. Gold chains hanging around his neck jump around as he jumps. Various posse members, their faces hidden by black hooded sweat tops, stand glued to the spot within the warehouse, their heads bobbing to the beat. A camera on a tall crane pans around to film them in the background as a machine steadily pumps dry ice into the warehouse. But all attention is on the rapper in the middle and everyone has crowded round to watch him rapping and recording the video.

The film crewmen by the van stop playing with the guns. Drawn to the music and flood-lit filming, they leave to take a closer look. You can see the shiny guns sitting on the carpeted floor inside the back of the van. You don't need a second chance. Like a magpie drawn to silver you quickly walk over to the van.

You thought the guns might be more heavily safeguarded. But then why would they be? It's not like they're loaded. Not yet anyway.

With your fitted fleece gloves on you pick up a gun in each hand and size them up. You've brought a selection of rounds you'd bought from a gun shop online, but you figured they'd be using Glocks – the gangster's gun of choice. You deftly unload the blank bullets and quickly load each Glock with a round of steel tipped bullets from your tweed jacket pocket. The record label had been very helpful on the phone when, pretending to be from the security company, they'd told you The Nuff Respect Crew were shooting a video for their new single, *Bullets On Broad Street*. They were going to use guns with blanks, they said, for the fake shoot out being filmed for the video.

Holding the guns brings back fond memories but you're quick to stay focused on your mission, keeping an eye on the crowds behind you. They're still mesmerised by the video shoot. Even the security guards are watching. You take a cartridge of blanks with you, hide the rest of the blanks behind some film props in the back of the van, and walk around to the row of caravans, carefully checking nobody's watching. You pull your flat cap down and stroke your beard affectionately. As you amble old man-style towards the toilet you stop behind one of the other caravans to get a good view, still staying out of sight.

The Director shouts into his megaphone. "Cut! That's great, Whitey."

MC Whitey. The leader of the Nuff Respect Crew. You stop and watch him through a gap in the caravans.

"That's the one. That's the take," shouts the Director. "Right, can we get MC Rock and DJ Spin lined up for the shoot out please. Thank you everyone."

The floodlights get dimmed again, the music stops and people start looking busy. Several of MC Whitey's crew crowd round and pat him on the back. Film crew race around measuring where the hooded posse members are standing on set, others are moving cameras, and sound men follow them. It's organised chaos. MC Whitey gets a large padded jacket put around his shoulders to keep him warm and someone hands him a can of Stella. He greedily drinks his lager and walks... no, *limps* away from the set. He wasn't limping earlier. Is he limping on purpose? What's that all about? He's limping like one leg has a kink in it. What a tit.

MC Whitey sleazes an arm around a near anorexic, young blonde with a belt-sized skirt and cropped white fluffy jacket exposing her fake tanned tummy. She giggles as he whispers something in her ear.

MC Rock and DJ Spin are handed a gun each as they walk on to the warehouse set. Male bravado takes over and they weigh up the silver tools in their hands like they were born to hold them. MC Rock points his gun towards the back of the warehouse, he closes one eye and takes aim at one of the floodlights. He makes the noise of a gun being fired then smiles to himself. DJ Spin gets a feel for his gun, holding his arm out straight, showing off by pointing it at some of his Nuff Respect Crew. They laugh nervously.

"It's alright, players. They're filled with blanks!" shouts DJ Spin.

You've untied Sadie now and hold on to her lead. She sits patiently at your feet. You watch from behind the caravan as MC Rock and DJ Spin get shown their positions on set. The music is cranked up. The opening beats of what you assume is *Bullets On Broad Street* boom out of the speakers. The floodlights are fired up as MC Whitey takes centre stage. He jumps up and down on the spot even before the cameras start rolling.

"Okay, get ready guys. Annnd ACTION!"

MC Whitey raps in time to the music, bounding around, staring down cameras as they fly around his head. MC Rock and DJ Spin are stood about twenty yards either side of MC Whitey, cameras zoom in to their scowling faces, and then zoom in on their guns. They're both holding them across their chests, nodding to the music as the cameras pan around.

MC Whitey launches into the chorus.

"Bullets on Broad Street. There's bullets on Broad Street. Bullets on Broad Street. There's bullets on Broad Street..."

MC Rock and DJ Spin slowly raise their guns, arms held out straight. MC Rock holds his gun at an angle, leaning his head to one side. Both take aim on MC Whitey. He's still ferociously rapping to camera. You lick you lips and rub your fake beard.

"Bullets on Broad Street. There's bullets on Broad Street..."

You'd carried out a lot of research on the Nuff Respect Crew. All their interviews in magazines and newspapers, their (two) albums, online facts about each of the twenty-eight posse members, lyrics to songs... you read and listened to the lot before making your decision. Head wannabe gangsta rapper MC Whitey was the obvious target. An easy target. But too easy.

You could've popped him on your list and not thought twice about popping him. But you realised from your research, from reading between the lines, he isn't the one with all the power over the posse. He's merely the front man. He doesn't write any of the wannabe LA gang banger lyrics or create any of the heavily sampled/stolen break beats. MC Whitey isn't the danger. He isn't the backbone or future of the crew.

That's the duty of MC Rock and DJ Spin.

It was a TV interview they'd both done that had swung it for them. MC Rock and DJ Spin and their Midland accents had actually compared themselves to hip hop gangster greats like LA's Ice-T and Ice Cube, and name dropped the likes of Doctor Dre and 50 Cent. They even talked about being like the incomparable Public Enemy; MC Rock believed he was as powerful and political as Chuck D, DJ Spin thought he had the turntable and mixing skills of Terminator X. Not *influences* of theirs – they thought they were on the same level as such hip hop heavyweights. But their lyrics and beats just don't stand up. Rapping about the streets of Kidderminster ain't the same as rhyming about Compton – they have guns, we have water pistols – and mixing Rick Astley samples ain't the same as samples of Rick James.

Bands, or crews, or singers don't get to draw their own comparisons. Their peers, the public and press, they all decide for themselves. You'd already decided. You wanted them dead. So they made it on to your Top 10 Hit List. In at No.7 with a bullet.

The Director helpfully counts them down before they fire their guns in time with the chorus.

"Bullets on Broad Street. There's bullets on Broad Street..."

"3...

2...

1...

Now!"

Their timing is impressive. MC Whitey dives out of way as MC Rock and DJ Spin fire two rounds off each simultaneously.

Blam. Blam.

They take a bullet each in their stomachs, then as they're both knocked backwards, and the guns and their aims are raised, a bullet explodes into MC Rock's chest, and another punctures DJ Spin's upper body.

Glocks and gangstas in motion.

MC Rock hits the ground first, flat on his back. DJ Spin drops to his knees, then falls face first with a crunch as his skull hits the ground. Their bodies lie lifeless on the cold concrete floor.

There's a cheer, followed by a round of applause. "That was awesome boys! Great job!" shouts the Director. "Great dive Whitey. Just what I wanted."

MC Whitey nods at him appreciatively as he picks himself up.

You join in with the applause. Although to be honest, even if nobody else had clapped, you would've started anyway. You're chuffed how your little shoot out worked so well. Both boys did you proud, especially managing to get off another round even when they'd already taken a bullet each. If that doesn't deserve some praise you don't know what does.

The flood lights stay on but the music stops. Gradually the applause subsides.

"They wos wicked," you hear MC Whitey say. He looks at his MC and DJ on the floor. "Dead realistic."

Couldn't've put it better yourself.

"Dat blood looks well real don't it?" says MC Whitey.

The applause has stopped. The crowd become silent.

"There wasn't any fake blood," says the Director slowly. "We were going to add that afterwards."

Neat pools of dark red blood start to form underneath MC Rock and DJ Spin's bodies. There's a few mumbles throughout the crowd.

"Why ain't they movin'?" says MC Whitey, visibly panicking. "Shouldn't they be movin' now? Blanks don't fire anything do they!?"

"Why's there blood!?" shouts the Director.

The two crewmen who'd been handling the guns are gobsmacked and silent. They both walk then start running towards the bodies lying on the floor. They kneel on the ground and frantically start trying to shake the life back into MC Rock and DJ Spin. As they pick them up by the shoulders their neck's fall limp. Blood drips from MC Rock's mouth. Probably the most powerful thing ever to come out of it. You can see a fleshy, plate-sized hole in DJ Spin's back as the crewman holds his body up. Bullet exit wounds are always bigger than people think.

"They're bleeding!" shouts one of the film crewmen. No shit.

They shake the bodies some more, slap MC Rock and DJ Spin's faces, and shout at them. Not text book paramedic procedure, but nonetheless fun to watch.

Even though this feels like a movie set, this isn't the movies. This isn't where characters take multiple bullets to the body then carry on for another hour, shooting hundreds of bad guys in the process. This is real, and in real life you know from experience it only takes one bullet to explode into the body to kill. Two bullets and you'll die even faster.

The crewmen slowly give up on reviving the bodies.

"They're... they're d-d... they're dead," says one of the crewman.

"I think... they've been shot!" says the other crewman.

And the penny drops.

"What da fuck? WHAT DA FUCK? Why are they dead? WHY THEM?" shouts MC Whitey.

If you didn't know better you would say MC Whitey sounds jealous he wasn't the target.

Screams erupt all around you. Some of the posse run towards the bodies, others run in the opposite direction. The film crew buzz around, fiddling with cameras, others look lost. It's disorganised chaos. The Director pleads with everyone to be calm over the megaphone, although his shaky voice sounds anything but. You feel very calm. You walk over to Sadie and rub behind her ears. You untie her lead and pull your flat cap down and simply walk off the set, disappearing behind the caravans and lorries. Nobody noticed the old man shuffling about before, now you're practically invisible.

You walk to the gate and clamber over like an old man. Sadie crawls under the gate, and you both walk back across the fields to your car. Not once do you speed up, an old man wouldn't speed up. Stay in character until the coast is clear. Back at the car you dry the dew off Sadie with an old towel from the boot. She wags her tail as she hops on to her rug on the back seat.

"Guns don't kill people, rappers do," you say to Sadie.

She snaps at you, a low, growling bark.

"Yes. I know. Bullets kill people too."

You drive off, back the same way you came. A pair of cop cars scream past you heading in the opposite direction, sirens blaring and blue and whites flashing.

A grin of satisfaction appears under your fake grey beard.

Another successful hit, and you didn't even need to lay a finger on them.

No. 6

I want something good to die for, to make it beautiful to live
Go With The Flow, Queens Of The Stone Age

L-N-B-M-Y-E-A

What the hell am I supposed to do with that?

I scratch my head. I'm already 40 points behind and can't just roll out any four-letter word rubbish. I need to think big. I swig at my can of Guinness and place it slowly down on the carpet next to the board. We're spread out on my living room floor. Sophie's shoes and my trainers are dotted about. Our clothes are strewn over the chairs and sofa. I'm sitting in just my fitted black boxers, Sophie has a little black T-shirt and pretty pink knickers on, and a small orange sock on her left foot. Zero 7's latest CD is playing quietly in the background.

It's Saturday and it's been one of those cold, rainy days that seemed to get dark around mid-afternoon. Sophie and I had cracked open a nice bottle of red to warm our cockles. Seemed like a nice thing to do. Then we opened another, and shared another over dinner. It's now close to midnight and I've finished one four-pack of Guinness and I'm happily breaking the back of the second. Sophie is quietly polishing off a bottle of vodka, mixing increasingly stronger measures with coke.

I stare at the board. My brain isn't playing ball. The stout had 'helped' initially – Guinness is good for you, right? – but now my delicate mind is wandering. The third joint of the night isn't recharging the old grey matter like I'd hoped either. Instead it's blending it up magnificently. I pass the joint over to Sophie who's staring at her letters with a look of confusion and amusement. My head sways, I burp, then scratch my naked chest.

"Is there such thing as a Ambynel?" I enquire politely.

111

"Nooo!" replies Sophie. It's the fourth time she's had to say no and, even though she's smashed and stoned, my clever, perceptive side tells me it's becoming a little tedious for her. Still, she looks at me and giggles. She's also poo-pooed Ambley, Yembal and Nabymen. But she doesn't rush me. She just takes another long drag on the joint and sits back against the sofa, exhaling slowly.

I groan out loud. I can't think of anything worth more than ten points. Using the 'L' from Sophie's 'LOVELY' for the third letter I eventually concede and take my turn.

B-E-L-L-Y

It's enough to set me off. The word belly seems like the funniest thing in the world in my blissfully mashed state. But it only scores me ten points. No double word score, no nothing. Belly, belly, belly. Even though I'm laughing I've had a belly full of this game. I'm beginning to realise why they're called board games. I'm bored stupid. I look at the game's box. It says, *'The world's leading word game'* on the side. It's a little misleading, and what does the world know about leading words anyway. I rub my naked belly and wonder if the Guinness is doing it any good. It is if you count making it grow steadily as good. I lean over and pick some more letters out of the little green bag.

Sophie studies her letters, moving them into different orders on the tiny green rack. She smiles to herself. But this is no ordinary smile. It's bigger than a slice of melon. Mmm, melon. As she lays her letters out across the board, I can't help but watch. I notice goose pimples appearing on Sophie's bare legs. She continues to lay her letters down one by one, utilising the 'B' from BELLY.

S-C-R-A-B-B-L-E

"There. Can you believe that? Can you!?" she screams.

No, I bloody well can't.

"No, I bloody well can't," I say, just in case her ESP's turned off.

"And as I used up all my letters I get a 50 point bonus, so, er, that's 14, plus a double-word score, 28, that makes… 78 points! Yippee! Yayyy!!" She starts laughing and slapping her hands on the floor with excitement.

"You! You jammy… you jammy cow!" I shout.

"Check me out. I wonder if it's a British record or something, actually scoring with the word scrabble while playing the actual game. I wonder if Norris McWhirter still works for the *Guinness Book of Records.*"

"He's dead isn't he? Anyway, you can't have that. It's a name. It's the name of this damn game. This stupid, boring, board game."

"Bollocks. I can! Off they come, mister!" she says, pointing her eyes excitedly at my pants.

"Bloody game."

"C'mon, get 'em off!"

"Yeah, yeah, yeah, alright…" I mumble.

I stand up and slip off my boxers and they fall around my ankles. I shake them off and kick them across the room. I stand proudly with my hands on my hips, legs a couple of feet apart. A dirty, drunken look appears in Sophie's eyes. For some reason this makes me start dancing. Zero 7's still playing yet I ignore the chilled out tunes and find myself breaking into some kind of bump 'n' grind 'n' rock 'n' roll routine. I'm in full swing and so is my under carriage. Sophie's eyes are now standing out on stalks, both her hands covering her mouth. I'm not sure if she's amused or disgusted so I stop dancing as quickly as I started and sit back down, cross-legged, with my hands hiding my pecker. It's an awkward moment.

"Wowzers!" she says still with both hands over her mouth.

I look at her, and look at myself.

"Not sure where that came from," I say softly. I point at the board. "But it's still a name. You can't have names."

"Oh, balls! I am the greatest Scrabble player to ever walk this Earth. Ever. Ever. Ever. I'm the winner, and you're the loser!"

"Yeah, yeah, that's me. Hardy the loser." I look her in the eye. "Bed, then?"

"Not yet, darling. Not until you've done your forfeit. That's what we agreed at the start of the game. The winner picks a forfeit for the loser."

"What about my little impromptu naked jig?" I was hoping she might've forgotten about the flipping forfeit.

"Doesn't count. I didn't pick that."

"Oh," I say, putting on a little sad face.

"It doesn't count!"

"Okay," I say. "So what do you have in mind?"

"I want you to run down to No.78 completely naked and play Knockout Ginger on them."

"You fucking what?"

"You heard. C'mon, off you trot, down to No.78."

"Why No.78?"

"It's my new lucky number. Now, go on, get going!"

Why not? I'm game.

"Why not," I say.

It seems like a fun idea in my boozed-up, stoned state. I stand up and proudly stretch to reveal all my manliness. I feel pretty confident and the rain has stopped outside. I have a nice, warm, boozy glow and I'm sure the darkness will give me some cover. Plus I can run pretty fast barefoot: it'll be like running around the park in the summer only without any clothes on and without the warm-your-cockles weather. I walk out of the flat and towards the front door of the building. Thankfully none of the neighbours are around. Sophie, following close behind, starts giggling. As I open the front door I turn to her and do that loud drunken whispering that's actually louder than talking normally, "Not a buggering word, alright? You've got to keep you mouth shut."

She just giggles even more while gawping at my naked bum. I peer out into the street. The coast it clear so I make a dash for it. The cold, fresh air hits me, tickling the hairs on my chest and down below. I jog past the other flats on Camden and towards the rows of houses on the way to Larkhall. The streetlights are on but I can't see or hear another soul.

"Wayhey! Naughty sexy naked man!" I hear Sophie holler behind me.

The cow. But she thinks I'm sexy, so I let it slide. I take a deep breath and start running faster down the pavement in search of No.78.

My balls start bouncing all over the place, but I feel in control. Although that doesn't explain why I'm banging into the parked cars. Is it possible I'm a teensy-weensy bit wasted? Surely not. I slow down to a jog but still seem to be moving sideways rather than forwards. I can barely walk, let alone run, and with every lungful of air I'm careering off in all directions.

I promptly whack my knee into the bumper of a parked Mercedes.

"Bollocks!" I scream as I lunge on to the bonnet. The car alarm goes off immediately. It's deafening. I instinctively jump off the car, and my bare arse lands straight onto the bonnet of a Ford something parked behind me. Off goes a second alarm, higher pitched and more piercing than the first.

"Big bollocking bollocks!" I shout, rubbing my knee, and sliding off the bonnet back on to the pavement.

I look back and can just about see Sophie still dressed in her skimpy knickers and T-shirt, standing in the doorway, lit up by the light from the hallway. From the way her body is contorted it looks like she needs to pee. The bedroom lights of No.53 and No.55 come on across the road. A middle-aged man appears in a doorway right in front of me.

"Oi! What the bloody hell... " he shouts.

I almost forget I'm naked. I look back at my flat. I've gone too far to turn back now. I leg it further down the road, jogging as fast as my lurching legs will carry me. I narrowly miss a few more parked cars as I hear the man shout after me, "You maniac!"

The car alarms are still blaring as I start counting door numbers. As I jog I start to feel more stable and confident. No.70, 72, 74... then No.76 comes into view. I start to sprint. I know No.78 is next and decide to take a short-cut. This would be one of the worst decisions I'd made that night, only just ahead of playing Strip Scrabble. I leap into the air in at attempt to vault the garden wall. I'm going to make it. I'm flying. Sadly my judgement is at least six feet off. I land before the wall, instead of after it, and smash my shinbone into brickwork, tumbling into someone's front garden. The grass is wet and freezing and not at all welcoming for a naked body, but I'm not stopping. Momentum carries me in a cartwheel through a line of dense rose bushes, ripping the skin off my chest, arms and legs. I don't slow down – why am I not slowing down? I crash noisily into a bunch of milk bottles on the doorstep. I finally stop moving when my head clatters into the hard, wooden front door.

I see stars, literally, as I lie flat on my back looking up at the night sky, then more stars as my head begins to spin wildly. My breathing feels heavy as my body throbs on the cold concrete path. The salty taste of blood appears in my mouth. I feel totally exposed, yet I still manage a dizzy smile.

The last thing I remember is a small, grey-haired old lady with bright white false teeth opening the front door and saying, "Les! Les! There's a naked man on our doorstep. Come quickly, Love!" I'm sure I catch her checking me out, then I hear her say, "Oooh, that reminds me, I'd better get the sausages out of the freezer for breakfast."

Then I pass out.

I wake with a start. I don't move, I just open my eyes. I'm naked in bed with Sophie by my side. She's gently snoring, and I can see she's still wearing yesterday's eyeliner. She still looks edible. I peck her on the cheek (upper, left). My head starts pounding as soon as I move but my bladder's fit to burst so I gingerly climb out of bed. I wince. My head feels ready to fall off, and my body feels like it's been run over by a lorry. I rub my hip. It's incredibly sore. I look down and see a big black bruise on my right hip, and a big, bloody cut on my left knee and shin. My elbow looks like it's been bleeding, and why are there scratches all over my chest, arms and legs? My stomach grumbles. I feel more than a bit nauseous.

Jesus, I haven't felt this much pain since that Ronan Keating concert I went to last year.

What the hell did we do last night anyway?

I remember we'd had some red wine. I remember we'd played Scrabble. Not sure. I scratch my cranium trying to diffuse some of the confusion. My fingernails feel gritty. Closer inspection reveals lines of mud underneath. I can feel soil in between my toes as well. I painfully lift each foot up in turn and discover both soles are dirty and black. I don't remember doing any gardening. I don't even have a garden for starters, not even a neat little window box.

Even the short trudge across the landing is hard work. I stagger into the darkness of the bathroom, and towards the sink. Only I don't make it. I skid on a damp flannel lying on the tiled floor and promptly flip on to my back. For reference, tiled floors don't make soft landings. As I hit the floor I crack the back of my head. I start to whimper.

I stand up and try to rub the soreness out of my throbbing head. What was a distant ringing has been replaced by deafening chimes. I shuffle backwards and cunningly step on a tube of Aquafresh lying on the floor. The cooling, menthol toothpaste oozes steadily in between my naked toes.

"Wank!" I shout.

I give up on any more complications and shakily clamber into the shower. I stand very still under the hot deluge of water and moan and groan for the next ten minutes. As the water washes away the dried blood I'm able to examine my war wounds and bruises. I prod them with my finger and instantly wish I hadn't. If I was meat I'd be tenderloin. Each pat with the towel afterwards hurts so I head for the safety of the bedroom.

"Morning, daredevil!" says Sophie brightly, sitting up in bed. She's wearing my old, red Doors T-shirt.

"Morning, er, sweet angel?" I say feeling bemused.

She smiles at me.

"What happened last night? My whole body is cut to buggery, there's mud in strange places and I ache from my big toe up to here." I hold my hand up level with my forehead.

"Ahh, my poor baby. I didn't realise you'd done so much damage to yourself. Let's have a look at you," she says sympathetically.

I show Sophie my cuts and bruises. She gets some antiseptic cream and plasters from the bathroom cabinet and gently rubs it into the grazes on my chest and back, sticking plasters over the bloody bits on my elbow and knee.

"So what happened?" I say again.

I sit on the bed and Sophie fills in the blanks from the third bottle of red wine to losing at Strip Scrabble and the attempted Naked Knockout Ginger.

"Christ. I won't be able to show my face around here again."

"It's your arse I think you won't want to show again," says Sophie. She smiles. It could almost be a 'I'm proud of you' smile. She wraps her arms around me and kisses me on the lips. Her mouth feels warm and inviting but I think even the most energy-saving sexual positions will hurt my battered body today.

I stand up, throw on my dressing gown and head to the kitchen to cure my pain.

I down a pint of squash, and another, and stick the kettle on. I neck four pain killers and a Berocca multi-vitamin. I ignore the pile of fruit in the bowl and make a round of toast with chocolate spread on top. Why do I always feel like eating junk after abusing my body? I ignore these thoughts as I wolf down the toast and crack open a can of coke from the fridge. I guzzle down half the coke and get a nice sugar rush.

I need more sustenance. I'm willing to try anything to sort myself out. Well, not anything. I couldn't eat a shoe, for example. Not a whole one.

I think about poaching some eggs. That would involve cracking them. I pour the boiled water from the kettle into a saucepan and plonk four eggs straight in. Boiled eggs it is. I look at the clock on the wall. It's 10:06. Is it three or four or five minutes for boiled eggs? I put some more bread in the toaster for me, and Sophie too, and decide the eggs will be done when the toast pops up.

When I think I can handle some light sounds I switch the radio on in the kitchen. I get Bath FM. The nasal rapping of the Nuff Respect Crew emanates from the tinny-sounding speaker. It doesn't help my nausea. I tune in another station. GWR is playing the same Nuff Respect Crew song as well. I keep flicking channels. They're all playing the Nuff Respect Crew. I can't stand their half-assed gangsta rap crap – that rhymes, am I a rapper now? – even if me and MC White Nigel are now best mates.

I tune in Radio 1 as it cuts to the news. I leave it on and listen with as much attention as I can fathom, which isn't much. I'm not really sure what they're saying.

Perhaps I should go back to bed and start again.

I make soldiers and serve up breakfast for two. My two eggs don't touch the sides, or stop the hollow feeling in my stomach, so I scoff Sophie's as well while she's still in the shower.

You snooze you lose around here. Or, you shower you lose. But that doesn't rhyme.

I give up on the radio and flick on the TV in the lounge to try and ease myself back into reality. Every channel has 'Live news' and 'Breaking news' splayed across the screen. I settle on BBC1 and sit down and attempt to take it in. They're talking about the Nuff Respect Crew and a photo of MC Whitey appears on screen.

MC Whitey is dead.

Oh God. I start going dizzy and sweat appears on my brow. A mixture of paranoia and panic overwhelms me. Not another one. Has he been killed because I'd interviewed him? Is the psycho Hitman killing everyone I come into contact with? Should I be thankful he's got rid of the wigga? Should I have some more chocolate spread on toast?

"He strikes again," I say to the TV.

I think about shouting to Sophie but I hear the burr of the hairdryer in the bedroom.

My non-existent attention span returns to the TV to see more photos of the Nuff Respect Crew and MC Whitey. BBC keeps showing photos of two other boys from the crew but I don't recognise them. I can't believe he's dead. MC Whitey is dead. Nigel is dead. He was a chavving chav and a wannabe gangsta, but still, does that mean he deserved to die? I'm not sure. I shouldn't ask myself such meaningful questions when I'm feeling meaningless.

I turn the TV volume down low and make Sophie's breakfast (again). I make myself some tea and put five sugars in it. I don't need the sugar, I'm sweet enough already, and I'm shaking all over too, but I figure it'll help switch my brain on. It only switches me back to thinking that MC Whitey is dead because of me.

A mobile phone starts ringing. My mobile phone. I follow the ringing to my jeans lying screwed up behind the sofa. I pull my mobile out of the pocket. I don't recognise the number on the display, but answer it anyway. I'm crazy like that.

"Hardy Matthews?"

"Speaking."

"It's DCI Johnson."

Excellent.

"Why is it that whoever you've been around ends up dropping down dead shortly afterwards?"

I can picture Johnson in his brown shirt and brown trousers with his brown aura.

"Christ knows," I say. If he's going to cut out the pleasantries with me I figure I may as well do the same. "It's worrying me too."

"Is there anything you're not telling me Matthews?"

I think about telling Johnson I got another email from the Hitman about No.7 and No.6 on his Top 10 Hit List, but I don't like his tone. I haven't been called Matthews since school, and I didn't like it much then either. It doesn't make me want to cooperate.

"No, there's nothing I'm not telling you. I don't know why MC Whitey was shot."

"What!? MC Whitey? He hasn't been shot," says Johnson.

"Don't piss about."

"I don't, as you say, piss about," says Johnson.

"But the news said about the Nuff Respect Crew, and MC Whitey, and something about a shooting, I figured the Hitman had struck again, and I put two and two together."

"And got five," he says. "MC Whitey's not dead."

"Thank fuck-a-doodle doo for that."

"But MC Rock and DJ Spin shot each other, and *they are dead*."

"Oh," I say, pausing briefly. "Poor buggers. Why would they want to shoot each other?"

"Indeed," he says.

I must stop jumping to conclusions. I must learn to watch the full story on the news instead of catching a glimpse of the headlines then freaking out like a complete freakazoid. But news is so dull to watch sometimes, even with the dramatic graphics and glamour-puss presenters.

"And the Hitman hasn't shot anyone?" I say.

"It doesn't look like it. But we're not counting out his involvement."

"I see. Okay, well, sorry Johnson, there's been a terrible mix up," I say. I can feel relief rising through me as it sinks in that MC Whitey's not dead. He's not dead. It's not because of me.

"You don't seem particularly upset that MC Rock and DJ Spin are dead."

I'm not upset, that's why. I'm too happy that MC Whitey's not dead. "I didn't know them did I?" I say.

Johnson doesn't respond.

"Best be cracking on then," I say. "Lots to do. Speak soon."

"Hang on a second Matthews. Look, well, we know you're not the Hitman, but, you're a well-connected man…" Johnson pauses "…have you any ideas who might be behind all this? Do you know who the Hitman could be?"

The police need my help. They need *my* help. What a laugh.

"You see, it happened on a video shoot. The guns were meant to have blanks in, but they'd been replaced with real bullets. It seems too clever for a gang killing. They like to shoot other crews, not set other crews up to shoot each other."

I think Johnson's confiding in me. I keep silent.

"My detectives and constables are spending all their time and available manpower talking to everyone who was on the set at the time of the shootings, and all we've got was something from one of the security guards who saw 'a nice old man and his dog'."

"Hardly a prime suspect, unless he had a hit squad of sheep with him."

Johnson ignores my facetious jibe.

"So we think it's the Hitman. We think MC Rock and DJ Spin were No.7 on his bloody Hit List. But we don't know how he got on set or who he is."

"I'm sorry Johnson, but I haven't got a clue who your man is."

"Excellent," he says sarcastically. "Whoever he is, he's professional. There were no fingerprints on the guns or on bullets left in the gun chambers. Just like there were no prints left on the amps on the West Side stage, at Abbey Road or at The Royal. He never leaves any sodding evidence."

I nod but I don't think Johnson can see it from his end.

"Even the two strands of gel-covered hair CSI managed to find at The Royal in Sean Bates's room were no good to us."

I don't need to ask him what CSI stands for as I've seen the show on television. "Why's that? Because of the gel?"

"No, because they weren't his hairs. They were real hairs, but from the wig he was wearing. They were actually female hairs," says Johnson exhaling loudly. "He always seems to wear a bloody different disguise, and that's making our job very difficult."

For some reason I like the idea of the Hitman dressing up.

"Well, if you think of anything, anything at all, please give me a call."

"Okay."

I hang up before he asks me anymore questions. I log Johnson's number on my mobile so I'll know it's him next time he calls.

Sophie joins me to watch the over-sensationalised TV coverage of the Nuff Respect Crew murders. Every channel seems to have replaced their reliable, level-headed reporters with unreliable headless chickens.

After the initial shock of learning of Hit No.7, Sophie soaks up all the facts, while I sit in a daze.

"So he's using guns now then," says Sophie coolly.

"Yes. Well, no. He's not using them. He cleverly got MC Rock and DJ Spin to use them on each other," I hear myself say.

"But still, guns are a step up for him. Wonder how he'll knock off the next lucky lot. If he gets to knock them off..."

I can't think. My brain's turned to cheese and it's too stuffy inside.

"I need some fresh air. Fancy going for a walk?" I say. Sophie's just turned over to watch *Hollyoaks*.

"You don't go for walks, Hardy. You don't like walking, unless it's to a pub," she says with half a mouthful of breakfast.

"I know. But I need to clear my head. A walk will help, I think. It's nice outside." I pull the curtain back to reveal blue sky and sunshine. "See?"

"Cool. Okay, let's go. My head's a bit cloudy too," she says.

We wrap up with scarves and cosy jackets. Spring's on its way, but it hasn't sprung yet. So it's still bastard cold outside. We trot down Lansdown Road to The Paragon and past the Curfew pub. It's only 11:30am but I could do with hair of the dog. Not sure how dog hair helps hangovers, sounds a bit too chewy and, well, hairy.

We carry on and walk past the fire station to pick up the canal path that will take us out of Bath and into the countryside. The air is bracing but as we walk with the canal by our side I can feel some life re-entering my body. Sophie slips her hand inside mine. It's warm. I can feel what she's thinking.

"Cold hands, warm heart," I say.

"My hands are warm. Does that mean I have a cold heart?"

"Let me check," I say.

We stop and I put my hand inside her jacket and blatantly grope her left breast for a while in a mock examination kind of way. She doesn't flinch, she just smiles with her head tilting to one side.

"Well, Doctor?" she says.

"Feels quite warm to me, Ms Cooper. Get plenty of rest and lay off alcohol for a while. If you feel you heart turning cold come back and see me and I'll prescribe something."

"What would that be, Doctor?"

"Two gropes three times a day should cure things."

We carry on walking past a series of long canal boats lining the side of the water. They have odd names like 'The Badger', 'Watson's Wanderer' and 'Luverly Jubberly'. But I'm not interested in barge monikers, I'm interested in brutal murders.

"I still can't believe the cops haven't managed to produce anything," I say. It's been on my mind since Johnson called.

"Bless them. I'm sure they're trying," says Sophie sympathetically.

"Four bands have been hit, seven people are very dead, and yet they haven't been able to find one single lead."

"It's crap, but I'm sure they're investigating everything they can," says Sophie.

"I don't think they are. I don't think Johnson knows how to handle a serial killer in the music industry. Cops don't know pop," I say.

"That rhymes."

"They need to get inside the killer's head. Think like him. Understand what motivates him. What music he hates. What bands might be next on his Hit List."

"Get you," says Sophie.

"We could do a better job than them," I say.

I think I actually mean it.

It's funny how walking gets me talking, gets me thinking. The fresh air's doing the trick, my head's starting to feel less fuzzy.

We pass a man on the canal path with a Sherlock Holmes-type tweed hunting hat walking a pair of Spaniels skipping along. The hunting hat's not walking the dogs, and neither are the dogs skipping, with ropes or anything. Just to make things clear.

Three brightly coloured, fit looking mountain bikers overtake us and zoom off up the path, weaving in and out of the pedestrian traffic, leaving a trail of dust behind.

"Bloody cyclists," I say.

"You don't like cyclists?" says Sophie.

"Fitness freaks, aren't they? What's the bloody point? You need to increase your heart rate? Just eat a big fry up. You need to sweat? Get a hot 'n' spicy curry down your neck."

"You're so wise, Hardy Matthews," says Sophie tugging playfully on my hand.

"They only thing I hate more than cyclists is bloody joggers."

Two joggers promptly overtake us. They're even more brightly coloured and fit looking than the mountain bikers.

"Bloody joggers," I say under my breath.

"Hardy, shush. Let's just enjoy the walk. It's a nice day."

Half an hour's walk brings us conveniently to The George pub at Bathampton. If American tourists knew about this picturesque place by the side of the canal, with ivy-covered stonework, a pub garden looking out into the rolling hills and a perfect little church by its side, they'd say 'Gee, ain't it quaint'. Thankfully they don't. It's too far away from the Roman Baths and Royal Crescent for the open top bus tours. As it is, this classic country pub with low beams and warm, old fashioned décor gets packed with Bathonians anyway. No room for tourists. Although when I order us a couple of pints at the bar I'm served by a cheerful Australian. But everyone knows Aussies make the best barmen in the world, so I don't complain.

We manage to find an empty table in one of the many rooms hidden away. The ceiling is so low even I have to duck under the exposed beams. An old couple with grey hair and grey faces are sat at the table opposite. The woman is reading *The Mail on Sunday*, the front page headline says *'Rap Crew Shootings'*. *The News Of The World* is lying on their table. There are pictures of MC Rock & DJ Spin, Dazza, Hoodwink and Sean Bates, and the headline underneath says *'Wanted: Hitman & Top 10 Hit List'*. Underneath in smaller writing it says *'Who will be next…?'*

It was only a matter of time before the Hitman and his Top 10 leaked out in to the mainstream press. Trust *The News Of The*

Screws to get there first. I wish I'd got that exclusive out there. I wonder, did Johnson sanction it.

The old man seems content to sit without a care in the world and puff on his pipe. It's a long necked one. You don't see many of those about anymore. Come to think of it, you don't see many pipe smokers these days either.

"Do you mind if I borrow your *News Of The World*?" I say to the old man.

"Help yourself young man, it's the pub's paper. Doris and I don't read such tat," he says smiling and puffing on his pipe.

Sophie and I read the front-page news together. It's not really news to us: we already know all about the Hitman on the loose, and the story doesn't tell us anything new. Although it does make it more real reading about it in the papers. What interests me is the 'Who's next on the Top 10 Hit List?' angle. It's a well-known trick in the press to use numbers in articles – we do twenty one best this and top ten worst that in the magazine all the time. I start thinking about my Top 10 as I look around the room, but I find myself staring at the pipe smoker.

"Something very weird is going on around here, Sophie," I say quietly. "Is it National Sherlock Holmes Day or something?"

"Sadly, I don't think there is such an annual celebration."

"What's going on then? We've seen hunting hats, Watson's canal barge and long-necked pipes. Is someone trying to tell us something?"

"I saw it all too," says Sophie staring down at the menu on the table. "I didn't want to say anything in case you thought I was some sort of fruit cake."

"Is Sherlock Holmes trying to tell us something?" I say for a laugh.

"Doubt it. But they *were* hefty hints."

"Hints signalling that we should maybe do some detective work."

We let it hang in the air for a while. We drink our pints. They go down far too nicely and far too quickly. I go to the bar to get a couple more and order two roast dinners; turkey for me, pork for Sophie. The old man and his wife leave. He puffs on his pipe and nods to me as he walks past. I don't need anymore signs. I sit back down with our drinks.

"Fuck it!" I say. "I think we'd make a great pair of detectives."

Sophie laughs out loud. I don't say anything. I just look at her.

"You're so funny sometimes," she sniggers.

I continue looking at her, and raise an eyebrow.

"You're being serious aren't you?" she says.

I look away to the pictures on the wall behind her. They're mostly of horses and dogs on a hunt. I wonder why there are never any paintings of foxes. I like to think that I'd make a good fox; a sly fox, a sleuth, hunting from the shadows.

I still don't say anything.

"Oh my God. You are. You're serious," says Sophie, her mouth hangs open ready to catch flies.

"Let's at least have a go," I say. "We'd bag an exclusive to end all exclusives if we catch the Hitman in action."

"Are you taking the piss?"

"No. Come on, what's the worst that could happen?"

"We try to stop the Hitman and end up being killed ourselves."

"There is that. But let's not think like that. Let's think about how we can track him down," I say. "I think we could find him before the cops do and get a scoop every newspaper in the country would pay big money for."

"I'm not sure about this," she says.

"I could be the brains, you could be the brawn," I suggest.

"Beauty!" she says, thumping me on the arm.

"Okay," I say.

"Okay!" she says.

We grin like fools.

"So what next?" she asks.

I put on my best serious face.

"We need to think like the Hitman, like a murderer. We need to get inside his head."

"And how do we do that?"

"Hang on."

I pop to the bar and ask for some pens and paper. I slap them down on our table and sit back down.

"We write down our *own* Hit Lists."

I could be wrong, but I'm sure Sophie looks at me with an expression of pride. Either that, or she's got trapped wind.

"What, like a pub quiz?" says Sophie.

"No! To see if we can predict who the Hitman's going to bosh next," I say. "Look, even the newspapers are thinking about it." I hold up *The News Of The World* and point to the front page story. "We can skip No.10 to No.7 as he's done them. Let's starting at No.6 and work down to No.1."

I quickly start writing. If I'm honest I've been thinking about my own Hit List since I got the first Hitman email. My list would've included at least two of the bands and singers he's already killed off. West Side and Sean Bates were obvious choices. Hoodwink had it coming it as well. The Nuff Respect Crew weren't so obvious, although I can totally see his point. I keep writing. No.5, No.4 and No.3 all come to me in a flash.

Sophie's looking at what I've written. It feels like a test at school and I childishly shield my paper with my hand and arm so she can't see. I write No.2 with my nose almost touching the table.

"Spoil sport," she says. I see that her page is still blank.

I smile the smile of the smug. Although I'm not finished yet. I put my hand over what I've written. No.1. Numero Uno. Who deserves to be at the coveted No.1 spot? I look around the room for inspiration, but don't find any. Sophie starts busily writing.

"I'm done now!" she says proudly. A desperately annoying artist pops into my head. I can't believe I didn't think of them sooner. I quickly write down my No.1. "Me too," I say.

"If you'd like to now swap your answers with the person sitting on your left please," says Sophie in her best maths teacher voice.

We compare and contrast each other's lists. We both have a different band as our Hit No.6, but we both have the same singer at No.5.

"Great minds," says Sophie.

"Indeed," I say.

We have different choices for No.4, but the same at No.3 and No.2. At No.1 we've both picked different solo male singers.

"Interesting choice at No.1, Sophie," I say.

"I just can't bloody stand him. You know when you just look at some people and think, 'I just don't like you'? That's how I feel about him. Plus he can't sing for shit."

"Same as my boy at No.1. Can't stand him either. Gormless, arrogant little tosser. Thinks he's God's gift to the pop world. The charts would be a better place with out him and his cheesy pop crap," I say.

"So, detective time. Do you think we follow what your No.6 is doing or my No.6?"

"That's easy. Mine. We did a little news story on your lot recently and I don't think they're playing many live shows this year, too busy being photographed shopping and clubbing," I say.

"Okay, clever clogs. We'll check out your little lot."

"Good. We'll go and see my lot sing in London," I say. I know they're playing there as I had an email with concert and TV studio dates. "We can do some snooping and spying backstage. See if our Hitman is about to do anything naughty. This is how we catch him. We just need to be in the right place at the right time."

*   *

You enjoy crossing off another hit on your Hit List. A line of ink now strikes through No.10, No.9, No.8 and No.7. You look at your

Top 10 you memorised long ago then fold it up and put it back safely in your pocket. It feels good to finally be doing something positive with your life.

You've been reading music magazines, watching the chart movements and checking out the web news and press to see how your Hit List is going down with the public and pop industry. On the whole, as far you're concerned, it's having a positive impact. You've read about tributes by traumatised Hoodwink and Sean Bates fans and heard something about MySpace being a very busy place to be online. You're surprised there hasn't been any tribute sites set up for you online yet. In time, in time. The artists' funerals have all been private affairs so far although some fans think they should be made public so they can make their grieving even more visible and melodramatic.

The music scene and music channels are still playing boy band/ girl band and talent show dysentery around the clock, and you've also learned of the *wonderful* news that West Side plan to release a special CD dedicated to Dazza with all of his favourite West Side tracks. At least *he* can't release new material anymore.

But all this just makes you more determined to keep going.

No.6 on your Hit List. This is one pop act you've had to build up to. You couldn't have named them at No.10, that would be too soon, and they didn't deserve to be in the top five either. So, the girly girls of Kitty Bomb find themselves at the tricky No.6 spot on your Top 10 countdown.

You wonder if anyone appreciates the thought you put into your Hit List. Probably not. People don't appreciate thought these days. They haven't got time for it. Haven't got time for great music. Haven't got time for great tunes, great melodies, great lyrics. People haven't got time for anything worthwhile anymore. It's thoughts like these that spur you on.

There is part of you that wanted to keep your Top 10 to boy bands and fake male musicians. But that isn't very PC of you. You want to keep all things equal. So you judge the girls of Kitty Bomb with the same contempt you used for West Side, and Sean Bates, and MC Rock and DJ Spin. You judge them on their musicality, and lack of it, and their desperate hunger for fame and fortune, blind to the fact they don't have a harmonious muscle between the three of them. It's songs like Kitty Bomb's *Da Bomb* that got them on your Hit List. It's the half rap (half crap) and half singing that winds you up.

But the great thing about girls is, from the point of view of a real man like you, you can judge them on their looks and sexuality too. Sadly, for Kitty Bomb, they have a look, but it isn't sexual. To put it bluntly, Kitty Bomb are three dogs from Dagenham.

Rough round the edges, class-less pop star wannabes who don't know the difference between seduction and writing melodies, and sucking cock and writing cheques. There are other talent-less girl bands more interested in celebrity status and shopping than writing songs or playing a piano, but they're easier on the eye, and you don't mind a bit of eye candy. Kill off a pretty girl band? Now *that* would be wrong. You're not some kind of sicko.

You freely admit you were stuck for a method to murder the three Kitty Bombers. You wanted to do it right. There won't be no half-assed way out for this girl group. You want to show them that you care. But you couldn't think of how. When all along you just needed to listen to your instinct. Actually, all you needed to do was listen to your radio. It was on an afternoon Radio 1 show when you heard their cover version of *Hanging On The Telephone*. It goes without saying that the three little pigs aren't a patch on the young, sexually-charged Debbie Harry who drove grown men to weep and young boys to masturbation. Kitty Bomb's cover curdled your blood, but it also got it pumping. Their modernised version with compulsory dance floor-friendly beats and whining, passionless vocals spoiled the sassy Blondie classic to the point of insult.

So, you figure you'll add fatal injury to insult and murder them with their own song. After all, they started it by murdering Blondie's.

*   *

It's a Saturday morning and summer's approaching. It's been over six weeks since we drew up our very own Hit Lists and now we're absurdly excited about playing detectives for the day. We're like Holmes and Watson, if Watson was a woman. We're like Inspector Gadget and his little niece, if I was half robot, and Sophie was half her age. We're like Starsky and Hutch, if we could only find some impressive knitwear, and Sophie had shorter, more manly hair. We're like Dempsey and Makepeace. That's it. If only I was American, and Sophie was blonde... These comparisons aren't really working are they?

TV detective comparisons or not, we've been keeping our eyes peeled for anything suspicious backstage and front.

We were up and on the road at 7am and I drove us up to London to arrive at the TV studio at 10am, two hours before the girl band were due to take the stage. We scoped out the dressing rooms, the corridors, backstage, side stage, front of stage, the main entrance and side entrances, fire exits, even the toilets. I've seen enough movies to know that toilet windows are popular for getting in and out of places. Out back I've been scanning everyone and anyone, sussing out if they belong or are intruders or potential murderers. The pop bands stand out – they have that over confident aura – plus I recognise most of them.

The roadies and TV crew blend into the background, lugging drum kits and amps this way and that, but I keep an eye out for anyone *just* looking busy. It's an art form I've mastered when in the office so I know the tricks to look out for when people are just pretending. It's all in the shifty look in their eyes. Back out in the crowd I've been checking out security staff and anyone hanging around where they shouldn't be. Nobody is wearing a trench coat and shades or looks like they're concealing a shotgun or large bomb on their person.

Sophie and I have covered everywhere with the Chief of Security, Simon Rumbles, who's one of those unassuming blokes who doesn't look very big until I'm up close and realise he's a foot taller and a foot wider than me. Earlier on I'd said, "We're doing a mag feature on how security has been stepped up in light of the pop star murders and how the general public don't need to worry because security guards like you are making the music world a safer place."

Rumbles puffed out his chest proudly and said, "I'm just doing my job. But I have doubled my security work force here at the television studios in light of recent events."

The uniformed security guards stood out easily, obviously, and Rumbles pointed out one of three undercover security guards, a middle aged man trying too hard to fit in by wearing a teenager's flashy jeans and layered T-shirt. I was able to pick out the other two. Mainly because they're stood on their own, looking shifty and uncomfortable like paedophiles at a pop concert, and dressed in fashionable clothes that obviously weren't their own.

The only people missing here this morning are the police. I'd thought about telling DCI Johnson about our little detective plan, how we're going to track down the Hitman with our own Hit Lists, but after ten seconds of deep thinking, I thought better of it. Johnson and his detectives would only cramp our style and I don't intend to miss out on another exclusive.

While I've been casually checking out dark corners to see if anyone's hiding, ready to pounce on the unsuspecting three-piece girl group, Sophie's been taking rounds of photos as the public walk in. She's firing off photo after photo until she's happy she's got most of the 300 or so people that have either walked in the front or back. Many of the young girls walking past Sophie can't help themselves by posing and pouting for the camera, desperate to find some kind of easy fame as they imagine Sophie's photos appearing in tomorrow's papers or celebrity rags.

We're watching everything and everyone. I've got my back to the wall and, like all good undercover security I'm eyeballing everyone from the crowd to door staff to roadies to cameramen. I'm also watching the floor manager energetically directing the crowd, and the dumb dance act that's performing their latest single before the girl band come out and sing their charmless, ineffective pop ditty on stage. But I'm playing it all suave and sophisticated. I'm blending into the background, acting the part, pretending like I'm not interested in anyone, when I'm interested in everyone. Because anyone could be *him*. At any moment *he* could strike.

But when the Hitman shows up we'll be ready for him.

*　　*

The TV set of Music:UK feels much bigger than you remember. On your previous late night reconnaissance when the set was empty, it had felt immense inside, but even now on Saturday morning when it's packed with camera crew, production staff, hundreds of rosy cheeked fans in the crowd, bands on stage, and presenters on podiums, it still feels vast.

You're hanging around near the back of the teenybopper crowd with one eye on the stage and another eye on the green room door, with the occasional peek across at the pretty presenter talking to camera. She looks more orange in person than she does on TV. She's shorter too. You know it's not live as Music:UK goes out at mid-day and it's only 10.45am.

"Excuse me, love, you'll need to stand over there when the next act comes out." A middle aged security guard dressed in a white polo shirt and black trousers puts his hand gently but firmly on your arm, pointing towards the green room door and then the crowd of kids.

"Oooh, okay dear, no problem. I just didn't want to get in the way," you say in character. Robin Williams would be proud of your voice skills that you've been practicing at home to get right.

"You'll be okay if you stand over there on the edge of the crowd." Again he touches your arm with his hand, indicating with his other where you should be. Normally you wouldn't let a man like him touch your arm, normally you'd break theirs. But as you're in character, and deep in disguise, you make an exception.

"Okay, dear. I'm Mandy's mum. From Kitty Bomb. I come to what gigs I can," you say in your realistic old lady's voice with a slight Liverpudlian accent. You give him a closed mouth smile through your makeup. "Thank you. I'll stand over there."

"Sorry, love, I did wonder what a, er, mature lady like you is doing in a place like this. I'll take you to the green room where Kitty Bomb are if you like."

"It's okay, dear, I've already wished the girls good luck. I'll be fine standing over there."

"Okay, love." He gives you a friendly smile as he walks off.

Love? You're being treated like an old dear. But then, if you will dress up in disguise as one, people will treat you as they see you. You pat your lightly greyed wig down and play with a ruby earring dangling down. You're wearing a pair of skin-coloured silk gloves that remind you of your old Aunty Caryl.

Being a bodyguard has meant you've managed to pick up all sorts of tips along the way. Like a sponge you soaked up the makeup methods used by some of your older celebrity clients who relied heavily on war paint before greeting their public. You picked a baggy, flowery dress to subtly, cleverly hide your physique, with a long-sleeved cardigan over the top. You've used the thick-walled makeup methods over your face and neck, and gold-rimmed glasses (with clear lenses) to put the finishing touches to your fifty year old lady outfit. With a stooped body posture, even you were convinced by your reflection in the mirror at home.

You take in the crowd as there's some hustle in front of you as kids jostle for position nearer the stage. The presenters gee the crowd up, as if they need to be worked up into anymore of a frenzy. You stand waiting patiently.

"Who's ready for Kitty Bomb?" shouts the pretty presenter and her grinning male co-presenter into their flashy silver microphones.

The crowd reply with adolescent screams and whoops of joy. You think of joining in and cheering and jumping up and down for the hell of it. But you don't think that's the correct behaviour of an old lady, plus you would be faking your enthusiasm for the three white trash witches... actually, witches is a bit strong. They're not witches. They're not complex and clever enough to be witches. Bitches? No. Not got it in them. They're too simple. They're just three dumb blondes who got lucky with a recording contract.

The presenters turn to camera as Mandy, Sharon and Zoe totter up on stage. On cue the crowd bop up and down as the presenters blab away to camera. Even over the screams you can her what they're saying as it's piped through the TV studio speakers.

"Now we've got the pleasure of three sexy kittens from Kitty Bomb performing their new single..." says the pretty presenter.

"...*Hanging On The Telephone!*" says the male presenter.

The crowd dances and claps and cheers just like the board prompts held by the production staff tell them to. The lights flash sporadically as spots shine down on the three Kitty Bombers on stage. A telephone dangles by the side of each of the girls from long phone wires hanging from the gantry. There's no real backing band like Blondie, instead a backing track starts thumping out of the speakers. The guitars are more studio replicated rather than rock-fuelled as Kitty Bomb proceed to sing over the top in unison. No, actually, not sing. Mime. Fucking mime. You know this because their lip-synching is slightly out. It's obvious when you're there in the studio – there will need to be some post production TV tweaks to fix the timing before it goes out.

Three chicks all miming to a song they didn't write by a band they never met. As they get to the chorus, they dance around the phone lines and pick up the phone and sing, sorry, *mime* their version of the chorus into the receiver.

"Hanging on the telephone,
Hanging on the telephone"

The kids in the crowd love all this show-woman shit and display their appreciation by clapping and cheering even louder.

You keep to the edge of the studio, one eye on the stage, and another on the studio fuse box on the wall. You know where it is thanks to your earlier recce. As Kitty Bomb mime their way through the next verse, you check that the smiling security guard and production staff aren't watching you – they're not, they're all watching the slags on stage – then shuffle up to the fuse box and open the metal door.

You timed your moves at home and know how long the song lasts, and when each verse and chorus starts and ends. Your cue is the first of three lines of *'Oh why can't we talk again'*. You know the song's only 2:22 so you have to act decisively. Your instincts take over as you close one eye and swiftly pull the fuse for the lights out. The studio is plunged into darkness but the music continues. The crowd changes from cheers to sneers while a few people start shouting and screaming. You open your closed eye as your pupils adapt to the darkness instantly. In a flash, and impressively for an old dear, you run across to the stage and jump up between the Kitty Bombers. You can hear them bickering in the blackness between themselves as the song continues to thump out of the speakers.

"Hanging on the telephone"

"What's blimmin' going on Mandy?" says Sharon or Zoe, you're not sure which.

"How the hell should I freakin' know? It's gone all dark innit!" says Mandy or Zoe.

"I can't see a flippin' fing. Let's keep dancin' and that innit," says Zoe or Sharon.

The crowd continue to shout and complain.

"Hanging on the telephone"

"I'll hang you on the fucking telephone," you snarl. You almost start laughing, but check yourself: you're too professional to take your eye off the target.

"Who said that?"

"Eh? Who's that?"

"What's going on? I can't see a flamin' fing!"

While they're still standing on stage in perfect darkness wondering what to do, you take the first phone wire dangling down from the ceiling and quickly tie it tightly around Kitty Bomber No.1's neck. She holds her hands up to her neck and screams. You take the second phone wire and promptly wrap it tightly around Kitty Bomber No.2's neck and tie it tightly. She kicks out at you and screams. You dodge her boots as she lashes out and take the third wire to tie it quickly and tightly around Kitty Bomber No.3's neck. She resists and tries to scratch your eyes with her fingernails, but you overpower her easily and give her a quick bitch slap.

The crowd start screaming and jeering.

You quickly jump off stage and find the three wire's pulley mechanism attached to the rope you'd scoped out earlier on. You untie it from the steel catch on the wall behind the stage backdrop. You quickly and silently heave on it as production staff run past in the darkness oblivious to your presence. The weight of three skinny slappers is probably about twenty two stone, but your strength, adrenaline and determination enable you hoist the girls about a metre off the ground. You pull hard on the rope and tie it back up to the catch in a double bowline knot just as someone puts the light fuse back in. You're already in position on the outer edge of the crowd as the lights gradually blink back on throughout the studio. The chorus continues to pour out speakers.

"Hanging on the telephone,

Hanging on the telephone…"

You're not sure which is louder, the screams of the crowd or the screams from the production staff and pretty presenter. The three girls aren't screaming. They're quietly choking. It's almost beautiful. You'd always thought they should bring back public hanging. Perhaps it'll catch on?

Production staff try frantically to untie the rope but you know from experience you won't be able to undo that knot until the weight on the rope has been completely unloaded. Security run around, some try to undo the knot while others attempt to steer the screaming crowd towards the exits. The two presenters don't know what to do, neither do the cameraman. They all simply look on in disbelief.

It doesn't take long for the girls' choking to stop and for all three of their necks to fall limp, their arms hanging flaccidly by their sides.

"Hang up and run,
Whoah, hang up and run,
Whoah oh oh oh"

You look at the three girls hanging from their gallows. One of the girl's legs involuntarily spasms. You smile. They won't be running to anyone now. As the song fades out, a gold bracelet falls off Mandy's wrist and clunks down on the stage floor.

Security and staff try to get under the girls to lift them up and to take the weight of their nooses, but they're all too late. These cowgirls have been hung out to dry.

Your work is done here.

You keep out of the way and slope out of the fire exit that a young security guard is showing people towards. The kiddie crowds file out. Some of them are crying.

You leave the Music:UK studio and walk around the corner to your Astra parked in the disabled spot where you'd left it – your car is complete with fake disabled parking badge and fake number plates. You wave at the old, overweight security guard on the gate – who's oblivious to the commotion around the corner – as he lifts the barrier for you on your way out. As you drive past he winks at you and smiles. You think about stopping the car and wiping the smile off his fat puffy face, but instead you encourage the randy old sod by winking back.

As you slip the car into second gear, and blend anonymously into the heavy Saturday morning London traffic, you're greeted by the pleasant realisation that you're halfway through your pop project.

It's a game of two halves.

Five down. Five to go.

No. 5

I'm just a soul whose intentions are good
Don't Let Me Be Misunderstood, The Animals

"Well, that was rubbish," I say into Sophie's ear as the youthful crowd scream and cheer all around the TV studio.

"Ladies and gentlemen, boys and girls, give it up for Star Bright!" shouts the young, boyish C4 presenter in the yellow and green shirt now standing on the studio stage. Sophie and I reluctantly join in and clap along with the crowd as the young girl trio of Star Bright skip off the stage.

Star Bright have performed two of their hits for the crowd as well as their latest single, *We've Got The Soda*. Their performance will be shown on Pop It! on C4 later on today. If their single was a vegetable, it would be celery; snappy, bland and ultimately pointless. But the young kids cheered on happily enough when prompted by the TV floor manager.

At one point a kid dancing by us excitedly shouted, "This is the *good* shit!"

I had to the correct the little urchin.

"No. This is just good, old-fashioned *shit*." I said with a little more venom that strictly necessary.

Star Bright leave the stage without a death in sight and I'm disappointed. In fact, really disappointed. I now know why nightclub doormen are so twitchy and eager to kick off. I've been ready and waiting impatiently in the wings for the Hitman to do his thing. But he hasn't shown, and even though it's anti-climactic, my adrenalin is still pumping. I need a release.

Sophie follows Star Bright back to their little dressing room safely behind their bodyguards. Nothing happens. I jump about and watch their bodyguards escort them to their chauffeur driven car outside as studio security holds the doors open for them. I see them drive off and safely leave the TV studios, but it's all very boring: their car doesn't explode into a fireball or anything.

Where are you Hitman?

When we get outside after the uneventful C4 TV show, there are lots of camera crews and TV vans rushing out. I switch my mobile on and it starts ringing immediately. It's Gary from the office. "Where the hell have you been Hardy!? I've been trying to call you for the last hour!" he shouts.

I take a deep breath. I won't give Gary the satisfaction of winding me up, even though I'm about to burst because of the pent up adrenalin. "Inside the Pop It! TV studio. Everyone has to turn their mobiles off before they're allowed on set. You know how it works. Why, what's up?"

"What's up!? The Hitman's struck again, that's *what's up*. Barely an hour or so ago. Kitty Bomb have just been murdered on stage in front of a live Music:UK studio audience."

"Big fat cocks," I say flatly.

"What was that?"

"Opportunity knocks," I say quickly.

"Eh?"

"Never mind. I can't believe Kitty Bomb are dead," I say, sounding suitably upset. And I am upset. I can't believe the Hitman's been at work in a different TV studio. There's no point explaining to Gary that I'm only sad because I was hoping Star Bright were next on the Hit List. I'm not about to tell him about our little detective agency and exclusive hunt either.

"Yes, deader than dead. My production contact at Music:UK called me straight after it happened. It's unbelievable, they were hung live on stage by phone wires while they were singing their cover of Blondie's..."

"*Hanging On The Telephone*. I know, I've heard their version. I can see why someone might want to stop them ever singing again," I say.

"Hardy! Our readers wanted to be Kitty Bombers."

So what. I'm pissed off. The Hitman's hung them and not Star Bright. Although I've got to hand it to him with the prime-time public hanging. A nice touch.

"How'd he manage to string them up..." I ponder out loud.

"Apparently the girls were dancing around phone lines on stage, the lights went out, and when they came back on all three girls were strung up."

"Wow," I say. "All in front of a studio audience and cameras. Surely *someone* saw *something*?"

"You'd think so. But, no. With the lights out it was pitch black, and it was all over so quickly. Nobody saw anything."

"Seems like we've been in the wrong studio then," I say cheerily.

"You could bloody say that," he says, exhaling loudly. I don't think he's upset about Kitty Bomb being murdered either. He's more annoyed I missed all the action.

"What are you so worried about? The mag's already selling like it's cover-mounted with free money. We'll be outselling the daily papers soon."

"Funnily enough, that's the new sales target set by John."

"That's greedy."

"What?"

"That's great," I say unenthusiastically.

"Well, at least you're up in London's TV land. Get round to the Music:UK studio and see what you can dig up. Our press deadline is Monday so get something together, write it up for an exclusive for The Insider section, and email me with it tomorrow morning."

"Okay, Boss Hogg," I say.

I picture him in a little white sheriff's outfit complete with cowboy hat. Gary hangs up without saying goodbye.

I guess we didn't have everything covered after all. I guess we weren't all set. Feeling deflated, I tell Sophie the bad news as we walk off site.

"I knew Kitty Bomb would get it next. See? That's what I wrote on my Hit List. You should've listened to me," she says slightly joking, slightly angry – which makes her look slightly sexy.

"But!? But... You didn't even protest. You just agreed with me to go and see what happened at the Star Bright show."

"You said Kitty Bomb weren't playing in the UK, you said..."

"I know what I said. And I was wrong," I say.

We get outside C4 and I flag down a cab to take us to the Music:UK studios. We jump in the back and continue arguing.

"You were very wrong," says Sophie.

"Yes," I say.

We share an uncomfortable silence, staring out of opposite windows. After a while Sophie says, "We need to be in the right place at the right time."

"We got the right time. And nearly the right place." I offer.

"Nearly ain't good enough, mate," she says looking me straight in the eye. "It's a bad start for the H&S Detective Agency," I say.

It's only a short drive to Music:UK. I pay the cabbie and we get out and walk through a steady flow of teenage girls and a few boys coming out of the entrance looking shell-shocked.

"Oh well. At least we were in the right town," I say.

"London's quite a big *town*, though, isn't it?" she says.

"Quite, yes. At least we got the TV studio thing right."

"But not right enough."

"No," I say.

"No," she says.

"We're always one step behind," I say.

"Yes," she snaps.

It's bedlam inside the Music:UK reception. A large group of teenage girls are sobbing in the corner, Music:UK cameramen are trying to get out, but the police won't let them leave. Meanwhile, security guards are trying to fend off BBC news cameramen trying to get in. News travels extra fast in media land. A group of women who look like mums are shouting and demanding to know why the police haven't got the Hitman yet. Several paparazzi photographers try to slip through into the studios unnoticed but get spotted and a pathetic attempt at a brawl ensues. At one point I think a photographer strikes a security guard with his handbag.

"This is nuts," I say.

I try and talk to the receptionist explaining I'm a very important journalist. "Might be best of you come back later… or tomorrow," she says, in case I hadn't noticed the face off beside me. "We're not letting any press through."

At that moment a police riot van pulls up outside and Sophie and I take that as our cue to leave. "Pint then?" I suggest.

"No," she says, still a bit mad at me.

We walk out of a side exit door as policemen file through the main entrance.

"No?" I say.

"No," she says, a little less mad.

"Please?"

"Oh, okay then."

A little drink always makes things seem better. After Sophie has bought the second round our moods start to lift. No point dwelling on the past. Time to move on. Spies like us don't give up after one minor error. Admittedly, three girls being hung live on stage in a TV studio might not be seen as minor to some, but it's a setback that the H&S Detective Agency will endeavour to sweep under the carpet.

Spring is in the air, the sun's out, and we've managed to find a London pub garden that's warm enough to sit outside. With coats on, of course, this is Britain we're talking about.

"Who have we got next on our Hit List? Who did we have at No.5?" I say.

"We both put down the same singer. Look." Sophie unfolds her list from her pocket. I get mine out and unfold it from my wallet.

"Ah, yes. That arse wipe."

"It's a no-brainer. Our Hit Lists have settled it for us. We will go and pay him a visit," says Sophie.

I check the web on my phone. "He's touring oop North at the moment. Got gigs in Manchester, Sheffield and Blackpool next month…"

"All up North? Isn't it grim up there?"

"Not anymore. It's *great* up North. I've made many good friends up there. They all had indoor toilets and none of them ever flew any whippets or walked any pigeons."

"A flying dog would be amazing," says Sophie dreamily.

I scroll through the web text pages on my phone. "Then the middle of the following month he's playing down in Liverpool, and then Birmingham."

"Where shall we go then?"

"Blackpool, next month. It's the English equivalent of Las Vegas. All those lights, all that tat, all those half-dressed drunk people."

"And that's just the grandparents," says Sophie.

"Plus there's Blackpool Tower to go up," I say.

"To Blackpool," says Sophie raising her glass.

"To Blackpool," I say.

*   *

You've been feeling a bit down. You didn't know what to do with yourself after the Kitty Bomb mission. Even a month later everything has felt like a chore, and even though summer's arrived and the weather's warmed up, you've found yourself staying in, pumping some weights, pottering about your flat. You're not sure why. Everything had been going so well.

You've been enjoying the whole process of your little pop project: from picking the next victim off your Top 10 Hit List to planning the method of murder to show time. Being around the music industry again, seeing stages, crowds and lights, though, has been dragging up old memories. More than once you've found yourself thinking way back to when you had dreams of becoming a rock star.

From when you used to bang your toy drum kit and play with your red plastic, battery-operated guitar, to your early teenage years in school music lessons, you just really, really wanted to be a rock star. It wasn't a fad with you. Other friends tried to match your love of rock music, but they just didn't share your drive and ambition. That was alright, you didn't hold it against them, you knew nobody else would understand what it meant to you.

Least of all your parents.

Mum's false encouragement was far too infrequent, while Dad was too busy getting pissed up the pub and would only ever offer words of abuse on his return. The usual, "Turn that racket off before I crack your skull open with that bloody guitar," and the heart felt, "We never should've given you pocket money to buy that guitar."

But that only made you more determined to prove them wrong.

But your hobby turned into an obsession after one particularly bloody row with your drunken Dad late one evening. He tried to break the neck of your guitar. You stopped him by trying to break his neck. You did okay for a boy of fourteen and your well-timed flying kick saved your first acoustic guitar. But your Dad did one better by insisting on splitting your lip, dislocating your jaw and covering your body in pretty little bruises. You didn't want to punch him back in case you damaged your guitar playing fingers. Instead you tucked your hands tightly under your armpits, curled up and simply closed your eyes.

Which is why, years later, when The Good, The Bad, and The Ugly were playing regular gigs and filling up pubs, it felt all the more satisfying.

People wolf-whistled, girls stared at you and danced to your songs and a few would shout out their favourite song – "*Hot Dog*! Play *Hot Dog*!" It was always *Hot Dog* – and most clapped and cheered. People would buy you pints long into the night.

You always remember the night you played your local rockers' pub in Liverpool and a few old school mates showed up. People were queuing out the door to try and cram into the sweaty little room. The landlord said he'd never seen the bar so busy as everyone struggled for elbow room to sip on their pints, while you set up nervously on the tiny little stage. But from the first chord to the last chorus you felt ten feet tall. You felt at one with your guitar and you didn't have to think about playing the notes. They just flowed from within. You rocked that night.

But that was your best gig, and the high point of your rock career. You tried to release another single, *Ten Gallon Hat*, but it seemed the pop and rock charts weren't ready for The Good, The Bad, and The Ugly. It didn't even make it into the top 100. Your rock star dreams started slipping away. It would be smoky, little, local pub gigs for the rest of your guitar-playing years. Your drummer, Jim, and bass player, Steveo, were happy with that. But you weren't. You wanted more. You'd always imagined touring the world and playing on big stages to big crowds in the UK, in Europe, and down in Australia. You even dreamed that one day you'd conquer America.

But it was never to be.

You soon got bored and disillusioned with the pub circuit and started making excuses to avoid band practice and gigging. The guitar case started gathering dust in the corner of your bedroom. You never felt like playing. What was the point?

You felt lost.

So you figured you'd try to find yourself. You avoided the usual Asia and India travelling route. Too many hippies and students. So instead you joined the army.

You found yourself then alright. You discovered a whole new Mac. You knuckled down at training camp. You enjoyed having a focus. You even liked your hard-assed superiors and soon found yourself climbing the ranks to sergeant. You loved the macho 'we're real men' lifestyle. But what you loved most of all was the combat. The Gulf War was a harrowing, disastrous, life-changing experience for most soldiers. But for you it was life changing for a different reason. It gave you the excuse you needed to unleash your killer instinct.

Your gun replaced your guitar. It became a new obsession. You volunteered for any missions in the Gulf if you knew you'd get to see some action. At first you used to add up your kills but you soon lost count of how many bullets hit the target. You got a rep and some nicknamed you Rambo. You pretended you didn't like the label, but behind closed doors you would smile to yourself and pose with your gun in front of the mirror. You became a killing machine. And it just felt so right.

You'd never been happier.

Those days seem such a long time ago as you sit drinking a big mug of black coffee in your flat in the middle of a Thursday. The curtains are half-drawn. Once in a while the warm sun comes out to send a shaft light into the living room. You have a bite of your cheese and tomato sandwich.

You didn't think your Top 10 Hit List was going to be easy. You didn't think it could be so much fun either. But now you need a boost to get kick started into the second half, your Top 5 Hits await.

You have an idea.

You call your phone network's helpline. You don't have a problem with your phone, you just think customer services will have the desired effect.

Naturally it's an automated helpline with recorded messages explaining what number to select to sort out your problem. You try and speak to someone about overpaying your bill. You haven't. You just know it's bound to take ages to get through to speak to them about paying you back. You get passed around various departments, being put on hold each time, with painfully naff hold music. Then they cut you off. Again you go through the automated service, pressing number two for this, number five for that.

After fifteen minutes you feel yourself getting agitated.

After twenty minutes you start clenching the phone until the plastic creaks in your grasp. After thirty minutes you're ready to throw the phone through the window. You're transferred then put on hold again for another five minutes. It's working. You soon feel the warm, familiar anger bubbling up inside.

Honestly, it's enough to make you want to strangle someone.

Perfect.

You smash the receiver down and start making plans for Hit No.5.

*   *

It feels funny – funny weird, not funny ha ha – being back in the office after being on the road and playing Hunt the Hitman with Sophie. Gary wanted me back in to work on some features and for a Monday morning planning meeting. I avoid these meetings wherever possible as there's far too much wanking over each other's ideas or discussing the magazine design layout in mindlessly minute detail.

"Should we make the *TOP 10 HITS* logo slightly curlier with a serif font? I think it could help make the magazine feel a bit younger," says a senior designer in sharp spectacles.

"But how much younger do we want it to be?" says a senior editor in a sharp shirt.

I think it would be dangerous if it were any younger. There's only so much immaturity one man can take. I keep my mouth shut.

"I think we need to be aiming about two years younger than where we're at right now," says Gary. "We need a font that looks good for fourteen *and* eighteen year olds. How about slightly curlier, but not really curly wurly."

"Something more expressive and passionate. We want the words to shout out to readers. Something bold," says a man whose name I can never remember.

"Not a tall, thin grown-up font, something fatter and more kid-friendly. Where the numbers one and zero work with the words," says the senior designer.

"It needs to be on-message."

"And on-trend."

I exchange bemused glances with my team-mates Robin and Jane.

"Not too psychedelic. Like a daisy age font, but without the flowers. Everyone clear, yeah?" says Gary. "Now, what colours should we be using on the cover logo? White can look too serious, bright lime green is much more accessible..."

"...and what about exclams?" says the senior designer.

Media abbreviations. I loathe them.

"...I like them, but they can read like we're shouting rather than sounding excited."

"Use them. But don't over use them..."

This goes on for three hours. The only slightly redeeming part is that I get a pat on the back for bringing back some top stories and insider info from the front line.

In the afternoon I make myself busy by writing some words, surfing the web, checking out images, drinking tea and nicking other people's chocolate biscuits. Around 6pm I check my emails one last time before shutting down and heading to the pub. I filter through a few jokes to find an email from 'Hitman'.

I thought I might get used to these emails, but every time I see his name in bold on a new email, my heart starts thumping and I have to remind myself to breath out.

I click on it and see what the Hitman's got to say this time.

Subject: Top 10 Hit List
From: Hitman <top10hitlist@gmail.com>
To: Hardy Matthews <hardy@top10hits.co.uk>

How are you and Sophie? Hope this email finds you in good spirits.

Just a quick update on my little pop project. After those gangsta wannabes came in with a bullet (or two) at No.7, I decided not to hang around and got those dumb blondes dialled in at No.6. Which brings me to the halfway point with five to go.

Of course I won't tell you who's next at No.5 or No.4, as I'm sure you're both having lots of fun trying to keep up. But I will tell you that a hit will drop out of the charts this weekend.

143

Feel free to spread the good news. But be careful how much you share with your friendly neighbourhood DCI Johnson. We don't want to give the game away just yet do we?

The Man With No Name

I automatically click on reply and start typing as if replying to a friend, but I stop myself when I realise there's no point. He won't reply. He's a crap email mate. Instead I forward the email to Sophie, telling her I'll call her about it tonight.

I head to the pub with a couple of workmates. On the way I wonder how the Hitman knows about DCI Johnson contacting me.

And what's the The Man With No Name all about? He's not signed off with that before.

I only stay for a couple of pints before heading home for a night of quality time with me and my thoughts of serial killers. I phone the local curry house as I leave the pub. By the time I've walked through town and up Lansdown Road, my takeaway's ready to collect. I scoff the lot at home and mop up the remaining Balti sauce with my garlic nan bread. Afterwards, I crack open a beer and give Sophie, my detective partner, a call.

"Hello, H&S Detective Agency?" she says obviously having seen my number appear on her mobile.

"Is that Makepeace?" I say.

"Yes."

"It's Dempsey here."

"Hi."

"Did you get my email?"

"I did."

"What do you think?"

"I think it's from the Hitman."

"Cor, there are no flies on you."

"It's just a quick update really isn't it?" says Sophie. "He confirms he set up gangstas MC Rock & DJ Spin to shoot each other for his No.7 and that he strung up Kitty Bomb at No.6."

"He does tell us Hit No.5 is planned for this weekend," I say.

"He does. So how does he know about DCI Johnson?"

"Because Johnson's on telly as the head of the investigation and the Hitman's figured he must've been in contact with us as we were in Cardiff and at The Royal etc."

"You don't think he's bugged your mobile or linked to your email somehow?"

"Unlikely. If he'd got that close he would've done more than bug me."

"You're right. But it's a horrible thought to think he might've been in your flat while you're asleep, watching you as he inserts a bug into your mobile," says Sophie in a creepy voice.

"Alright, alright. What are you trying to do – scare the shit out of me?"

"Sorry, got carried away there."

"So what about his new sign off?"

"So what?"

"So what about it?"

"So what about what?"

"His new sign off: he's ended with *'The Man With No Name'*. He's never put that before," I say.

"I did notice that."

"And?"

"Didn't really think much about it to be honest."

"C'mon Makepeace," I say raising my voice. "This could be a vital clue that could lead us to him."

"Maybe," she says, "or the Hitman's getting sloppy."

"No way. He doesn't do sloppy," I say. "I think it's a clue worth checking out."

"If you say so, Dempsey."

"Hang on, I'll ask the internet about The Man With No Name and see what music related stuff it brings up." I put down my beer and with my free hand I fire up my laptop's browser and type it in.

"Any luck?" says Sophie after a while.

"There's lots of links to Clint Eastwood Westerns…" I say as I read, "but the only music-related stuff it's bringing is a site or two about a trance album from 2003 called The Man With No Name."

"Has he brought anything else out recently? Is he a man with a violent past or a huge chip on his shoulder about the pop scene?"

I don't think the website will tell us that, but I read on anyway, trying to find anything to say if this particular Man With No Name has a penchant for trance by day and murdering by night.

"Doesn't seem to have done much since 2003," I say after reading most of the websites.

"We're not really getting anywhere here are we?" she says, and yawns dramatically like Bagpuss.

"No," I say

"No," she says.

I close my laptop.

"I'm tired. Let's sleep on it," she suggests.

"Okay," I say.

"I'm doing a shoot late tomorrow, I'll come over on Wednesday night and we can discuss our next move, Dempsey. I'm going to run a bath now and have a nice long soak."

I picture Sophie naked and lathering up in a hot tub. "Can I join you in the bath?"

She lets out a little dirty laugh as she hangs up.

"That'll be a no then," I say even though Sophie's gone. I feel horny but humbled.

I get into bed and wish Sophie was beside me with her clean, naked body. I could take pleasure in getting her all dirty again. She could distract me from thinking there's a Hitman in the corner of my bedroom waiting for me to fall asleep before injecting me with poison.

After two days of semi-working in the office and dodging deadlines, I'm still trying to link the Hitman and The Man With No Name. They say two brains are better than one – *they* say a lot of things – however, I'm hoping Sophie and I can bash something out between our two brains this evening. I could call it brain-bashing.

It's Wednesday evening and we're in my lounge drinking a glass of red wine. We have one each. I'm not tight. I'm hoping the wine might lubricate our thought processes. In fact, it just lubricates the dirty side of our minds and instead of talking about the Hitman With No Name, we strip each other and have a very steamy shag on the sofa. Afterwards, I spoon her warm, post-coital body.

"It suits you being naked," I say reaching around and stroking her bare abdomen.

"What does that mean?"

"I'm not sure. But I've said it," I say. "I mean it in a good way."

"Okay."

Sophie reaches around and kisses me.

"Thank you," she says.

I climb over her and off the sofa and put my jeans back on. I leave my pants on the lounge floor – it's nice to go commando sometimes – and pull my T-shirt on.

"Right, back to tonight's topic," I say. "After doing some more online snooping, I've bloody well come to the conclusion that the Hitman's a Clint Eastwood fan. The Man With No Name is Clint's character in Sergio Leone's Spaghetti Western trilogy: *A Fistful Of Dollars, For A Few Dollars More...*"

"...and *The Good, The Bad, and The Ugly*," says Sophie.

"Exactly."

Sophie stands up, confident in all her naked glory, then puts on a blue hoodie and grey tracksuit bottoms of mine lying around.

"But it's got to be music related. Something to do with a song or band. He's a Hitman but he must be something do with the music industry," I say.

"Wonder if it's something to do with the Gorillaz song, *Clint Eastwood*?" says Sophie.

"A song that has nothing to do with Clint or cowboys? They also called one *Dirty Harry* that wasn't anything to do with Clint's loose cannon cop who carried a Magnum 45."

"What then?" she says. "Wasn't there that Clint film about an obsessive fan stalking a music DJ?"

"Yeah, *Play Misty For Me*. But that wasn't Clint's Man With No Name character."

I pull my laptop out and do some online investigating. I've already tried checking this but with Sophie by my side reading through the web links as I scroll through, she might see something I've missed.

I put in 'Clint Eastwood music'. It brings up lots of film links and an official Clint site, and scrolling through the pages, eventually a link about his jazz songs and details about Clint singing on a few of his films, but little else.

"I'll try putting in The Man With No Name again," I say.

It still just brings up links to Clint's Spaghetti Westerns. I'm not sure what I'm expecting – the Hitman's website with a helpful 'Contact Me' page with his address and telephone number?

"What about searching under the cowboy film titles to see what comes up music wise?" suggests Sophie.

"Okay," I say. I try 'Fistful Of Dollars' and it just shows web pages with all sorts of sites about the films, where to buy the DVDs, online reviews, but nothing helpful.

"Do you think money is his motivation?"

"Fistfuls of money from other band managers for killing the competition? Could be, but I doubt it," I say.

I search for sites and clues under 'Few Dollars More'.

"Arse. Nothing there either," I say. Just the same sites about buying the films. "I'll try 'The Good, The Bad, and The Ugly' for what it's worth."

There are the usual links to film-related sites, DVDs and soundtrack CDs and fan sites, but as I scroll down Sophie points to the bottom of the screen. "What's that about an old British band?" she says.

Crikey.

"Pea-ow!" I say in my best impression of a bullet ricocheting off a rock in the Sierra Nevada plains.

"What is it, gun slinger?" says Sophie.

"Some old links about an British band called The Good, The Bad, and The Ugly," I say reading the home page of Disbanded.com.

"That could be something. Are they still playing?"

"Don't think so. It says here, *'British pub rock grunge act. After mild success with a single called Hot Dog and an unnamed EP they dissolved into the musical graveyard along with all the other nearly-made-its and not-quite-good-enoughs'*. That was over sixteen years ago."

"Sounds interesting," says Sophie.

I scroll down to another link and manage to find an old fanzine site with the names of The Good, The Bad, and The Ugly band members: Steveo, Jim, and McNamara. Must be the leader singer with a name like that. I try doing searches on them, but get nothing. We need surnames or Christian names or something.

"Do searches on band members' names," says Sophie.

I put them into the search engine each in turn but only get stuff about someone from *Jackass*, stuff about Jim Morrison, and a rugby league manager from up North, Steve McNamara.

"Nothing that's shouting 'pop killer' really is there?" says Sophie.

"Maybe not," I say staring at the screen, "but it's something."

"And all we've got," says Sophie.

"We need to find out what The Good, The Bad, and The Ugly are up to today. You never know, one of these old ex-rockers could have turned sadistic."

"Sadistic enough to kill several pop artists?" says Sophie.

"Sadistic enough to keep killing," I say.

I close the laptop and sip my wine.

"I think I might call Fat Pat. See what he can dig up on them. See if this old band are still in the UK. If they have any violent records," I say.

"What, as in some angry fighting songs?" says Sophie.

"Yes. Wise ass. That is what I meant," I say.

I call the man who can. Fat Pat's not surprised to hear that I'm after something. I think he likes our give-and-take relationship. I give him requests and then I take his answers. I fill him in with details about the Hitman's latest email, The Man With No Name, and The Good, The Bad, and The Ugly's band members. I give him their names.

"As it's you, Hardy, I'll see what I can do," says Fat Pat.

It's around midnight on Friday when Fat Pat rings me on my mobile. I'm home alone and halfway through enjoying *Once Upon A Time In The West.*

"Good evening," I say.

"I've had a very productive two days of investigating and you'll be pleased to know my sources have come up trumps," says Fat Pat.

I know better than to ask who his sources are these days.

"The bass player, Steveo, and drummer, Jim, both hold down middle class jobs in middle class medicine and architecture. Steveo is married and has 2.4 children. Jim is married with one baby girl."

"Good cover if they were killers, possibly."

"Possibly, but unlikely."

"None of them got any criminal records?"

"Like any Cliff Richard, Bros or Craig David records?"

He's nearly as funny as Sophie. "Yes, very good. You know what I meant, Tarbuck."

"No, apart from a drink driving charge for Jim back in the mid-nineties, they're both good boys."

"However, it gets interesting with the man who's simply known as McNamara. He was the lead singer/lead guitarist, he left the band and joined the armed forces and was promoted to train at Hereford…"

"The SAS base?"

"Right."

"Which means he's *nails*."

"Hard as, yep. He then did some service out in the Gulf in '91. He was a very professional solider from what my mate heard on the army grapevine, very respected by his peers and a real force when it came to combat."

"Shit the bed."

"Somebody said McNamara would be the one volunteering for kamikaze missions, just so he could use his gun."

"Sounds like a regular psycho."

"And he's now, by all accounts, a security guard."

"Sounds like he's laying low."

"Sometimes he's a bodyguard."

"Laying low in the public eye."

"Sometimes he's a bodyguard to musicians."

"Ah."

"Ah in-facking-deed."

"He'd certainly have the skills to kill and the contacts to find bands and singers," I say thinking out loud.

"I think we have our Prime Suspect No.1 right there, Hardy my boy."

"Does that mean we need to call Helen Mirren?"

"Hope not. She was fit a few years ago, but now I wouldn't touch her with yours."

"I'd touch her with yours though," I say. "She's still well sexy."

Neither of us say anything for a while. I feel a little embarrassed.

"Seriously, Pat, do you think McNamara could be the Hitman?"

"Not that I'm familiar with serial killers, but it looks like a big possibility. And it's all you've got to go on for now."

"So if Steveo the doctor is The Good, and Jim the architect is The Ugly, that means McNamara is... The Bad."

Fat Pat whistles the eerie Ennio Morricone theme tune then says. "I think we can safely say that McNamara is one bad motherfucker."

I get a tingle down my spine and across my shoulders.

"His last known address was Manchester about two years ago. But he's been linked to just outside Liverpool too," says Pat. "I couldn't get an exact address."

"I don't think I'd pay him a visit at home just yet anyway," I say. "I wonder what he looks like now. All I've got to go on is an old website image of him playing in the band. He looks studenty, skinny, and has greasy, shoulder-length hair."

Fat Pat says, "I didn't look into recent photographs..."

"...Not that a recent photo will help, even if McNamara really is the killer, as the Hitman's always deep in disguise when he strikes. That's why they can't ever catch the bastard."

We both stay silent for a few seconds.

"You know I could use all this information to score a big scoop myself don't you?" says Fat Pat

"Of course I do. But you won't, will you?" I say, hopefully. I cross my fingers.

"As it's you I won't step on your toes. You saved my life and my job that fateful night in Brixton, mate, and I will always remember that. You can have this exclusive," says Fat Pat.

"Thanks for the info Pat. You're a star player," I say.

"Use it wisely, Hardy," he says in a wise old man's voice.

"I'll try," I say. "I owe you another pint now."

"That's about twelve pints you owe me, Hardy," he says.

"It'll be quite a good session next time I'm up in London then."

"I won't hold my breath, country boy."

He hangs up before I can say goodbye. People keep doing that to me. It's so rude.

I think about calling DCI Johnson despite the Hitman's threats. McNamara fits the bill to kill. It all adds up. This could be my chance to shop the serial killer. Or a very strong potential suspect at the very least. I could possibly stop all the murder in the music industry, and all the madness in the media and across the nation.

But I'm not going to call Johnson.

I'm not going to tell Gary.

I'm not going to tell anyone.

But I am going to tell Sophie as I want us to get the exclusive of the century. And this is one cowboy the H&S Detective Agency can bring to justice. We can sell our front page news to every paper across the land for a big fat fortune.

*   *

You remember the first time you saw Danny Stone on TV. He was in his mid-teens when he started on *Argyle Street* as the junior mechanic working in his Dad's garage. He soon became part of the furniture in Britain's most popular TV soap. He was harmless enough when he started, but five years later you could tell he was an arrogant little shit. Actors can only act so much. After a while they just become themselves on screen as they mature into and, eventually become, their character. Especially soap stars who live in character week in, week out. Danny Stone's Scott soon became the character you loved to hate on *Argyle Street*.

Then at the height of his popularity, when you couldn't open a newspaper without seeing photos of him on another boozy night, Danny Stone decided to jump ship and start a career in pop.

It didn't seem to bother him that he couldn't sing or play a guitar. Although it bothered you very much. You can't believe the mentality of actors who think, 'If I can act, I can sing – it's all show business.' They get greedy and want it all, the acting career and the pop star lifestyle, regardless of how disinterested we are in hearing them sing. The problem for Danny Stone stemmed from all manner of 'yes men' from his agent and adoring soap fans to middle-aged mums and his family telling him "Yes, you've got a lovely voice" and "Yes you can become the next big pop star."

You'd love to be a 'no man'. Be the one to tell them 'No, of course you can't sing. What were you thinking? Have you heard yourself? You're terrible! Don't give up the day job. Now piss off.'

You remember the last time you saw Danny Stone on TV as well. He was performing his new-at-the-time single, *Drink Drank Drunk*, on one of those cheap breakfast shows where they're interviewed before they sing. The single was languishing around No.21 in the charts. Danny took great delight in explaining what the song was about – drinking, perhaps? – and padding out his bad boy persona. He believed his lyrics were "real life social commentary, and stuff". You think the female presenter may have blushed as he blabbed on, sitting back and showing off too much chest with his shirt undone, tactically revealing one of his many obligatory tattoos. He then bounced up on the fake TV stage and struggled through one of the most mediocre, music-by-numbers rock-lite you've ever heard. The desperation in his eyes as he sang into the camera made you want to vomit. He looked at you longing to be loved, trying to be cool, so desperate for attention.

The final straw was Danny Stone's latest excuse for a single, *Pump Me With Your Love*, which you heard recently on your car radio. It has everything you hate in a song: dumb dance beat, tiresome bass line, irritating Gerry Rafferty sampled horn loop, nasal vocals and so-cheesy-they-stink lyrics.

Man, I'm on the brink
I could really do a drink
Pump me, pump me
Pump me with your love

I'll hit all the bars
Hang out with the stars
But I'll be looking for love
In all the nightclubs

Pump me, pump me
Pump me with your love
I'll wear you like a glove
We'll fly like white doves

Bring your pretty face
Back to my place
You can rub my back
And then we'll hit the sack

Pump me with your love
Pump me with your love

Enough was enough. This sappy actor turned pop idiot was just asking for it. You promptly put him at No.5 on your Hit List. Probably the highest chart placing he was ever going to experience.

Man, I'm on the brink
I could really do a drink

So, Danny Stone likes a drink does he? You're sure you can arrange that.

*   *

After much deliberation, and in light of the new information that our Hitman With No Name may be called McNamara, and may be somewhere up north, Sophie and I agree to stick to our original plan and find out if his Hit No.5 is the same as the one on our list.

I decide to drive us up to Blackpool. I figure we can make a bit of a road trip out of it rather than sitting on a train staring out of the window, getting a bit drunk on cans of beer, eating crisps, and playing cards… actually, that sounds ideal. Why did I want to drive again? Oh yeah, the road trip, and so I can pleasure Sophie's ears with my music collection.

It's a bit of a way up country to Blackpool from Bath via Bristol, but we set off after Friday evening's rush hour to avoid the traffic. I stretch the legs of the Golf and cruise around 100mph all the way up. I figure we're basically above the law now we've set up the H&S Detective Agency. Of course we haven't bothered with any of the paperwork or legalities (or got any fancy silver badges), but we don't need to bother with that sort of admin. We haven't got time for that anyway: we've got a Hitman to catch.

I've got my iPod rigged up to the car stereo and have primed Sophie so she knows this is all about *my* music for *her* benefit. With the music set to shuffle, our conversations go like this as we eat up mile after mile of the north-bound M5.

"Who's this?" asks Sophie.

"Black Rebel Motorcycle Club," I say.

"What's this?"

"*Wish You Were Here*! Have you never heard any Pink Floyd?"

"Who's this?"

"Aim's *Cold Water Music*. Haven't heard this for ages."

"This sounds ace," says Sophie.

"It's Mars Volta. A great mixture of raw rock and beautiful blues."

"Didn't know you liked hip hop, Hardy."

"Only old school stuff like this from Cypress Hill."

"This is mellow. I like this."

"Turin Brakes' first CD. They went from mellow to melancholy after this."

"This is lovely… proper dirty, sexy blues," says Sophie.

"The Black Keys. One of the finest guitarists of our generation."

"Ah, I love Jimi Hendrix," says Sophie.

"One of the finest guitarists of *any* generation," I say.

I crank up the stereo as Hendrix plays his hits for us up the M6. I can't decide which solo is the best, the short yet smooth-as-silk guitar on *The Wind Cries Mary* or the bluesy, unmistakable riffs through the solo on *Hey Joe*. Both are sonically satisfying so I don't worry about it as Sophie and I sing along like fools, making up lyrics when we're not sure what Jimi's singing. Like on *Purple Haze*…

"*Excuse me while I kiss this guy.*"

"Excuse me while I piss in your pie."

We make it up to Blackpool in under three hours, and I pull up outside a medium-sized hotel on the sea front. I feel I have successfully introduced Sophie to some new music.

"I'll pick the music on the way back, eh?" Sophie says.

We check into the hotel then check out Blackpool. The night is marching on but it still feels like day: I've never seen so many lights illuminating one street. They're flashing, blinking and dazzling the entire street. The electricity bill must be extortionate. We walk past bars with their charty dance music blaring, and the stalls and shops selling touristy tat. We weave in and out of the crowds of hen parties and stag dos. Around ten girls stumble past clutching bottles of alcopops with straws in. Some are cackling, looking cross-eyed drunk, and some are slurring through *Is This The Way To Amarillo*.

The days are getting warmer and longer as summer does its best. The evening air feels pleasant but there's a fair wind and it's still not exactly tropical. Yet that doesn't stop the gangs of fake-tanned girls wearing Union Jack bikini tops and white 'belt sized' mini-skirts. More than once the wind blows their skirts up to reveal G-strings. Unfazed and laughing, the girls bend over in unison and flash their various sized arses while boys drinking lager out of cans cheer and old ladies look the other way. I can't help but stare. Although I think I've managed to keep my mouth closed.

"Getting a good view of the night life there, Hardy?" says Sophie.

"Eh?" I cough. "Yeah, it's quite colourful round here."

Sophie shakes her head. I turn my attention back to her and slip my arm around her shoulder. She rests her head against my chest and we walk – well, shuffle – along the promenade towards Blackpool Tower.

As a group of girls in pink cowboy hats walk past, I start thinking again about Clint, and The Bad, and McNamara. I wonder if he ever wears pink. Unlikely.

We walk up to the foot of Blackpool Tower and lean back to take it all in. It's a vast structure that soars up into the sky, an impressive industrial feat, covered in lines and lines of bright lights. Nearby a spotty lad with a crew cut and ill-fitting shirt chucks up his night's overindulgence. He's got the Puker's Pose perfected, with one hand high up against a wall, while his body's bent over double, legs wide apart to avoid any splash back. He's not holding back, either, giving it as many grunts and groans as he can.

It's nearly as impressive as Blackpool Tower, if I'm honest.

We walk up to the front entrance, past the queues of people waiting to get in, and I speak to the head bouncer, explaining who we are, flashing my press ID. I explain that we need to speak with the head of security, and use the same spiel I used at the C4 studios to flatter his muscular ego. The head bouncer waves us in, acting like he knows us. He walks us through reception, up some stairs and down a few corridors, and introduces us to Jon Peters, a tall, brick-shithouse of man in his thirties. He has the crooked nose and mangled ears of someone who played second row in their day, and probably enjoyed the punch-ups more than the rugby.

"Welcome to Blackpool Tower," says Peters. "Allow me to give you the tour."

The pop singer we've come to see isn't performing until Saturday night, but we figured it would good to check out the venue when it's busy to scope out potential weak spots and places a Hitman might hang out. We don't tell Peters our theory on our prime suspect, there's no point causing any extra security problems. The H&S Detective Agency can deal with him.

"Tomorrow night's sold out. He's a big star compared to the usual performers we have playing here," says Peters. He's a big something, that's for sure.

Peters shows us around the dressing rooms and backstage, pointing out where extra security will be tomorrow. Out front in the auditorium, the garish, gold-coated stage design and surrounding decorations lend the place a certain, if utterly outdated, charm. I think our star singer will be right at home in this wonderfully tasteless arena.

On stage, a local duet are singing their way through a show tune megamix. The grey-haired crowd are lapping it up, joining in and clapping along in time.

"The oldies love this set," says Peters as we stand to the side of the stage.

"Nice to see them enjoying themselves instead of moaning about buses and dodging coffins." I find myself blurting out.

Peters glares at me, Sophie digs me in the ribs with her elbow. He leads us up into the top tiers of seating and points out all the entrance and exit points. Even though we now believe we're looking for some ex-rocker, ex-army psycho it doesn't make it any easier wondering where he's going to make his entrance. Or if this will be the venue of his next hit. I make a few notes. Sophie takes a few photos with the smaller of her digital SLRs, then we thank Peters for his time.

We head back to the hotel and take in a nightcap in the bar before heading up to our room an hour after midnight.

In the hotel room Sophie drops her clothes on the floor. She gets in the shower and beckons me to join her with a lazy, sexy look. We're too knackered to speak, but not too knackered to slowly shag each other senseless. With clean bodies, but dirty minds, we jump into bed and continue riding each other like cowboy and cowgirl. I just about manage not to think about The Good, The Bad, and The Ugly until afterwards.

*   *

You're really looking forward to being back in Blackpool. It was one of the venues you enjoyed playing the most – outside of Liverpool – and although the pub crowd were mostly smashed that evening way back when, you felt like you rocked a big one.

For tonight's mission you're toning down the disguise and going back to basics. You've left the wigs at home, and instead you've died your short hair to a bleach blonde, adding gel for a spiky effect. You look and feel totally different, and only a smattering of your natural dark roots show through. You're wearing a tight black, sleeveless T-shirt showing off your biceps, de-stressed and faded (that's what the label said) blue jeans and a pair of flashy, bright white trainers. You felt a bit pale so you've rubbed in some subtle fake tan to give your face and arms a bit of colour. You admire your new look in the mirror, flexing your biceps you've been building up, showing off your arm tattoos you got when you were in the army.

Your only secret weapon is the 'liquid skin' you've procured from your Hereford days. You've painted your hands with it so your fingerprints won't show up on anything because you won't be able to wear gloves tonight.

You haven't gone on a hit this underdressed before, and yet you've never felt more in disguise and more confident.

As you drive your Astra up to Blackpool you shout along to punk songs on your car's stereo, sipping on some vodka straight out the bottle. It's ideal for getting yourself into character so you'll hit the booze running when it's time to make friends with Danny Stone.

You park on a side street a mile from Blackpool Tower. Checking your spiky hair in the mirror, you lock your car and walk into the first pub on the promenade. You order a pint of strong lager and down it in one. You leave and walk into another pub, squeezing through the crowds to order another pint. You take your time with this one, taking two big gulps instead of one. You notice a pair of young punks drinking next to you. Their hair is bright green and pink and the Mohicans are old school spiky and at least a foot tall.

They're leaning with their backs against the bar and wearing matching T-shirts: they're white with the shoulders ripped off, and on the front in big red handwriting it says 'We Love You Top 10 Hitman'. The 'love' is done as a heart. You knew you'd build up a fan club one day. You want to say hello and offer to sign their T-shirts, but you've got another pop star to kill.

You stride down the promenade with a smile on your face. It's Saturday night and the streets are heaving with groups of boys and girls dressed up and pissed up. You walk up to Blackpool Tower, walk past the main entrance and bouncers managing the queue of girls with some boyfriends in tow, and march down to a VIP entrance on the side. You join the queue at the end and, with the added assurance of the drink, you casually make friends with a group of tarted up girls who fall in behind you. You don't have to charm them much. Everyone's friendly when you're VIP. You stick by the girls as you give the bouncer your VIP ticket. He pats you down as he gives you a full a body search. He won't find any concealed weapons as you're not carrying any. You only have a sachet of medical alcohol strapped to your calf and you know it will feel like muscle through your jeans as he touches it. Satisfied you're clean he tears your ticket, sticks a VIP badge on your chest, and waves you through.

Sometimes the best way to get into a place unnoticed is to become a paying punter. You'd bought the VIP ticket just like anyone else, over the phone, about a month ago. The only difference was you bought it using a false name, fake credit card and someone else's PO Box address. It's the second credit card you've got through your bodyguard mate's dodgy contacts in Manchester.

Once you're inside you head to the VIP bar and spot Danny Stone's bodyguards straight away. It takes one to know one. Apart from their big build emphasised by tight polo shirts, and the way the pair of them are strutting about like they own the place, it's the subtle earpiece/microphones hidden by collars and gelled hair that are a dead giveaway. If someone wasn't looking they probably wouldn't notice, but it's the first thing you look for. You buy a pint at the bar and gulp half of it down, keeping an eye on the bodyguards and another on the door to the dressing rooms; you remember where they are when you played here all those years ago. An old place like Blackpool Tower doesn't change its layout often.

You hang around with the girls who are giggling with excitement about the chance to "Say hiya to Danny before he sings on stage". As if on cue, Danny strolls in, checking people notice his arrival while acting like he doesn't want any attention. He's a terrible actor. He's wearing a chocolate brown shirt with white writing all over it; it's ripped at the arms to show off what looks like a couple of freshly-drawn tattoos. His hair's heavily dishevelled, his skin's deeply tanned and his jeans and trainers look expensive. Danny gladly accepts a pint from the pit bull look-alike bodyguard. As he's drinking his pint he takes a whiskey chaser from another guy and necks it.

"I can't believe we're standing this close to Danny frigging Stone off *Argyle Street*," says a blonde girl from the group. You notice how the women seem so obsessed with celebrity status, and it's not lost on you how much of an aphrodisiac it appears to be too.

The girls gravitate towards him so you tag along, blending in like a boyfriend in the background. The striking, brunette leader of the girls gets his attention.

"Hey Danny, how's it going? How's about a quickie before you go on, like?" She winks, and holds up her digital camera and flashes him a big smile.

"And a quick photo too!" shrieks the blonde girl. They all cackle like mad.

Danny eyes them up and down before smiling and saying, "Sure thing, anything for my gorgeous female fans." He hands his drink to the pit bull.

"Will you take it for us please, handsome?" says the brunette to you as she hands you her camera.

Nobody calls you handsome. You know she's just saying it for effect in front of Danny.

"Yeah, of course," you say, happy you won't be in any photos.

Danny poses with a few girls either side of him, the brunette under one arm, the blonde under the other. You watch as his slimy hands slip down to grope both girls' bodies. The girls don't even flinch. Danny looks as happy as a pig in shit.

"Say doggy style," you say to them.

"Doggy style!" say the girls, laughing and smiling. Danny doesn't say anything, he just grins. You click off a couple of photographs.

"Nice one mate," says Danny as he winks at you. He grabs his drink back and walks over as you give the brunette her camera back. The girls huddle together, eagerly checking how the photos have come out. Danny ignores the girls and says, "I like your tattoos, mate. Nice, nice." He nods and shifts from foot to foot.

Usually you'd accuse a bloke of being gay if he'd just asked you about your tats, but this is part of your plan, so you just say, "Cheers."

"They look real old school. I like that," says Danny. You think he's swaggering around to see if you notice his tattoos. You ignore them, but notice he's wearing make-up including some thick black eyeliner. "Yeah, I got them when I was younger. I was drunk for every single one," you say.

"A man after my own heart," he says holding up his drink.

"Apart from this one," you say, pointing at the tattoo of a naked girl riding a camel on your left bicep. "This one I got done when I was unconscious."

Danny loves this and throws his head back with laughter. You down the remaining half of your pint. "Drink?" you say to him, waggling your empty pint glass.

"Yeah, sure…" he says, just as the pit bull appears by his side.

"Danny, we'd better get going," he says, pointing his thumb back towards the dressing room. "You're on in ten."

"Ah, best crack on, mate. I need to powder me nose before the show." Danny pauses to wink. "We're having a little party after the show. Stick around for drink."

"Cool," you say.

Sure, you'll see Danny Stone after the show for a little drink.

*   *

"If anybody unauthorised or without a ticket tries to get through any entrance or fire exit, we'll be the first to know," says Peters proudly.

Sophie and I are stood in the main reception hall of Blackpool Tower on Saturday night just before ex-soap star pin-up Danny Stone is due to take to the stage.

I, for one, believe Peters. He's got so much security on each entrance and fire exit, as well as lining the front and back of the stage, and along the sides of the seating areas, it'll be hard to miss anyone getting to Danny Stone. He's got his own bodyguards in tow as well according to Peters. Sophie and I have already given the behind the scenes a once over. We also checked all the toilets and toilet windows. I checked the gents, Sophie checked the ladies. I felt better when I saw the windows were nailed shut. Although in the gents they could do with being open a smidge just to get some fresh air circulating.

"Okay ladies and gentlemen, can you please make your way to your seats. Danny Stone will be on in five minutes," bellows one of Peters' security staff to the crowds milling.

"Showtime," says Peters.

Sophie and I take our seats high up in the gods. Peters has arranged it so we're at the front of a balcony overlooking the right of the stage. From here we can see the main seating area below, as well as the entrance and exits upstairs and downstairs.

"I've got a feeling he's going to be here tonight," I say quietly in Sophie's ear.

"Let's hope you're right," says Sophie. She pulls down the peak of her red cap and twiddles the focus on her camera lens.

The crowd is mostly young girls and older mums, with a few boyfriends and husbands dragged along. Looking around I can see some women have made an effort, with several wearing some ropy old outfits and ill-advised make-up. Sophie's brought a long lens and is scouring the crowds with her camera, looking for anyone in suspicious places. I'm looking for *anyone suspicious* in any places. We've got suspicious minds.

We're looking for someone in disguise. But don't know what disguise. The Hitman could be dressed up as Elton John for all we know. I quickly check the crowd but relax when I can't see anyone in a large, flamboyant wig, wearing fifteen-foot high boots, a sequined jacket and giant glasses.

I vaguely recognise the tune that starts booming louder and louder out of the speakers as a series of lights sweep across the stage. Various, anonymous band members take their positions behind drums, keyboards and guitars. They all gradually join in with the opening tune, giving it some body. Then Danny Stone runs on stage, almost skipping, almost dancing, as he grabs the microphone and starts singing.

I can tell you the first song Danny Stone sang. It was *Drink Drank Drunk*, and I can tell you the last, *Pump Me With Your Love*. But I've no idea what other songs he performed in between. Partly because I was surveying the crowds and doors, checking out whoever was at the side of the stage, but mostly because I'm not interested in his brand of low-grade pop music. I think at one point my ears tried to seal themselves shut rather than listen to such plop. I thought, as an actor, he'd be able to perform and turn it on a bit better. But, no. I found myself wishing for someone to jump on stage and unleash a flame thrower or attack him with a Samurai sword, just to put an end to it.

More than once I had to remind myself I'm on his side and that, if someone was trying to kill him, I would bolt down to the stage and attempt to save his life. Or, at least, tug on a security guard's shirt sleeve and ask them politely to stop the Hitman.

I look at the crowd and their smiling, shiny faces. Once again I'm amazed at what certain people will sit through. Perhaps it's because they've never been to a see a real band or really talented singer so they don't have anything to compare it to. The crowd are still cheering as Danny finishes his encore, waves and skips off stage.

"Well that was a load of bollocks," I say.

"His singing?"

"That, and the fact the Hitman didn't show," I say.

The stage lights are dimmed, the main arena lights are turned up, and the crowd start shuffling out. Sophie scans the crowds through her telephoto lens.

"Let's get a pint."

"But he could still be in danger," says Sophie, lowering her camera.

"We can but hope," I say.

She gives me the evil eye. And then another one. Two evil eyes.

"Okay, alright. Let's get a drink in the VIP area. I'll check on Danny, and try and warn him his life could be in danger," I say.

Try being the operative word. How am I going to say that without smirking. It's not the sort of thing I say everyday.

*   *

After-show parties are sometimes better than the show itself. You certainly knew that would be the case with tonight's show. You gladly missed the naff actor's naff singing, and instead checked out the empty dressing rooms and the rider Danny Stone's got.

Riders are a band's best friend. The more famous you are the more you can demand what goes on it, from special drinks and cocktails to exotic foods and hard drugs. In a fair-sized, white-walled dressing room, Danny's rider is moderately exuberant and consists of a large-sized fridge with two shelves full of posh canned lager, twelve bottles of fancy cider, two bottles of vodka, two litres of coke, two bottles of white wine, two bottles of Dom Perignon, and a carton of orange juice. On a table next to the fridge are two bottles of red wine, four bottles of Jack Daniels, a big bowl of fruit, a bucket of ice, and a spread of food including chicken curry, pasta, cold meats, nibbles, dips, and sliced up baguettes.

On a smaller table are several bottles of mineral water and a pile of white towels next to a sink and mirror. A TV sits in the corner. On a shelf next to it is a CD player and speakers. You check out a small pile of CDs on the shelf; Danny Stone's CD is there, along with other CDs you'd be embarrassed to own. The least crap is a double-CD chart compilation so you put that on, although Danny singing live next door is drowning it out somewhat.

Your mission is to make this an after-show party to remember. You take two of the four bottles of JD and empty half of one down the sink and fill it with tap water, then partly empty the second one and fill it back up with sachet of 100 per cent proof liquid alcohol you had strapped to your leg. You make a tiny tear on the corner of the label of the first bottle, and two little tears on the corner on the second

161

bottle. You screw the lids back on and tip the bottles up and down slowly to mix the liquids without shaking bubbles into them. You tuck these two bottles behind the fridge out of sight.

You relax and make yourself at home, trying the nibbles, cracking open a can of lager and sitting on one of three sofas. Two roadies dressed all in black denim join you after a while.

"Blimey, mate, and we thought we'd be at the front of the queue!" says the fatter of the two, clocking your VIP badge that gives you access to the after-show party.

"I was wondering when you guys would get here," you say.

"We haven't got equipment to shift until afterwards so no point wasting a good feast," he says.

"A good, *free* feast," says the slightly less fat one.

You all laugh and tuck in. You know the chat, so you swap roadie stories with them, opening and toasting cans together. Slowly, but steadily a select few VIP badge holders arrive until there's about twenty bodies gathered around. You notice the music outside on stage has stopped and shortly afterwards the band walk in, sweating and smiling. A few people congratulate them on a good gig and give them pats on their backs as they mop themselves dry with the towels. A couple of security guards show up to watch the door.

Danny Stone isn't far behind, sweating and grinning with a few almost-glam groupies in tow. You recognise the brunette from earlier and his two bodyguards follow closely behind. Danny grabs a bottle of bubbly from the fridge and pops the cork much to the delight of the girls who scream and hold out empty flutes expectantly. He winks at you as he fills their glasses.

You squeeze in next to him and, even though you missed the whole concert, you say, "Well, you seemed to go down well out there."

"And let's hope one of these babes goes down well later, huh?" he says, squeezing the arse of the brunette who seems wildly excited to be in his presence.

"Nice one bruva," you say. "Now let's break the back of these beers before cracking on with the JD, eh?"

"Sounds like a plan, my tattooed friend," says Danny. "What's your name anyway?"

"Stan," you lie.

"Stan, my man with the plan, let's get wasted."

You and Danny mingle with the bodyguards, groupies and band members, joking and drinking your way into the night. You've already had a skin full, but if there's one thing you know how to do well, other than killing, it's drinking.

*　　*

162

Sophie and I catch up with Peters in reception and congratulate him on a security job well done. I tell him we'll be featuring him and his security crew in an in depth – yet non-existent – article in the magazine soon.

"It was a successful night. And nobody died," I say, trying to hide my disappointment.

"That's how we like it," says Peters. "Well, thank you for coming to Blackpool Tower."

"No. Thank *you*."

"Right, I suppose I'd better go and look in on Mr Stone," he says, sighing, and checking his watch.

"Don't bother. Danny will be fine now. He's got his bodyguards and band protecting him," I say confidently.

"You think so?" says Peters, looking towards the bar, obviously keen to call it a night.

"Yeah. Go and put your feet up, have a drink. He's safe now. The Hitman only strikes when the stage is hot," I say.

Peters scratches his chin thoughtfully.

"We're off to have a quick chat with Danny before we leave anyway."

"Okay, great. All the best," he says almost running towards the bar.

As the last of the crowd files out the exits, we walk against the stream and head backstage to the main dressing room, nodding to a couple of Danny's security staff on the dressing room door. We walk in and, like all freeloaders, head straight to the drinks. There are some beers in the fridge so Sophie and I grab a couple and check out who's hot and who's not. I look around the room to see it's full of the latter.

The biggest of the lot, Danny Stone, is across the otherside of the room chatting to some toned guy with spiky bleached-hair and tattooed arms. Probably a bodyguard. Stood and sat around us are backing band members, roadies and groupies. Some chart pop is playing on a CD player.

"What do you reckon, sweet cheeks?" I say hinting to our fellow freeloaders, "I don't think there's much of a threat for Danny here."

"Just seems the usual after-show hangers-on," says Sophie.

"Why don't we drink a couple more freebies, warn Danny about his impending death, then clear off back to the hotel."

"Okay, baby, as along as you talk to Danny," says Sophie, knocking her can against mine.

It's funny. The room is full of pop's low level shakers, but even if it was full of top movers from the music industry, I'd still just want to chat and drink with Sophie. As she's surveying the room, I steal a long look from her lips down to her hips. Her mouth is half-open, half-smiling. She looks beautifully sexy.

Another drink later and we're doing a bit of light mingling with the guitarist, Vince Harris. "To be honest, I can't stand churning out the crap Danny's had written for him," says Vince, surprisingly candid, "but it's a chord in the right direction."

"Step in the right direction?" I say.

"That's what I said," slurs Vince loudly.

He seems nicely oiled so I ask him what he thinks of the greasy Danny Stone.

"He's a nice enough guy... actually, that's ball sacks. I don't know how he gets away with it. He can't sing, he can't perform, he wasn't even a very good actor on *Argyle Street* if you ask me," says Vince, half focussing on us, half focussing on his vodka and coke. "I can't stand him to be honest, none of the band can, we're only at this party now for the free food and beer. I'm gonna piss off soon..."

Sophie looks at me, smiles, and steers me sideways and away from Vince. Another drink later and the after-show party seems to be flagging, half the people have slipped away, and we're nowhere nearer to talking to Danny. "Sod this. I'm bored. Let's go and talk to twat features and get out of here."

"Okay."

We walk over to Danny and his crew. "Hey Danny, sorry to interrupt, we're from *TOP 10 HITS* magazine and just wanted to say hello," I say.

"Hi guys," he says not looking at us. Close up, he's smaller than I thought he'd be. Actors always are smaller. Or taller. Or exactly as I imagined. One of the three. His hair's rigid with gel and he's had his teeth fixed to ultra white.

"Hi," I say.

"Sorry, what are your names?" he says. His eyes are vacant and he stares straight through us. Which is weird, because he's the one with the transparent personality.

"Hardy," I say.

"And Sophie," says Sophie. She's got her camera around her neck but with the lens cap still on.

"You're not going to pap me in here are ya, darlin'?" says Danny oozing smarm.

"No, don't worry, that's not my style. I won't take the lens cap off. Promise," says Sophie sweetly.

"Good girl," he says in a condescending manner. He turns around and says, "Hardy, Sophie, this is Stan the man." Danny points to the bleach-haired bodyguard guy. "And these are my old mates, Cav and Oz." Danny points at the two other men stood nearby. They're a pair of well-built roadies who look like they enjoy their cooked breakfasts and free beer. Both of them are wearing flowery Hawaiian shirts.

"Hello," Sophie and I say together, smiling politely.

We all share a few beers and talk shop. Sophie tells pop photography tales, while I politely compare Danny's gig to other 'pop greats' I've seen – I can lie along with the best of them – and only gently take the piss out of his pedestrian performance. Danny seems fairly plastered, and Cav and Oz are like a double act, encouraging each other and laughing at their own jokes. Stan is drinking steadily, but he's quieter about than the others. The other bodyguards don't seem bothered about drinking on duty either. I notice a brunette and a blonde hanging around in the background.

A lull appears in the conversation, so I quickly say, "Danny, can we have a quiet word?" Stan looks up at me as he drinks his lager.

"Yeah, sure, sure." He puts his arm around my shoulder and guides me, and Sophie, over to the other side of the dressing room so we're out of earshot.

"This is going to sound crazy, but we think the Hitman, the pop star killer, has got you next on his Top 10 Hit List. We think your life could be in danger," I say as sincerely as possible.

A big grin appears on his face. "But the Hitman's only after rubbish acts! I don't need to worry. I'm far too good for his Hit List!" he says boldly.

Why is it that deluded sorts like Danny Stone believe they're untouchable?

"Hey! Lads! Get this. Hardy over here thinks I'm danger from the pop star Hitman! Classic, huh!?" Shouts Danny, proud as punch, winking towards his cronies. All of them lap this up, laughing their various shaped heads off.

"We know it sounds mad," says Sophie. I look at his crew of beefcakes and can't help agreeing he's never been in a safer place.

"But you're a journalist, and you're a photographer. Why should I believe either of you? It's not like you're private detectives, is it?"

Sophie and I look at each other.

We don't mention that he's talking to the H&S Detective Agency.

"And if I'm in danger, why aren't the police here?" says Danny.

"They can't be at every pop concert protecting every band and singer in the charts. They don't know where the killer's going to strike next…" I say. I don't tell him I neglected to share our Hit List predictions with the cops.

"Now, don't get me wrong, but I've never heard such a load of old shite," says Danny, quietly, drunkenly. "I'm flattered someone feels strongly enough to kill me, but I've got my boys with me, we've got some drinks to get drunk, so would you be so good as to piss off?"

"Right," I say. Sophie doesn't say anything, she just takes my arm and leads me away. I look back and Danny winks at me.

"You're such a winker," I say.

Danny grins and returns to his stooges.

"Hope you die soon," I say as an after thought.

His bodyguards are too far away to hear. Danny isn't, but he doesn't seem to care. Stan stares at me as I'm walking out the dressing room.

We walk down the corridors, and past the stage and rows of empty seats. A couple of cleaners are sweeping and vacuuming up all that's left of the show. We walk past the main bar and, through the windows in the entrance door, I spot Peters and a few of his security staff propping up the bar, smoking and drinking. I check my watch and it tells me the little hand is on the one and big hand is on the six. When we get through to the reception there's nobody around, not even a doorman to bid us good evening or a bouncer to stare down their nose at us. We let ourselves out and walk along the promenade back to our hotel.

After a while Sophie says, "I can't believe a man so small could be such a big nob head."

"He was small wasn't he?" I say.

"At least we tried to warn him," she says.

"Maybe we've got it wrong again," I say. "Maybe he's not in danger at all."

*   *

Danny Stone may've been on *Argyle Street* but you should be getting the actor's award for the turn you're doing. The journalist and photographer never had a clue they were sharing a beer and a joke with you, the 'Hitman'. You're proud how you kept it together and didn't flinch when they showed up.

But how did they know Danny Stone was next on your Hit List? You're sure you didn't leave any clues in your email about your Hit No.5.

You're buzzing inside, but blending in with the bodyguards. Everyone thinks you're cool because Danny likes you so much. You laugh the hardest when Danny shouted across saying that he was 'in danger from the Hitman'. Of course he's in danger, the arrogant dick.

You slip out of the party for a quick piss. You're glad Danny got rid of Hardy the journo and Sophie the snapper, and it's good she didn't take any photos of you with Danny. Although you'd doubt anyone would recognise you, the spiky bleached hair and fake tan is so far removed from how you'd normally look. You'd doubt if even the boys from the barracks would recognise you in a line up looking like this.

You don't want Hardy and Sophie spoiling your best laid plans. You wouldn't mind sacrificing them, nothing's going to stand in your way of reaching your No.1. But they're not part of your plan for now. You noticed their body language and how Sophie looked at Hardy. Maybe they're getting closer. What concerns you is how they'd got close to you, and how they'd known to warn Danny.

They're helping your little pop project for now. You're using them as a PR machine, but you make a mental note to be ready for them next time.

As you finish pissing, you twig. It's obvious. They're in contact with the same singers and bands as you are, and see lots of gigs. You realise tonight they just got lucky. Or unlucky.

Back at the party the numbers have dwindled and most of the band have disappeared. This mission is really testing your patience but you're not about to ruin it by rushing. Danny's security guards watching the door have disappeared. You walk over to a semi-paralytic Danny sat on the sofa. He greets you with a JD and coke.

"Cheeee-eearrs eaaarzzz..." stammers Danny.

"Cheers ears!" you say.

You've been enjoying blowing off some steam. You haven't got pissed properly since your little project got off the ground. But you still know you've got a job to do this evening. Danny's bodyguards are having too much fun drinking to worry about intruders. You'd never drink on duty like that but you're glad they're a pair of slack asses. You notice Cav and Oz are sharing one of the bottles of JD, and Danny is holding the other. You pick at some of the food on the table and take a casual glance around the back of the fridge to check the other two bottles of JD are safe.

An hour or so later and Cav and Oz have finished their bottle and both have their arm around the blonde. Danny fills your glass up with JD, then you subtly take the bottle from him and make sure he gets the lion's share of the liquor, mixing more coke with your drink than his. The brunette is still hanging around, perched on the arm of the sofa, but Danny's smarm sorts her out.

"You two still here," he says trying to focus on her chest, "why don't you two come out to play?"

The brunette is drunk, but not that drunk. She doesn't respond. You don't say anything either.

"Let me introduce my Russian alter ego," says Danny. "His name is 'Slobberdownmycock Youbitch'."

"I thought you'd be cool, but you're nothing but a charm-less cock," says the brunette. She downs her drink and storms out. Cav goes after her, no doubt to give her a shoulder to cry on, and something to ride on afterwards.

The blonde bounces over to Danny.

"I'll still do you, like," she says.

"No ta, love, I don't do blondes," says Danny.

She looks fit to blub. Oz notices this. "Let's go and find your friend," says Oz. He puts his arm around the blonde, and leads her out the door, and probably into his bed. You wonder if Cav and Oz do this at every concert.

This leaves you and Danny, and the two bodyguards across the other side of the room. They're big built but are the sort of muscle-heads who don't know their own names three beers down the line. You've been counting and both have had at least six cans each now. You take the last four-pack of lager from the fridge and give it to them. "You deserve this boys."

"You can bugger off for the night boys!" Danny shouts, slumped on the sofa. "You lightweights won't be able to keep up anyway."

They grit their teeth, nod towards him, take the lagers, and promptly leave. You close the door behind them and, with your back to Danny so he can't see, lock the door and put the key into your pocket.

"Now the party really begins," you say.

Danny's got the bottle of JD and up-ends it as the last few drops drip onto his tongue. "Shit! There's no JD left, Stan the man," he says, swaying around but still sat on the sofa. He makes you feel sober.

"Allow me, Danny boy." You reach behind the fridge and pull out the two stashed bottles of JD. You keep the bottle with one small tear on the label, handing Danny the second bottle.

"Good job Stan the man!"

"Let's do one each. It's the rock 'n' roll way," you say. You know he won't be able to resist it.

"Yeah, man! Rock 'n' roll!" He says jumping up off the sofa.

You take a glug – but you're really taking a sip – from your bottle. Danny takes a glug from his bottle. He doesn't seem to notice the pure alcohol going down his neck. You take a sip, he takes a glug. Your watered down JD tastes weak but as you're working, you don't mind tonight.

Danny puts on his own album in the CD player and turns the volume up. "This may sound big headed." He pauses drunkenly. "But I think I sound foooooking grrrreat!"

Now you're alone, you drop the matey act. No more Mr Nice Guy. "It does sound big headed. You'd sound shit without all that studio production."

Danny thinks you're joking and starts singing along to his own song. Narcissus would be so proud.

"Get it down you, Danny boy!" you say holding up your bottle.

His eyes are all over the place. He downs another mouthful but chokes on it. "It tastes so strong."

"You not man enough, Danny *boy*?" you say, making a point by emphasising the 'boy'.

"'Course I am, Stan the man!" he says slurring the 'man'.

Danny starts dancing and bumps into the table of food. A couple of plates and glasses crash on the floor. Danny's oblivious and continues singing at the top of his voice. He downs some more JD without provocation.

"Have you ever heard yourself sing, Danny?" you say.

"I'm listening to myself now," he says. "I sound grrrrreeeeat."

You stare at him.

"Y'know, theeeese people think I'm kind of a big deal."

"What people, Danny? There are no people here now."

He ignores you and carries on singing and dancing. You've had enough of Danny Stone. You put your bottle of JD down and stride over to him.

"I've suffered listening to your music, so now it's your turn."

"Eh? To what?" says Danny.

"To suffer," you say.

You yank the bottle of JD off him and ram the neck down his throat. The bottle clatters against his teeth. He chokes but you grab him by his collar with your other hand and make sure he stays up and the alcohol goes down. He slaps you wildly around the face trying to fight you off. You feel it, but it doesn't hurt. Danny gags as he tries to say something.

"Don't speak with your mouth full, Danny boy," you say.

He tries to scream in-between gagging but chokes instead. He tries to spit out the JD, so you massage his throat to make sure he's still swallowing. When you're satisfied he's had enough, you tug the bottle from his throat, and pour some alcohol in his eyes. He screams and coughs and doubles over, rubbing his eyes. The music blasting out of the CD player helpfully drowns out his cries for help. Danny staggers to his feet then tumbles backwards over the table of food and gets curry all over his shirt.

"W-what the fuck are you doing, man!?" he spits, blinking, coughing.

"You're always saying you like a hard drink," you say.

"W-w-what the...!?" He retches but nothing comes out. He slumps down so you grab him and lift him up. You want to keep him upright so he's not sick and wastes all that precious alcohol.

"Come on, Danny, you're the big man always saying you like a drink." You grab the JD, clamp his mouth open with your fingers, holding his body upright at the same time. You pour the remaining alcohol down his throat. He coughs and splutters. You let go of his mouth and Danny collapses on to the floor. You instinctively kick him in the stomach a couple of times while he's down.

"W-w-hat you doing!?" he manages to spew out.

"Something I should've done much earlier," you say.

His eyes start rolling back and his body sways around as the alcohol hits him. You'd better put an end to his pain. The surgical alcohol will poison and kill him but there's no harm in just making sure. You turn the TV on, and drag Danny by his collar across the floor and make him sit up. He looks at the TV but he's not focussing.

"You should've stuck to the TV acting. People need to know their limitations. The pop world doesn't need actors like you thinking they can sing."

You pick the TV up off its stand, swing it high above your head and bring it crashing down hard on top of Danny's skull. The TV screen shatters and he's left wearing a TV-shaped helmet. But as it's still plugged in, the electricity gives Danny the shock of his life. Followed instantly by his death. The weight of the TV pulls him over to one side. His legs kick out involuntarily a couple of times, sparks fly from inside the TV, then nothing.

You leave the TV on and turn the CD player off. Quiet at last.

Out of habit you check his pulse.

Danny Stone is dead.

Time to move.

You unlock the door, check the corridor is empty and lock the door behind you, putting the key in your pocket. You walk quickly towards the fire exit. There isn't any security around. You check the door isn't alarmed, then push on the fire exit bar and let yourself out. There are no bodyguards, no bouncers. No Hardy, no Sophie. Nobody. You close the fire exit behind you and simply walk up to the promenade and blend in with the last of the booze-heads falling out of the clubs, buying chips, and wobbling home.

No police, no press. Nobody.

They keep underestimating you, Mac. It's how you'll always stay one step ahead.

NO. 4

If you tolerate this then your children will be next
Manic Street Preachers

"I had a lot of respect for that new band Bundy when they stormed off stage in Manchester last month," I say.

"I thought it just made them seem like egotistical brats," says Sophie.

It's Monday and it's been a week since we were in Blackpool. Sophie and I are having a liquid lunch. She was on a photo shoot in Wiltshire in the morning taking some quick pop portraits, and dropped in to see me in Bath on her way back to Bristol. We're both drinking our second Guinness sat at a table in The Raven, a pub around the corner from the *TOP 10 HITS* office.

"Why are you on their side for refusing to play to a crowd of people who'd paid to see them?" she says.

A pair of suits walk in and order a bottle of wine and sit at a small table in the window. Up until a couple of years ago The Raven used to be a rough-round-the-edges pub called Hatchets, frequented by bikers, rockers and punks. You wouldn't have been able to order a bottle of wine back then. Suits didn't darken their door either.

"Picture the scene: Bundy survey the crowd before they start their first song. The band can't wait to start playing, but the crowd are all getting lairy, and essentially full of lager louts who're drunk and pissed off after Man Utd lost. A few punters throw cans full of lager on stage. Lots of them are wearing football shirts, spitting on each other, and trying to spit on the band."

"Sounds lovely."

"So, they take a good long look at the crowd while they give their instruments a final tune up. As the lead singer adjusts the mic stand, a can whistles past his ear and thuds into the amps behind him. Someone shouts, "Get on with it shit face!" While a group wearing white caps are jumping up trying to gob lager on him. A few others are already fighting with each other. There aren't any bouncers to stop it, it's only a small venue and it's not usually that sort of pub. They get more heckles. But the lead singer doesn't give in and just crash into the opening number. Instead they stand there, looking for a source of recognition, not someone they know, just someone they can *relate* to. A look, a face, something. But nobody. There's not one face they can look into and think, *'Yeah, that's the sort of person we want listening to our music'*. So they unplug their instruments and walk off stage."

"The crowd must've gone berserk."

"They exploded. Lager went everywhere. Although most of them took it out on each other. There were some nasty scenes inside and out that night," I say.

"Did the police show up?" asks Sophie.

"Eventually. But by then the damage had been done," I say. I take a sip of my stout. "I had to respect Bundy for what they did."

"Well, I still think it was arrogant," says Sophie.

"No, it's almost the opposite. They were very humble when I spoke to them about it the following day. They just made a decision that this particular crowd didn't deserve their performance because they weren't there for their music."

"It wasn't even like they were established and successful enough to be able to do what they did," says Sophie.

"It doesn't matter. It could've been a new band at their first gig. The point is they made the decision that they didn't need this crowd. They didn't like them, didn't want these people as fans."

Sophie responds by taking a sip of her pint. I sip mine too. It tastes creamy and velvety.

"I can't imagine any of today's pop bands having the balls to do that. They're too greedy for success and fame. They'll play to anyone who turns up and pays them. They don't care if their fans are twelve year old thieves, forty-two year old heroin whores, or twenty-two year old football hooligans, they'll play to whoever's stupid or tone deaf enough to want to buy a ticket or CD."

"You're forgetting, Hardy. You don't get to choose your fans."

After a long lunch, Sophie and I kiss goodbye, and I head back to the office hoping for a lazy afternoon. As soon as I walk in Gary's on my case.

"Hardy, can you take this call?" he says with his hand over the receiver. "It's Sharon's mum... Sharon from Kitty Bomb. She's pretty upset but wants to tell us her side of the story. As she's called, can you quickly interview her now? Let's do a side panel on this in the news pages."

"Great," I say indifferently. "Put her through to my extension." I sit down and pick up my desk phone. "Hello. This is Hardy, thanks for calling *TOP 10 HITS*, Mrs…"

"Mrs Strong."

"Mrs Strong. Okay. And you're Sharon's mum, Sharon who is… sorry, who *was* in Kitty Bomb," I say, tucking the phone against my shoulder, attaching my 'bug' microphone to the phone receiver. I connect it to my Dictaphone and press record.

Mrs Strong doesn't respond.

"Mrs Strong?"

I hear her sniff. "I'm sorry. I'm still well upset. I still can't believe our Sharon's gone," she says between sniffs.

"That's okay. You take your time."

After lots of pauses and occasional tears from Mrs Strong I get enough answers from her for a 300 word Q&A in the news section.

After I hang up, I feel weird. After a while I realise what I'm feeling is remorse. I couldn't care less about Kitty Bomb living or dying. I didn't know them, I think I'd only seen them perform once live, and didn't care about their music or (lack of) values. They were all about making money, whether through music sales or merchandise. But I feel remorse because I can't help feeling sympathy for Mrs Strong. She's lost her daughter. She doesn't understand why, and there's nothing she can do about it.

Feeling distracted, I try to start tapping out one of two short features Gary's commissioned me to write about the *Pop Factory* winners of the last three years. I could sum it up quickly in one paragraph:

'They all disappeared into obscurity after a couple of forgettable singles that flirted with the Top 40, proving once again that the manufactured music industry isn't producing top quality pop performers, regardless of what the TV talent show egos try to make us believe.'

I press delete and start again. It's too honest for the young, fickle readers who buy our mag, and I don't think it's the sort of angle Gary had in mind. After twenty minutes of typing and deleting, I give up and browse the web. Somebody's emailed me a website address I want to check out anyway; it's called www.whosnextonthehitlist.com. It's a darkly comic read and although the forum is full of people listing their own Top 10 Hit Lists, I don't join in and post mine online. I log off and check my email. I sift through the usual concert invites, press releases, new singles and rude jokes from mates. And then I stop.

Here we go again.

Another email from the Hitman.

I hesitate before opening it. I look over my shoulder to check nobody can read what's on my screen. They can't. My heart starts pounding as I click to open the email.

Subject: Top 10 Hit List

From: Hitman <top10hitlist@gmail.com>

To: Hardy Matthews <hardy@top10hits.co.uk>

Nice to meet you both the other night at the Danny Stone concert in Blackpool. Did you and Sophie enjoy yourselves? You two seemed cosy.

I had a top night on the sauce. Too bad our pop star singer Danny can't handle his drink. He's got terrible TV watching habits too.

You'll be pleased to know preparation for the next Hit is moving along swiftly.

No doubt see you around.

Holy heck. When the hell did we meet him? Was the Hitman in the crowd? Is he McNamara? Was he at the after show party? Was he disguised as security? Has he killed Danny Stone? Did we miss a really good piss up after all? And, more importantly, did Sophie and I miss the big scoop we're hunting for?

Before I'm able to answer any of these questions, my work phone starts ringing. I think about ignoring it then pick it up.

"Hardy Matthews," I say.

"Matthews, DCI Johnson."

"Hello Johnson, are we well?" I say. The more unfriendly I feel towards him the more friendly I am. He seems to have that affect on me.

"Cut the crap, Matthews. You are not a man lucky enough to be in my good books."

"Oh Johnson, but I thought we were bestest buddies."

"Matthews," he says in his sternest voice. "Don't try my patience."

"But I did think we were buddies. We've been getting on so well."

"Matthews, do you realise I could arrest you for murder on the evidence I have?"

That shuts me up.

"Danny Stone was found murdered the night after his Blackpool Tower concert."

The Hitman strikes again.

"And surprise, surprise, guess who was there that night?"

"The Scarlet Pimpernel?"

"Guess again," he says ignoring my attempt at wit.

"Me?" I say tentatively.

"You."

"I didn't kill Danny Stone," I say not so tentatively. I look around to check none of the *TOP 10 HITS* crew can hear me. Luckily Gary and Jane are out of earshot looking over a cover design on Robin's computer.

"Are you sure?"

"What a stupid question. Of course I'm bloody sure," I say as quietly as possible. "You don't kill someone then forget about it. I was with Sophie the whole night. We left the after-show party early. There were loads of people still drinking when we left, and Danny Stone was alive and kicking then."

"How do we know you didn't go back there later?"

"Because I spent the night with Sophie in our hotel."

"You spent the night with your photographer? Do you share hotel beds with all your work colleagues?"

"That's none of your business."

I'm not about to tell the cops the finer details of my love life. Johnson doesn't say anything and I can tell a creepy smile is crawling over his face.

"You can't seriously think I killed Danny Stone?"

"All I know is that when a pop star is murdered you're never far behind," says Johnson quietly, sternly.

"There must be some witnesses who saw something? What about all the people still there after we left the party?" I try to picture who was there and who might have been the Hitman.

"I've talked with his bodyguards. They were pretty sheepish as it seems they left him alone to get drunk with..." I hear Johnson flick through some paper work "'A well-built man with spiky, bleach-blonde hair who we thought was one of Danny's best mates.' Apparently he had arms full of tattoos."

"I remember the guy. I thought *he* was one of the bodyguards."

Is the spiky-haired, tattooed dude, the Hitman With No Name? Is he McNamara? I don't let my theory slip to Johnson.

"We can't find anything on the spiky-haired man, we've nothing on record that fits his description. It is possible he's the Hitman. Again there were no fingerprints or DNA prints left anywhere, and the only strand of bleached hair CSI found was so dead it wasn't any good to us either," says Johnson. "At least the strands of hair we found at Music:UK after the Kitty Bomb hangings were real. Although CSI traced the DNA profile back to Lucy-Ann Loftus, a woman from Alabama who'd been dead for five years."

Does that mean the Hitman's wigs are actually from the heads of dead Americans?

"The last the real bodyguards saw of him was with Danny Stone drinking Jack Daniels at the after-show party. Nobody saw him leave," says Johnson.

It sounds like the Hitman, disappearing into the background without trace, quietly marking another Hit off his Top 10.

"What about the Blackpool Tower security staff? Did they see anything?" I say.

"I spoke to head of security – a Mr Jon Peters – and he says they were reliably informed that Danny Stone was in safe hands with his own bodyguards at his after-show party," says Johnson. "I don't know what idiot told them that."

That would be me. I steer the conversation back around.

"Do his bodyguards remember seeing me and Sophie leave?"

"They confirmed they saw you both leave the party early on in the evening."

"So why are you giving me so much shit?" I shout. I see Jane stand up and look over from across the office, and sit back down.

"I need to check all possibilities. I needed to hear your story of events," he says.

"I think we both know I didn't kill Danny Stone, but it's bloody likely that the spiky-haired Hitman did. He's the one with a Top 10 Hit List," I say more quietly.

Johnson doesn't say anything.

"Hang on, I don't even know how he was killed anyway," I say.

"His body was found in his dressing room with an abnormal amount of alcohol in his system and a television smashed over his head."

"A television?" I say.

"A television," says Johnson. "With the amount of alcohol he had in his blood stream he was already dying, but the big blow to his skull and being electrocuted by the television killed him first."

"He was alive when he was battered with the telly?"

"We believe so, yes."

"That's rough," I say. '*TV kills TV star*' headlines flash through my mind.

"And you think the Hitman did this?"

"We believe so, yes."

"So why question me so much?"

"Because you're always bloody close by when there's been a murder, what else are we to think Matthews...?"

"That I'm innocent until proven guilty?"

Johnson doesn't say anything.

"How did he get in?" I'm more than a little annoyed he got in without us catching him.

"That is simple. Through the front door with a legit VIP ticket."

"Clever. Are the VIP tickets traceable?"

"I've got a detective sergeant looking at everyone who bought VIP tickets, but it's unlikely we'll find anything. He probably stole the tickets or something."

My question-asking nature keeps going. "Why are you calling me about this a week after the incident anyway?"

"The music industry and the media are already having a bloody field day, that's why. We have to be careful how we release the details. The Hitman is big news and the media will run and run with Top 10 Hit List stories. If we tell the nation another one's dead from his Hit List there will be mass panic. We're not telling the press and papers for another week, and have only just started telling a select few: that includes you." Johnson suddenly sounds all professional.

"You won't be able to keep it quiet for that long. What about Danny Stone's other shows or his PR and celebrity appointments?"

"We've cancelled the next few concerts and media commitments with his A&R agent saying that he's been suffering from a severe headache," says Johnson.

"It's almost true. You've just missed out the bit about the telly that caused the headache and that it was so severe he's now dead," I say.

"Excellent, thank you Matthews," says Johnson. "As before, if you print any of what we've talked about I'll shut down your publishing company quicker than you can say 'lawsuit'."

It's a big threat but that's all it is, a threat.

"So how are you going to catch the Hitman?" He needs a Top 10 Hit List like us.

He ignores my question. "Listen Matthews, I don't know what you and Sophie are up to...." Johnson trails off.

I realise how guilty we must seem and quickly gloss over it. "We both work in the pop industry. We go to gigs all the time. It's just a weird coincidence ," I say. I'm not about tell him about the H&S Detective Agency.

"Okay, but if you two are found near a crime scene again I'm going to arrest you myself and drag you both in for questioning."

I don't agree or disagree to back off.

"Are you sure you don't want to tell me anything before I hang up?" says Johnson, all softly-softly.

"What, like, tell you where to go?"

Johnson snaps. "Watch it, Matthews. I've had just about enough of the media. You're all giving us a kicking for not producing the Hitman out of thin air. I've had record label execs threatening legal action if we don't find a murderer overnight. Plus I've got Chief Superintendent Bishop breathing down my neck demanding results, and as long as he's on to me, I'll be on to you. If I find out you're hiding evidence or information, you and I are going to fall out."

I'd be scared if it wasn't for the fact my Dad used to threaten me like that when I was young and naughty. I smile and say, "Don't blame me because of Chief Super Ted and the TV and newspapers."

People always lump journalists together in one big dirty den. I'm always getting shit for what the papers or celebrity gossip mags have printed even though music magazine media is completely different. We don't go out to try and expose the police's or pop stars' shortcomings. It's just not our style. Although I'd be the first to sell a revealing story to the tabloids if I thought they'd pay for it.

"You're skating on very thin ice, Matthews."

Dad used to say that too. My smile turns into a grin. I think Johnson can tell. "I'm serious, Matthews," he says. "I'll come down on you like a ton of bricks."

And another classic Dad line.

"If I think of anything I'll call you," I say, doing my best not to call him Dad before I put the phone down.

I sit at my desk and stare at my screen but think about Danny Stone. Not how he was killed by a television, but how they'd found 'an abnormal amount of alcohol in his system'. My mind flicks back to my latest email from the Hitman.

Too bad our pop star singer Danny can't handle his drink.

It's a nice touch to let me know he killed Danny Stone. I wonder if the bleached hair and tattoos were real or a disguise?

I look over and see Gary, Robin and Jane still pouring over the cover design. They'll be there for hours tweaking headlines and images by miniscule increments. I don't bother them with information about Danny Stone's death for now, instead I pick up my iPod and mobile phone and slip off home.

I walk up Milsom Street. Apart from Waterstones, most of the shops are closed for the evening and the usual busy pavements are virtually empty, so I browse quietly in the window before remembering the pile of new books in my bedroom I'm still yet to read. Not that I want to buy what's on offer in the window today; it's all celebrity autobiographies from footballers' wives, girly pop acts, TV chefs and some bloke who was on a reality show for ten minutes once. They're all in their early twenties – surely they haven't lived enough to have anything interesting to say to fill a whole book? They just want to shout and remind us they're celebrities in case we've forgotten.

In the adjacent window are books with titles like *As I Watched Dazza Die On Stage* and *Our Sean: A Tribute To A Wicked Pop Star* and another by Hoodwink's manger simply called *We Were Hoodwinked*. Next to them is a book by the Hitman's wife called *So I Married A Hitman* and in the bottom corner is a small book snappily titled *Dealing With The Loss Of A Celebrity – 100 Ways To Help With Your Misguided Grief!*

I might've made up the last two.

I walk to George Street and head on up to The Circus. Not the sort with clowns and dancing bears, this is a circular street in Bath with huge, vastly overpriced Georgian houses. Badly dressed tourists stare in through the windows, and well-dressed businessmen and wealthy old women stare back out. In the middle is a large grassy circle with five enormous Chestnut trees. I sit on the lone bench that faces back towards the city centre as leafy branches sway above me. It's a warm, balmy evening which needs a breeze to take the edge off. A teenage girl drives past with both her windows down and her stereo turned up so loudly that unfortunately I'm able to hear Kitty Bomb blaring out. The girl's wearing a pink cap and singing along at the top of her voice. I guess you could call it grieving.

Once she's driven away I call Sophie's mobile while thinking how to tell her the news about Danny Stone and DCI Johnson's threats.

"Hello you," says Sophie as she answers her phone.

"Are you free Thursday night?" I say.

"Ooh, I don't know. Let me think," she says, pausing briefly. "Sure. Shall I come and stay? I could stay Friday night too, actually. I'm only working in Bristol on Friday morning. I've got to photograph the guilty coming out of the Crown Courts on Small Street."

"Great. I'm going to take you out for a nice meal. Bring something sexy to wear."

"Oooh, okay. That sounds exciting," she says. I picture her on the other end of the phone.

"See your pretty face tomorrow," I say.

"See you tomorrow cheeky chops," says Sophie.

"Oh, Sophie, I nearly forgot," I lie. "Danny Stone was killed after we left Blackpool Tower last week, and DCI Johnson will arrest us if we're found anywhere near a murder scene again."

"Y'what!?" screams Sophie.

"Right, best be going, I've got another call coming in," I lie, again. Twice in a row but they're only little white ones. "I'll speak to you tomorrow sweetheart."

"Hardy!?" she says as I hang up.

There, I think Sophie took the news rather well.

I've booked a table at Hudson on Walcot Street in Bath for a real meat-head meal of fine steak and finely cut chips. I'm smartly dressed in a black shirt and Sophie's all sexed up in a fitted, chocolate coloured dress. She's wearing her hair up with a few curly tendrils hanging down.

"You look bloody beautiful," I say.

"Thank you," she says, and reaches up on her tiptoes to kiss me warmly on the lips.

Before dinner I take us out for some cocktails at the Grappa bar. We find a table in the corner where the lighting is low. Conservatively dressed, middle class men and women sit around us. I'd rather be in a dirty pub but I think Sophie appreciates the gesture of going out somewhere nice. A Singapore Sling, some Sex On The Beach and a Long Island Iced Tea later and our senses are comfortably numb. It seems the ideal time to discuss matters of murder.

I tell Sophie all I know about Danny Stone, his alcohol levels and the TV, and that the Hitman was there all along. I tell her about his latest email, and what the bodyguards didn't see, and the threats Johnson laid down. She takes it well, although she orders another round of cocktails from a passing waitress to help swallow the facts.

"I can't believe we met the Hitman and let him slip away right under our bloody noses," says Sophie quietly. "You'd think we would've noticed a man with bleached-blonde hair and tattoos."

"We noticed him. I just thought he must've been one of Danny's bodyguards."

"Do you think it was McNamara then?"

I've been thinking about that. I think about little else these days.

"Yes, I think it was McNamara," I say. "If he's ex-army it's likely he'd have a few tattoos. And he was pretty well built."

"He had big arms, I remember noticing."

"Alright. So he's got some muscles. I thought he was kind of funny looking…"

"No need to get jealous, Hardy. Serial killers aren't my type."

Sophie slowly sips on her cocktail. She looks stunning in her dress. It's low cut, showing off a tasteful amount of cleavage. She tucks a few strands of black curly hair behind her ear. The low lighting shows off the shape of her cheekbones. She looks dreamy. Who wouldn't get jealous?

"You should take it as a compliment that I might get jealous sometimes," I say under my breath.

Sophie reassuringly strokes my hand on the table. A tanned man in a loud shirt is stood at the bar... I mean, a man in a tan shirt is talking loudly at the bar, and he's looking over at Sophie. She's oblivious but I give him the proud look men give each other when our women are being checked out. It says, *'I can see you looking. She's very pretty isn't she? Well back off, mate, she's mine.'* He gives me back the *'I wasn't really looking and I don't fancy her anyway'* look. Who says men can't communicate?

Sophie steers the conversation back to more important matters.

"So, McNamara is the Hitman," she says softly.

"McNamara," I say slowly. "The Hitman With No Name now has a name."

We let it hang in the air for a while. I shudder, but it could just be the taste of gin in the cocktail.

"So where does this leave the H&S Detective Agency?" she says, chewing on her straw.

"One step behind as usual," I say.

"Johnson's put us on a short leash as well."

"He can try. I say, let's ignore Johnson's threats. He's only stressed out and pissed off we've been getting closer to McNamara than he has. Let's trust in our Hit Lists. We've got to strike it lucky soon."

"Our Hit Lists!" says Sophie mockingly punching the air.

"Exactly. Let's beat him at his own game."

"How do you mean – start killing bands ourselves? I don't know if..."

"No. I didn't mean it like that. Let's catch the bastard in the act."

"Can we catch him *just before* the act? I'm not being girly, but I'm not a big fan of watching a man get killed to death by a television or seeing a man thrown off a balcony tied to a rocking chair."

"Good point. Let's catch the bastard right before he strikes next," I say.

I've no idea how you stop an ex-army killing machine from killing, but right now, full of cocktails, I'm almost looking forward to it.

We walk down to the Hudson for our feast of meat and luxurious wine. The Hudson is an upmarket bar and grill that was once the infamous Hat & Feather before it got taken over and given a makeover. The pub was all about hard drinking, scoring drugs, rubbing shoulders with Walcot Street's finest crusties, and listening to all sorts of random and brilliant music. The Hudson bar now attracts a more salubrious clientele who enjoy fancy cocktails and the hush-hush tones of live jazz in swanky surroundings downstairs, and expensive but excellent steak dinners upstairs. I preferred the Hat & Feather pub crowd, but I'm a sucker for top steak, and as Sophie and I walk in I get the impression she's happy we're here.

We avoid the offer of more cocktails at the bar and take our table upstairs. I browse the menu and feel sorry for my paltry journalist's salary. Then I remember I've still got a good wadge in the bank thanks to the generous cut from what Sophie made on her front page photos of Dazza. The show back in Cardiff seems like a lifetime ago. Time flies when you're having fun. We go wild and order the best wine we can buy, the first time I've ever ordered from the bottom of a wine menu, and choose two suitably extravagant steaks, medium rare.

"God damn! That is some mighty fine wine," I say after taking a big sip.

"You funny boy," says Sophie smiling.

"What? It is fine wine," I say taking a smaller sip.

"To the H&S Detective Agency and our next move," I say, toasting Sophie. We clink wine glasses.

"At least our next move is easy," says Sophie. She pulls out a crumpled bit of paper from her handbag. "This time we go with *my* culprit at No.4 on *my* Hit List."

"But…"

"No buts," she snaps.

"I was going to say, I thought we should go with your Hit List choice this time anyway."

"Did you now?"

"Yes, I did. Honestly. I even checked tour details online earlier. He's playing football stadiums at the moment."

"They're big venues aren't they?"

"They are if you're the main attraction. He's more like the main distraction – he's singing before kick off. It's common practice when blooding new singers these days."

"What an apt phrase."

"Indeed. They shove the fresh meat out in front of a big crowd of football fans who couldn't care less who's singing – they're there for football – and see if they perform well or get eaten alive. If they can handle that, they'll go down even better when they sing in front of a crowd who's paid to see them."

"It toughens them up then," says Sophie.

"Exactly," I say. "Although your man seems to have pretty thick skin already. I remember a performance on *Pop Factory* when he tried to sing a Duran Duran number and it went down very badly. The judges really got stuck into him, but he couldn't've cared less. He didn't seem to take in what the judges said about his singing, or notice the terrible reaction from the crowd. He was wrapped up in his own little celebrity dream world."

"Which is why he was so stunned when he didn't win."

"Even though everybody else saw it coming weeks before," I say.

"So where's he playing?"

"In London before the Arsenal and Tottenham games pretty soon, but he'll be playing before a Friday night Liverpool game in month or so."

"Our man McNamara lives near Liverpool doesn't he?"

"We don't know that for sure. Fat Pat said his last known address was near there but he could live in Scotland for all we know."

"What? And commute down here for a spot of serial killing before retiring to his country retreat in The Highlands? Hardly, Hardy," says Sophie, laughing at her own little joke. "I think he's still living around middle England. I've got a gut feeling. Let's go to the Liverpool game next month and stop McNamara knocking off my man at No.4 and get that big scoop we keep dreaming about."

I simply say, "Okay."

After we've devoured a juicy chunk of cow each, Sophie and I share some sweet, delicately-made pavlova. We have a long spoon each and take our time enjoying every mouthful.

"My ex-boyfriend wouldn't let me eat dessert." Sophie says suddenly, playing with the edge of the pavlova with her spoon.

Where did that come from? She's never mentioned her ex before. I don't know what to say, so I say nothing.

"He didn't let me do a lot of things," she says softly. "That's why I like you, Hardy. You let me be myself."

"I wouldn't want you to be anyone else," I say.

She smiles and her eyes go a little watery. Happy tears.

"I wouldn't want you to be Ann Widdecombe, for instance."

Sophie laughs and a happy tear rolls down one of her glowing cheeks. She picks off a piece of pavlova, letting it melt on her tongue, and looks me straight in the eye.

"What?" I say.

"Nothing," she says.

"Go on."

"I was just thinking how handsome you look tonight. You've shaved, you smell nice, and you look really good in your black shirt."

"Cheers," I say. I'm trying to keep cool but the sexy girl in front of me paying me compliments is making it hard. Don't be rude. When I say hard, I mean difficult. Not that I was getting a massive erection. Honestly, grow up!

Sophie looks down at the pavlova, then looks up.

"I've fallen for you, Hardy Matthews," says Sophie.

She smiles but hides her shyness behind her curly locks.

"I think I love you."

She says it softly, and I can tell it's from the heart. She looks up at me with the sweetest expectant look in her eyes.

But I'm dumbstruck.

For once I'm lost for words. Actually, I know the words, I just can't find them to say them back to her. I've fallen for you too. I love you too. There they are. That's all I have to say. Come on, just say it. Sophie looks at me, waiting for a response. She takes a sip of her wine.

I've fallen for you too.

She looks away and hides her blushes behind her curls.

I love you too.

The waitress appears at our table, and cuts through the tension by saying, "Here's your bill." She puts the bill down on a saucer with some gold covered chocolate mints and some hot flannels. I grab one of the flannels and hide my face and shame.

I love you too.

That's all I have to say. I'm not even saying it first. She the one who's been brave enough to bare her feelings. How hard can it be? She loves me. Just bloody say it.

I love you too.

But instead I say, "I'll get this. My treat. For a very special woman."

Sophie smiles and says, "Thank you." But it's obvious she doesn't care I'm paying, she just needs some indication that I feel the same way about her.

I love you too.

I pay on my credit card and leave the waitress a tip in the saucer.

On the pavement outside I put my arm around her shoulder but she doesn't cuddle in close like she normally does. We don't say anything as we start walking home. Well, I start walking.

"Let's get a taxi," says Sophie.

"You want to get a taxi?" I say

"Yeah, it's miles to walk home."

"A mile. It's one mile. It'd be quicker to walk it." I'm always astounded how lazy women are when it comes to walking.

"I spent all afternoon walking around the shops before buying these strappy shoes to look nice for you," she says, showing off a pair of pointy little things barely covering the bottom of her feet.

"So you're happy to walk around the shops all afternoon, but you won't walk ten minutes home now?"

"Don't be silly. I can't walk in these shoes!" she says.

"But they're shoes! What are they for, standing in?"

Sophie ignores me and flags a passing taxi down. The driver pulls the car into the kerb immediately. They never pull over that quickly for me. She wobbles a bit in her heels and falls into the back of the car. I reluctantly follow. Barely a minute later we're back at my flat.

"That'll be £4.80," says the taxi driver.

"You'll be paying the man, then, sweet cakes," I say as I climb out of the taxi.

We ignore each other indoors. I go and lie on the bed with my shoes still on. Sophie takes her heels off and uses the bathroom. After she's finished we swap places. When I get back to the bedroom the main light is off and Sophie's tucked up in bed with her back towards me. I can only see her mane of dark hair tucked around her neck. I get undressed and slide under the duvet. I lie on my back and wait for Sophie to roll over and lay her head on my chest like she normally does. She doesn't roll over.

I love you too.

I want to tell her how I feel but something's stopping me. I think about rolling over and spooning her, but instead I switch off the bedside light and lie on my side with my back to her. Why can't I just say it? Why did I have to be such a twat about getting a taxi home? I was just angry with myself for not having the guts to say what I really feel. What's wrong with me?

Before I drift off to sleep, Sophie rolls over and slides across, pushing her body next to mine. I can feel her soft breasts on my back and her freezing feet on my legs.

"It's just because I'm cold," she says.

I love you too.

*   *

Being a professional footballer is a lot like being a rock star. Both get paid vast amounts of money to perform to thousands of adoring fans and they only have to play for around 90 minutes once or twice week. Both have pretty blondes hanging off them, both love scoring (goals/ drugs) and both can be self-absorbed and intellectually challenged. They both get away with having ridiculous haircuts, both are interested in their positions (in league tables/pop charts) and both have that dual attraction that makes men want to be them and women want to be with them.

This is what you're thinking about as you flick the long, blonde hair off your face and drive towards Anfield in a red Lotus Elise. You're wearing your long-sleeved Liverpool replica shirt, a pair of smart Armani jeans, your lucky Liverpool football socks and smart

Puma trainers. You've had the professionally-produced wig on since mid-afternoon. You like being in character from start to finish. You were wearing the whole getup earlier when you picked up the Lotus from the sports car hire centre using a fake driver's licence and fake credit card. Your mission is proving pricy at times but your army savings are still going strong and you're not about to cut corners and jeopardise your Top 10 Hits.

You've got your football boots in a boot bag on the passenger seat and a big kit bag with towels, toiletries as well a spare pair of jeans, a T-shirt and trainers to change into if necessary. A suit, shirt and tie are lying on the back seat, a pair of black leather shoes sit behind your chair. It's just gone 8pm.

You timed your arrival for just after the evening game had started. You waited in the car in the darkness around the corner until you heard the cheers from the crowd as Liverpool kicked off, before you pulled up to the security gate outside the VIP car park, revving the Lotus's engine. A red-faced, ginger-haired security guard looks your way but is obviously more interested in watching the game on the portable TV you can see just inside his little office. He pokes his head out with one eye still on the TV as you hear the crowd cheer in the stadium illuminated by towering floodlights only 100 metres away.

You push a button and the electric windows slide down. Flicking your floppy hair about, you put on a Danish accent a bit thick and confidently say, "I am, how you say in Britain, better never than late?"

Act like you belong and nobody will question you.

He looks at you in your Liverpool shirt, looks at the car, and looks at the suit on the back seat and boots on the passenger seat inside.

"I have boots all clean, ready for when I go to pitch at half-time for penalty shootout challenge," you say proudly, in broken English with a Danish accent, enthusiastically patting the boots bag next to you.

"Ticket and ID please," he says looking back at his portable TV.

You hand him your real VIP ticket you'd bought on eBay – posting cash to the seller – and your fake ID.

"I'm Magnus Brock, Marketing Manager from Carlsberg in Copenhagen," you say. "We sponsor the Liverpool."

"Oh, yes, right Mr Brock. You don't have to explain," says the security guard as he looks at your ID and quickly hands it back with your ticket. "The game's already kicked off. You'd better get a bloody shift on."

He presses a button to lift the security barrier and you say, "Thank you, yes, my friend."

You rev the engine a little more than necessary, driving quickly without wheel spinning into the car park, and stop abruptly without skidding like how you imagine a Danish man would drive. You switch the lights off and notice you're sandwiched in between a Jaguar and BMW. You can smell the wealth of Anfield's richest. In the rear view mirror you see the ginger security guard shaking his head at you. You grab the boots and kit bag and walk past the door marked 'Strictly Players Only' and in through the VIP entrance. You quickly look back to see the security guard returning to his TV.

You show your ticket and ID to the young, blonde haired man behind the counter at the VIP entrance. You spot a CCTV camera in the corner of the ceiling. This will be part of the challenge of slipping in and out of a Premiership football club. You're looking forward to outsmarting their so-called all-seeing eyes. The young man slides back your ticket and ID across the counter and waves you through.

You walk along the brightly lit corridor and resist the urge to go upstairs and join your fellow Danish work colleagues in the VIP box for the first half, instead making your way to the main seating area via a series of corridors and stairs behind the stands.

You know where No.4 on your Hit List will be sitting. You've already spoken to his manager, Richard Long, who's sitting with him and expecting you. He was only too happy to meet you when you mentioned the idea of Hit No.4 singing a new Carlsberg ad campaign jingle when you'd called. You walk up the stairs past the empty bars and head towards the cheering fans and floodlights. You show the thuggish security guard your VIP ticket and he waves you through turning his attention back to the game without even checking your bags.

The Kop is, and always has been, an impressive stadium and it seems to get better and better every year. You walk out between the rows and rows of fans in red with scarves and flags and hats, and breathe in the evening atmosphere. It's so loud and masculine and intimidating. You feel completely at home. You'd love to watch Gerrard and the mighty Liverpool knock three goals past the cockneys and mockneys of Chelsea, perhaps have a punch up with the away fans afterwards, but today you've got a job to do. You walk down to the row you're after and spot a man in a suit on the end with an empty seat next to him.

"Richard?" you ask in your Danish drawl as you reach him.

"Magnus, great to meet you."

He stands up, grabbing and pumping your hand like you're his long lost cousin.

"Sit down mate!" says a fan sat behind him. Richard sits back down, you squat down beside him, still clutching your boots and sports bags.

"Where is Mr Jimmy?" you say.

Richard rolls his eyes and says, "You've just missed him. He said he's gone to freshen up in the VIP area. He's not really a football fan I'm afraid, but he is a fan of Carlsberg. He always drinks it. Yeah, he loves Carlsberg our Jimmy. He loves singing too."

"I'm sure he does," you say. "I go find Mr Jimmy and drop these down there as well I think," you indicate towards your bags.

"I'll come with…"

You politely interrupt. "This is okay. You wait here and enjoy game. We, how you say, catch up at half the time."

"Okay, magic. See you in a bit Magnus," he says. The crowd start cheering. You look down to the pitch to see a long cross into the Chelsea area get snatched out of the air by their keeper before a Liverpool player gets a head or boot on the ball. The home fans shout and jeer. You reluctantly leave your team to battle on and walk back out to the VIP area.

You retrace your steps back down and walk along a red carpeted, white walled corridor dropping down some stairs to the VIP toilets. You notice a small sign for the players' changing rooms off to your right. You've always wanted to have a look. You've got a minute before you find your target, checking nobody's around, you slip inside the door marked 'Home Team'.

It's empty. Everyone from players and subs to managers and backroom staff are all on the pitch or pitch-side. The changing room floors are pristine white apart from the odd bit of mud left behind from football boots. It smells of muscle rub and deodorants. You quickly toss a white towel from a bench over a CCTV camera high up on the wall. You relax and have a look around the changing rooms where many a living legend has pulled on their boots then played their hearts out for Liverpool FC.

Suddenly you hear someone… and they're whistling. You walk towards them, towards the toilet area: there's no separate door just doors on the WCs. You edge silently, cautiously, to look around the corner and see the back of a man. He's whistling while he washes his hands. You recognise the tune. The man's whistling his latest single, the one he's probably just performed. He looks overly tanned, he's wearing a light blue shirt, black trousers and his hair looks like it's been blow dried and covered in hair spray.

Jimmy Fink.

You can't believe your luck. He probably thinks the players' changing rooms are part of the VIP area. He's obviously not a football fan if he's down here mid-game, but you're glad you didn't have to track him down at half-time and drag him off somewhere quiet. You put your bags down gently and quietly walk towards the pop star-shaped carrot dangling before you.

*   *

Football's a funny old game. It can be the most scintillating sport known to man, and it can be the most boring. Today, sadly, we're watching the latter. Under the dazzling floodlights, Liverpool are trying but failing to break Chelsea's defensive line and after 20 minutes of the first half we've not seen one shot on goal.

"Is it always this exciting?" says Sophie, tugging on my arm. She's got her red cap on and is wearing a tight, long sleeved red shirt, and her trusty Diesel jeans. She looks sexy cool. A camera with a modest sized lens and flash hangs around her neck.

"No. Sometimes it can take until the 90th minute before someone scores," I say.

"Fab," she says flatly, holding both thumbs up.

We're sat under the floodlights for a Friday evening game. Sat on Sophie's left are three chubby Liverpool fans dressed in identical red outfits. They've all got scarves around their necks, even though this September evening is warm enough for T-shirts, and all three are wearing bright red trainers. Two of them stare at Sophie then focus back on the game.

"Anyway, what are you worried about? I thought you were happy keeping an eye on your Hit No.4." I say. "That was the deal. I look this way at the football and you look back behind us to check Jimmy Fink's okay."

"He's not budged since he sat down after that embarrassing pre-match singing. God, you think he would've improved since we saw him support West Side. His voice has actually got worse," she says stroppily. "He's got his mate-turned-manager with him anyway. And he's boring and not very attractive to look at. There are lots of fit thighs to look at down there." Sophie hints towards the pitch.

There's a cheer from the Liverpool fans as a winger skins a Chelsea player and dribbles close to the sideline. With the ball, not out of his mouth. The ref blows for a throw in and a round of 'Who's the wanker in the black?' starts up. I join in, and Sophie frowns.

We're sat middle left, midway up. We needed to be high up so we can casually look back on Jimmy Fink as well as watch the game. I turn around and lean back in my seat to check on him. There's an empty seat next to Jimmy's manager-mate.

"Sophie, he's not there."

"What?"

"I thought you were keeping an eye on him?"

She looks back with me at the empty seat.

"He was there two minutes ago."

"Well, he's not bloody there now," I snap.

"Oh dear," she says coyly.

I grab my backpack, grab Sophie by the hand and lead us past the rows of fans. We squeeze past most but stand on the toes of a fair few. We get a couple of "Watch its!" and one "Twats!" shouted at us to send us on our way.

"Where are we going?" says Sophie trying to keep up with me, holding on to her camera.

"Wherever Jimmy's gone," I say as I march down the steps. "I reckon he's gone to buy a drink."

"Well, I'm sure he'll be fine then," she says as I pull her down the steps with me.

"Not if McNamara's buying," I say.

*   *

"Jimmy Fink. A chancer if I ever met one," you say, leaving Magnus and his Danish accent outside.

"You what?" he says looking at your reflection in the mirror above the basins. He doesn't bother turning around or seem that worried you've caught him in the players' changing rooms.

"Listen mate, I'll be straight with you. I'm here to kill you because you're a talent show reject who should never've taken up singing. You've been hurting my ears for months so I'm gonna kill you before things go too far with your farce of a pop career."

"You what, mate?" he says turning off the taps and shaking the water off his hands.

"I'm here to kill you because you're a talent show reject who should never've taken up singing," you repeat.

"You're a killer? Good one. You're a football fan, mate," he says.

"It's my disguise," you say tapping the side of your head. "Do you like it? I think I look fantastic. This hair's not mine, you know." You tuck a few blonde strands behind your ears.

"So you're going to kill me?" he says drying his hands with a paper towel and smirking.

"That's it. You're gradually picking this up," you say all chirpy. He begins to look uneasy. Your bubbly demeanour is clearly unnerving him.

"Is this some kind of joke?" he laughs.

"No. I take my music very seriously."

"C'mon, where are the cameras?" says Jimmy looking around the walls and ceilings. "Who do you work for BBC, ITV... MTV?"

You shake your head and stare at him without saying anything. You can tell by the shifty look in his eyes he thinks you're a mentalist. After a while he quietly says, "You don't work for any of them do you?"

You shake your head and continue staring at him.

"I've got to get back to my seat. My manager will be worried about me," he says as he looks at the silver watch on his wrist. He makes for the door.

"I've already told Richard we'd catch up with him at half-time," you say quickly, and move to block his way to the exit.

"How do you know his name?" he says.

He stops. He looks perturbed.

"I know everything," you say as you walk towards him.

"Who are you?" he says.

"I'm the band manager to die for," you say proudly.

"I've already got a manager thanks," he says eying up the door.

You reach down, without taking your eyes off him, and subtly pick up your boot bag from the bench.

"I would love to stay and chat, but I really should get back to Richard," he says, making for the exit.

You grip your boot bag tightly in your right hand. There's a loud cheer outside that catches Jimmy's attention just he tries to dodge past you and reach the door. You swing your boot bag around swiftly on its cord and catch him on the side of his head, knocking him towards the benches.

"What's going on..." He pushes himself back up and rubs his head. You move in closer and Jimmy suddenly swings his fists at you. You dip out of the way and get your own back by thumping him repeatedly around the head with your boot bag, making sure the studs make contact.

Jimmy puts his hands and arms up to protect his face.

"Stop... please... stop..."

*   *

We dash down underneath the stands and jog towards the bars and toilets. I readjust my trainers from slipping off my feet. One day I'll grow up and tie the laces properly. I can see four bars, two either side of us, all are deserted except for a couple of Chelsea fans drinking lager out of plastic bottles at the first bar to our right. Both of them are bald, about five-feet tall and in their mid-fifties.

"No Jimmy," I say, "and looking at them, I'm pretty sure no McNamara either."

"Where then?" says Sophie.

"The pissers," I say.

I run into the first toilet and check the urinals and cubicles. Empty. I run out and in to the next. A lone Liverpool fan is taking a leak. He's short, skinny and probably just taking his GCSEs. No McNamara. I check the cubicles. And no Jimmy. I run out and look around as Sophie stares at me. She looks concerned. I dash to the only other toilet on our level and our side of the pitch. My heart's pumping and I don't think it's because I've been running.

I've got a bad feeling about this.

I barge through the door and find a line of empty urinals. I check the cubicles. The first one's empty, the second one's empty, but the third's engaged.

I knock on the door and shout, "Jimmy is that you in there?"

"No it bloody isn't. It's Dave," says a rough old voice, "and he's having a shit."

I picture an old man in his sixties, and don't want to picture anything else.

"Sorry," I say.

"Piss off and leave me in peace."

I walk back out and I'm greeted by Sophie's worried face.

"Anything?" she says.

"Nothing," I say.

"Bollocks. Where then?"

"The VIP area."

*   *

You stop hitting Jimmy and drop your boot bag on to the tiled floor.

"Now do you think I mean business?" you say coldly.

"Yes, Jesus, yes," says Jimmy nervously as he slowly pushes himself up off the bench. A trickle of blood runs down his forehead.

"Now we both know there's no point shouting for help as the crowds will only drown you out. Don't try and go for the door again otherwise I'll give you a kicking with the boots on my feet next time," you say staring at him.

"Who do you work for? Who sent you?"

"Nobody. I work alone. I'm killing people like you for the greater good of the music industry."

"But... What? But? But why me?" he stutters and rubs his head.

"Because you have no musical talent."

"But I can sing. You just heard me."

Jimmy rubs his head. When he removes his hand more blood runs down his face.

"I know. It was awful. You must've paid *them* to sing here," you say. You didn't need to hear him to know he was terrible.

"But I was on *Pop Factory*," he says meekly.

"But you didn't win. You came third," you say, "and that bimbo who came second and the pretty boy who won it weren't much better."

"I was robbed. I deserved to win," he says softly.

"The judges didn't think so. I tend to agree."

You walk over to one of the large players' baths and turn on the hot and cold taps. You're wearing 'liquid skin' again so you won't be leaving any prints. Jimmy's not paying attention, he's too stunned to notice or move. You spot another camera and throw a towel up over that one as well, although you can guarantee security are too busy watching the fans on CCTV to bother with the changing rooms.

"Well, I showed everyone by releasing an album," he says, still rubbing his head.

"I've seen it in bargain bins in Woolworth's already."

"I've got a new single out."

"And it's still well outside the top 20," you say.

"I supported West Side," he says.

"Dazza thought you were so shocking he electrocuted himself on stage," you laugh.

Jimmy looks at you but doesn't laugh along.

"Look, I'll make it real simple for you. I'll prove you have no talent."

"Try me."

"Did you write any of the songs on your album?"

"Well, er..."

"Yes or no?"

"I co-wrote..."

"Yes or no."

"No," Jimmy hangs his head down on to his chest.

"Did you write any of the lyrics?"

"They do that for me."

"No, then."

"Can you play a musical instrument?"

"I've bought a piano."

"But can you play it?" you say as you look over to the bath. It's nearly half full.

"I like to sit in front of it."

"Don't take the piss. Can you play it, yes or no?"

"No," he says quietly.

"Can you read music?"

"No," he says quietly.

"There. That's proof you have no talent," you say, "and you didn't win *Pop Factory*."

"So?" says Jimmy staring into the distance.

"You're nothing but a glorified karaoke singer."

"I love karaoke. I've won loads of karaoke competition finals, and I can sing loads of songs, without looking at the screen and everything."

You pick up the boots and give him two quick lashes, around the face this time.

"No, please, no more..." he says. He holds his nose as blood starts dripping on to the tiled floor. You drop the boot bag and stare at him. He looks every inch the prepubescent pop twat.

"I've never told anyone this, but since I've been trying to break into the pop industry, I've always felt like I'm at a party full of adults, and I'm the odd kid in the corner," he says.

A cheer goes up outside on the pitch. Why aren't there any windows? You could see if Liverpool have just scored. Although windows would mean people could see in, and you don't think they'd like to see what's about to happen.

"That's because you don't belong in the pop industry," you say. You hope the immature little prick doesn't continue with this confessional.

"I know, I know..." He stares at the blood dripping onto the floor. The bath is three quarters full now. You leave the taps running.

"I've thought about killing myself, you know."

"That's the spirit," you say.

"But I could never do it," he says, quickly looking at you, shaking his head.

"That's okay. I can help you out."

"I only ever wanted to be famous," he says, staring blankly at the blank wall.

"That's the great thing. This way you'll be more than famous," you say. "You'll be dead famous."

You could just knock him out, but it's much more fun watching the human spirit drain out of him in his punch drunk state.

"Dead famous," he says, trying it out for size. "I like the sound of being dead famous."

Jimmy has no idea what it really means to be dead famous. But you encourage him nevertheless. "Good, I can sort that out for you."

The clock on the wall tells you there are fourteen minutes to go before half-time. You check your watch. It says the same time. You'd better get on with it.

"I'll help you. Come on, let's get this over with," you say in a soothing voice.

You grip his shoulder and point him towards the bath.

"Come on Jimmy."

He's so dazed he doesn't even bother to resist.

*　　*

We both run down the stairs and along the corridors until we reach a security guard outside the door leading to the VIP area. He's short and has a large chubby face.

"Tickets?"

"We're press," I show my NUJ card and so does Sophie.

"I really need your tickets as well," he says.

"We just need to pee," says Sophie smiling.

"Go on then," he says smiling back and enjoying having the authority to allow us to go to the toilet.

"Cheers," we both say.

The large VIP room has red carpet on the floor, player's photos line the otherwise white walls, and apart from a few grey-haired old boys drinking bitter and watching the match through the large windows, it's empty. I dash towards the gents.

Thirty seconds later I'm back outside to find Sophie stood outside the ladies.

"Anyone?" she says.

"No Jimmy. No one," I say.

"Oh God. Where is he?"

I think for a second. I don't need long sometimes.

"The players' changing rooms," I say. "He might've gone down there thinking he's too famous to piss with the public. It's the equivalent of a pop star's dressing room."

*　　*

"This is going to hurt me more than it's going to hurt you." You've always wanted to say that but never had the chance.

Jimmy hasn't said anything since you put him in front of the bath.

"I've run a bath ready for you." You turn the taps off. It's the perfect depth with the water level just a couple of inches below the overflow.

"I like baths," he says hypnotically. His eyes are glazed over.

"Good, good. In you get then."

Jimmy squats down near the edge of the bath. You can see blood matted in his hair.

"It feels nice and warm," you say squatting beside him and swishing your hand around in the water.

Without allowing Jimmy to get undressed or even slip off his shoes, you push him head first into the bath. The water soaks his blue shirt turning it almost black as it clings to his body. He tries to stand up and starts shouting, wiping the water out of his eyes. You kneel down by the side of the bath and grapple his neck firmly with both hands and push his head under the water. His legs kick the water up and his hands start flailing as he tries to grab the sides of the bath. You shuffle along on your knees and roll him over so he's facing down, moving your grip around so you're still holding the back of his neck firmly with your thumbs and gripping his throat with your fingers. Jimmy splashes water over you and the sides of the bath as he struggles against you. His fake tans starts rubbing off his neck and face and it turns the water a muddy brown.

You squeeze his soft throat in your hands and force the life out of him. Jimmy doesn't resist for very long. You feel his body go limp and give in, his neck goes floppy and his arms drop down by his sides.

A huge cheer erupts from fans outside. Even down here it sounds deafening. You wonder if Liverpool's scored.

You really feel you're helping Jimmy Fink. Putting him out of his music career misery. You push his head down until it hits the bottom of the tiled bath, getting your upper arms and shirt sleeves wet in the process. You watch as the last of the bubbles from his mouth rise up to the surface and burst, one by one.

*   *

I grab Sophie by the hand and we run towards the players' changing rooms. As we leg it towards the changing room door we get a glimpse of part of the pitch from the players' tunnel. Chelsea are attacking but a Liverpool defender hacks their striker to the ground. The home crowd cheer. The referee runs over and hands the defender a yellow card. The crowd boos.

I briefly think about all the great players who've run out on to the pitch at Anfield. Kenny Dalglish, Ian Rush, and then there's that other Liverpool player... the one who scored all those goals. I've never been one to remember names.

We walk quickly to the door marked 'Home Team'.

Sophie and I look at each other. She looks scared.

"Here goes nothing," I say.

I open the door and we walk inside. I can hear what sounds like someone splashing around in water. We follow the noise around the corner to find a blonde-haired man in a Liverpool shirt kneeling down next to a big bath. He's got his hands gripped around a man's neck and is forcing him under the water as he vainly thrashes around. I don't think he's being given swimming lessons.

We stand silently glued to the spot. The man underwater is still fully clothed. I recognise the blue shirt. I know who was wearing a shirt like that earlier.

Jimmy Fink.

The strangler might have long, blonde hair, but it's obvious who he is. The bit of murdering he's doing is a slight giveaway.

The Hitman.

*   *

You hold Jimmy Fink's head under for another few seconds then release your grip from his neck. His body floats face down, lifelessly, in the bath. The fake tan has rubbed off on to your hands. You lean over and feel for a pulse on his neck. You don't find one.

Jimmy Fink, once deluded, and now dead.

You stand up and turn around to find a man and woman looking at you. Make that a shocked-looking man and woman. You know the man with slouching shoulders and a pack on his back, and you'd recognise the woman anywhere with her red cap and camera around her neck.

Hardy and Sophie.

"McNamara," says Hardy.

How does he know your name?

Sophie looks ready to scream but nothing comes out. She puts both her hands over her mouth anyway. Hardy's eyes dart from you to Jimmy and back to you.

He knows your name.

It stuns you for a split second but you don't let it show. You are genuinely pleased to see them. Although you're not going to have time for pleasantries today.

"Hello you two. Fancy seeing you here," you say warmly. "I wondered when we'd meet again."

"I could be wrong, McNamara, but I think it's traditional for men to normally *sing* not *sink* in the team bath," says Hardy looking over at Jimmy.

"Young Jimmy Fink had already done enough singing for one lifetime."

So now he knows your name. Your brain starts racing. You're sure you didn't let anything slip out when you were in Blackpool. Of course you didn't. Did you leave something in your emails?

"And they usually take their clothes off," says Hardy, making a move towards Jimmy's body in the bath.

"I knew you'd be a smart arse, Hardy," you say, quickly adding, "Don't bother trying to resuscitate him. You won't be able to breathe any life back into him now."

"Are w-w-we t-too late? Is Jimm-my... dead?" asks Sophie while looking at Jimmy's floating body. Her voice sounds high pitched like a little girl's and she's shaking like a shitting dog.

"You could say you're a bit late," you say cheerfully.

"You've got a w-w-warped sense of humour," says Sophie with a hand over her mouth.

"I've got a great sense of humour. Haven't you been following my little pop project? I've injected humour everywhere I go." You look at her camera and hope she doesn't take your picture as your mind continues doing overtime. Now you remember. Your last email. The Man With No Name. You used to sign off with it back in The Good, The Bad, and The Ugly days. Hardy could've linked them together and traced your name from there. Brainy little bastard.

"Everywhere you go you've injected death," says Hardy.

"Well, injecting humour, injecting death – they're two sides of the same coin."

Your brain keeps racing. You're only chatting to distract them. So they've come to your door. That's okay. They're not going to stop you. He's only a journalist and she's only a photographer.

"I've often thought the music scene needed to be flushed free of all the shitty singers and crap bands..." says Hardy looking straight at you.

"Exactly!" you say interrupting him. "Everyone shouts at the TV or radio saying 'God I hate this band' or 'I wish this band would piss off and die'. Well, that's where I come in. I'm doing everyone a favour."

"...but there are other ways of making a point without Top 10 Hit Lists and serial killing," says Hardy. He seems to be gritting his teeth.

"I thought you two were on my wavelength," you say.

You look at the clock behind them. Better get a move on.

Hardy looks over at Jimmy's motionless body floating on the surface.

"Jimmy Fink had it coming," you say. "Y'know, he actually wanted to die. In the end he didn't even put up a fight."

As if the word triggers something primal inside Hardy, he lunges himself at you.

The problem with people who don't know how to fight is their poor weight distribution. Someone can have all the anger and strength in the world, but if it's misdirected it doesn't count for shit. You sidestep Hardy easily. As he glides past, off balance, you punch him on the back of the head just for the hell of it. He tumbles forward and his face crunches into the tiled wall before he's able to put out a hand. You hear the home fans start to sing outside. Sophie screams but doesn't move. Hardy turns around and fixes his eyes on you.

"Great! I haven't had a good scrap in ages," you say. You rub your hands together.

"Me neither," says Hardy as he wipes some blood from his mouth on to the back of his hand.

Hardy comes at you again, this time more guarded. He feigns with his left fist and manages to give you a glancing blow to the side of the head with his right. The boy's got guts, you'll give him that. But you scarcely feel it and quickly retaliate. You keep a solid stance, tuck the hair out of your eyes, and shuffle towards him. You crack him on the nose with a hard right jab, following through by fully extending your arm. His head reels backwards. While he's off balance, you follow it up with a fast upper cut to the chin. You punch him so hard his whole body lifts off the ground, bizarrely leaving his trainers behind. A good old-fashioned punch on the chin gets them every time – it forces the jaw to stun the brain into shutting down. Hardy lands flat on his back with a thump, right alongside Jimmy still taking a bath. Hardy doesn't budge. He looks funny as he's still got his backpack on. You knew a journalist wouldn't be able to stop you.

"Oh my God. Oh my God. What have you done?" screams Sophie.

"He started it," you laugh.

"Oh my God. Oh my God," she screams. Sophie puts her hands over her mouth and stays rooted to the spot.

You stand over Hardy. His eyes are half closed as he fights to stay conscious.

"I could kill you easily but it's your lucky day: you're not on my Hit List. Instead I'm going to take Sophie hostage to stop you interfering anymore. If you so much as fart in my direction, I'll kill her. If I see Johnson and his merry men anywhere near me, I'll kill her. If you mention anything in the press about me, I'll kill her. You tell no one I was here and you tell no one that I've taken her. Nobody's going to stop me reaching my No.1. The fun's over. Stay out of my way, Hardy, you're way out of your league."

Hardy groans, lifts his head slightly, but it's too much for the lad. It drops back to the floor, his eyes close, and he promptly passes out.

You hear a cheer from the crowd. You turn your attention to Sophie. She's not moved, her hands are still cupped over her mouth. You're not sure if she heard what you just said or not.

"What have you done to Hardy?" Sophie runs over to crouch besides him.

"He's just unconscious."

"You're an animal," Sophie hisses. She looks up at you, at Hardy's body, and at Jimmy's.

"Why thank you," you say.

You stare at her. "The first time we met it was a coincidence, but a second time... well, that's a mistake."

"I knew you'd be here today to kill Jimmy Fink. I know how you think," says Sophie. She stands and squares up to you. Her camera's hanging around her neck but she's taking the weight of it in her hand.

"I doubt that very much," you say. You look at the clock. One minute to go to half-time. "Now, I'm on a bit of schedule so shall we make this quick?"

"Make what quick?" she says. "Taking your photo?"

She holds her camera up in both hands and you hear the shutter clicking several times. You leap towards her and grab her right wrist with your left: she lowers her camera down, and you punch her square on the chin with your right. Her eyes roll back inside their sockets and her body wilts. Two for the price of one. She falls backwards but you've still got hold of her wrist. You pull her towards you, bend down, and lift her on to your shoulder in one movement. You can hear the whistle go and a cheer outside on the pitch. Half-time. You've only got seconds to get out before the players come in. You run towards the door, snatch it open, and run down the corridor with Sophie on your shoulder, holding her camera in your hand. Just as you make it safely around the corner you hear the 'clackity clack' of football boots on the tiled floor.

You run out of the 'Strictly Players Only' door and close it behind you. You look around. The car park is empty as streetlights show off the shiny paintwork of the expensive cars. You spot the CCTV camera pointing in the other direction and quickly shuffle over to the Elise. You press the button on your Lotus keyring, flip open the boot and roll Sophie off your shoulder and inside. As you tuck her legs neatly inside, you notice a phone shaped bulge in her back pocket. You slide her mobile out, switch if off, and close the boot.

You look around again. Not even the ginger-haired security guard is in his little office. What's the catch? There is no catch. You're just a Danish Marketing Manager about to drive home. You're just a little early to be leaving the game... No, you're beating the rush! You jump in the driver's seat, start the engine and drive off. You swiftly drive up to the barrier and it automatically rises to let you out. You stroke some blonde hair out of your face.

The roads are deserted, everyone's either at the game or watching it on TV. You jump a couple of red lights just because you can, and to get as far away from Anfield as quickly as possible.

When driving along the Mersey you wind your window down and, checking nobody is behind you or on the street watching, you sling Sophie's camera into the drink. You see the tell tale splash of white water pop up as you look over your shoulder.

You're annoyed. Your plan wasn't to leave Jimmy Fink's body behind, let alone in the players' bath. You hope the Liverpool boys and The Kop can forgive you. Kidnapping the photographer was never part of your plan either. You're no good at kidnapping. You're only good at killing.

*   *

What's that noise? It sounds like a herd of cattle tap dancing and breathing heavily from above. Only the cows are talking to me. They're calling me "mate".

"Hey, mate, are you alright, like?"

I never knew cows could talk.

I know I'm lying down on my back, but I'm not sure why. My back feels cold and wet. The floor feels hard.

"Hey, mate, are you alright, like?" says one of the cows.

"Yeah, I'm fine, my mooing mate."

"Open your eyes then."

I open my eyes, smiling, expecting to see a herd of friendly cows stood above me. Instead I'm surrounded by the entire Liverpool team staring down with bright fluorescent lights glaring from above. Some faces look concerned, some look scared, and some are angry. How long have I been out?

"You're not cows," I say. I feel my jaw ache as I talk.

"'Course we're not fooking cows," says one of the confused-looking players. Why wouldn't he be? There's a strange man lying on his changing room floor at half-time... Is it still half-time?

Dozens of football boots clatter around on the tiled floor. A few footballers are still staring at me but most are steering clear. I recognise a few of the faces. Some of them play for England, one or two play for France, or Spain, I can't remember, but they definitely look familiar. They seem to be gathered around one of the baths next to me. I try and sit up but my head's throbbing so much it feels like it's full of water.

Water.

Jimmy Fink.

I look over and see Jimmy Fink's dead body still floating in the bath next to me.

Where's Sophie?

Where's McNamara the Hitman?

I quickly look around and in-between the players, but it's obvious McNamara's disappeared, and true to his word, he's taken Sophie with him.

My Sophie.

I didn't get to tell her I love her.

The twisted, twisted bastard better not lay any one of his fat fingers on her. My mouth goes dry as I picture him with her.

I try to get up but my head starts spinning so I flop back down on the floor. The Liverpool players, managers and coaches look at Jimmy's body but try not look at the same time. They don't know what to do. Neither do I. My chin and jaw are throbbing. I clench my teeth together and pain shoots from my jaw up to my ears. I look down at my feet and can only see my socks. I spot my trainers across the other side of the changing room. How did they get there? Or how did I end up here? What happened?

The Hitman happened.

I can see now that the H&S Detective Agency was hopelessly unprepared. We hadn't really thought this through had we, Sophie? It was all meant to be a bit of fun to get the big exclusive. I figured we'd photograph McNamara in the act, and I'd somehow overpower the SAS hard man-cum-serial killer, or he'd give up easily or something, then we'd call the cops and they'd take him away. But this ain't no TV detective show.

"Alright boys, alright, out of the way. Make some room for the police please boys," says a voice from behind the footballers. "Where are they?"

Speak of the devils. A familiar face pushes through the players and stands above me. DCI Johnson. He's flanked by three armed, uniformed PCs in bullet-proof vests, and two plain-clothed detectives. Johnson looks at me, looks across at Jimmy in the bath, then back at me. One of the detectives, wearing rubber gloves, turns Jimmy's body over so he's facing up. His eyes are open but lifeless. His face looks very pale. The detective lifts one of his arms up and feels for a pulse on his wrist.

"He's dead, sir."

"Well I didn't think he was just taking a bath, Detective Sergeant Denning."

The players and managers gasp as uniformed PCs usher them away from the baths and out the door. Johnson puts his hands on his hips and looks down. He shakes his head, and says, "I warned you, Matthews."

"You're too late, Johnson…"

"I know we're too late to stop you killing Jimmy Fink, but I always knew we'd catch you," he says, putting one foot up on a bench.

"Me killing? Catch me!? But…" then I remember what McNamara said before I passed out. I can't let him hurt Sophie. I can't run the risk of telling the police. I keep quiet.

"Hardy Matthews, I'm placing you under arrest on the suspicion of murdering Jimmy Fink. You do not have to say anything…"

Oh bollocks.

No. 3

You can't always get what you want, but sometimes,
you just might find, you get what you need
The Rolling Stones

I really enjoy interviews. I've done hundreds as a journalist. I've asked pop's biggest players all sorts of questions in all sorts of places. I enjoy the whole process. Especially the revealing answers I've received after probing yet another self-absorbed pop celebrity.

But not since I've been on *TOP 10 HITS* mag have the tables been turned.

I'm sat in a medium-sized interview room at Bridewell Police Station in the centre of Bristol very late on Friday night. Two plain-clothed detective sergeants are sat across from me, and I'm beginning to feel more than a little nervous. Sweat's starting to drip down my back and it's not just because it's a warm night. Perhaps it's my usual suspicious reaction to the police that's making me feel the heat.

Who am I trying to fool? I'm feeling totally on edge because I've been arrested for a murder I didn't commit, and because Sophie has been kidnapped by the Hitman and I don't know what to do about it other than say nothing for the sake of her safety.

I'm not the only one keeping quiet. The detective sergeants haven't said anything since they came in and sat down. They're men in their late twenties, one's well built, the other's more lithe. Both have that hooded, unfriendly look in their eyes. We're waiting for DCI Johnson. We're back in Bristol because that's where Johnson's based, and he's still heading up the Hitman investigation, even though he's just arrested the wrong man.

At least the handcuffs I was forced to wear in the back of the cop car all the way down here have been taken off. I massage my wrists where they were rubbing too tightly. I stroke my jaw. It still feels bloody tender. Exactly how hard did McNamara punch me?

I notice my hands shaking. I've not stopped trembling since I saw Jimmy Fink's dead body in Liverpool barely four hours ago, and my head's still not right after McNamara knocked me into next week, but it all seems irrelevant because beautiful Sophie's been kidnapped. I want to think about her, but I have a panic attack every time images of McNamara and Sophie swim around my mind, and I think of what he might be doing to her. I try to think of nice things, but that's hard when I know McNamara's idea of doing something nice with someone is to drown them. I keep picturing Jimmy Fink's body in the bath full of water. Thinking about water makes my mouth go dry.

I keep trying to tell myself I've no reason to be nervous. I may have been arrested and I may be sat in a police interview room, but I'm not guilty. I'm not a killer. But Johnson doesn't know that, and I can't tell him either. God knows I want to tell him. I want to tell him everything as soon as he walks in so he can go and catch McNamara and save Sophie. Then he can let me go and Sophie and I can go home and look after each other and nurse my bruises. Perhaps we'll cry as we cuddle, I'll run her a deep bath and get in with her, and afterwards I'll open a bottle of wine and cook her a nice meal, and when the timing is right I will tell her that I love her.

How did we end up apart and in such a mess?

It's all because we got greedy. We wanted to bag the biggest exclusive of our lives to make a pot of money.

I can't tell Johnson about that either.

Greed is not good. I've always known this. So why did I not realise that before blindly leading us into the hands of a killing machine like McNamara? We're lucky to still be alive.

That's if Sophie *is* still alive.

I try and picture her pretty smile, but McNamara appears and wipes it from her face.

My mouth feels so dry. I can't seem to swallow. I wish Johnson would hurry up. I don't know how long I can keep this brave face on and bottle up the biggest disaster of my sad, stupid life. I wish my foot would stop tapping, and why won't my hands stop shaking? I put my hands in my lap under the table and will them to keep still, just as Johnson finally marches in.

"Hardy Matthews," he says.

"Johnson, dear chap. Milk and one sugar, thank you."

Johnson ignores my sarcastic request. He sits down opposite me so we both have a sergeant each side of our table. I've got the well-built DS Cheadle on my side so if it boils down to a fist fight I think we could take him and Denning. Johnson opens up a box file full of paperwork and reports. As he flicks through I see some of the reports are headed up with the name HOLMES. It's good to see Sherlock's still in action. No wonder they're arresting the wrong people and letting a Hitman roam free if they've got a fictional detective in charge. I look closer and can make out Home Office Large Major Enquiry System on the reports. Yellow Post It notes with handwritten remarks on them are stuck to a couple of HOLMES reports, but I can't read the writing.

"Hardy Matthews," says Johnson, rearranging the reports. "Chief Superintendent Bishop himself wanted to interview you. You wouldn't like to be interviewed by our Chief. He'd scalp you. But, you're lucky. I said I'd deal with you."

The sergeants both smile to each other. I don't feel very lucky.

Johnson presses record on a large double-tape deck sat on the table. It looks like the sort of machine I had in my bedroom when I was fifteen.

"Friday..." Johnson looks at his watch. "Saturday the 13th of September at 12:37am. For the purpose of this interview, Detective Sergeants Cheadle and Denning will be present, and we shall record all conversations in their entirety on this tape recorder."

I pull my Dictaphone from my pocket and put it on the table. It's the only possession I was allowed to keep as my backpack and laptop, keys, mobile, wallet, coins and chewing gum were taken off me when I was searched and checked in. They also took a mug shot and blood sample, I had to rub a swab inside my mouth to give them a DNA sample, and remove my shoes.

"Don't mind if I record this interview as well do you?" I smile. "Journalist's habit."

Johnson glares at me, but I know he can't do a damn thing about it. I can legally record the interview as well if I want.

"Right, Matthews..."

"Please, call me Mr Matthews," I say. I know that if I'm going to get through this I'm going to have to get cocky to hide my anxieties. They say that arrogance is a form of shyness. Right now I'm going to have to start acting like one of the biggest arrogant pricks in Britain. I picture Danny Stone and think of what he'd be saying if he were still alive.

Johnson ignores me again and says, "Where were you on the afternoon of Wednesday 26th of March? The afternoon when Darren Cox from West Side was electrocuted on stage in Cardiff?" Johnson says and looks me in the eye.

Hit No.10.

"I was in the press area with all the other journalists and photographers," I say. My hands are still shaking in my lap.

"Were you with anyone specific?"

"At the time of his death I was with Sophie Cooper, a freelance photographer. She does lots of photos for *TOP 10 HITS*."

"Okay. We'll come back to Ms Sophie Cooper later."

My foot starts tapping again. I picture Sophie's face and can hear her laughing in my head. I hope she's laughing wherever she is. I hope she's laughing her head off. I hope she still has her head. As long as I don't tell on McNamara he won't hurt her.

"Where were you on the afternoon of Saturday 29th of March when the three members of Hoodwink were murdered in Abbey Road Studios?"

Hit No.9.

"In the Pulteney Arms in Bath with my mates Richie and JP."

"JP?" asks Johnson.

"John Paul. Not the dead Pope, my friend is called John Paul. John's spelt J-O-H-N."

"Excellent, excellent."

"Johnson, you've got the wrong man. I didn't or haven't killed anyone. Surely my nonexistent criminal record gives you an idea what sort of man I am. I'm not a murderer," I say.

"We'll be the judge of that," says Johnson. "Where were you on the evening of Monday 31st of March when Sean Bates was pushed off a 12th floor balcony at The Royal Hotel in London?"

Hit No.8. How could I forget?

"On an eighth floor balcony in the same hotel. Sophie and I saw him drop by as we were having a drink," I say. "That was the first time we met."

"We? You and Sophie?" says Johnson.

Me and Sophie. Will there ever be a me and Sophie again? Or will there just be me, and Sophie in a coffin at her funeral? I didn't even get to say I love her.

Focus, Hardy, focus. I will see her again. I hope I will.

I *know* I will. Focus, focus. I will not break in front of Johnson for Sophie's sake.

"No. Me and you, Johnson," I say.

"Yes, yes. I remember," he mumbles.

"So you'll remember what my alibi was that night won't you."

"We have to go over everything again Matthews," says Johnson.

"How exciting," I say, deadpan.

"Where were you on the afternoon of Saturday 26th of April when MC Spin and DJ Rock accidentally shot each other on the Respect Enough Crew music video shoot in Sutton Coldfield?"

"You mean MC Rock and DJ Spin from the Nuff Respect Crew…" I say.

The poor wiggas of Hit No.7.

Johnson stares at me. I don't think he appreciates the correction. He makes a note on his report.

"Where were you that afternoon Matthews?"

I picture the afternoon and evening of Strip Scrabble and Naked Knockout Ginger and give Johnson an edited version.

"I was with Sophie at my flat in Bath. We cooked a meal and played a few games of Scrabble. We had a couple of glasses of wine and an early night."

I think of her half dressed and how much she laughed as I ran naked into the street that night. McNamara better not be undressing her. Not even mentally. If he so much as looks at her body I will find him and I will rip his eyes out and stamp on them.

Focus, focus.

"Excellent. And where were you on the morning of Saturday 7th of June when the three members of Kitty Bomb were hung on stage in the Music:UK studio in London?"

The girl band at Hit No.6.

"You know where, but for the benefit of the tape recorder and your two sergeants, Sophie and I were in the C4 Pop It! studio."

"Just down the road from the Music:UK studio?"

"Yes."

"Excellent. And where were you on the evening of Saturday 19th of July when Danny Stone was killed at Blackpool Tower?

Hit No.5.

"In a hotel with Sophie."

"And where was the hotel?" Johnson smiles. He already knows the answer.

"Blackpool."

"And had you been to see Danny Stone at Blackpool Tower?"

"Yes."

Johnson waits for me to expand on my answer. I don't.

"Excellent," he says.

"And, now bringing us up to date on the pop star murders. Where were you when Jimmy Fink was drowned earlier today... last night... in the Liverpool players' changing rooms at Anfield football stadium?"

Hit No.4 in a bath tub.

Have seven pop acts really been murdered?

"We were at Anfield. But Jimmy Fink was dead when we reached the changing rooms."

"So how did you end up in the changing rooms, Matthews?" says Johnson.

We went there to catch the Hitman in action to nail the biggest scoop of our careers and make a bundle off the world's press.

My mouth dries up and my foot starts tapping under the table as my mind accelerates. I feel dizzy. I hold on to the table which at least hides my shaking hands.

When did I become Mr Greedy? Is that what all this whole shit storm is really about, bloody money?

Blood money.

I think I might be sick in my lap. Focus, focus.

"We ran down to the changing rooms because we thought Jimmy Fink's life was in danger. We were trying to warn him he could be on the Hitman's Hit List."

"How could you possibly know that?" says Johnson shifting about in his seat.

I think of McNamara and his emails and his Hit List, and mine and Sophie's Hit Lists.

"We had a hunch he might be on the Hit List," I say.

"I'd've put Jimmy Fink on my Hit List," says DS Cheadle out of the blue. It's the first time I've heard him speak. He has a soft Bristolian accent. "The wife liked him but I couldn't stand him. He was rubbish on *Pop Factory*. I sing better than him at our annual Christmas Karaoke parties..."

"He is quite good believe it or not," says DS Denning, pointing to DS Cheadle.

"Yes, thank you both for your valuable contributions, Sergeant Detectives Morecambe & Wise," says Johnson, practically snorting out of his nose. They stop and stare at the table and Johnson continues the interrogation. "So you thought you'd drown Jimmy Fink and make out he was the Hitman's next target. Yes?"

"No. We didn't drown him. I didn't drown him. He was dead when we arrived. I wouldn't know how to drown somebody," I say acting dumb and innocent. "Don't you need to submerge the whole body or something?"

"You only need a teaspoon of water to drown," says DS Denning. I think I see some steam come out of Johnson's nostrils.

"Surely you need at least a *tablespoon* of water? So you can take a proper dive into it," I say.

"No, you only need a teaspoon of water to drown, because drowning is simply choking on water," says DS Denning proudly. We all look at Denning and then look at the tape recorder. Johnson gives him a look that says 'Pipe up again like that and you'll be back on the beat quicker than you can say *The Bill*'.

Johnson stares at me intensely. "So, you're telling us, you and Sophie walked into the changing rooms and found Jimmy Fink's body already floating in the bath."

"Exactly. He was already dead. We were too late."

"And there was no sign of the Hitman?"

"No sign at all," I say.

"So how were you knocked unconscious?"

"I slipped on the wet tiles and landed on my head," I say. I rub my chin and jawbone without thinking about it. I quickly add, "I landed face down, but on my head."

The sergeants look at me. Johnson looks at me.

"You slipped backwards but landed on your face?" says Johnson.

"I slipped, yes."

Johnson pauses and checks his notes. He exchanges a glance with the sergeants and takes a moment.

"You were in the vicinity for five out of seven the Hit List killings. That's more than a coincidence isn't it?"

"We work in the pop industry. We go to lots of pop concerts. It's not a coincidence. It's our job."

"You keep referring to 'we'. We meaning, you and Sophie Cooper. And where is Sophie now?"

Where is Sophie now? Wouldn't I like to know.

She's with mad-man McNamara and they could be half a world away by now.

One half of me is screaming to tell them, so they could attempt to track down and catch McNamara and save Sophie and put an end to all these Top 10 Hits. But my other half is repeating what he said to me when I was half conscious.

"If I see Johnson anywhere near me, I'll kill her... You tell no one I was here and you tell no one that I've taken her..."

Sweat continues to run down my back.

"Where is Sophie now," repeats Johnson.

I quietly say, "I don't know."

"You don't know?"

"I don't know," I say. "She freaked out when she saw Jimmy's body and ran away. It's not everyday you see a dead body is it? I went to have a closer look, but slipped and knocked myself out. When I came around she was gone, the changing room was full of Liverpool players, and then you showed up."

"Have you heard from Sophie?" I ask hopefully.

I know I'm clutching at straws.

"No we haven't," says Johnson.

He looks at me and I see a flicker of sympathy in his eyes. Johnson quickly covers it up by rubbing his forehead and frowning at me. But he manages to say, "You might like to know that we've got two squad cars doing the rounds near Anfield and the pubs in Liverpool for her, but they haven't found anything yet. A squad car checked her Bristol address before I came in here but she hasn't been back home."

"Are you sure you don't know where she is?" he says.

Tell them, they can help.

I can't. I can't risk her life.

"I wish I did," I say. I take a deep breath and concentrate on staying calm. I put my hands back in my lap.

"How do we know you're not covering for her and she's actually the murderer in all this?" says Johnson. His eyes are bulging in their sockets.

She's not a murderer. She could be *being* murdered right now.

Focus. I remember what Sophie said back when we were staying at The Royal.

"Women wouldn't murder pop stars like this," I say. "They wouldn't have the strength to throw them off balconies and drown them for starters."

"How do we know you didn't kill Sophie and stash her body somewhere?"

Don't talk about Sophie like that. If he wasn't flanked by two sergeants I swear I'd knock his ruddy block off. I take another deep breath and don't answer. It's the first time I haven't answered one of his questions. He makes a note of it and then thumbs through his pile of HOLMES paperwork.

"Can I say something?" I say.

Three pairs of eyes tell me to do otherwise, but that only encourages me to say my piece. I compose myself and lean in a little closer to the tape recorder.

"I would like to state for the record that I did not kill Dazza from West Side. I did not kill the three members of Hoodwink. I did not kill Sean Bates. I did not put real bullets in the guns that killed MC Rock and DJ Spin. I did not hang Kitty Bomb. I did not kill Danny Stone with alcohol and a TV. I did not drown Jimmy Fink, and I certainly did not kill Sophie Cooper." I pause briefly and take a deep breath. "I think we all know that you should be looking for a professional Hitman with tattoos and a Top 10 Hit List. I'd appreciate it if you'd stop taking your frustrations out on me just because he's not been leaving any clues behind for you lot."

"Excellent. Thank you, Matthews," says Johnson smiling through gritted teeth.

He stares across at a blank wall for a full minute. The sergeants fold their arms. I look at a poster on the other wall that says 'The Police Are Your Friends'.

"Let's say you're not guilty. So who is the Hitman with the Top 10 Hit List?"

"I don't know," I say. "Isn't that your job?"

"Are you sure you don't know?"

McNamara you bastard.

"Yes, I'm sure," I say, and stare at the table.

There's another moment of silence, then Johnson says, "It's late. That's enough for now." He looks at the clock above the tape recorder. "Interview terminated at 1:48am on Saturday the 13th of September." Johnson switches the tape recorder off.

"You'd better be telling the bloody truth, Matthews, for all our sakes. I don't bloody trust you. You're not telling us everything. Take him to his cell but don't give him any supper," says Johnson. No supper? Who is he, my Dad?

I nearly stomp my feet and say 'That's so unfair'. But instead I say, "I am not a liar DCI Johnson," and hold up my Dictaphone that's still recording. Johnson clocks it and his cheeks turn red. The sergeants don't say anything as they lead me to my budget accommodation for the night.

I feel battered and exhausted as I look around the basic jail cell. Single bed, thin mattress, flat pillow, one white sheet and one grey blanket. A dim light is recessed into the ceiling. And that's it. No table, no chairs, no basin, no toilet, no porn mags, no books and no Sky TV. No spoons and soft walls to dig my way out like the escapees from Alcatraz. No laptop or mobile phone either. Along with my other worldly possessions, they have been locked safely away.

After a light supper of tea and a biscuit, I get to make my one telephone call from the cell phone in the corridor. Not cell as in cellular telephone, cell as in the communal police cell phone. A uniformed officer stands nearby as I try Sophie's mobile number. It goes straight to her answer phone. Her recorded message is short and sweet but it's so good to hear her voice. So good that I find myself choking back tears.

I will not break down in front of the police.

I want to hear her voice message again but it will only remind me she's not here with me, she's somewhere else with McNamara.

I hang up and saunter slowly back to my cell and the officer locks the door behind me. I sit on the bed with my back against the wall and think of Elvis and his Jailhouse Rock. The last thing I feel like doing is rocking and rolling around this jailhouse. I want to be out. I want to be free. I want Sophie.

The sound of the officer's footsteps fade as he walks down the stone corridor, and then my brave face dissolves and I start blubbing like a big girl. I drop my head on to my knees to hide my face as tears run and run.

I don't think I've been this upset since Robbie left Take That.

At some point in the night I stretch out on the single bed and try to get some rest. I attempt to think about something other than McNamara pulling Sophie's teeth out with a pair of pliers.

I wake up early on Saturday morning with sunshine streaming through a small window with bars in front of the glass. It's light and hot in the jail cell. Typical that I get arrested when it's warm and sunny outside. I feel starving yet sick to my stomach. I think I drifted off for half an hour in the night, but I mostly tossed and turned, thinking about Sophie, and going over my story in my head again and again.

My head aches and my mouth still feels dry as toast when I'm summoned to the interview room at 9:15am. The two sergeants are there waiting with Johnson. He goes over exactly the same questions, but in so much detail I think my brain's going to make a run for it by creeping through my body and crawling out my arse. For Sophie, and my arse's sake, I stay strong and focused. I'm so frazzled I'm amazed I'm able to remember everything I said late last night, but somehow I keep it together to repeat my story without slipping up on any of Johnson's banana skin questions.

I ask if there's been any word on Sophie in Liverpool or Bristol but Johnson just shakes his head. I picture her body floating along the Mersey and have to stay focused to stop tears from welling up.

We have a quick break and the DS's and Johnson slip outside to inhale their cigarette smoke in the fresh air. I have the luxury of being confined to my cell. Jail food is less exciting than it sounds but I greedily gobble down the odd combination of a toasted chicken sandwich and orange juice. My hollow stomach still feels empty afterwards and it's all I can do to stop myself from chucking up.

The morning's interrogation continues with Johnson trying a more aggressive approach while DS Cheadle and Denning, and I, look on.

"You must have insider knowledge. You were there for Dazza's death. How could you know Sean Bates was at The Royal? And you were there for Danny Stone's murder and Jimmy Fink's drowning. You're not telling us all you know, Matthews." Johnson stands up with his fists resting on the table. He's virtually spitting in my face. The baddest bad-ass cop routine. By now I'm too knackered to be tense.

"I've told you everything I know, why would I want to hold anything back...?"

There's a knock at the door and in walks a plain-clothed policeman who I assume is another detective. He looks young enough to still be getting pocket money off his parents.

"Sir, can I have a word?"

Johnson walks to the door but keeps it open so I overhear the underage detective say, "A sports bag and a pair of football boots were found in the changing rooms at Anfield last night."

"And!?" says Johnson, obviously annoyed he's been interrupted. "Isn't that normal for a football club changing room?"

"Nobody at Liverpool FC claimed the bag or any of its contents, sir. We think they were part of the murderer's disguise, sir. We think he left them behind in a rush to escape."

"I don't like you lot thinking too much. I do the thinking," Johnson says.

"I just spoke to the security guard who was working on the VIP gate yesterday. He remembers a blonde-haired Danish man from Carlsberg driving into the car park in a Lotus Elise just after the game kicked off," says the young detective. "Sir, the security guard said he had football boots and a sports bag with him."

"Carlsberg? Danish?" says Johnson.

"Liverpool's main sponsor, sir," shouts Cheadle from his seat next to me.

"Maybe the kit bag and football boots were part of Matthews' disguise?" he says turning around and glaring at me.

"Sir, the football boots we've found are size 13."

Johnson spins around and both he and the youthful detective, and Cheadle and Denning, look down at my feet. I pull them out from under the table so everyone can have a good look. They still haven't given me back my shoes in case I beat myself to death with them so everyone's now looking at a pair of faded black socks.

"What shoe size do you take, Matthews?"

"Size nine, Johnson," I say smugly in my best 'told you I wasn't guilty' voice.

Johnson glares at the detective and says, "It's not conclusive evidence that Matthews didn't…"

"Sir, the boot bag had traces of blood on the outside," says the detective. "We believe it was the weapon used to beat Jimmy Fink."

"Whose blood is on it?"

"It doesn't match Matthews' blood sample," says the detective. "As we thought, sir, it matches Fink's."

"What about Matthews' DNA on the boots or bags?" asks Johnson.

"We've had it checked and only Fink's DNA showed up. There were no traces of Matthews' DNA of any of it."

That one little sentence hangs in the air and for the first time in two days I begin to smile. From where I'm sitting I watch as Johnson's neck changes from pink to red to purple.

"In fact, nobody else's DNA showed up in the tests."

"Nobody else's DNA? Are we to suppose Fink beat himself with the boots!?"

"The Hitman never leaves any indication of his DNA behind at the scene, sir..."

"Thank you sergeant. That will be all for now."

Johnson closes the door firmly and slowly walks back over to the table. "Interview terminated on Saturday the 13th of September at 11:13am." He stops the tape player recording. I've still got my Dictaphone recording on the table.

"Matthews, in light of the recent evidence, you're free to go... for now."

"Excellent," I say.

For the first time Denning and Cheadle let out a wry smile.

"Like Danny Stone's death, we'll be keeping Jimmy Fink's out of the press for as long as possible. They're like wolves baying for more blood out there. I'm beginning to think the media actually want more celebrity murders. Meanwhile I'm getting pressure from the music industry and band managers who want the killer's head served up on a bloody silver plate..." says Johnson drifting off. He snaps back to reality and points a finger at me. "So keep your mouth shut, Matthews."

"I can't stand media types, don't worry," I say.

"Detective Sergeant Denning, please sign Matthews out."

I stand up and head for the door. Before I leave I have to ask.

"What was the score?"

"Eh?"

"The football score. Did the game continue, did Liverpool win?"

Johnson ignores me, but Cheadle seems very keen to talk. "The Liverpool players had to go back out there – everyone would've gone nuts and wanted to know why we'd cancelled the match..."

"And we weren't about to announce Jimmy Fink's death live on Sky Sports," says Denning.

"Exactly. So, Liverpool were one-nil up at halftime, but with the players' minds obviously elsewhere, Chelsea came out and scored two easy goals," says Cheadle, getting animated. "Amazingly Liverpool managed to dig deep to get one back then Gerrard scored a blinder with two minutes to go to win it 3-2. Get in!"

Johnson gives us all a look that could turn meeker men to stone. "Get out of my sight, all three of you," he says.

We walk away and I have to stop myself jumping with delight. Not because I'm a Liverpool fan, but because I've escaped. DS Denning signs me out, I get my shoes, backpack and other possessions returned, and walk free.

Outside Bristol's city centre cop shop, the late summer sun is pouring down on hordes of shoppers taking advantage of the weekend and the warmer weather. I walk off in the direction of Bristol's harbourside without a clue what do with myself. Every step I take I feel the relief of escaping Johnson's grasp. But it only takes a few strides before my attention switches to Sophie.

Beautiful Sophie.

Is she still alive...?

I try calling her mobile but get her answer phone message again. I listen to her voice and it makes me feel more helpless.

I walk and walk, not really knowing where I'm going. I walk around in circles until I end up at the Old Duke on King Street. It's a pub that plays live jazz and blues and its drinkers happily spill out on to cobbled streets and pub benches across the road from the dockside. I buy two pints of Guinness and some crisps and find a bench in the sun, away from other early birds nursing their drinks. It's only half past mid-day. I sup steadily on the first pint. I'm in no mood for necking it quickly. I stare into space.

As my empty glass is taken away by the barman I start on the second. It's then, as I'm relaxing, that my guard comes crashing down all around me. I've had it up all morning, but now I'm melting as my emotions bubble up inside.

Tears start trickling down my cheeks. I don't bother to wipe them away. I look at the empty seat opposite me and realise I've never felt so alone in my life.

Where are you Sophie?

I'm going through the biggest crisis of my life and I can't tell a damn soul about it. Even Fat Pat's out of circulation as he's in the States working and will be asleep because of the time difference.

A kind looking, round-faced woman in her mid-40s is sat on a bench next to me. Her blonde hair is held up with a few black clips and she's smoking a roll up.

"Are you okay?" she says, smiling politely.

"Yeah."

"You're not convincing anyone. Are you sure you're okay?"

"No, not really," I say. Her kindness sets me off again and fresh tears fall down my face.

"It's usually only girl trouble that drives a grown man to tears," she says.

"It's girl trouble alright," I say.

"Would you like to talk about it?"

I would love to. But I can't. I just can't. Can I? I look at her round face and figure, what the hell, I'll try my luck.

"My girlfriend has been kidnapped by a serial killer and I can't

217

call the cops otherwise he will kill her. I don't know where she is and I don't know what to do."

It feels so strange to say it all out loud. I let out a half-hearted smile as I wipe some tears from my cheeks.

The round faced woman looks at me for a while, then smiles. "Good one. You nearly had me. Kidnapped indeed. What's really the matter? Been dumped?"

I look at her kind expression and realise there's no point persisting with the truth. It's easier to lie. "Yeah, sorry, was trying to be funny. I've just broken up with my girlfriend. I've only known her a six months, but I felt like I'd known her forever."

"Did you love her?" she says.

Two tears start to run, one falls on to my lips. It tastes salty.

"Yes," I say softly. "But I never got to tell her."

*   *

You wouldn't say you feel sorry for Sophie but you admit kidnapping wasn't on your agenda. But that's life. You make plans and things change. It's how you adapt that's important. You've adapted by taking on the psychotic torturer role like a natural. Even if, bizarrely, you have Monty Python's *Always Look On The Bright Side Of Life* playing continuously in your head. There are worse songs to be humming when you're about to torture someone, you suppose.

You've been remembering the stories from soldiers after they'd been tortured by the Iraq lot and wondering if you'll have to step up your technique and what household implements you could use.

You slap Sophie around the face. It's an open handed slap. You've been aiming at her pretty left cheek for the past ten minutes. It's gone red but there's no blood just yet. You think about slapping her right cheek but you've never been very good with your left hand when it comes to violence. Your left hand is your creative hand. The one you used to pluck and strum your guitar strings when you were still playing.

It's 1:17pm on the day after you drowned Jimmy Fink and you're in the dining room of your flat. You've zip-tied Sophie's wrists behind her back and zip-tied them to a dining room chair. You've tied her legs together and tied them to the chair legs. You've let her keep her clothes on, but you've taken the cap off her head. You've kept your blonde haired wig glued on. It adds to the 'Evil Danish' character.

"I've already told you," says Sophie angrily.

"I can slap you around all day, darling," you say.

Sophie looks at you like you're an annoying bit of dog shit on her shoe. You're impressed that this posh piece of totty hasn't

218

cracked yet. After a shaky start in the changing rooms yesterday she seems to have found a new resolve today. Must be bred from good, strong stock.

"Come on, let's make this easy for both of us then this will all be over."

"I've already told you. It was just potluck. We thought Danny Stone might be on your Hit List and out of all his concerts we decided to go to Blackpool Tower."

"Sophie, darling, I'm just not buying this pot luck thing," you say. You're not. You think she and Hardy have somehow worked out who's on your Hit List.

"It's the truth," she says, staring at the floor.

"How did you know I was going to be at Anfield to meet young Jimmy Fink?"

Sophie doesn't say anything. She just looks at the floor. Last night you left her tied to the chair to get an uncomfortable night's sleep. You're hoping it's worn her down and that she'll soon reveal the truth.

"Tell you what. Why don't you tell me who's next on my Hit List?" you say.

"Who's going to be Hit No.3?" says Sophie quietly.

"Yes, tell me who it's going to be."

"Candi & Carmel?" says Sophie quietly.

"Speak up girl," you say.

You heard, you just want her to say it again.

"Candi & Carmel?" says Sophie a little louder. "It's who we thought you might have next on your Hit List."

"The pretty vacant twin act from Lancashire?"

"Yes," says Sophie.

That's not a bad shout. Candi & Carmel had been on your initial Hit List funnily enough but they didn't make it on to your short list. Not because you like them, you hate them alright, you just hate other pop bands more.

"Okay," you say, "I'll be honest with you. They're not on my shopping list."

Sophie stares at you. You're not sure if she's surprised Candi & Carmel aren't next or not. Perhaps she really doesn't know who's on your Hit List.

"I just want you to be honest with me. I'm all about honesty," you say.

"I've already told you what I know, ram rod."

"Ram rod? That's not very nice."

You slap her hard across her right cheek, drawing a little blood from her top lip. She licks it off, and gives you her best dirty look.

"Come now Sophie, just tell me what you know."

"I've bloody well told you a hundred bloody times already. We just got lucky. We thought about who you were likely to hit next and bloody went to their next show."

You remember something your captain said when you were on a reconnaissance mission in Belfast. You were there to rescue a female hostage. Actually, maybe it wasn't your captain. Maybe the kidnapper said it when you'd rescued the hostage from him, just before you cracked his skull with the butt of your rifle. Anyway, one of them said...

"Like children and dogs, women need boundaries."

Sophie doesn't say anything. Perhaps she agrees. Although her look of contempt says otherwise.

"Women need boundaries. If you don't have boundaries you run loose like a dog. Barking at everything, eating anything, shagging anything. You need to know who's in charge otherwise you don't know how far you can push your luck. In this instance, I'm in charge. I'm The Boss."

"Like Bruce Springsteen, only uglier?"

"Play nicely now, doggy, otherwise I'll put your collar on and lock you in your kennel," you say. "I'm The Boss, and I set the boundaries. And if you know where the boundaries are then you'll be happy."

"I don't feel so happy right now, to be honest."

"And are you honest?" you say.

"Yes, McNamara. Yes I bloody am."

You have a thought. What if she's telling the truth? She looks completely bushed and must be too tired to lie by now. Maybe Hardy and her did just show up in Blackpool and Anfield by chance. "Are you telling the truth? Was it really pot luck you and Hardy found me at Anfield?"

"Yeeeeees."

"Swear."

"Big fucking dog's cock."

"No," you laugh. "Do you swear?"

"I swear."

"I'm not getting it," you say. "Do you swear on Hardy's life?"

"I swear... on Hardy's life... that I'm telling the truth."

"Okay. No more slapping," you say. You're still not sure whether to believe it was potluck that brought them to your missions, but for now, it'll have to do. "However if I find out you're lying to me, Sophie darling, you'll get more than a slap. And lover boy Hardy 'n' all."

At least the kidnapping hasn't been a total waste of time. By keeping Sophie here you're controlling Hardy again. So what if he's stopped acting as your publicity agent, and tried to put an end to your little pop project, he won't be getting too involved and trying to stop you anymore. He won't dare shop you to the police either. So what if he knows your name, that's all he knows. There's no way he'll predict your next hits now. Even if eventually he breaks and lets your name slip, the police won't find you here. You're living under a false name and none of your neighbours know you.

But you're prepared even if the police do show. You've already put plans in place and lined up your next hits, your last three, only two steps away from Hit No.1.

You cut the zip ties on Sophie's wrists and legs with a pair of pliers and stand back from the chair to give her some space.

"Come on, Sophie, you can make lunch. It'll be in keeping with your boundaries and you get to go in the kitchen. Every woman's favourite place," you say.

You sit with Sadie in the kitchen and occasionally rub her belly while keeping an eye on Sophie preparing the food. You put Radio 4 on in the background and pour yourself and Sophie a beer. She finishes her pint before you've even got two thirds through yours. You watch Sophie standing quietly, chopping up the vegetables, putting them into a saucepan. You hope she doesn't come at you with the knife. You're not worried, it would be easy to disarm her and slice up her neck just like she's slicing up the carrots. But you hope that doesn't happen. It's nice to have a pretty woman about the place.

As you reach down and rub Sadie behind the ears, you notice the chopping noises have stopped. What happens next is so predictable your instincts are already primed to react. You quickly stand up and grab Sophie's right wrist before she's able to clout you with the saucepan she's brandishing above her head.

"That was a bit obvious," you say. Still holding her arm you swiftly crack her hard across her chin with your free fist.

"Get off me you bastard! Get off me! Let me go!" screams Sophie.

"Be quiet and let the saucepan go." You squeeze her wrist until your hear it crunch in your grasp. She grits her teeth but eventually drops the pan on the kitchen floor. You grab her other wrist and pull her in close to head butt her on the nose. Not to knock her out but hard enough to stun her. Blood starts dripping from her nose.

"You silly bitch. You definitely need boundaries. It's early to bed for you now."

Sophie looks at you with her watery eyes and bloody nose. It's the first time today she's looked really scared. That's more like it.

*　　*

221

I don't finish my second pint. If my mates heard about this my reputation would be in tatters. I feel broken. In my mentally and physically empty state I walk around the docks, watching swans and seagulls fight over scraps of last night's discarded takeaways, and slowly make my way to Temple Meads.

As I walk into the train station I pass three young girls wearing matching yellow T-shirts with 'We Miss U Hoodwink' in black lettering. I briefly check the afternoon editions of the papers in the newsagents. Two of the red tops have both broken stories of Danny Stone's murder – DCI Johnson will be pleased. Although they don't have – or don't publish – the full details of how. Wonder how long it'll be before Jimmy Fink's front page news too. I walk out without bothering to buy a paper.

I stare up at the bank of screens and check the train times and destinations. I've no idea where to go although my options are plenty.

Where are you Sophie?

While staring vacantly at the screens, my mobile rings. Without checking who's calling I answer it.

"Hardy where the cock are you? Why's your phone been switched off?" It's Gary. And he's angry. "You're meant to be at the X-Festival. Carly from Power's been on the phone saying you're not there. What are you playing at?"

Oh… shit. What do I tell him? I witnessed the Hitman doing some murdering, Sophie's been kidnapped, I was arrested? Say nothing. Keep it bottled up, Hardy.

"I'm in Bristol. I got delayed after being at a gig last night up north. I'm at the station on my way to the festival now," I say. It's the best my addled brain can come up with.

"Wise up, Hardy, you should've been there yesterday." Gary breathes out loudly. "Okay, look, it's early afternoon, if you catch a train to Exeter now you should be able to watch the majority of decent bands playing today. But make sure you watch the lion's share of tomorrow's line up. There's a lot of material there for the mag, you know that. Call Carly and sort it."

Gary hangs up. At least he didn't give me the third degree about Danny Stone's death.

My mobile immediately starts ringing. It's Gary again. I grudgingly answer it.

"Forgot to ask, do you know anything juicy about Danny Stone's murder?"

I don't tell Gary I was in Blackpool and nearly saw it all. I do tell him I'll dig around and write a quick news story for the mag. At least he doesn't know about Jimmy Fink's murder. Yet.

So, I'm off to Exeter. A quick call to the X-Festival PR contact, Carly, and a bit of chat and false excuses for my tardiness, and I've arranged to pick up my VIP ticket on the gate.

I hang up, and immediately feel guilty. I know I should be doing all I can to save Sophie instead of running scared to a music festival. But whenever I think of her I think of McNamara and feel the fear. Besides, I haven't got a Scooby Doo where they are. Even if I could somehow miraculously track down McNamara to find Sophie, he could murder her just because I show up. I try not to think about it and think about going to watch some bands in a field.

I wait for the train in a station café that's got WiFi. Over a double espresso, I rapidly write an Insider piece on Danny Stone's death on my laptop and email Gary the copy. Afterwards I nervously check to see if McNamara has anything to say on email. He doesn't. Three different companies offering to help with my erection problems do, though. I've also been sent batches of emails about the MySpace and Facebook tribute site activity for Hoodwink, Dazza and Kitty Bomb, and it seems Sean Bates' record label is re-releasing all his CDs with new packaging. And I've got emails from two different newspapers wanting to talk to me about the 'Musician Murderer'. I ignore them.

I join the other festival goers from Bristol getting on the Exeter train as they clamber on with their tents and backpacks filling the seats and luggage compartments. I find two empty seats around a table and dump my bag. As the train rattles away in a south westerly direction, I nip to the food carriage and buy a four pack of beer and some crisps. When I get back a young girl is sitting in the seat next to mine. Her dark hair is in pigtails and she's wearing black nail polish and pink lipstick. I plonk myself down, crack open a beer and start power drinking. She starts talking energetically about the X-Festival and, as we chat and I glug beer, I find my dilemmas slipping to the back of my mind. She's eighteen and called Pansy and it's nice just to talk about music because I want to rather than because of work. Two beers in and I'm doing really well, until I call her Sophie.

"I'm Pansy. Who's Sophie?"

Instead of making something up or just saying she's my girlfriend, I can't help staring past her and out of the window.

"Who's this Sophie then?" says Pansy, tilting her head to one side, a sweet smile on her face.

I try to speak but nothing comes out. I'm desperate to talk to someone, anyone. Even Pansy would do if I thought she could help. Usually if I have something on my mind, I'm not the sort to bottle it up or quietly solve problems on my own. If I have a problem, I bore anyone who'll listen... and then solve it. But now I don't know what to do when the only person I can talk to is the person who's missing, and the one who's the problem in the first place.

Where's Sophie when I need her?

Pansy's still smiling patiently and looking at me.

"Sophie's my long distance girlfriend," I say. "I just miss her that's all."

Four very quick beers later and our conversation dries up along with my brain cells.

As the train clatters along the tracks my eyes close over. I end up having half-broken dreams about a longhaired football fan swimming the channel in his Liverpool shirt. The water is red and it matches the colour of his shirt. I'm in a rowing boat behind but he's a strong swimmer and I don't ever catch him. I wake up and my forearms are rigid from clenching my fists so tightly.

With blurry eyes, I crawl off the train at Exeter. I tell Pansy to have a good time, wave goodbye, and get a taxi straight to the festival. On the way there I try Sophie's mobile. I get the recorded message. I'm too comfortably numb with booze to cry now at the sound of her voice. I switch off my mobile and stuff it in my backpack.

I think I need to get *uncomfortably* numb.

A warm, late afternoon breeze swims around in the air as Moby performs on the main stage at the X-Festival. He's asking everyone why does his heart feel so bad. I know how he feels.

Why do song lyrics always mean so much more when I'm depressed?

But I'm here to try and forget about girlfriend kidnappings. I'm determined to check out some bands, and drink and party like it's 1999. I just won't be wearing any purple, or raspberry berets.

Armed with my ticket I find the VIP area which is at the back of the Square stage. Inside I have access to the backstage bar and access to the very front of the stage for a clear view. I don't have to mix with the peasant crowds if I don't want to. It's beer o'clock by my watch so I grab one and start doing the press bit by chatting with PR girl Carly. She has her blonde hair in a ponytail and is wearing a tight chequered blouse, a mini-skirt short enough to see some high thigh and some cowboy boots. Cowgirl boots. Whatever.

I try to be polite and interested but I make sure I have a can of beer in each hand at all times. We can see the front side of the stage from where we're standing, but as we're outdoors and not in the direct line of audio fire, the sound isn't shaking our socks off. As Carly chats about the artists, I check the line-up for the rest the weekend's music in the X-Festival programme. There aren't any bands playing that would make it on my Top 10 Hit List. Most are solid indie and rock stalwarts who are happy to play their music to grateful crowds.

I glance around the VIP area. There are a couple of hundred press and muso types milling about with various hangers-on.

"Who haven't you met yet?" says Carly.

I look around and see a few X, Y and Z-list celebrities from various reality shows. Before I can say I'd rather talk to my can of Red Stripe, she says, "I've got to introduce you to Rob. You'll love him. He's a riot, I'm telling you. He cracks me up."

"Rob! Rob sweetheart! Come and meet Hardy, yeah?" says Carly.

A tall-ish, scruffy looking twenty-something ambles over. He's got a bottle of lager in one hand and a roll up in the other. He's wearing his unwashed hair long, and his fringe is messy enough to touch the top of his retro-style shades. He's got a faded Beatles *Revolver* T-shirt stretched across his scrawny chest.

"Rob's from *Enemy* magazine," says Carly before going off to circulate.

"Hi, Hardy, from *TOP 10 HITS* magazine," I say, resisting the urge to ask him what time his parents are picking him up later.

After some brief getting-to-know-each-other waffle, Rob launches into one of his obvious passions.

"...their debut album hit the British music scene just when we needed it. The charts were full of lightweight dance music and moaning rock bands all drowning in the aftermath of the grunge, post-Cobain era. We all needed something new and optimistic. Then along they came, these Beatles-look-alikes, with their mod clothes, the hair, their uplifting guitar melodies and sing-along-able lyrics. And Liam? What a fucking front man, huh!?" Rob pauses to suck on his fag, squinting unnecessarily.

Rob is a wannabe rock 'n' roll star/music magazine bore, and a music journalist's nightmare.

"Erm, yeah." I greedily drink my third can of Red Stripe, and look around the other journalists desperately trying to find anyone else to talk to. Unfortunately, everyone else looks equally annoying.

"...Noel Gallagher said *Definitely Maybe* was about trying to become rock 'n' roll stars, and that *Morning Glory* was when they'd *become* rock 'n' roll stars. Not sure what *Be Here Now* was though. Personally I felt it just about held its own, although there's a lot of MOR – that's Middle Of the Road, mate – tracks on there."

"Do you realise I couldn't give a pretty little shit about your theories?" I say. But Rob's not listening.

"...Noel brought a modernised Beatles' sound into the nineties and noughties. He's such a clever songwriter. Do you realise how hard it is to write a really simple pop song? I do, I've tried to write some stuff…"

"Do you ever pay attention to people's body language?" I say. Rob's not listening to me, and I'm not listening to him. It's your classic one-way media conversation.

"Okay, there's no denying it, Oasis are a fucking brilliant rock 'n' roll band. They could do no wrong at the start, they hit a lull in the middle, but now they're back on song, rocking out better than ever," I say. But Rob's not heard me.

"…I wish I was still a student. I could spend all my time writing music instead of writing about music…"

"Sod this," I say. I grab Rob's bottle of lager.

"It's not dead yet, mate, still half full…"

"I know."

I quickly put my thumb over the end, shake it up, and fire the frothed-up lager over Rob. It's like dowsing a verbal fire. I keep shaking and spraying until the bottle's empty and his face and T-shirt are soaked. For the first time, Rob's speechless. He stares at me and pulls at his wet Beatles T-shirt which is now sticking to his bony chest. Several journalists and media blaggers stop talking and look at us.

"See you later cheese dick," I say, and walk out of the VIP area and off in search of something less boring instead.

I'm hungry so I have a hot dog. I put on extra ketchup as I figure the tomato in it will act as one of my five-a-day. By now I've finished seven or eight cans of Red Stripe. I don't even like lager. I don't feel drunk either. I'm almost in danger of sobering up. Annoyingly, lots of people seem to be bumping into me. Maybe I'm in the way. I need something stronger.

I end up back at the Square stage VIP area and squeeze my way to the front of the bar, ignoring the insults I get as I push in.

"Two double vodka and cokes and two pints of Guinness."

"No Guinness, babe," says a girl with several piercings in her face.

"Beer…? Y'know, bitter?"

"Beers, and vodka and cokes it is."

I count her piercings as she pours my drinks. She has fourteen in total. Two in each nostril, one in her bottom lip, one in her chin, one in each eyebrow, and three in each ear. They don't do anything to take away the fact she is a very pretty girl.

I carry my little cardboard tray over to a slightly raised mound that's getting the evening sun and drink a vodka, a pint, a vodka, a pint. I get to my feet. Who's feet would I get to? I decide as I'm able to stand I must still be sober. I head off in search of something stronger still. I need to find *him*.

People repeatedly walk into me as I leave the VIP area and join the general public.

I like festivals for the mixture of people and the X-Festival is no different. Middle-aged, middle-class men and women sit on rugs and sip chilled wine from glasses next to rock boys and goth girls drinking warm cider out of the bottle. Groups of glammed up, messy haired students stand and watch an indie band on stage, next to half-dressed chavs and townies in football shirts drinking lager from cans. Fashionable thirty-somethings in expensive T-shirts and jeans chat among themselves drinking bottled beer as crusties and leather-clad, bearded biker dudes pass a hookah pipe around and swig on straight Jack Daniels. But he's not here.

I walk and walk until I'm busting for a wee wee. After opening and closing three portaloo doors – because they're already full of God knows what – I find one that's got a semi-clean seat. I get past the smell and noise of fellow festival goers going next to me by shoving toilet tissue up my nostrils and in my ears.

Feeling lighter, and light headed, I reach the big, red and blue Vodafone tent. I nick someone else's beer from the bar at the side, while people are looking the other way, and catch the last couple of songs by a punk rock band I can't remember the name of. They are very good though, but whenever I try to make my way nearer the front of the stage, people seem keen to knock into me. Where is he?

I have a look around, pushing through the crowds and stepping on people who have decided it's a good idea to sit down in the middle of the tent, but I can't find who I'm looking for. I still feel too straight. I need to get numb.

I head to the dance tent and finally spot who I'm after: a giant Rasta in a green and yellow hat with dreads creeping down his back. He's wearing a big, black leather trench coat even though it's summer, and he's got some bright yellow rimmed sunglasses on, even though it's pretty much night time by now. His honey coloured, pockmarked skin is covered by a fine layer of sweat. He's stood on his own, dancing occasionally to the big beat music, but generally looking around and looking shifty. It's so blindingly obvious he's a drug dealer I wonder if he's dressed up like it for a bet.

"Alright?" I say.

"Alright, man. Yeah, all good in the 'hood," he says.

He doesn't bang into me like the others, which is nice, but he seems to be swaying around a lot. "Got any pills?" I say.

"I wouldn't know too much about that sort of thing," he says. "But if you come around the back of the tent I might know someone who does. After two minutes, follow me."

After two minutes I walk around the back of the tent. The someone he knows is himself. Perhaps he's a schizophrenic. "I may be able to sort you out, geezer," he says. His coat's flapping around in the breeze like a cape. He looks like a Super Rasta. I wonder what super powers he would have. Magic dreads?

He charges me £15 for four ecstasy. Seems a fair deal to me. I hand over the money. As he hands over a small plastic bag of pills, I feel the roughness of his skin in my hand. He doesn't look me in the eye the whole time, he's too busy checking nobody's watching.

"They're tip top, these are," he says looking over my shoulder, "and they're pretty trippy, man."

The big beats aren't any smaller outside so I can't really hear what he's saying. "I look like a hippy man?" I say.

The Super Rasta shakes his head and flies off to save any pill heads in space who are in danger of coming back down to earth.

All day I've been functioning on a mixture of adrenalin and alcohol but now I'm so tired I'll take anything to keep me awake. I can't remember the last time I did a pill or if I used to do half a pill at a time. My drunken logic is saying it's probably easier to have whole ones, so I pop two in my mouth and wash them down with a can of Red Stripe. I put the other two in my wallet and wander off in search of adventure.

After checking out a really loud thrash-rap band I can't remember the name of, I wonder if I've bought some duds. I couldn't get into the music and hardly danced. I did bounce up and down a bit, but apart from feeling nearly drunk, and nearly sick, I don't feel any sort of buzz.

I look around and decide which direction seems most appealing. It's dark now and the light show across the other side of the main field is spraying out of the dance tent and into the night sky. It looks amazing. I'm drawn to the lights. Bright light, bright light. I start walking, then do a sort of half-skipping half-walking dance all the way to the tent. Inside, the music's some repetitive cheesy house tat, but my body seems keen to dance so I don't argue. I'm soon arsing about with anyone and everyone, giggling and dancing until my jaw starts aching. I leave the dance tent, find a bar and numb my jaw with a couple of pint-sized, lager flavoured pain killers.

I stumble back towards the Square stage as I somehow remember the Arctic Monkeys are due on at 9pm. I look at my watch and for some reason the small and big hands are spinning around wildly. Helpfully, my watch speaks to me and confirms that it is 9pm. I start talking into my watch as he seems like the ideal new best friend. He's on my wrist and he's always on time! I ask him why everyone keeps barging into me and why the ground keeps moving. Are we at sea? I'm not sure but the crowd seems to be acting like one huge wave of bodies.

I weave mid-way through the crowd to watch Sheffield's finest on stage. They've set the new standards for everyone else to follow; from their wonderfully Northern vocals and insightful, witty story-telling to their melodies that leap from power pop to raucous rock in a chord change. No British band has made such a strong debut since Oasis. I keep my thoughts down in case Rob is passing and hears me.

The Arctic Monkeys rock like their lives depend on it. I sing along to the songs I know, and dance to the ones I don't. But the crowd go one better and bounce and sing along to every single lyric, as well as somehow singing along to the guitar solos. It's a bizarre yet beautiful experience and the whole time Alex Turner is on stage, singing and spanking his guitar, I notice a large halo hovering above his head. I'm not sure if it's part of stage lights or my imagination.

Mid-way through their set I neck another pill. I don't think the first two have had any effect other than making my left foot feel really light and my right foot feel really heavy. Everyone's smiling at me as I pogo around in circles, and I find myself chatting shit to anyone who doesn't fight me off. The Monkeys leave, and the crowd cheer continuously while I start chanting on my own trying to get them out for an encore.

"Will you come back and sing, for bananas and ice cream?"
Gradually a small group join in.
"Will you come back and sing, for bananas and ice cream?"
A few chants more and a hundred or thousand have joined in.
"Will you come back and sing, for bananas and ice cream?"
By the time the Arctic Monkeys come back for their encore, thousands of us are chanting. I feel special and ridiculous all at once.

They come back to mass applause and rip out a quick-fire medley. I have the urge to break dance to their punk rock. It feels like the most natural act in the world as I dive into a caterpillar. I whack my chin as I hit the hard-packed mud, but that doesn't stop me rolling back and flipping into a windmill of Dutch proportions. My body feels like a spinning top and my crazy legs go mental for it as people all around cheer me on.

I buy some water, and a lager, and neck the last pill by the side of a beer tent. I think I get some strange looks, but they're off people who're strange looking so I don't pay attention.

After that it gets a little hazy. I think I bond with some boys from Manchester in the Vodafone tent. They shout things like, "Your pupils are like saucers, mate!" After a while it feels like I'm bare foot on a hot plate. I don't normally dance to drum 'n' bass but I think a girl with a revealing bust keeps saying, "Give me some of those nasty moves!" While her friend is shouting "Have it large!" over and over. For some reason nobody is annoying me. If anyone bumps into me I just hug them. Even the most irritating tunes just make me move to the music.

I find myself drifting away in time to the beats and songs, and I go beyond listening to the DJ's set and actually start *seeing* the music. All types of fluorescent blue and effervescent green shapes pulse around my head. The repetitive beats keep on coming and I keep on dancing.

There's a break in the music and suddenly my mouth feels like it's on fire. Water doesn't cool it down. I need something else.

Will you come back and sing, for bananas and ice cream?

I go off in search of, and miraculously find, an ice cream van. At first I think it's a mirage but I'm able to touch the cool metal of the van, and the vendor inside isn't a camel, so I order a double coned Mr Whippy and stand memorised as the ice cream squirms out of the nozzle. The ice cream seems to be glowing but it tastes electric so I don't mind. It does the trick and my mouth starts to cool down, but then I feel like retching and the simple act of swallowing is proving tricky. So I sling the ice cream on the floor.

As I walk off my watch starts talking again. It's telling me it's late but never too late to dance.

The dance tent, let's go.

It's late and only the dance tent is playing music now as the festival's hardcore have it inside. It's rammed full of hot bodies bumping and grinding. The beat keeps pumping, my legs keep dancing. I close my eyes as the DJ breaks it down to a really simply, smooth bass line. Pump, pump, pump, pump. It sounds so good vibrating through my whole body. I could be the only person dancing in the tent. I don't care. I'm at one with the music.

Pump, pump, pump, pump.

The bass line stops to give way to a continuous, kinky little beep. The beeping stops, and it's replaced by a revving engine, and then some louder beeps. The beeping becomes more constant and I up my dancing moves, throwing all sorts of shapes. It almost sounds like a car horn. Beep, beep, beep, beep.

Beep-beep. Beeeep-beeeeeep!

I open my eyes, and turnaround to be faced with the headlights of a truck.

It appears I'm no longer in the dance tent. I'm on the track that runs through the festive fields. The truck driver beeps the horn again and I quickly move out of the way. Actually, I *dance* out of the way. As the lorry goes past I notice a big tank on the back. It says 'sewage' on the side.

At least I can say I haven't been dancing to any old shit. I've been dancing to *everyone's* shit... as it's being pump, pump, pumped from the toilets.

My watch tells me it's time for bed.

I fall over a couple of people's tent pegs in the VIP campsite landing on a couple of bodies already in their tents. It's all good fun. They shout at me, I laugh at them. The sky starts getting lighter, which is a great help as I can see to find my orange and black tent the PR company's sorted out for me. Eventually, after crashing into three more tents, I crash into my own.

I crawl into my sleeping bag fully clothed and want nothing more than to pass out. My body feels like it's done a marathon, and my hearing's numb from dancing too near the speakers, but my brain is still busy whirring away. I chomp on some fresh gum to stop me chewing the insides of my cheeks off. My hands are shaking and my feet are achy and twitchy. I lie back and stare at the roof of my tent and suddenly feel enormously guilty when realise I haven't thought about Sophie since I arrived.

I close my eyes and on the inside of my eyelids I'm treated to a double showing of *Nightmare On Hardy Street*. The main plot revolves around me going through a series of very long, very dark tunnels. Every so often a spotlight is switched on and Sophie appears wearing a Liverpool shirt, and little else. Her eyes look like black marbles. She smiles at me, but she looks upset when I notice half her teeth are missing.

I hug myself tightly and will my brain to sleep.

I can't sleep.

Still can't sleep. Perhaps the pills weren't duff after all. Now I get to enjoy some sleep deprivation. I remember now why I don't do pills anymore. I'm too tired to sleep.

When Sunday morning properly comes around I realise I've had my eyes closed for hours but haven't snatched any real sleep. My jaw feels even more sore than when McNamara knocked me sideways, my eyes feel full of dust when I blink, and my tongue tastes like a Mexican grave digger's flip flop. I met a Mexican grave digger once, and I saw his flip flops. Believe me, they were dry, sandy and smelled of gone-off nachos.

My brain feels like I've borrowed a large potato for the day as a replacement. I feel like a vegetable. I feel... out of focus. Not my vision, my whole body *feels* out of focus. Out of touch with reality: half asleep, half awake, half pissed and half depressed. That adds up to two people but I feel a shadow of my former self so it's probably about right.

To stop myself sulking, I crawl out of my tent and stand still while my head spins round. After a few minutes I have a go at walking. I only trip over one tent's guide ropes so it's an improvement on last night... well, earlier this morning. It must be breakfast time. My watch says it's 8am but it's not talking out loud anymore. Avoiding everyone's glares in the VIP camping area I find a hot food van and buy a bacon roll. I eat half of it, throw up as discretely and quietly as possible behind the toilets, and shuffle back to my tent.

Despite the white noise inside my head, I'm so shattered I manage to drift off into a hazy sleep. But even as I'm sleeping I know I'm not myself. I'm on a come down, even in my dreams.

*   *

"Daddy's got to go to work now, darling," you say. You feel like you should kiss her on her forehead. So you do, just a little peck. "Unfortunately these pop artists won't kill themselves."

You stand back from the bed and admire her dark curly hair contrasting with her fair complexion. There's a little dried blood up her nostrils.

"I'll be back early tomorrow afternoon and we can have a nice cooked lunch together. I'm sure we'll both have worked up an appetite by then."

Sophie doesn't say anything. She can't. You've put a gag in her mouth. She looks confused, still half asleep. She tries to stretch but the ropes stop her spreading out. You've tied her ankles and wrists with zip ties and rope equal distance from each corner of the bed.

"Actually, I suppose I'd better let you go to the toilet before I leave." You undo each rope in turn, and leave the zip ties around her ankles and wrists. She's still wearing her jeans and red top. Her cap is on the bedside cabinet. You've switched off and stashed her mobile in a shoe under your bed.

You remove the gag and Sophie sleepily says, "You're too kind."

You hold her arm and walk her to the bathroom. Like before you don't let her close the door, but you do wait around the corner in the kitchen. You know she won't be able to escape. The bathroom windows are locked with a key you have in your pocket, plus you're on the first floor and it's a long way down to the ground.

You walk Sophie back to the bedroom and retie her securely to the bed. You double check all the ropes are really tight.

"Take one of these before I go, there's a good girl," you say showing her a packet of over-the-counter sleeping pills. "Look, I'm pressing them fresh out of the sealed packet. They'll only help you sleep."

Sophie can't move to sit up.

"But it's 10am. I don't want to go to sleep again now," she says.

"I don't want you walking off when I'm at work," you say.

"You work on Sundays?" says Sophie, yawning.

"No rest for the wicked," you say. "Take these, it'll make things easier for you."

Sophie realises she's not really in a position to argue. You hold her head up, pop two pills on her tongue and help her with a glass of water. You notice how beautiful her lips look as you put the gag back in her mouth and tie it tight so she can't talk. Sophie lies back down but keeps her eyes open. She wriggles and stretches as much as the ropes allow.

You check the bedroom windows are still locked and that the three security bars on the outside are in place. You installed them last year after you were burgled. How you would've liked to catch the scum that broke in and stole your DVD player and TV. You keep the curtains drawn.

"Sweet dreams," you say.

You close the spare bedroom door behind you. You slide the two big bolts across that you fitted yesterday.

In your bedroom you remove the blonde wig you've kept on for Sophie's benefit, and start getting changed into your disguise. It's a part of the mission you've learned to enjoy. You never really liked fancy dress parties but these disguises have a purpose.

You run a thin line of glue around your hair line and pull the long, black wig on to your head. It's sort of wavy and shoulder length. You put lines of glue on your upper and lower lips and chin, and push the black goatie on to your face. You press on the beard and check yourself out in your bedroom mirror. Eddie Vedder would be proud. Or is Chris Cornell the one with the beard? You shake the hair around and laugh as it falls on your face. You're glad you invested in professional wigs – the real hair means nobody will question your rock credentials when they see you. You put another layer of your trusty 'liquid skin' on your hands. It dries quickly. You pull on an old and worn Black Sabbath T-shirt, some baggy blue jeans and Converse trainers, and you're ready to rock.

Before you go you make a Hitman's lunch in the kitchen. It's a little like a ploughman's, only with an extra special ingredient. You make some ham and tomato sandwiches, on granary bread, with salt and pepper and mayonnaise. You seal them in a sandwich bag and place them in your blue, non-translucent Tupperware sandwich box, and put your loaded Glock 17 and silencer next to them. You put some cheese and onion crisps on top, fit a Granny Smith in the corner and seal the lid on.

You put some dog food in Sadie's bowl, and top her water bowl up as she wolfs back her breakfast. You like the way she doesn't care what disguise you're wearing. She senses it's you from your manner and smell. You don't like leaving her alone, but she's used to it now, and you've house trained her to use the 'dog litter' tray in the corner.

You lock up behind you and walk down to your Astra parked across the road. You put your sandwich box on the passenger seat and drive to work. Your new job will take you two days as you're driving down to the south coast to kill a quartet of wannabe punk rockers later on tonight, staying over in a Travel Inn, then driving back up in the morning.

You pull on to the motorway and settle into driving, flipping the sun visor down as the morning rays light up the road. As your speed increases you turn up Led Zeppelin on the CD player so you can hear Plant howl and Page's quick and clever riffs over the sound of the tyres on the tarmac.

Dazed and Confused builds up and you sing along, doing the guitar parts with your fingers on the steering wheel.

*   *

I wake up and sit bolt upright. I'm breathing hard and my chest hurts. Slowly I get my bearings inside the tent and realise I was just having a nightmare: I was swimming underwater towards Sophie tied up at the bottom of the ocean, but a shark circling around her wouldn't let me get close enough to rescue her.

My watch says it's 11:45am. It's still not talking to me and I decide that's a good thing. I shuffle out from the tent and stagger to my feet. No need to get dressed as I didn't get undressed earlier and I don't have any spare clothes with me anyway. I have a shower and clean my teeth. Well, I splash water on my face from an outside tap, run my fingers through my hair and pop some chewing gum in my mouth.

I mooch around the campsite stepping over Saturday night's carnage. Beer cans and plastic glasses are lying all over the grass. A few bleary eyed campers are cooking food on gas stoves. On the sun-dried grass a small crowd are sat around a boy strumming on an acoustic guitar. I home in on the hot food van, narrow my eyes, and order a bacon, sausage and egg sandwich. I hold it down this time without so much as a retch.

Meandering about I catch up with Carly hanging out near the bar. She's stood with the guitarist from The Strokes, the bassist from The Hives and the singer from Franz Ferdinand. They look like they've just won first, second and third in a 'I've got the skinniest legs and tightest jeans' competition. Carly's already supping on a cold one.

"Fancy a drink?" she says. Two days of heavy festival action don't seem to have had any adverse effect on her. Her eyes are still as bright as they were yesterday. Somehow, her legs seem even longer and her mini skirt seems even shorter.

"I promised myself I wouldn't today," I say looking over at them. "Over did it a bit yesterday." The skinny-legged amigos slope off, presumably to find tighter pairs of jeans.

"Oh yeah!" says Carly excitedly, with her hand over her mouth. "I saw you in the dance tent. You were flying across the dance floor like a kamikaze pilot!"

I don't remember flying. Although I have vague recollections of trying to take off.

"I like a good bop every now and then." I actually say 'bop'. I sound 65 years old.

She smiles at me and finishes her drink. It makes me thirsty.

"I'm just going to the bar then I'll be right back. Sure you won't have a drink? They're free today," she says mischievously.

I have the hangover from Hades, a hole in my stomach, and the love of my life may be being tortured or dead, so what do I say?

"Go on then. One won't hurt."

I'll just have one to take the edge off, then go home and get my head straight and work out what to do next.

When the sun starts setting it dawns on me that Carly and I haven't really left the VIP area all day. Actually, we haven't left the free VIP *bar* all day. We've been chatting about stuff and nonsense, avoiding annoying journalists, telling silly stories, and forgetting that some of the world's best bands are performing around the corner. We saw a folk band briefly as they played on the Square stage. They sounded brown. We also checked out The White Stripes for half of their set earlier. They sounded red.

Carly has turned out to be great company. I like it when she screws her nose up when she laughs, and I've only thought about Sophie three times. Each time it's happened I've gulped the thoughts away with more beer. It seems to be working.

I think Carly's been trying to flirt with me. More than once I've caught her looking at me and standing a bit close and in my personal space. She said, "You have really nice blue eyes," at least twice, she's not left my side all day and made sure I've always got a drink in my hand. Perhaps she's trying to get me drunk. But the only reason an attractive young girl like Carly would be interested in me is because I'm not interested in her. I must be exuding that *'I'm disinterested because my girlfriend's been kidnapped and I can't stop thinking about her'* aura.

But I'm not thinking about any girls right now. I've been tucking lots of thoughts away in the bottom drawer of my brain over the last two days.

"So any girlfriend back home in Bath?" asks Carly as she hands me yet another free drink.

I take a big swig of beer and force Sophie to stay down in the bottom drawer.

"Yeah," I say, then I don't know what else to say so I just say, "I like her."

"That's nice," says Carly. "Why haven't you brought her with you?"

I can hear Sophie banging away inside the drawer.

"She's working away at the moment," I say.

The drawer pops open and Sophie climbs out. Another big swig but it's no use. The drawer gets bigger. I take another swig but can barely swallow.

Sophie, lovely Sophie.

"Are you okay Hardy? You look a little… sad," says Carly.

I thought drinking all day would help me forget. It has, but now it's turned around and tricked me.

"Are you alright Hardy?" says Carly, putting her hand softly on my arm.

Sophie's staring at me, holding the empty drawer up in her hands.

"No. No I'm not," I say. An army of tears get the better of my defences and start marching down my face.

"It's okay," she says standing close. "You can talk to me."

Talk. It's good to talk.

"Can you keep a secret?" I say.

Thirty minutes later and I've told Carly everything. I started with seeing Dazza die in Cardiff and the Top 10 Hit List email, and brought her up to date with Danny Stone being crowned with a TV. Then I told her what I'd been wanting to tell somebody since being arrested in Liverpool. I tell her I saw the Hitman drowning Jimmy Fink, and I tell her about Sophie's kidnapping and the Hitman's death threats. It wasn't as hard as I thought it was going to be – is it ever? Sure, it was helped by the fact that I'm plastered but I've been telling people bad news for months. It's like bad news has become a friend.

It's a lot of murder and mayhem to take in and Carly's bright eyes have filled with excitement and worry all at once. She's a good listener, although I don't know whether she believes how heavily involved I am with the Hitman and his Top 10 Hits. Danny Stone's death has been released to press, but Jimmy's hasn't so that shocked her, but not as much as Sophie being kidnapped.

"I'm so, so sorry Hardy. I feel so sorry for your girlfriend. It's awful," says Carly. "I can't believe she's been kidnapped. Has the Hitman sent a ransom note?"

"Nope. No ransom. He's not motivated by money or anything, just murder."

"You must be worried stupid."

"This may sound weird, but I think I know she's alright," I say. It's what I want to believe and, for now, it's all I've got.

Talking it out somehow made more sense of the situation. It also made it more real, but I feel like I can deal with it now.

However, I don't think I picked the best place to talk openly about a Hitman and a top-secret kidnapping with the nation's press stood all around us in the VIP area. It's dark now but that doesn't mean people can't hear.

I'm just looking around and feeling uneasy when a voice says, "I couldn't help overhearing. Did you say you've met the pop star Hitman!?"

I turn all the way around, then look down to see a severely short, pretty girl with a jet black bob haircut stood next to us at the bar. She's the perfect height to rest a pint on her head. If only she had a beermat-shaped hat. I've no idea how long she's been there.

"Did you say you've met the actual Hitman, the one with a Hit List?" she says.

"Yes!" blurts out Carly.

I glare at her. "I thought you could keep a secret?"

"Sorry. It's just so mad and scary."

"You've actually met the Hitman murdering all the pop stars!?" says the miniature black bob girl. Her mouth hangs open as she puts her hands on her tiny hips.

"He's met him twice! Even had a drink with him!" says Carly.

"Carly, will you shut up," I say, letting out a fake little laugh. I put my arm around her and squeeze her shoulder hard as I smile through gritted teeth. "She's just messing about."

Carly puts her arm around my waist. "We're just drunk and talking bollocks," I say, still squeezing her shoulder.

"You guys! I did wonder. Okay, sorry to have butted in," says the black bob girl. "Do you mind if we get a quick photo for the paper anyway?"

"Yeah, of course," says Carly before I have a chance to say no. Black bob girl points at us, and a photographer appears as if by magic to snap off a few pictures. He disappears just as quickly.

"Which paper do you work for?" I ask casually.

"I'm the showbiz editor for *The Sun*," she says and walks away.

Oh dear. Oh bloody dear. This is not good.

"Keep it sleazy," I say.

"What's that?" she says looking back.

"Take it easy," I say.

Partially satisfied she walks off.

I turn to Carly. "I need another drink or ten. But not here."

"I'm up for it," says Carly. She links her arm with mine and we leave the VIP area for the first time that day.

* *

You've never been to Bournemouth before, but you navigate the modern roads among the old and new seaside buildings easily. You park your Astra on a side street off the sea front and on the edge of town. It's Sunday evening so there's no parking to pay. You tuck your long, wavy hair back behind your ears and rub your goatie. You pull a notepad and pen and a small black Dictaphone from the glove box, tuck your sandwich box under your arm and head off to catch up with No.3 on your Hit List.

If there's one wannabe band that really deserves to be on your Hit List, it's Dragonfly. You'd seen them play on TV and knew something wasn't right – and it wasn't just their punk-lite music. It was when you were working as security at one of their gigs late last year you found them out. As a guitarist you noticed that Dragonfly's lead guitarist wasn't playing the right chords. In fact, he wasn't playing any chords whatsoever: he was miming. As you checked out the rhythm guitarist, bass player and drummer you realised *none* of them were playing. They were all miming to a backing track. You had to admit their timing was fairly good, but not quite good enough. Only the singer was really singing, although miming would've made him sound better.

You couldn't believe they'd managed to fly under the radar for so long and not be exposed for what they really are; four posh, public school mime artists who wouldn't know punk if safety pins were shoved up their arses.

As you walk along Bournemouth's sea front you go over the wannabe punk rockers' names in your head; Julian the 'guitarist',

Rubin the 'bassist' and Miles the 'drummer'. But it's Mikey, the lead singer/lead 'guitarist' you've seen most of, mainly when watching the odd episode of *Celebrity Love Shack* on ITV. You've never heard one man talk about himself so incessantly. Mikey revelled in all the TV attention that went with being on *Love Shack*. Even if that meant that TV viewers got to witness his girly hissy fits and constant posing in front of mirrors – he used hair straighteners and wore make-up everyday – and hanging around in the sun by the pool trying to be a player in front of the bikini-clad girls.

Over the last six months you've noticed a couple of Dragonfly's commercial punk-lite songs have cropped up on car and mobile phone TV adverts. Real punk rockers would never sell out like that.

You stand on the sea front and breath in the fresh, salty sea air as the waves roll in for the evening. A few seagulls float around on the warm evening breeze, occasionally diving underneath the pier. Joggers run along the sandy beach below as the last of the day's beach dwellers pack up their towels and shake sand out of their shoes. Groups of students walk hurriedly towards a bar with a 'Happy Hour' sign outside, as grandmas and granddads hobble home for *Corrie* and cocoa.

But you're not here for sightseeing. You've got a job to do. You walk off towards Bournemouth University to bring some justice to the pop world. First stop, Dragonfly's band manager.

From the university entrance you can hear Dragonfly already playing inside. You recognise the song from the car advert. It makes you want to drive a car off a cliff. Maybe later. A few students are smoking out the front and you spot the Dragonfly tour bus parked around the side. It's an inconspicuous, tall white coach with various-sized windows, and doesn't have Dragonfly written down the side, but you've seen enough tour buses to be able to spot one from 500 yards. You approach the bus driver/security guard and his beer belly waiting near the bus.

"Is Brian on the bus? I've arranged an interview," you say playing up to his security guard role. Brian is Dragonfly's manager.

"Yeah, hang on here," he says. "Oh, what's your name?"

"Hardy Matthews, from *TOP 10 HITS* magazine." You've got his girlfriend so you figured he won't mind if you take his name as well.

You hear a brief exchange and the driver steps back off the bus. "No problem, Hardy. He's been expecting you," he says.

He looks at your tattoos on your arms and says, "Oh, what's that?" He nods at your sandwich box. "We've been warned by the police to be extra careful on account of the rock star Hitman."

Rock star? You haven't killed any rock stars.

"You can never be too careful," you say, and hold up your blue sandwich box in one hand, and Dictaphone and notepad in the other. "Just my dinner. I hate cheap takeaway food."

He looks hurt. You look at his belly and realise he probably has a deep love affair with takeaways. He briefly pats and searches you before waving you on. You step onto the bus and close the door behind you. A rank of spots light up the black leather interior. It smells new. You walk past a few rows of seats, through the corridor in between six bunk beds, and to the back where Brian is sitting alone in a large, crescent shaped booth. He's perched on big padded seats behind a wooden-effect table. There's a TV flickering in a corner and a glass of red wine on the table. You notice an empty bottle next to it.

"Hi Hardy, nice to meet you. Please take a seat," says Brian. He has a thin, hooked nose and his beady eyes are small and dark like a chicken's. His blonde-grey hair looks false but you don't take the piss because you quite like wigs these days.

"Hello Brian. Thanks for giving up some time to speak to *TOP 10 HITS* magazine."

You shake hands and sit down by the side of him and put your sandwich box, Dictaphone, and notepad and pen on the table.

"Might as well crack on," you say pressing record on your Dictaphone. "I'm writing an article on the role of modern-day band managers and how they differ these days with so many manufactured musicians around."

"Okay, great," says Brian. "Glass of wine?"

"No, I don't really drink," you find yourself saying. "So, how do you feel the band manager role has changed over the past decade? It used to be that someone would start playing the guitar, after a while he'd get a band together with his mates, they'd write some songs, play a few gigs in a few pubs, then when they achieved some form of success they'd look for someone to manage and organise them. That seems to have reversed…"

"Yeah, of course, the music industry's changing. Now managers come first and the bands are created afterwards. It's well known that I held auditions around several of the big public schools and universities to find Mikey, Julian, Miles and Rubin for Dragonfly. It was a long process, but I felt they looked the part, everything else can follow after that."

You make some notes on your pad you've got on your lap out of Brian's eye line. You're glad you're not using a pencil otherwise you'd have snapped the lead off. You take a deep breath.

"Everything else?" you say.

"Yeah, the songs, the music, that can all follow. It's all about image these days."

You write some random profanities on your pad. Brian finishes his wine. You wonder if his tongue's this loose when he's sober.

"So Dragonfly weren't a band before you picked them out?"

"No, not at all. They knew each other from Durham Uni. They were good dancers, and looked great together, but none of them could sing brilliantly. Mikey had the foundation to become a lead vocalist but he needed a lot of training. He's still learning. But that's how a large part of the industry works now."

"Do any of them write songs? What about Mikey?"

Brian reaches across to a box on the seat next to him and pulls out another bottle of red wine. It's a screw top. He undoes the cap and fills up his glass. "Sure you won't have a glass?"

"Just a small one, thanks." He pours you a glass and slides it across the table. You don't touch it. You think you might spit it out over him if you do.

"Where were we?"

"Do any of them write songs? Such as Mikey?" you say.

"Mikey's written a few lyrics but, to be honest, off the record, they were really weak – just about his student days or pulling birds on tour. We've got a team who write the lyrics and write the music. It works better that way and it gives the boys more time to live the celebrity high life," says Brian. He plays with the wine glass in between his fingers.

You write some more swear words on your pad, in capital letters this time. You're sure band managers shouldn't admit this much in an interview. You bet Hardy would love to be getting all this. Too bad it's never going to get used.

"But they can all play instruments, yes...?"

You already know the answer.

Brian doesn't say anything so you fill the silence. "I've heard a rumour they can't play at all. They're just miming on stage."

As slippery as a greasy politician, Brian slides around the question. "Playing on stage isn't all about the music, and about the instruments, it's about the performance as a whole."

"So they can't play instruments?"

Brian takes a sip of his red wine. "Next question," he says.

"So Dragonfly are playing all these university gigs right now. You'd think that some of the great future minds of Britain would realise they're watching a bunch of fraudsters just miming on stage?"

"I don't think the students care either way. They just want a good night. They're probably too pissed on snakebite and trying to pull Sally from Sociology to notice that the band aren't playing properly."

"So you admit they can't play?" you ask writing down more expletives on your pad.

241

Brian takes another sip of his red wine. "You seem surprised, Hardy. Surely you see these sort of boy bands all the time when working for *TOP 10 HITS*?"

"I see talent-free boy bands far too often these days," you say.

"There have been boy bands since the seventies. What's so wrong with boy bands today?" says Brian

"Everything," you say. You remind yourself you don't have to justify anything to this tosser, but you'll indulge him for now.

"There were the Osmonds, the Jackson Five, the Bay City Rollers back then. What was wrong with them?"

"Apart from the Jacksons, what was right with the others? Not their teeth or outfits. And the songs? Don't get me started." You quite liked the Osmond's *Crazy Horses* song, as it goes, but you're not about to admit this to Brian. You take the lid off your sandwich box that's now on your lap and put the crisps on the table. "I'm starving, I'm going to have a sandwich," you say. "I can't stomach the junk food they sell at these gigs."

"Carry on," says Brian. You take a bite of sandwich as he carries on. "In the eighties and early nineties there were Wham, Bros, New Kids On The Block, Backstreet Boys, Boyzone, Take That. All great, great boy bands," says Brian.

"Depends on your definition of great," you say.

"They were all great successes."

"Depends on your definition of success," you say.

Keeping your sandwich box on your lap and below the table, you have another mouthful of sandwich and quietly screw the silencer into your Glock. Brian's too busy talking to notice.

"They all made millions. They sold millions of records and made millions on merchandising. What other definition of success is there?"

"But your definition is all about making money."

"Yes, of course," says Brian.

"It should be about making music, not making money."

He puts his glass on the table and shakes his head. "You poor, deluded idiot."

"I am neither deluded nor an idiot," you say.

You raise the gun above the table and shoot him in the head. Two quick shots in the centre of his forehead. The silencer nicely muffles the sound of the bullets impacting into his brain.

Next time you'll shoot first and ask questions later. It'll save a lot of time.

Adrenalin rushes through your body as you stand up and hold the Glock by your side. You love the way it suits close contact work. The Glock's a great bit of kit that can carry seventeen bullets but works better with only fifteen in the magazine to avoid jamming. You have thirteen lucky bullets left now.

Blood trickles out of the two, neat little holes in Brian's forehead. His body stays upright as his head rests back on the seat and his dead eyes stare straight up at the roof of the bus. There's no need to touch him.

You quickly draw the little tour bus curtains making sure nobody can see in through the small windows. You click on the safety catch and hide the gun under a pillow on one of the bunk beds. You put the sandwich box behind the driver's seat along with the pad and Dictaphone. The key is in the ignition. Checking the fat driver's looking the other way, you tuck the key in your pocket.

As you step off the tour bus, closing the door behind you, the big bellied driver turns round. He's eating a bag of chips by putting two in his mouth at a time.

"All done?" he says, showing you a mouthful of mash.

"Not yet," you say. "Brian's dead on his feet."

"Oh, wanted to have a kip did he?"

"Something like that," you say.

"He can't handle Dragonfly's rock star lifestyle that one."

"Yeah," you say. "I'll be back with the Dragonfly boys later to finish the job."

"Alright."

"Brian asked not to be disturbed by anyone."

"Okay I won't let anyone disturb him."

Good idea.

*   *

It's getting late and Coldplay, the final headline act of the X-Festival, are doing their thing on the main stage. Their emotional, atmospheric rock is creating an emotional atmosphere as people passionately sing along. I've not been singing but for the last hour I've felt emotional. I've felt like crying. Really crying. Proper guttural wailing and thumping-the-ground bawling. Sophie is out there somewhere and I hope to hell she's okay. When I think of McNamara I feel like punching someone or something. Anything would do. Anything to make the pain go away.

Coldplay's music seems to be filling up the air space. It's so full of sound. From where I'm standing mid-way back from the stage, swaying in between the swarms of people, Chris Martin looks about two inches tall. I've heard on the celebrity circuit that he's much taller up close. Carly's leaning on me and I'm propping myself up on her shoulder. I'm not sure who's supporting who. Today I think I've managed to drink about one beer for every year I've been alive – it's not even my birthday – and now, consequently, I feel ready for dead. Or bed. Or both. One of my legs keeps giving in at the knee and it's taking a lot of effort to keep my head up.

I'm boozed in and partied out.

"I want my bed," I say.

"Me toooo," says Carly.

"You can't have it. It's my bed."

"I meant... I don't know what I meant. I'm v-v-very dru-unk-unk y'know," says Carly, with one eye open.

My watch won't tell me what time it is but I think it's about 10:30pm.

"I'm going home now."

"But Coldpants have only sung half their songs."

"I'm sure Christian Martian will forgive us. I'm going home. Right now. I'm going," I say.

"Okay," says Carly.

*   *

You walk into the student union bar without so much as a rub down from the two hairy-faced bouncers. The rock look of long hair, goatie and tattooed arms is doing the trick. You get yourself a pint and stand near the bar and a crowd of students, so it's not obvious you're on your own. It's 11:07pm.

The not-so-fab four of Dragonfly are at the other side of the bar, drinking and celebrating another fraudulent show. You heard Mikey say on *Love Shack* that he, "likes to mix with the fans after concerts to prove to them that he's an alright bloke, really." He's surrounded by and chatting to a group of voluptuous student girls. No doubt so he can prove to them, "he's an alright shag, really." Other students are trying to be cool by not paying them much attention. They seem to be doing this by looking at Dragonfly every five seconds.

Dragonfly has just played to a medium-sized Bournemouth university crowd, about half of which are hanging around for cheap drinks afterwards. You sip on your pint and wait for an opportunity to present itself. You order another drink and do some half-hearted mingling with some boys half your age, while keeping an eye on your Hit No.3. Half an hour later you spot Mikey going to the bar. You quickly slip through the crowd and stand next to him. He orders four pints and picks two off the bar. As he turns round you knock your elbow into him so he spills them down his front.

"Watch it you moron!" he barks.

"Sorry."

"Sorry's not good enough. Look what you've done," he says looking down at his saturated shirt and jeans. He puts the near-empty glasses back on the bar.

"I said sorry. Who do you think you are anyway?"

"Do you know who I am?" says Mikey. The look on his face is incredulous and priceless.

Be patient and an opportunity will present itself. You leap at the chance.

"Do you know who I am?" he repeats, standing with his feet unnecessarily wide apart.

"Nope."

"I'm from Dragonfly?" Annoyingly Mikey's voice goes up at the end of his sentences so it sounds like he's asking you a question. "I'm leader of the band?"

You humour him and look blank.

"I was on *Love Shack*?" he says.

You keep up the blank expression.

"You still don't know who I am?"

Celebrities, honestly.

"You don't know who you are?" you say loudly. "Everyone! Excuse me! Excuse me! This man doesn't know who he is? Can anyone help!?"

A few students look around and stare at Mikey. For once he doesn't look impressed at the attention.

"Ladies and gentlemen, can I have your attention?" you shout. "This man doesn't know who he is. Can anyone help him out? He just said to me 'Don't you know who I am?' Can anyone help?"

The tension in the room is almost unbearable.

You love it. You smile.

"Does anyone know who he is?" you shout.

At first people don't know how to react. Slowly they realise you're joking. A few students at the front start giggling, and gradually the tension fades around the bar as people chuckle and cheer. Mikey looks at you. "Very good, wise guy, very good." His mouth curls into a small smile.

"Sorry about that, Mikey. I couldn't resist it."

"That's okay. Don't let it happen again," he says with the air of someone used to calling the shots.

"Let me buy you some more drinks," you say. "I'm Hardy, by the way. I'm a journalist on *TOP 10 HITS* magazine."

"I've seen your name in the magazine," says Mikey, quickly realising it's probably good to be polite to a music journalist. "My name's Mikey. But you knew that all along didn't you?"

"Might've done."

You buy Mikey two more pints, and one for yourself, and walk with him back to his fellow Dragonflies. Miles and Rubin quietly look you over. Julian is chatting to a girl who's nearly wearing a short tartan skirt. Her breasts are trying to climb out of a white shirt and black bra that are two sizes too small.

"So are you writing a review of our gig for *TOP 10 HITS* then?" asks Mikey.

"Not a live review exactly," you say. "Put it this way. There will be something big about Dragonfly in the magazine very soon."

"That sounds very cool," says Miles.

"Listen, I feel bad about taking the piss. Can I make it up to you? I've got something for all of you. But not in here."

"What is it?" says Mikey.

"Coke?" asks Miles excitedly.

"I could do a few lines," says Rubin.

"Even better than that," you say. "Let's go to your tour bus."

"Okay!" says Mikey.

"What is it?" asks Miles impatiently.

"I bet it's some 100% Columbian," says Rubin. Julian overhears and joins in. "Have you got some gear?" he says to you.

"It's a surprise," you say, raising an eyebrow.

You start walking away. The intrigue is too much to resist as Mikey, Miles, and Rubin follow you outside. Julian says goodbye to the girl and catches you up. You get outside and let Mikey show you the way to the tour bus. The driver is eating a burger now. He nods with his mouth full as you all walk past. You let the four boys walk on to the bus in front of you, and close the door behind you.

"What is it?" says Mikey, excitedly rubbing his hands.

"It's a surprise. Not here. Past the bunk beds right at the back," you say, indicating behind them.

They head to the rear and you follow them, surreptitiously sliding your Glock out from underneath the bunk-bed pillow and clicking off the safety.

One by one you hear them scream.

"What the hell!?"

"Holy shit!"

"Oh my God!"

"Jesus Christ!"

All four turn around to find their exit is blocked by you, and your gun.

"Don't you love a good surprise!" you say.

"What the hell's happened to Brian!?"

Mikey spots the gun in your hand.

"What the fuck's going on?" he says.

"I thought you four are meant to be well-educated public school boys," you say. "Isn't it obvious?"

Neither of them answer.

"I've shot him!" you say brightly.

You quickly shoot Mikey and Rubin twice, a bullet in each thigh, they fall back on the seat next to Brian's body and start crying with pain. Miles and Julian come at you together. You whack Miles around the ear with the butt of your gun and kick Julian swiftly in the bollocks. It's not pretty, but it is effective. While they're down you shoot them both twice, once in each thigh. Again the silencer on your Glock successfully suppresses the sound of the bullets. Miles and Julian stumble back next to Mikey and Rubin. Like you've flicked a switch, they all start screaming. You're glad you're at the back of the tour bus and well out of anyone's earshot.

"Alright boys, don't run off anywhere now – okay?"

You quickly unscrew the silencer from your Glock. It feels good to have fired a gun in anger again. You can see why the Glock 17 is the police force's gun of choice. It's so neat and efficient.

"What sort of fucking journalist are you!?" spits Mikey.

"The type who's trained to kill," you say.

As Mikey clutches his leg wounds, blood seeps out between his fingers. You march to the front of the bus, switching off the spotlights so nobody can see in easily. You can see the back of the driver looking towards the student union bar. He's still eating – you notice the sides of his belly sticking out – and hasn't heard the boys squealing at the back of the bus. You slide into the driver's seat. Your gun's still got five bullets left so you put it and the silencer in the sandwich box and place it on the seat behind you. You look in the rear view mirror and can only see two of the boys, but you can hear all of them either screaming or moaning as you turn the key in the ignition. The driver turns around outside and ambles over to start banging on the windscreen. You ignore him and drive off.

You drove tour buses around when you were a bodyguard and thirsty drivers were too drunk to see the road. It all comes back to you as you select second gear and smoothly drive the bus out onto the main road. You glance in the wing-mirror to see the driver half-heartedly waddling after you. After about 50 yards he gives up. You think you see his belly carry on wobbling even after he's stopped. He'll probably think you and Dragonfly are just 'being rock 'n' roll' by driving the bus off somewhere. You switch the headlights on and change up into third gear.

"Why are you doing this to us!?" shouts Mikey.

You ignore him. The traffic is light – it's after midnight and most of Bournemouth are sleeping before the dreaded Monday morning alarm. You drive along the coastal road, sticking to the wider A-road, keeping the engine revving.

"Why are you doing this to us!?" shouts Mikey again.

You look back to see him gritting his pearly-white teeth and wincing with pain.

"What have we done to deserve this!?" shouts Julian in between moaning.

"The pop world doesn't need fraudsters like you. You're just a bunch of mime artists taking the piss."

"Y'what!? I can sing!" Mikey manages to shout in between screams. "That's debatable," you shout back.

"We rock when we're on stage," shouts Julian, or Rubin, you're not sure.

"Don't make me laugh," you shout. One of them moans loudly. You look in the rear view mirror and check the boys aren't crawling towards you. They're not.

"Please... take us to... a hospital... we're losing blood..." One of them begs in between short breaths.

You ignore their request.

"I'm a great... guitarist!" screams Julian.

"You can't play a note! I've seen you on stage! You're all miming to a backing track!" you shout, changing into fourth gear.

"Be honest now, can any of you play the guitar, or bass, or drums?" you shout.

Silence. They even stop moaning briefly.

"You've not even tried to learn how to play them properly, even after playing all these gigs?" you shout.

No answer. More silence. You stop at a T-junction and indicate to turn right, waiting for a couple of cars to pass.

"Where are you taking us you freaking psycho!?" You hear one of the boys half shout and half scream. You think it's Julian.

"We're all going on a summer holiday," you shout back.

"Where!?" shouts another.

"We're going to a nice spot by a cliff," you shout as you drive up and along a winding coastal road.

"Please... please can you take us to a hospital?" one of the boys begs as another screams out with pain. "Just drop us off... we'll say we never saw you."

"No, no. That's not how it works," you shout.

They all start screaming at you.

"We're all going on a summer holiday. No more working for a week or two. Fun and laughter on our summer holiday," you sing. "Come on, kids. Sing along."

The screams get louder. They must be enjoying it.

"We're going where the sun shines brightly, we're going where the sea is blue." You sing even louder to drown them out. You wonder why nobody has ever released a rock version of *Summer Holiday*. It's the sort of cover Dragonfly would release.

You stop singing and stick the tour bus stereo on. Dragonfly's latest single booms out of the speakers – another band playing their own fucking songs! You let their excuse for punk rock play to remind you why they're so high on your Hit List.

You turn right at the helpfully named Highcliffe, and drive down a small, narrow coastal road. You pull into a field running next to a golf course and drive around the perimeter until you get to another hedge. You find a gap of sorts and force the coach through the hedge. You continue a little further then stop about 200 yards from the edge so you have a clear run facing directly out to sea. From your research you know it's a good 100 yard drop down to the ocean below, and the water's the same depth again. You leave the engine running.

"Right, this is where I get out boys," you shout to the back.

"You're going to leave us here!?" shouts Mikey.

"No. As listening to your music has sent me over the edge, I thought I'd return the favour and send you over the edge too."

"You're going to drive off the fucking cliff!?"

"I won't be driving, boys. But I'm going to start you off okay?"

"You can't kill me! I'm a celebrity rock star!" shouts Mikey.

"Don't do it... don't do it!" shouts one of the others, possibly Rubin.

"Look at it this way: you've tried and failed to rock, so now you must roll... off the edge of this cliff!" You make a note to work on your pre-death jokes.

You press the button that opens the front-side door. You stick the bus in second gear and rev hard. You drop the clutch and actually manage a wheel spin. You speed up to 30mph. At 100 yards from the edge you slip the bus into neutral. You leap out of the driver's seat and quickly grab your sandwich box and Dictaphone from the seat behind you.

"Good luck!" you shout and jump out the door. You tuck and roll away from the bus and finally stop about twenty yards from the edge and long drop into the ocean. The bus continues steadily and drives straight over the edge.

Darkness falls as the bus's headlights disappear. There's a sinister stillness when all you can hear is the fading engine noise through the air and the waves crashing into the cliff face. Suddenly there's a giant eruption as the bus splashes into the sea below. You run then scrabble quickly on your hands and knees to the edge, and lie down to peer over the cliff. The moon helpfully highlights the bus as it faces nose down. Huge ripples pan out as white waves gush into the bus and coastal wall below. The bus slowly sinks until its back end disappears beneath the surface like a big metal whale's tail. You watch as the red rear lights fade down into the depths, and then it's gone.

You stare down at the dark waves as your hands grip the grass and sandy soil. As your breathing slows you realise how quiet it is. All you can hear are the waves below and the faint sound of a ferry's horn in the distance. Several seagulls swoop silently around the cliff face. You're glad you didn't just shoot all the boys in the head. It's been so much nicer to give them a burial at sea. Two seagulls land on the waves right above where the bus sank. Perhaps they like to eat dragonflies. You become transfixed as you stare at the waves rising and falling. You look down for eight minutes to make sure none of the boys somehow swim out from the back of the bus.

They don't.

They're long dead.

You wonder how shrivelled their bodies will look in the morning when the tide goes out. You pick yourself up and breath in the salty air as a fresh coastal wind swirls around.

Hit No.3. Done. Only one more to go before your No.1.

You pick up the sandwich box, pad and Dictaphone scattered a few yards away and start the four-mile coastal walk back to your car parked in Bournemouth. With the moonlight for company, you quick march and start to sing quietly to yourself.

"Oh I do like to be beside the seaside. Oh I do like to be beside the sea."

No. 2

We could be heroes, just for one day
David Bowie

There's something deeply erotic about watching a fit, young girl who I've only just met, get undressed and stare at me as she walks naked and confident across her bedroom towards me. I know she's got undressed for me. I know her naked body is for me. I know she wants me. I know we're about to have hot, wild sex. She knows all this too. Which makes it even sexier.

I'm trying to act cool as I recline on Carly's bed. She's young, single, blonde, attractive, wears short skirts, and screws her nose up when she laughs. She likes all day drinking and music festivals. I know this much.

But what I don't know is what I'm doing here.

I feel mad drunk. Dizzy drunk. I can feel a helicopter head coming on. I touch my forehead and realise I'm sweating. When I sit up in bed a line of sweat dribbles down my bare back. I've undressed down to my boxers. I look at Carly standing before me. Her perky breasts sit expectantly and her pink nipples are pointing at me. She turns around and looks back over her shoulder, smiling, teasing me. Her blonde hair's long enough to cover her shoulder blades. I follow her curves down to her slim hips and naked bottom. It's peachy. I want to eat it.

"Do what you want to me," she says, looking over her shoulder and biting her bottom lip.

No. I can't. But I start nodding. My mind is staying no, but my body's saying let's go, let's go.

Carly turns away. When she turns around again her head has been replaced by Miss Piggy's. She still has her own voice and she starts singing, staring into my eyes, beckoning me towards her.

"Stop making the eyes at me, I'll stop making the eyes at you," she sings.

I'm confused. Sweat dribbles onto my eyebrows and around and down my temples as I stand up.

Her pink piggy nose twitches and her voice changes to Miss Piggy's. Which seems to make more sense.

"What it is that surprises me, is that I don't really want you to," she sings.

I stand still as her body changes before me. Her breasts morph into a row of funny little Miss Piggy teats. I count six of them, they look like they're made of felt. She still has Carly's long legs. They're brown and look like well-cooked sausages. I can see her blonde pubic mound.

I walk towards her and she walks backwards, teasing me. Miss Carly Piggy screws her nose up, laughs, and starts singing again. I can't quite place it. Strangely I still find her very attractive. I have to concentrate. The song sounds so familiar.

"Just banging tunes in DJ sets and dirty dance floors and dreams of naughtiness," she sings.

I'm sure I recognise it.

"I bet that you look good on the dance floor," she sings.

Now I recognise it.

"I don't know if you're looking for romance or..." she sings.

Is she an Arctic Piggy?

"I don't know what you're looking for," she sings.

I walk towards her but I'm not getting any closer as she keeps walking backwards. Her bedroom goes on, forever fading into darkness. She's slipping away.

"Where are you going?" I say.

She carries on singing, carries on slipping away.

"I don't know if you're looking for romance or... I don't know what you're looking for."

"Where are you going?" I say loudly.

She's slipping away. She has Miss Piggy legs now.

"WHERE ARE YOU GOING?" I shout.

When I wake up I'm breathing frantically and standing in the middle of my bedroom. My heart's racing and my entire neck is pulsating. It's dark. I'm in Bath. I'm wearing one sock and an old, blue *Star Wars* T-shirt. My naked arse feels cold. My duvet is lying on the floor by the side of the bed.

Miss Carly Piggy has disappeared. I am alone.

I wipe the sweat off my face with the sleeve bit of my T-shirt. I feel faint.

It seems I made it home on my own after all. I don't know whether Carly wanted to be in my bed, or why I've just dreamt about her with Miss Piggy tits, but I'm hoping I was strong enough to resist any sex that may've been on offer.

I look across my room and see half a pizza on a plate. Next to it a large bottle of white rum stands upright on top of a speaker. If I was feeling optimistic I'd say it's half full. But I'm not. It's half empty, just like me. The orange from the street light outside is creeping around the edges of the curtains. There's a pint glass of water nearly full to the brim sat on top of a two-foot high pile of music magazines. I pick it up and shakily down the lot in one. My mouth still feels like sandpaper afterwards.

I pick the duvet up off the floor, wrap it around me and shuffle back on to my bed. Even this tiny act makes my head throb like... like Miss Piggy is repeatedly karate chopping me around the skull.

"Bizarre," I say to myself. "I always thought I fancied Janice, the groovy, blonde guitarist with the big red lips. Not Miss Piggy. She's a pig for Fozzie's sake."

"Stop talking to yourself." I actually say this out loud.

I start panicking and wonder if I will ever be able to stop talking to myself. Bloody booze. The evil drink. I roll over. To the left, to the right. I turn the pillows over so they don't feel so hot on my face. I'm still sweating but I start shivering even though I'm hiding under the duvet.

I sit up, wide eyed. Is it classed as being unfaithful if I have sex with a Muppet? Better than sleeping with Carly, I guess. I feel guilty even having thoughts of infidelity.

I lie back down and close my eyes and all I can see is Carly's pretty head on Miss Piggy's pink, felt body. It doesn't help me get back off to sleep.

After an hour or so of not sleeping, I remember what I used to do when I was young and couldn't sleep. I pick up my pillows and move them to the other end of the bed and shuffle round. I pull the duvet tight around myself, and lie very still.

"Sweet dreams, Hardy."

As I drift off I'm not sure if I just said that or if it was Miss Piggy.

Take two. I open my eyes. I blink a few times. I lift my head off the pillow and it doesn't fall off or start throbbing so badly. I'm in my room, but everything's in the wrong place... then I realise I've been sleeping at the other end of the bed. Miss Piggy isn't in bed with me. Thank God. Kermit would go crazy. I relax a little. I swallow and it feels like I've got sand instead of saliva in my mouth.

"I'm never drinking again. Hardy, you're such a twat."

I must stop talking to myself.

I've still got severe sleep debt, but I can't face any more weirdo nightmares and I know deep down that I need to get up. There are important problems to solve.

When I've been standing under the shower for over fifteen minutes I guiltily remember why I got so hammered at the X-Festival.

To try and forget about Sophie. Beautiful Sophie.

She's been gone for three days and I haven't done a damn thing about it.

McNamara. Bloody McNamara.

I find myself punching the tiles on the bathroom wall as water runs down my face. Left, right, left, right. I'm not sure how long I pound them for. It doesn't hurt, or I can't feel anything – is that the same thing? I stop when the water running down and around my feet turns red. I watch the water as it races down the plughole.

My life's going down the plughole. The shower washes all over my face so I'm not sure if tears start to run down my face or not. What's wrong with me? I feel so numb. I need to have a word with myself. It's not on. I need to sort my head out. Sophie needs me.

"Think Hardy, think. Where would she be? Where would a killer turned kidnapper like McNamara take her?"

I don't mind this sort of talking to myself, it's just thinking out loud.

I have a shave in the basin. It takes a while to scrape off the week's growth from my face. In the small shaving mirror I get glimpses of the huge dark rings around my eyes. I look like a panda.

"Where would he take her? What's he doing to her?"

Dried and dressed, I set to work on Hardy's Hangover Cure to get rid of the toxic taste in my mouth and rotten feeling in my stomach. I down four pain killers, two multi-vits, and make myself drink a glass of fresh orange juice. As some bacon's grilling I scoff two bits of toast, then make a bacon sandwich and scoff that too. I drink a glass of milk, followed by a glass of cold water. I feel sick, but a satisfying round of burping stops me losing my breakfast.

I quickly check my email to find out if McNamara's been in contact. The clock in the corner of the laptop screen says it's only 8:35am. I don't even get up this early for work. My hands start tapping the table as my email account launches. I look down to see that I've now got a line of pretty, red grazes decorating my knuckles.

I want an email from McNamara, but I don't want one. I only want one if it's good news. But I need to know the news even if it's bad.

No emails from the Hitman today. He's not been very chatty since Anfield. Dejected, I shut my laptop and pace from room to room.

"Is she still alive?" I say as I look in the long mirror on my bedroom wall. The reflection staring back at me looks haggard and disorderly. Weekend benders aren't good for the appearance. They're even worse for the soul. I stare at myself and try and find some inspiration. I feel embarrassed looking so deeply into my own eyes, but it's time to take a long, hard look at myself. While I've been getting all sorts of mashed, for all I know Sophie has been getting all sorts of tortured. It's my fault we got involved with a Hitman. It was my idea for us to play detective. It's my fault Sophie's been kidnapped.

It's time to start accepting responsibility. It's time to stop running scared. So what if McNamara threatened to kill her if I do anything. He might've killed her already. I need to sober up. I need to start acting like a real man.

"I need to find Sophie," I announce to myself.

"About fucking time too," I reply.

I take myself outside from some fresh air. As I march my way down Lansdown Road, the warm September sun begins to thaw out my brain that's been frozen since Liverpool. I walk purposefully past people on their way to work and gaze out and across the city of Bath as Monday morning goes about its business. Sunshine lights up the sand-coloured brickwork of the higgledy-piggledy rows of Georgian architecture down below.

I walk and try to coerce my jaded, sodden mind into action.

Come on brain. Do something.

*   *

You never understand people who complain that they can't sleep. Are they stupid? You just go to bed and fall asleep. You never have problems switching off. Even the late night bombing raids in The Gulf couldn't keep you awake.

You rise after a fitful night's kip in your firm but comfy bed in the Travel Inn just outside Ringwood. You're only about ten miles from Bournemouth, but far enough away not to get caught in police blockades should they be set up when the Dragonfly tour bus is found at low tide. Dressed in your T-shirt and underwear, you do 100 push ups on the bedroom carpet, followed by 100 sit ups with your feet tucked under the bed, and 50 tricep dips using the edge of the bed. It's 9:05am. You'd never sleep this late normally, but you didn't get to the Travel Inn until gone 3:30am. You prefer getting up at 6am. You get so much more done when you're up early.

You carefully shower without getting your face or wigged hair wet – you're keeping the black goatie beard on but will be wearing a cap over the long wavy wig today. You inspect your fingers and remind yourself to reapply some 'liquid skin'. As you're drying yourself there's a knock on your door.

"Morning papers, sir."

"Leave them outside."

You give it five minutes, making yourself a coffee, then open your door and pick up *The Daily Telegraph* and *The Sun* from your door mat. You sit on the bed and flick through the broadsheet. There isn't anything on Dragonfly's tour bus at sea. It only happened about nine hours ago after all. There are a couple of stories about Danny Stone, and a few photos of his ex-colleagues from *Argyle Street* with quotes saying, *'How shocked, upset and grief stricken we all are at this great loss to the acting world.'* Not that actors would ever overact, obviously. There's an official release from his record label saying, *'We're all devastated and distraught at the loss of Danny Stone, someone so young and talented with a very promising music career ahead of him.'* Reading stories like this reminds you why you started your little pop project.

There's also a story comparing you with other serial killers who've been caught and jailed. That's one place you plan to stay well away from. Your meticulous planning will see to that. You put *The Telegraph* to one side and check out *The Sun's* front page. There's a photo of a drunk-looking man with his arm around a slim, pretty bird in a mini skirt. She's smiling, he's not. You read the headline and it makes you stand up. You read it again.

'HITMAN & HIM!'

The caption reads *'Journalist Hardy Matthews is mates with the Hitman.'*

You have a mate? And it's Hardy fucking Matthews?

"What are you playing at, Hardy my boy?"

The front-page story says: *'Hardy Matthews, a journalist for music magazine TOP 10 HITS, has exclusively told The Sun that he's mates with the Top 10 Hitman. In confidence at the X-Festival yesterday, Hardy told us he has witnessed two of the recent pop star murders, including the murder of The Sun's much-missed Danny Stone...'*

Hardy wasn't there when you did Danny Stone. Has Hardy been telling porkies... or has *The Sun* not got its story straight?

You read on: *'Hardy, from Bath, told us he's met the Hitman on several occasions, and has even been out drinking with him – although Hardy wouldn't reveal the Hitman's name or who might be next on the Top 10 Hit List.*

Hardy was at the X-Festival in Exeter yesterday drinking heavily in the VIP bar and getting friendly with blonde, leggy PR girl Carly –

they later left together. Meanwhile, we believe the Hitman was plotting his next pop star murder...'

Is Hardy to blame for these front-page antics or is this tabloid tattle? You'd warned him to keep his gob shut but who knows. Either way, you don't need him on the front page pretending to be your mate with some blonde bint in tow. You want dead boy bands and dead talent show singers as the headline news.

Even if Hardy hasn't mentioned your name or Sophie being kidnapped, you'd warned him not to talk. You can feel the fire welling up.

"I told you to keep your trap shut, Hardy," you spit through gritted teeth, pointing at him on the front page of newspaper.

You clench your jaw and repeatedly punch the pillows on the bed until feathers start floating up in the air.

"I told you, keep quiet or I'll kill Sophie. You are about to find out that I am a man of my word."

You quickly pack your bags, shoving the papers inside and making sure you've left nothing incriminating behind. You pull on your black cap, pay up in cash at the Travel Inn desk and leave.

Behind the wheel of your Astra you join the Monday morning traffic. It's just past rush hour but the A-roads to Salisbury are still slow going and packed with cars and lorries. You won't be able to pick up the motorways until you get on the M4 near Bath. You shout at the cars in front to get a shift on, and grip the steering wheel tightly. Put your anger on the back burner. There's no point wasting it. You're going to need it when you get back home and deal with Sophie.

As you will be passing through Bath, why not pop in and murder Hardy?

It'll be easy enough to track him down in Bath through his magazine publishing office. Hardy's not on your Hit List, but neither was Sophie until half an hour ago. You're not going to let a bloody journalist ruin your master plan. You will reach your No.1.

Should you kill or should you go now?

There's no rush. You've got 45 miles to decide before you get to Bath. You put a Pink Floyd CD in the car stereo, sit back and wait for *Shine On You Crazy Diamond* to get going.

*   *

I pop in the local newsagents on Julian Road. I need chocolate to boost my sugar levels and to trigger my brain into action, and I need to check out the papers. I pick out a few bars of milk chocolate and a can of coke. I glance at the magazines and see our latest issue of *TOP 10 HITS* already on sale, an illuminated headline says *'Danny Stone is Dead: The Inside Story'*. I flick through out of habit and check The Insider piece I wrote hasn't been subbed to death. It's mostly how I'd written it, although I don't remember writing 'wicked' or 'super cool' or 'sexy' when describing Danny bloody Stone.

It amuses me that we were struggling to sell over 50,000 copies every two weeks but now that's soared to over 350,000 with my exclusive Insider stories on the Hitman murders. Who says crime doesn't pay? I put our mag back on the shelf and browse the newspapers. I thumb through *The Times* broadsheet in its tabloid-size. Broadloid? Tabsheet? There's the usual speculative guff trying to predict who's next on the Hit List. I scan the other papers' front pages for any updates by DCI Johnson or to see if Sophie's kidnapping has been mentioned.

Neither of them are on the front pages.

But I am.

On the front of *The Sun* is a full-page photo of me looking a bit drunk with my arm around Carly.

I've been papped. It's not a nice feeling. It's like being caught wanking by the whole country and having the evidence plastered across the front page. My cheeks redden and I check nobody in the shop has recognised me.

I've seen photos of myself in *TOP 10 HITS* and other magazines many times, and after a while, to be honest, it stops being exciting. However, seeing myself on the front page of Britain's best-selling national newspaper that over three million people buy everyday is in a different league.

I have an out-of-body experience as I stare at the picture. I hardly recognise myself: I've got a sunburnt face and a scruffy beard. My eyes look half full of booze, Carly's look half empty. You can tell from my expression that I don't want the photo taken, whereas Carly's smiling for all the attention of Britain.

But if the photo's scary, the headline's terrifying.

'HITMAN & HIM!'

Me and McNamara, together. I go dizzy at the thought. The main story is a mixture of lies and total fiction that I apparently exclusively told that poisonous little showbiz witch. I've been done over. I'm not happy about this.

More importantly, McNamara's not going to be happy about this.

Gary's not going to be happy about the negative press coverage of our youth-friendly mag. I can't imagine DCI Johnson's going to be too happy about my front page gossiping. I look at the photo again, and I look at my arm around blonde, long legged Carly.

Most important of all, Sophie's not going to be happy either. If I ever see her again before McNamara gets medieval on her ass. A wave of panic gushes over me and my legs start to shake.

I unsteadily buy the chocolate, coke and two copies of *The Sun*, and I pay the nice man in the shop who's oblivious that he's serving the Hitman's mate.

As I walk out of the shop, another wave flushes over me. Does this mean that I'm a celebrity now? What an ugly thought. I tuck the papers under my arm and shove chocolate down my throat, gradually walking faster and faster until I look like one of those annoying speed walkers.

I realise I haven't switched on my mobile phone yet. Shakily I turn it on and instantly my voicemail calls me. I have five new messages. The first is from DCI Johnson wondering what I'm doing on the front page of *The Sun*, the next two are from Gary wondering the same, the third is from Richie sounding excited, and the last is from my Mum sounding concerned.

She's not the only one. What's my new mate doing with Sophie? A third wave of panic washes over and over me.

As soon as I ring off, my mobile buzzes again. It's DCI Johnson. I don't answer as I break into a jog to get back to my flat. A minute later my mobile rings again with a new message from Johnson, and another from Gary. Fortunately, half way through listening to Gary sound agitated because Johnson's called him and threatened to close *TOP 10 HITS*, my battery dies. I sprint the last two hundred metres to my flat.

I need to get out of Bath, and quickly. I hurriedly pack a backpack of random stuff and jump in my Golf parked outside the flat. I wind down the windows and drive off, breathing in the fresh air, and wishing I'd stop sweating.

Just as a pull out of Camden Crescent and head up and away from town, I spot a blue and white cop car in my mirror as it turns into my road. I just know they're heading to my flat. I put my foot down and get the hell out of Bath. I feel my head clearing and the panic rising and falling as I attempt to occupy my mind with driving. This still means I feel empty headed, and I've started shaking thanks to a combination of the sugar, hangover and adrenalin. I put on Radio 1 to discover they're playing highlights from the X-Festival. I slot the Golf through the gears and drive towards the motorway, although I don't know where I'm going.

Actually, that's not strictly true. I do know where I'm going.

I'm going to rescue Sophie, God damn it.

*   *

When you're busy you make lists and prioritise what's most important. It's how you started with your Top 10 Hit List. You've decided that finding and killing Hardy is not a priority. Keeping your word and killing Sophie is. He's not top of your Hit List. You'll deal with him later, perhaps after Hit No.2, perhaps before. You're not sure yet. He may've blabbed to the press, but he doesn't know where you live and where you're holding Sophie. He's not a threat.

You've also heard Bath's full of posh, pretentious tossers anyway. You'd rather get back home to Liverpool. As you drive up the A36 towards Bath, you skirt around the edge of the city and follow signs for the A46 and M4. The traffic seems busy for such a small city so you do a few breathing exercises as you crawl in a queue behind giant BMWs and shiny 4X4s. You notice the Range Rover in front has a sticker in the back window that says 'Sean Bates R.I.P.' You resist the temptation to ram into the back of it.

Instead, you put a Guns 'n' Roses CD on and think about how you're going to get rid of Sophie's body after you've quietly killed her in the spare room of your flat.

*   *

I pull onto the west-bound M4 and join the fast lane. With one eye on the motorway, I plug my phone charger into the cigarette lighter socket. The moment I switch my mobile back on the voicemail rings with another message.

"Will you all just fuck off!"

I cancel the call.

What does a man do when he's in trouble? He's speaks to his mate. Not the Hitman one, the other one. I phone Fat Pat on his mobile. I hope to hell he's back from The States. I really need him now.

"Hello Sunshine," he says as he answers. "Well, I've just flown back in early this morning after a blinding weekend of top gigs in Las Vegas. What's new with you? Actually, I don't need to ask. You're on the facking front page of *The Sun* with your arm around some blonde. What have you been playing at, you marrow? What's happened to Sophie?"

"That's why I'm calling Pat," I say. "He's got Sophie."

I explain everything to Fat Pat. That McNamara's the Hitman With No Name, seeing him drown Jimmy Fink, kidnapping Sophie, and his death threats. I tell him about being arrested, but gloss over details of being wrecked for two days. I also explain the *The Sun* was a tad creative with its journalism.

"Figured *The Current Bun* had done a number on you," he says. "So... Christ... it is McNamara then?"

"Yep, and the bastard's taken Sophie. Now with *The Sun* doing its best to stick two of my fingers up at him, I've got no doubt that he's going to kill her."

"And he's very handy at that sort of thing."

"Thanks. As if I need reminding," I say. "I need to act fast and I need your help, but we've got to keep this under our hats."

"I don't wear a hat, Hardy."

"Neither do I. But the police do, and DCI Johnson and his detectives are crawling all over the place right now. The last thing I need is to be bloody arrested again," I say. "Look, I need to find out where McNamara lives, and quickly. Can you track down his old band mates and see if they have an address. We both need to call our industry contacts as well, see if they've ever heard of a bodyguard called McNamara."

The driving has finally kicked my brain into gear. It's time to get the H&S Detective Agency back on the road. Well, 50 per cent of it. I continue speeding in the outside lane towards the M4/M5 junction while looking out for cop cars.

"I can do that. I'll start with the band then I'll call a few bodyguards I know," says Fat Pat.

"Great, brilliant. If I can get hold of his home address I can pay him a visit and wing it from there. He's not a kidnapper, he's a killer. I've got a strange feeling he hasn't taken Sophie to some secret location. I think he's taken her home. It's the sort of twisted thing McNamara would do."

"I'll get right on it," says Fat Pat. "Where are you anyway?"

"Just pulling onto the M5. I'm driving to Liverpool. I'm hoping the bastard still lives there. I figured you could somehow source the address before I get there."

"No pressure then. But ten out of ten for initiative," laughs Fat Pat.

"I need to find him, Pat," I say. "I need to save Sophie."

"I'll call you back as soon I know something. Stay cool, Hardy."

I stay cool by driving the Golf at a steady but almost flat-out 125mph. At a contra-flow I slow down to 100mph but as soon as it's back to three lanes I'm back to 125mph. Screw the speed cameras. It's only the motorway patrol cars I'm worried about. I figure Johnson's put out a description of my car and number plate to bring me in so I eagerly play spot the cop car. The blue, white and fluorescent yellow ones are easy to spot, and l know from experience that unmarked cop cars are usually powerful saloons, and have two people dressed in shirts up front, and extra aerials on the back. I spot a blue and white siren on the hard shoulder just past Gloucester. I slow down to 80mph as an officer is busy giving a Jaguar driver a ticket. When they're out of sight I accelerate back up to cruising speed.

I ignore my persistent voicemails and make some calls. Using numbers from my address book and directory enquires, I speak to venue managers and heads of security from Cardiff International Arena, Hammersmith Apollo, Manchester MEN Arena, Birmingham's NEC, and all the Carling Academies from London to Bristol to Newcastle to Glasgow. I try outdoor venues like Milton Keynes' Bowl and the X-Festival in Exeter. Apart from a few crossed wires about Paul McCartney and Andy McNab, nobody has ever had a McNamara on their books.

I call Simon Rumbles from the C4 studio security team and Jon Peters from Blackpool Tower to see if they've heard of anyone called McNamara. They haven't. But Rumbles did know a McManaman and Peters has heard of a McMillan.

Undeterred, I stay positive and keep driving north. I turn the radio up every so often as the X-Festival highlights continue. I can't remember seeing half of the bands they're playing so it's nice to get a chance to hear them now. It takes my mind off images in my head of McNamara playing with Sophie's dead body.

I spot another blue and white cop car ahead so I slow down to 70mph and hang behind until they turn off. Then I'm back up to a comfortable 125mph. The old Golf engine continues to purr as it claws its way up the motorway.

My mobile keeps buzzing but I ignore all the calls until Fat Pat rings just as I drive past Worcester. "I've called every head of security at every venue I can think of and nobody's freaking heard of McNamara," I say.

"I managed to get hold of his old band mates on the phone," says Fat Pat.

"You're kidding!? And any joy?" I say.

"Nope. Neither of them have seen or heard from McNamara for at least eight years. Last they heard he was still in the army."

"Arse."

"But I have found someone who knows him," says Fat Pat in a 'I'm better than you at playing detective' kind of way.

"You taking the piss?"

"Nope."

"You beauty." Two words I don't normally say to Fat Pat.

"His name's Carney. He's an ex-rugby league player, he's been a bodyguard for a few years, and he did a couple of bodyguard contracts with McNamara early last year. From his description of a bitter Liverpudlian with tattoos and an army background it sounds like it could be the Hitman. Carney wouldn't say anymore to me, but he said he's willing to meet you to talk. I think that means he won't spill unless you bung him a wad. Grassing ain't cheap in this game."

"Okay. Where is he?"

"This is the best bit. He lives in Stoke-on-Trent, and you're lucky, he's got the day off. I'll text you his mobile number now. I said you'd give him a call."

"Pat, you're a legend."

"It has been said. This beer tally you owe me has got to be around the sixteen pint mark by now."

"You can count on it."

"Good luck."

"Cheers."

The instant Fat Pat's text comes through I call the number. After five rings a gruff voice of a man who I imagine enjoys his cigarettes says, "Yeah?"

"Carney?"

"Yeah."

"This is Hardy. I think you might have some information for me."

"I might."

"I'll make it worth your while. Can you meet now? I'm just passing Birmingham heading north on the motorway."

"Meet me in the Horse & Hound on Kings Street in Fenton in Stoke at 1pm. Don't be late," Carney says and hangs up.

I tear along the tired excuse for a motorway around Birmingham and speed in every sense of the word along the M6 until the first junction for Stoke. I turn off onto the dual carriageway leading into the town centre and notice that 70mph feels strangely slow. I've only got 15 minutes so I pull up outside a bank on the high street and park on some double yellows. I flick the hazard lights on and speed walk into the bank. There's only one old lady with blue hair before me in the queue, but typically she's paying in her life savings in two pence pieces.

When it's finally my turn I find myself saying, "I'd like to withdraw seven hundred and fifty pounds please."

"No problem," says a female cashier with mousy hair. "I'll be right back."

It's weird how I got a healthy bank balance thanks to Sophie's front page photos, and now I'm using the money to track her down after being given a kick up the arse by front page headlines. What goes around comes around.

The mousy cashier takes a while and I wonder if Johnson might be monitoring my bank account. The cashier may've seen something flagged up on my account and gone to tell her manager, who's calling Johnson right now while I wait like an idiot as my mug's being filmed by the bank's CCTV.

The cashier appears again. "Sorry about that. Just needed authorisation from my manager," she smiles.

I smile back but I'm not sure whether to believe her.

"How would you like the money?"

"Fifty pound notes please."

I don't know whether she's dobbed me into Johnson, but I don't care, it's a risk I have to take to reach Sophie.

I sign on the dotted line and ask the cashier to put £500 of it in an envelope, which I put in my pocket, and I put the other £250 in my wallet.

I speed walk out of the bank and jump in the Golf. As I pull away a traffic warden walks around the corner. I give the portly man with the moustache a wave. He shakes his head at me and waves a finger. I think about giving him a different finger back, but pull over, wind my window down and ask politely, "Do you know where Kings Street in Fenton is please?"

"Don't I know you? Your face looks very familiar," he says bending down to look in my window.

"No, I don't think so," I say, smiling. He looks like a *Sun* reader so he might recognise me. I am a celebrity. Oh crap. And I'm on the run. I'm not sure which is worse or if either dilemma would feel any less burdensome.

I look at my watch. It's five to one. "I'm sorry, I'm in a bit of hurry to meet a client. So, do you know where Kings Street is?"

"I'm sure I recognise you... Anyway, you need to carry straight here for about two miles. Right at the first roundabout, then after half a mile, right near the supermarket, and that'll lead you into Kings Street."

"Okay, cheers." I floor the accelerator and wheel spin not entirely inconspicuously away from the bank.

I screech to a halt outside the Horse & Hound, then realising I've got a minute to spare, I roll around the corner and neatly parallel park on a side street so the Golf's out of sight from the main road. I grab my notebook and pen, tuck the envelope of cash in my back pocket, and switch my mobile to silent and shove it in my front pocket.

The dark brown paint on the outside of the pub is flaking away from the woodwork and two windows have been boarded up. I take a deep breath. I attempt to appear confident as I walk into the pub, holding my head high, pushing my shoulders back. But instead I trip on a torn piece of carpet that sends me crashing into the double doors and falling straight into the pub. I look up from the grubby, worn out carpet to find two big faces staring down at me. Neither look friendly, but both are sort of smiling at me. This actually makes the two thickset, bald headed men with jutting jaws and leather bomber jackets look even more intimidating.

"That's funny, I normally only fall out of pubs," I say, picking myself up.

Clearly unimpressed they swivel on their bar stools and turn their attention back to their pints. I walk around to the other side of the L-shaped bar and glance around to see if someone looks like a bodyguard. The two bald blokes could be, and as I lean on the bar and look around and over my shoulder, I realise the chunky men dotted around at tables and at the end of the bar could *all* be bodyguards or bouncers. Or both. I've no idea which one is Carney and now I wish I'd asked him to wear a red carnation.

A blonde man is his forties in a fitted black T-shirt and jeans walks towards me. I do one of those 'smiles that aren't really smiles' in case he's not Carney, but thankfully he smiles back. I then panic and wonder if he's gay.

"Hardy?" he says. I recognise the gruff smoker's voice. He's got a fag on the go. Not a gay on the go, a cigarette.

I nod at him. "Carney?"

He nods at me.

"Buy you a drink?"

"Lager, cheers."

I buy a pint of strong lager for Carney and an orange juice and lemonade for myself. I can still feel my hangover bubbling underneath. A pint would take the edge off, but bad things happen when I drink these days. I need to stay sober.

We sit at a table in the corner by a window. Carney has a slim build, but as he picks up his pint I notice taught muscles along his forearms up to his biceps. His knuckles are unusually large and almost look swollen. I proudly display my own scabbed up knuckles on the table. A vein is sticking out the length of Carney's neck, he has a scar above his right eye, and the crooked nose of someone who played one rugby league season too many. I have no doubt he's been around the block and is also still the hardest in the 'hood.

"So, you know McNamara?" I say quietly.

"I know Mac, yeah," says Carney looking me in the eye. His green eyes don't exactly twinkle, but they do terrorize. He leans on the table and taps ash from his cigarette into the ashtray. "Mac and me worked together on a couple of jobs early last year. Doing personal security for one of them boy bands I can never remember the name of. They all look the bloody same after a while…"

"They all sound the same that's for sure," I say trying to be friendly.

Carney smiles and lets out the throaty cough of a dedicated nicotine addict.

"So, Mac…"

"Yeah, Mac. He was a solid bloke to work alongside. Very self assured. Very professional and someone I trusted. But I wouldn't want to get on his bad side. I saw him mess up three lads in an upmarket bar after they'd been getting verbal with our delicate little boy band. He was so fast and without even trying he broke one of their noses, another's wrist and bust the other's kneecap. Mac just laughed afterwards. We had to scarper pretty quick after to avoid the wrong sort of attention for the boys," says Carney, his eyes alight.

"Crikey," I say. I don't tell Carney I've already had the pleasure of being flattened by McNamara.

Carney sucks on his cigarette and blows smoke over my head. Better than blowing it up my ass, I suppose. "I don't think he even liked the boy band. He loved any excuse for a ruck did Mac."

I try the direct approach. "I need his address."

Carney inhales and exhales while looking me in the eye. "I know where he lives. I picked up him for a job once. But it goes with the territory that you don't give out a fellow bodyguard's address," he says as he stands up ready to leave.

"Would this help?"

I pull the envelope of cash from my pocket. I've got my back to the bar so I know nobody can see as I slide it across the table hidden under my notepad and pen. Carney sits back down and subtly slides the money on to his lap, leaving the pad and pen on the table. I imagine Carney's not very good at bluffing when he's playing poker because his green eyes bulge as he counts the cash. He quickly slips the money into his pocket, writes down an address and pushes the pad back to me.

Carney moves in close and says, "You didn't get it from me alright?" He downs his pint and looks to leave. "I don't know what you want with Mac, and I don't want to know, but I hope you know who you're dealing with."

I get in the Golf and look at the address on my pad. It's only an address, but it feels much more. I get a tingle in my shoulders and try and shrug it away. I knew it would be in Liverpool. I know McNamara. That's the scary thing – this address is my ticket to find

266

a trained killer poised ready to kill. I think about Sophie and try and stay positive.

I switch my mobile off silent and see that I've got twelve missed calls. Most are my voicemail persistently calling back. I ignore it and think about calling Johnson. The right thing to do would be to tell him the address and let him and his detectives rescue Sophie and catch McNamara. But there's a chance, even if Chief Supermarket sends in his best stealth shoppers, that McNamara will be one step ahead and reach the cash tills before they do. I think a lone gunman appearing quietly across the plains would be safer than the whole cavalry galloping into town. I can't take the chance that Sheriff Johnson and his posse won't spook McNamara into killing Sophie.

I avoid thinking up any more rubbish analogies, scroll to Fat Pat's number on my phone and call him instead.

"How'd it go?" says Fat Pat.

"Not bad. Carney gave me an address in Liverpool," I say. "Write this down. First floor flat, 36 Emerson Street."

"Got it," he says. "Can't believe it's a flat. Hitmen should have houses with gardens to bury body parts in. What kind of Hitman lives in a first-floor flat?"

"Either a very clever, confident one. Or a completely psychotic one."

"Which one's McNamara?"

"Worryingly, a bit of both."

"Figures," says Fat Pat. "You were right. It's in Liverpool."

"Seems that way. Can you look the address up on Route Finder online and text me directions from the M62?"

"I'll do it now. I'm on my laptop. I'll text you right back."

"Top man. I'm going to drive there right away and see what happens. If McNamara's seen the front pages there's every chance I'm already too late." Just saying it out loud makes me feel sick. I can't let Sophie down. She'll be counting on me. We're a team. We're the H&S Detective Agency.

"Watch out for those upper cuts, eh?"

"Thanks. Send out Johnson and his posse if I'm not back before the sun sets," I say, and hang up. It's such a cliché, but I'm only half joking. I hope Fat Pat realises I may well need the cop-sized cavalry later.

I drive out of Stoke and gradually speed up as I pull onto the dual carriageway. I watch my speed for now. I want to gather my thoughts. I need to psyche myself up. I need some music.

I pull onto the M6 and plug my iPod into the stereo, putting on some early Rage Against The Machine. As the guitars kick in and

Zack De La Rocha rages I gradually accelerate and turn the volume up. I accelerate a bit more, and turn it up a bit more. I'm soon at a cruising speed of 125mph and keeping an eye out for blue and whites as I drive north. The text from Fat Pat arrives with the directions and I read it a few times to memorise it before I turn off the M6. The early Monday afternoon traffic is quiet and light and the music is suitably loud and dark. I start singing along. Quietly at first. But as the Golf munches up the miles, I start singing louder, matching Zack's vocals as much as my larynx allows.

By the time I'm on the M62 and speeding into Liverpool, the nerves and hangover have been replaced by adrenalin and I feel ten foot tall.

Which is a good thing, because anything shorter and McNamara will beat me down to size quicker than I can say, "Let the girl go."

*   *

Should you shoot her in the head and put her in a sack with some bricks and toss her body in the Mersey? Or you could slit her throat after she's made dinner and bury her body in the back fields near Aintree. Choices, choices. You don't want Sophie to suffer *too* much. It's not her fault her boyfriend's tried to blow your cover by blurting it out to national press.

You're making pretty good time on the road even though you've been sticking to the speed limit to blend in with the rest of the motorists. The last thing you want is to be pulled over and searched. As soon as you reach the M6 you start to feel more at home, more relaxed. You allow yourself a break at Stafford services for a pee, and a coffee and sandwich, sitting out of the way on a bench outside. The dark, wavy wig feels sweaty and starts to itch a bit under the black cap but you resist the urge to scratch it in public.

You pull back onto the motorway and settle down to just above the speed limit. Should you suffocate her with a pillow when she's sleeping? It would be relatively painless, and a lot less noisy and messy than using a gun or knife.

*   *

I follow Fat Pat's directions and find my way to the south of Liverpool. I keep to 50mph along streets lined with red-bricked houses. People in work suits walk home and men in shell suits walk into pubs. Every so often I drive by teenagers and twentysomethings in red football shirts standing on street corners and hanging around in parks.

The sun is still shining, Zack's still rocking and I'm still shouting to keep my aggression up as I pull into Emerson Street. It's an innocuous road with large, three-storied, red-bricked houses down both sides. Each building is semi-detached and split into two houses. Most look to contain flats as they have three doorbells next to the front doors. I find No.36 half way down on the left, the houses either side have trees in their front gardens. I park up outside and turn the stereo down as a man in his sixties walks past with a Collie on a lead. It's late afternoon by now and the traffic is trickling past the top and bottom of Emerson Street.

I quickly check the address again on my notepad. First floor flat, 36 Emerson Street. I take a deep breath and get out of the car and walk straight up to the front door. I don't even lock the car or take the keys out of the ignition. If I'm going to do this it's now or never. If I think about something too much I'll end up not doing it.

There's no name next to the buzzer, but I can see 'Tony & Sarah' live on the top floor flat and 'The Ashtons' live on the ground floor. I ring the doorbell for the first floor to see if McNamara wants to come out to play. The faint sound of *Smoke On The Water* starts up, but I could just be hearing things. Nobody answers. McNamara's not home. Or he's here and not answering. Or, of course, he doesn't live here and someone who does is at work. Or possibly, Sophie's being held captive inside but McNamara's out doing murders.

See? When I start thinking too much it becomes complicated.

I ring again, wait a bit, then try the top floor flat buzzer. No reply. I try the ground floor. No reply either. I think about shouting out Sophie's name but that will only draw unwanted attention. I stand back from the front door to see if anyone's inside on the first floor. Strangely the curtains are drawn in one of the rooms even though it's daylight. All the windows in the surrounding houses have their curtains open. That's good enough for me. Somebody's inside. My heart starts thumping.

I jog down the side passage to the back of the house. There's a wall twice as tall as me surrounding the back garden so I can't see in or climb over. I find an old wooden door to the back garden that's rusted on the hinges and around the handle, which I try with no joy. I get a run up and hurl myself into the door. Apart from nearly dislocating my shoulder, the door doesn't budge. Fortunately I'm pumped with adrenalin so I don't feel the pain I'd usually scream about.

I leg it back around the front to work out how to break into the first floor. Security bars are running across both windows. I decide to go for the one with the curtains drawn as the flat-roofed porch is below it, and I think I could shimmy up on top of it and make it through the window.

I hastily dig around the boot of the Golf and find some high-tech rope that's been in there since I tried rock climbing about two years ago. I didn't like it: it wasn't the heights I was scared of, it was the ground way below.

I find a short, thick stick in next door's front garden and tie one end of the rope around it. I throw it up and, on the fifth attempt, the stick goes through the gap behind the three security bars in front of the window and falls down for me to catch. I've got metres of rope so I make a loop and pull it so it's tight around the bars, and then, as casually as a man can with a rope tied to a first floor window, I quickly tie it to the metal towing loop on the rear of the Golf's chassis. I slowly pull away from the house to take up the slack. As the rope goes taught, I balance the clutch in first gear and drive away looking back out of the window. To my amazement the rope doesn't snap and the three bars are yanked clean out of the wall, leaving the red brickwork almost completely intact. I quickly reverse back against the kerb. I gather up the rope and two of the bars and throw them into the corner of the front garden just as two middle-aged women in tabards walk around the corner. They're too busy gassing to notice an amateur burglar like me.

When the women are out of sight I swiftly chuck the third bar on top of the porch. I clamber up using the ground floor's window ledge and get on top of the porch so I'm chest-height with the first floor window. I can't see in because of the curtains so God knows what or who's in there. I ignore thoughts of finding McNamara with a gun, or worse, Sophie's dead, decaying body. Checking the coast is clear, and facing away from the window, I quickly smash the glass with the bar. Large pieces fall on top of the porch and smash on the ground below, but most of the window splinters fall inside the flat. No alarm goes off, no police arrive and no neighbours appear. I pull myself up onto the window ledge and squat with the bar up ready to cosh whoever's inside. I can feel my heart pumping against my T-shirt as I use my other hand to draw back the curtain.

*   *

You drive past The Dog & Duck and think about a quick pint. But it's not drink you need, it's food. You decide to call into the curry takeaway around the corner from your flat before you go home. You're starving and feel you can at least buy Sophie her last supper. You play it safe, avoiding a Vindaloo and Madras, and order a Bhuna and a Dupiaza, some rice, poppadoms and nan bread. You sit and wait for ten minutes. When the food arrives you ask for four bottles of Cobra lager from the fridge and pay the grey-haired Indian owner.

As you're leaving, you hold the door open as four rowdy, skinny lads in football shirts push past you without so much as a 'thanks mate'. A little anger rises up but you swallow it down, saving it for when you get home.

You put the beer and big plastic bag on the passenger seat and drive along the familiar and friendly streets that lead to your flat.

*   *

Holding up the bar ready to lash out, I peer into the darkness of what I discover to be a bedroom.

McNamara's not there. No Hitman and his gun awaits. Instead I can see someone lying on a bed. I look closer and realise it's what I've been dreading all along.

Sophie's body is lying motionless on the bed.

No, no, no. Lovely Sophie are you okay?

Her hands and legs are tied to each corner of the bed, which at least means I can check all her limbs are still attached. She's got a cloth gag in her mouth, and her eyes are open but she's staring at the ceiling.

I jump in through the window and her body starts to wriggle, pulling hopelessly on the ropes. She gives out a muffled scream.

She's alive. She's bloody alive.

Sophie looks petrified. She squints as her eyes struggle to adjust to the daylight pouring into the bedroom. I don't think she can see it's me. I can hear a dog barking somewhere.

"It's me. Sophie, it's me. I've come to rescue you," I say, gripping gently on her shoulders looking into her hard eyes. They soon soften and even with the gag I can see she's trying to smile. I quickly pull the cloth out of her mouth.

"You took your bloody time didn't you?" says Sophie, sounding tough, but her trembling body tells me otherwise.

"I've missed you too," I say.

It's feels so good to see her face again. I can see slight bruising on her cheek and there's crusty bits of blood around her nostrils. I touch her cheek gently with the back of my hand. She's still wearing the jeans and red top she had on at Anfield.

"No time for affection now," she says.

I look her up and down and down and up.

"Are you okay? You look okay. Are you okay? Where's McNamara? Is he here? You okay?" I say at a hundred miles an hour, buzzing with adrenalin.

"I'll be fine as soon as we get out of here it's okay he's not here but we'd better not hang about the psycho said he'd be back early

271

afternoon are you going to untie me or what?" she says at two hundred miles an hour.

I look at my watch even though I already know it's more like early evening. I try to untie the knots on the bed posts but can't. I pace around the bed and glance out the glassless window as a man in a black cap parks a white Astra on the other side of the street. For some reason I draw the curtains and run across the room to put the light on. I try the door handle but it's locked from the outside. The barking starts again.

"Back from where?" I say quickly, tugging on the ropes as hard as I can, "and has he got a big dog?"

"Work, he called it, yeah, his dog's called Sadie, but she's just big and soppy. The door's bolted from the outside. Are you going to untie me now or what?"

"I'm trying!" I say fiddling fruitlessly again with the knots.

"I shit myself when I heard all that noise outside, and then the bloody window caved in. I'd already heard the doorbell and I thought it was a scally burglar checking if anyone was home before breaking in. But I knew I wasn't going to be able to defend myself because I've been bloody tied to the bed by a Hitman kidnapper nutter who's obviously totally mental by the way..." Sophie gabbles again. "Are you going to untie me!? "

I look around for something sharp. The desk drawers and bedside cabinet are empty and the wardrobe just has clothes hanging up. I yank one of the shirts from its hanger and, picking up one of the larger shards of glass from the floor, I wrap the shirt around the end and start slicing as fast as I can through the ropes.

*   *

A blue Ford Fiesta and a red VW Golf are parked outside your house so you park across the other side of the street. It feels good to be back home. It'll be good to see Sadie, and Sophie too. You lock up the car and briefly glance up to the spare bedroom window and see the curtains still drawn. You wonder if Sophie's still sleeping.

As you're putting the key in the front door, you stop. Perhaps you should break her neck? She's a girl and it would snap easily. It'll still be mostly painless and quicker than suffocating her.

You walk upstairs and into your flat, putting the curry and beer on the side in the kitchen, placing the sandwich box next to it. You kneel down and rub Sadie's belly as she rolls over and pants, excitedly wagging her tail.

Yeah, break Sophie's neck. You haven't snapped someone's neck for ages.

I hurriedly slice through the last of the ropes and Sophie slides to the end of the bed and rubs at the zip ties still around her wrists and ankles. She finds her shoes at the end of the bed and quickly slips them on. Her hair looks tangled and her face looks pale, but she still looks beautiful. She pushes herself off the bed and jumps up, wrapping her arms around my neck to give me a smacker on the lips.

"I'm so glad you're here. I feel like I've been tied up for months," she says in a little voice, hugging me closely. Her body stops trembling once she's in my arms. Although that could be because my own trembling falls in synch with hers.

"I'm sorry I took so long." I squeeze her tightly.

The barking starts again.

"Did you hear something?" I whisper.

"Just Sadie barking," she whispers. "She barks at nothing I've noticed."

"No, something else. A voice."

We stand still and listen. I can hear Sophie breathing and feel my heart thumping. I reach over and flick the bedroom light off.

"Hello girl! Did you miss me? Daddy's home." The scary voice is all too familiar and it's coming from somewhere within the flat.

"McNamara," I say quietly.

"Oh God, oh God. He must be in the bloody kitchen talking to Sadie," she whispers. Sophie's eyes double in size and her hands start shaking.

"Let's get the fuck out of here," I say under my breath.

I open the curtains and quickly help Sophie out of the window. She drops down on the porch then whispers through gritted teeth, "My cap. On the bedside cabinet." I reach across and swiftly put it on my head and climb out of the window. Glass crunches under my feet as I drop down on top of the porch. I close the curtains behind me. It seems the polite thing to do. Sophie deftly climbs down from the porch to the window ledge below and I follow quickly, dropping down onto the path. Thankfully nobody's walking past to witness our great escape in broad daylight.

"Quick. To the car."

I run around and jump in the driver's seat, quickly opening the passenger door for Sophie. I turn the key waiting in the ignition, drop the clutch as soon as the engine fires into action, and drive off as quickly and quietly as I can. Sophie winds the window down and looks back as I look forwards.

You had better check on your guest in the spare room. You pull the two locks back and open the door. "Hi honey, Daddy's home."

It's dark in the bedroom so you flick the light on.

She's gone.

The ropes tied to the bed have been cut and there's glass on the floor beneath the window. The curtains flicker. You wrench them open to discover the window's missing. You look outside and see broken glass on the porch and ground below.

Who? What? How...?

Your brain clicks into overdrive.

In a flash you survey room. This isn't a police job. They would come through the front door. They would come for you first and save the girl afterwards. This is the work of a total amateur. Hardy. He came to get the girl.

"The cheeky bastard," you say to yourself.

You hear the rev of an engine. You jump to the window and see the red VW pull hastily driving away. You can't see the driver but you can see a girl with dark hair in the passenger seat. When the car's a little further up the street the girl sticks her head out of the window and looks back at you.

Sophie.

Where does the bitch think she's going?

*   *

I can't bloody believe it. As we drive off I really think we've done it.

"Oh God. He's spotted us from the bloody bedroom window!" shouts Sophie.

Or maybe not.

"Christ," I say gripping the steering wheel. Even over the vibration of the car's engine I can feel my whole chest throbbing.

"He's got on a black cap with long hair poking out underneath and a beard on his chin, but it's him alright," says Sophie with a shaky voice.

The man in the Astra.

"You can't let him catch us, Hardy, he'll kill us both," says Sophie tapping frenetically on the dashboard.

"Christ." It's all I can say.

At the T-junction at the top of the road I don't stop and give way, instead I nearly cause a major accident as I pull straight out in front of a van. Ignoring the beeping horns, I accelerate and drive the Golf like I've just stolen it. A few heads turn as I redline the engine and nudge 70mph up the street, overtaking cars when there's merely a suggestion of a gap. A group of teenagers in tracksuits on the pavement wave and cheer as I hammer past at over twice the speed limit. It seems car theft is still a popular pastime around here.

*   *

"The bloody cheeky little bastards," you say as you stare after them from the bedroom window. The sun's low in the sky so you have to shield your eyes to see which way they turn. They nearly collide with a white transit but you see their red car turn right.

You run out of the bedroom, quickly grab your car keys and sandwich box from the kitchen and run down to your car. You start the engine and get annoyed with yourself because you're not facing the right way. You know the street's too tight to turnaround. You stamp on the go pedal and as the Astra splutters into life, you accelerate hard and skid around the corner. You'll head them off using the back streets.

You won't let them get away. You can't let them.

"He's only a fucking journalist! She's only a fucking photographer!"

*   *

"Is he behind us? Can you see him!?" I shout as I overtake two cars in a row.

"I don't know," says Sophie jumping around in the seat and looking back behind us.

"What do you mean you don't know!?"

"He knocked me out after you at Anfield and when I came around I was bloody tied up in his flat!" shouts Sophie. "I don't know what car he drives."

"Okay, okay. You need to look out for a white Astra," I say as I swerve around two scooters buzzing along. "I saw him pull up before I closed the curtains in the bedroom."

"Why didn't you say anything!?"

"Because I didn't know it was him at the time because of his bloody disguise."

I overtake a powerful-looking motorbike and the rider in black leathers looks shocked that he's been overtaken by a six-year-old Golf. I keep driving like a mentalist until some traffic lights ahead turn red. Strings of traffic cross in both directions. I decide it's probably best

275

not to jump the lights at over 70mph so I hit the brakes to bring us to a halt on the white line. We both look behind us.

"I don't think anyone's followed us," I say.

"I don't think anyone could've kept up. Nice driving Schumacher," she says smiling and gripping my hand. "Let's get out of Liverpool and then can we pull over as I'm dying for a wee?"

"Okay, slack bladder. We can stop at the first services on the motorway," I say.

As I'm tapping the steering wheel urging the lights to turn green, I catch something out of the corner of my eye. I look to my right to see a white car flying up a back street towards us. Not off the ground and with wings and a jet engine, I mean it's travelling at great velocity. The car gets bigger and bigger until I can see the driver looking straight at me. I don't need to see the cap and beard to know it's McNamara.

I reach behind me and hastily put my seat belt on.

"Belt up, Sophie," I say calmly.

"I didn't say anything," she says.

"Put your seat belt on," I say, sliding the Golf into first.

"Oh, yeah. Oops, forgot," she says.

McNamara's white car gets bigger. The light's are still red. The traffic is still flowing across in front of us as a cop car drives past. I balance the revs on the clutch. McNamara's car gets bigger and all I know is I can't let him smash into the side of my Golf. It'll knock hundreds off the value.

"Hold on to something," I say as calmly as I can.

"Why?" says Sophie.

"McNamara's about to try and ram us," I say calmly.

"What!?" she screams.

I stamp on the accelerator and we jump the lights just as McNamara and his Astra launch out of the back street. I steer through the tiniest of gaps between a minibus and a taxi and somehow make it safely to the other side amidst a cacophony of car horns. I look over my shoulder to see McNamara's car shoot straight across the road, mount the pavement, and skid to a halt before narrowly missing an old lady and her poodle.

"Holy bloody smoke!" shouts Sophie. "That was a bit bloody well close."

I dip the revs into the red again and slip the Golf into third gear as we race up the high street. I look uneasily in the rear view mirror and Sophie twists around searching for McNamara. Behind us in the distance the lights turn green and a speck of white races towards us.

"We've got a Smokey on our tail!" I shout over the engine noise.

"Put that pedal down, Bandit," shrieks Sophie.

The rows of red-bricked houses flash by in a blur as I drive dangerously close to lines of parked cars. Without slowing down I overtake car after car in an attempt to put some distance between us. In the mirror I see McNamara doing the same a few hundred yards behind. I bully past two more cars by driving half on the pavement to put some space between us again. I keep the throttle busy and scream up the road as McNamara gets tangled up behind as the oncoming traffic thickens.

After another half-mile a sign says the ring road is straight ahead. I look in the mirror to see McNamara's white Astra looming, getting bigger. "Hang on!" I shout.

I take a chance and slam on the brakes, yank the car to the left and drift around the corner, feathering the accelerator to get the power and grip down. I just manage to straighten the Golf up at the last minute.

"Where'd you learn to drive like this?" says Sophie holding on to her seat.

"Back roads of Bristol," I say, "and on the PlayStation."

We shoot down a tight B road that looks to lead into the countryside as lines of houses are replaced by tall, green hedgerows. I keep the revs up as Sophie and I bounce along the uneven surface. In the fading sunshine, the Golf kicks up dried dirt from the road to leave a trail of dust. The road ahead is straight and empty so I gun the throttle as the speedo creeps past 90mph.

Now I'll lose the bastard.

*   *

You haul your car around the corner, nearly clipping a Volvo on the other side of the road. So the little twat thinks he'll get away on local country roads you know like the back of your hand? You know this only leads to a couple of farms and a small village pub at a dead end. They won't escape down here.

You give the Astra engine a workout and follow the dust trail Hardy's helpfully leaving behind. You check your sandwich box is within reaching distance on the passenger seat and think about using your Glock to fire a few warning shots. No point wasting bullets. Use them when you get a bit closer.

You hang back and give Hardy and Sophie some space.

You don't need to follow too closely now. Let them think they're losing you.

*   *

"I think we're losing him," shouts Sophie, looking out the back window. I can't see much behind because of the dust, but when it clears I can't see McNamara's white car.

"Let's keep on trucking just to make sure," I say.

I brake slightly and counter steer to power slide around a corner with gravel littered across the surface. I nudge the wrong side of 80mph. It feels more like 180mph as we whistle past the tall hedgerows. Sophie's knuckles are white as she grips the edge of her seat. I don't think she's enjoying the ride as much as me. I think it's brilliant: like playing an arcade racing game, only if I crash I don't get a second go by putting another quid in the slot. If I crash, we could die. And if we don't, McNamara could get hold of us and kill us. So we die either way.

I grip the steering wheel and resolve not to crash. I've been surviving on adrenalin all day, but now my body is pumping some extra strength stuff through my veins. My senses are so alert I'm aware of everything around me. I can even smell what's coming.

"Don't you love the smell of the countryside, sweetheart!?" I shout. I notice several fresh cowpats on the road have been squashed by some big tyre tracks.

"Fertilizer?" she shouts. "It's not an eau de toilette I enjoy."

As I weave through an S-bend, I cut the corner and a rear tyre flirts dangerously with the grassy verge. I have to fight to keep us online, but by keeping the power down, the tyres bite and the Golf lurches forwards once again.

"Don't get cocky, kid!" shouts Sophie.

I ease off and slow down a little. Which is lucky, as around the next tight corner a tractor's waiting for us. The farmer frantically waves his arms at us from the cabin. I slam on the anchors, but we're still travelling way too fast, and I really don't want to shunt into the back of a huge stationary tractor. My arms stiffen as I swerve blindly around the side of the tractor and quickly pray to God there's no oncoming traffic. He must be listening because there's no cars. But there is a herd of cows slowly crossing the road. I jerk the Golf to the right and pull on the handbrake to skid neatly sideways through a hedge, pirouetting a few times in a grassy field until we finally stop yards from the herd.

"Holy cow," says Sophie, taking her hands away from her eyes.

Feeling dizzy, but relieved, I drive the Golf slowly along the edge of the field away from the tractor and cows, and head towards an open gate about 100 yards back the way we came. In a moment of inspiration I decide we should hide from McNamara behind the dense hedgerows. I stop before the gateway making sure we're out of sight from the road, and out of sight from McNamara.

That's if he's still on our tail.

Sophie and I listen intently. Where is he? Then I hear the growl of a car engine gradually getting louder and louder. Through the hedge I watch a flash of white zip past on the road. It's quickly followed by the sound of screeching tyres, a loud thud, and an even louder crunch.

I pull the nose of the Golf out onto the road and we craftily look right to see McNamara's car lying on its side in a deep gutter by the other side of the road about 100 yards away. I think I can see a cow lying in the road. The tractor pulls alongside McNamara and the farmer climbs down from his cabin and stares at the mess with his hands on top of his head.

"I think the Smokey's crashed 'n' burned," I say in a dodgy Burt Reynolds accent.

"That's a 10-4. Let's roll, Bandit," says Sophie in her best Sally Field accent.

I take it as our cue to leave before McNamara climbs from the wreckage. I sneakily, quietly drive back the way we came.

*   *

You switch the engine off. There's no point chasing after them. They'll be miles away by now. Besides, your car's on its side and stuck in a ditch, and you think you may've killed a cow.

"The cheeky motherfucking bastards." You're slumped on your side and half upside down lying against the window. As you use the steering wheel to pull yourself upright you look up to see a farmer with a rosy complexion looking at you through the windscreen.

"You alright in there, like, mate?" he says.

You half stand up and wind down the passenger window that's now above you. The farmer helps you out as your car wobbles slightly on its side.

"What's blinkin' goin' on? What is it, like, you two just nicked these cars and thought you'd come and scare the cows for a laugh?"

You shake your head and resist the urge to shove his up one of the cow's arses. The farmer inspects the cow lying on its side. "She's gone. Oh well, like. For her size her deadweight price is around £500," says the farmer. "You can have her for £450 in cash if you fancy?"

What are you going to do with a whole dead cow? You shake your head.

"You're not very chatty are you? You're probably in shock."

You're not in shock. You're pissed off you've crashed and let Hardy and Sophie escape.

"Let's get your car out of that there ditch then shall we?" says the farmer exasperatedly.

After a bit of towing and reversing by the tractor, your Astra is soon resting back on its wheels on the road. It's got minimal damage and only the passenger door is superficially dented.

"Better call the police then," he says.

"I'd rather not get them involved," you say, smiling.

"Oh so you can talk," says the farmer. He looks at you, looks over at his dead cow and shrugs his shoulders. You pull your wallet out and hand over £170.

"It's all I've got on me," you say.

He shoves it in his pocket and walks away as the last of the cows cross the road into the farmyard. You've effectively paid for a third of a cow, but you leave the whole heifer behind, turn the car around and drive back home.

You start thinking. Hardy's stolen Sophie back from under your nose. Think. How did he find your flat? Think. Who told him where you live? Think. Hardy may've called the police and told them your address. Think. You need to shut up shop and get out of Liverpool.

*   *

I pick up the ring road and, still feeling paranoid, accelerate hard onto the dual carriageway that leads us to the motorway and to safety. Sophie looks behind us regularly, hanging her head out of the window, breathing the fresh air in deeply as the setting sun falls on her face. I look in the rear view mirror and speed up whenever a white car appears behind us. But McNamara doesn't show up.

It's only when we get ten miles down the motorway that I stop overtaking every vehicle in sight. I slip the Golf into fifth gear and relax to a steady 88mph.

*   *

You drive quickly but cautiously back to Emerson Street. Checking the old bill's not following or waiting, you park directly outside your house. You jump out of the car and up the stairs to your flat. In the kitchen Sadie is sleeping in her basket. You kick the outside of her basket, but she simply wags her tail at you.

You might be in a rush to evacuate but you can't waste a good curry. You greedily scoop up big mouthfuls of lukewarm Bhuna and rice using the nan bread and wash it down with lager. All the time you're eating, you're thinking.

Think, eat, think.

You need to find another base. Hardy may've tipped off the police, although if he had they would've been waiting for you here. But this doesn't change anything.

You're still going to purge the pop charts. You only have one more hit to go and then it's the big No.1.

Actually, make that three more hits before No.1. Hardy and Sophie have just made it onto your Hit List.

You dig out two big camouflage holdalls and swiftly start filling them with essentials, ignoring any sentimental items. You pack a few army supplies and some weaponry. You take a selection of disguises, your suit, one pair of trainers, and one pair of shoes, and make sure you've got Sophie's mobile phone from the shoe under the bed. It takes you two minutes to fill both holdalls.

You jog downstairs with one in each hand. Sadie follows you and you let her in the back of the car to curl up on her blanket on the backseat. She can sense you're moving. You take out your emergency petrol can from the boot and put the two holdalls in. You jog back up to your flat and find an old packet of cigarettes and a box of matches tucked in a cupboard and light one up. You haven't had one since your pop project started. You haven't felt the need until now. You inhale deeply and walk from room to room, shaking petrol liberally over everything from the furniture to your computer to the television. You take one last drag on the cigarette and flick it on to the sofa. Flames begin to flicker almost instantly. You light a few matches and throw one in each room, using the last to start a fire with some old Hit List plans on paper.

As the blaze starts taking care of itself, you leave your flat that's been home for the last three years. You're about to get in your car when a tanned man in his forties, wearing just tracksuit bottoms, appears on his garden path two houses down. He shouts from across the road, "Can you smell something burning?"

"I think next door's having a barbeque," you say, getting in your car. He gives you the thumbs up and walks back in his house. You look up and see bright orange, angry flames raging out of the spare bedroom window, and drive away.

You feel disappointed. Not because you've had to move out and torch your flat, but because you didn't get to break Sophie's neck. Not today anyway. You take the road around to the M56 and A55 and head south towards North Wales.

As you're driving, and the signposts start changing to show place names in English and Welsh, you think about ways to kill two people at the same time. Instead of two birds with one stone, two people with one bullet. That sort of thing.

The M6 traffic flows along at a steady rate and I keep the Golf at a middling speed in the middle lane as lorries slog it out in the slow lane. I've got the stereo on Radio 4 hoping that any newsflashes about me or McNamara will alert us to any police attention I'm about to drive into. Neither of us is making the headlines.

My mobile rings and Sophie picks it up from the ashtray I keep it in when driving. "It's DCI Johnson," she says.

"Don't answer it."

"I wasn't going to," she says, putting it back in the ashtray. "Although I wouldn't mind some answers. Like why didn't Johnson and the police come and rescue me? Why did I have to wait over three days before you found me? How did you find me anyway? It's not that I'm ungrateful. I was just so God damn scared. I really thought I was going to die back there. He really is properly nuts y'know... Where are the police when you need them? Not that the police were much cop – pardon the pun – our H&S Detective Agency has been far more successful. Anyway, what took you so bloody long...?"

"Have you finished?"

"Give me a break. I've been knocked out, kidnapped, smacked about, and bloody tied up on a bed on my own for over 30-odd hours in the dark."

I pull into the slow lane and reach across to put my hand on top of Sophie's. She looks at me, smiles, and starts crying.

"Everything's okay now. You're safe. You're with me," I say.

I hold her hand and then explain everything since she disappeared from Anfield, and why she's probably not safe with me at all.

I tell her about McNamara threatening to kill her if I told the police, about me being arrested and set free, about losing the plot and drinking to forget about her. I mention the X-Festival bender but leave out the front page antics for now. I don't want to overwhelm her. I explain how I got the address and drove up like her knight in a shiny red car. I explain that I've got the police after me, as well as my boss, and my Mum's worried sick.

"Well, that explains a few things," says Sophie after sniffing her tears back. "Are you okay?"

"Me? Yeah, God, I'm fine. I've had a field day compared to you," I say. I find a small packet of tissues and hand them to her.

"That's one way of putting it," says Sophie, blowing her nose.

"Did he... did he touch you?" I ask, holding her hand, looking over at her. I can see the bruises on her cheek as the last of the day's sunlight shines across the motorway.

"He slapped me about and made me make dinner. I went for him with a saucepan and he stopped me and hit me around the face, but he didn't abuse me sexually if that's what you mean. He also gave me some sleeping pills yesterday but that's it."

"Good. Well, not about the slapping, but about the lack of violating."

Sophie blows her nose again.

"We're a right pair, aren't we?" she says.

"We're a great pair," I say. "The H&S Detective Agency lives to fight another day."

My phone rings again. It's Gary. I switch it to silent. Then, as if she'd never been crying at all, Sophie says, "I'm bloody Hank Marvin. Let's stop at the next services and buy burgers and chips and coke, and beer and crisps, and tea and chocolate. In that order."

It never ceases to amaze me how quickly women's moods change.

We stop at the services near Birmingham and I cut the zip ties off Sophie's hands and wrists with some nail clippers I found shoved in my backpack. I put Sophie's cap on just in case Johnson's put my description out in circulation. Sophie's a little nervous going into the ladies on her own, in case McNamara's hiding in one of the U-bends, so I wait outside and promise to come in if she's not out in five minutes. Of course she takes longer, and when I go in, of course she's fine, and tells me to wait outside.

We order a mountain of food each in the restaurant. I pay in cash and choose a table so we can see any police or Hitmen walking in. As we eat in silence I look around at the mixture of glum faces dotted around the sterile service station. Services are such transitional places. Everyone's in a hurry to get in and get out.

With bellies full, I fill the Golf up with petrol while Sophie fills a basket up in the garage shop with six cans of full fat coke, two Redbulls, two bottles of water, chocolate, pasties, sandwiches, crisps, and a bottle of wine and four cans of beer. "Just for the journey," she says when I meet her at the till. I panic when I see the newspapers out on display, but luckily they've sold out of *The Sun*. I pay in cash and we hit the road.

We pull back on the motorway and Sophie cracks open a beer. I neck one of the Redbulls and sit back, bleary-eyed but focused, and start driving south.

As we head past Gloucester the moon has long replaced the sun and the sky is black instead of blue. Funny how that happens every night.

"I don't want to go home," Sophie says, opening another can of beer and a bag of crisps.

"Me neither," I say. "I'm sure McNamara wouldn't have much trouble tracking us down to my place in Bath."

"Plus Johnson will probably have his boys in blue waiting for you."

We drive on in silence for a bit as I follow the lines of car lights in front. After a few miles a solution comes to me. "Fancy a reclusive holiday for a month?"

"I'd love a holiday for a month anywhere. I don't care how reclusive."

"I just need to make a quick call." I pick up my phone and dial. I keep one hand on the wheel and both eyes on the road.

"Hi Mum, it's me." Sophie looks at me with a mixture of warmth and confusion. "Sorry, I've been a bit tied up recently," I say. (Sophie gives me a look that says 'you weren't the bloody one tied up.') "Yes, yes, I'm fine, I'm fine… You don't want to believe everything Marjorie reads in the papers… I can't talk long, Mum, I'm driving… Do you and Dad still have that nice cottage down on Bodmin? Yes please. Great, thanks… Is the spare key still in the bird box? Great… One last thing, Mum. If anyone calls asking if you've spoken to me or knows where I am just tell them I've gone to New York for a few weeks. Anyone at all, mates, workmates, the police, tell them I'm in New York… Okay? Thanks again… Say hello to Dad for me… Bye Mum."

I put my mobile down. Sophie starts smiling and bouncing around in her seat. "Brilliant! A holiday in Cornwall!"

"The parent's cottage is a cosy little place well out of the way. Ideal for laying low and out of the spotlight for a while."

"And ideal for spending some quality time with each other… and each other's bodies," says Sophie. She climbs out of her seat belt and leans over to kiss me longingly on the lips. Her warm lips taste of beer. They feel so nice I end up taking my eyes off the road. Sophie moves her head out of the way just in time for me to spot a Peugeot travelling incredibly slowly in the middle lane. I swerve into the slow lane and undertake.

"Wahoops," says Sophie, letting out a naughty little giggle.

A couple of hours later when we're miles past Bristol and heading south west on the M5, I feel it's time to tell Sophie about the front page story. At least she can't run away.

"I've got something I need to show you," I say, "but before you see it you have to understand it's not what it looks like."

Sophie's on her fourth beer by now. "What you on about, silly? What doesn't look like who?"

With one hand on the wheel I reach behind my seat and pull *The Sun* out from my bag.

"I made the front page news." I plonk the paper on her lap.

Sophie looks closely at the paper but it's dark inside the car. It's dark outside too, apart from the flashes of headlights from the other side of the motorway.

"This is you?" she laughs. "No way! It doesn't look like you."

I flick the internal light on. Sophie stops laughing. She holds the paper at arm's length, brings it right up to her nose and then puts it on her lap and reads in silence.

"How mad is that?" I laugh nervously. "That's me on the front page!"

Sophie doesn't say anything. She keeps reading and looking at the photo.

"That's why I had to find you. I knew McNamara – my mate according to *The Sun* – would freak and take it out on you if he saw it. I knew I had to rescue you today."

After an excruciating amount of time, she says, "So while I was being tortured and tied up you were getting pissed and friendly with a pretty blonde with six foot long legs?"

"It's not what it looks like."

"It's exactly what it looks like. There's you, and those six foot long legs," she says pointing at the photo. "Is that what you're like? I get kidnapped and two days later you run off with the first girl you can find!?"

"No! No, of course not."

"Stop the bloody car. I want to get out," she shouts, thumping the newspaper with her fists.

"I can't stop. We're in the outside lane on a motorway."

"How do I know you and Legs Eleven didn't get it on and the only reason you eventually came and found me was because you were feeling guilty?"

"What!? How would you even be able to even think that?" I say. I'm shocked.

"Stop. Pull over. I want to get out," she shouts. "I don't want to go on holiday with the Bastard of Bodmin."

"Don't be mad. Let me explain," I say. The road's become clearer the further south we get so I've let our speed creep up to 95mph.

"You'd better bloody explain. I was shitting myself up there. I cried myself to sleep every night as I wondered if I was going to wake up the next morning. Not that I was going to let that bastard know I was scared," she says. "But all the while you didn't have a care in the world. You were getting hammered and pulling a blonde bitch in a flipping mini skirt."

"It's not what it looks like," I say. Up to 100mph.

"You've got your arm around her."

"We were both totally plastered. We were just holding each other up," I say.

"How could you be so thoughtless and selfish? I thought you were different."

"I am different. I was so bloody miserable and lost without you."

"You seem happy enough with blondie."

"She was a PR girl at the X-Festival," I shout. 110mph.

"Carly," says Sophie. "Carly the pretty, blonde, leggy PR girl. It says you were seen leaving with her."

"And you believe that? I wasn't interested in her. I was just so frustrated I couldn't do anything to help you or tell anyone you'd been kidnapped. I was desperate to talk to someone. I'd been drinking all day and at the time it seemed a like a good idea to tell Carly everything. I told her how much I missed you and how helpless I felt. I was going out of my mind," I'm only half shouting now. We're still doing 110mph. "Then this tiny *Sun* reporter appears out of nowhere asking if it's true that I'd met the Hitman and the next thing I know a photographer's taking our picture. It was all Carly's fault."

"I'm sure it was," says Sophie.

"I didn't even want a sodding photo taken. Look at my face," I say. 105mph.

Sophie looks closely. "I suppose you're not exactly smiling."

"You for one should know what the tabloids are like. The whole story's made up. Exclusively told them blah blah... I mean, read the bit about me being mates with the Hitman and having drinks with him. Why would I say all that? And Carly and I only left together to share a cab to the train station. I went home to Bath, she went on to London. It's all bullshit." My heart's pumping doubly hard now.

"Now do you believe me? Because if you'd rather believe a tabloid showbiz story than me, then I don't think I want to go on holiday with you either," I say, raising my voice again. 110mph.

I think I've gone too far as Sophie's eyes fill with tears and she looks genuinely scared. But I need to know that she believes me.

"Okay, I believe you," she says quietly.

"Good. That's good. I needed to hear that," I say. 105mph.

"But I don't know whether I can trust you, Hardy," she says, holding up the newspaper.

I didn't need to hear that. Up to 115mph. I can't imagine my future without Sophie. I would fall apart without her.

"Of course you can trust me," I say as my stomach flips. I feel my back getting hot and sweaty against the car seat.

"Why should I? In my time of need you were pissed up and on the pull."

"I wasn't on the pull and when it really mattered today I was there. I showed up to your door... your window... and rescued you, my princess," I say. Up to 120mph.

Sophie lets out a little smile and a tear runs down the side of her nose. She thinks I don't see it as she tries to hide her face behind her long, curly hair.

We're both quiet for a few miles.

"You were amazing today. You were so manly. I forgot to tell you that," Sophie says after a while. 110mph. "I was so happy to see your face coming through the window. Every day I was captive I was waiting for you to come but this morning I really thought you'd forgotten about me." More tears starts to run. I feel my own eyes becoming wetter than necessary. 105mph.

"You can always trust me, Sophie. You can always rely on me."

"But how do I know that?" She sniffs.

"Because you can," I say. 100mph.

"But how do I really know that?" More sniffs.

I know what to say. Words, do not fail me now.

"Because I love you," I say.

She looks at me and I look at her and it's one of those moments that's so cheesy and clichéd it becomes just perfect. I feel warm and tingly. She starts sobbing and I'm not ashamed to admit that a few of my own tears escape. 95mph.

"I bloody love you," I say, loud and proud.

"Well, that's alright then," she says, and punches me on the arm. After a bit, Sophie slides across from her seat and, holding my face in her hands, gives me a big wet one on the lips. I kiss her back and promptly steer the Golf across three motorway lanes and back again. A Mercedes driver behind us beeps and flashes his high beam at us.

"Piss off," we both say as he overtakes.

Sophie holds my arm with both her hands, sniffing quietly, with a big daft smile on her face. "I've been waiting for you to say that," she says. Sophie slides back across to her seat and curls up into a ball, resting the side of her head against the seat so she's facing me, her legs tucked underneath her body.

"I bloody love you too," she says. She closes her eyes and her breathing starts getting even and heavy.

I sit back, emotionally and physically exhausted. My adrenalin has all run out. But I feel totally content and the happiest I've been all year. I sip on another Red Bull and munch on chocolate in a futile attempt to stay awake as the trusty Golf drives us down to the end of the M5. I know we pass Exeter and a couple of other small towns on the A30 towards Bodmin, but I'm so shattered I don't remember driving large chunks of our journey. Am I driving or is someone else?

I focus on looking forward to resting and catching up with Sophie in the cottage over the next few weeks. We've got lots of catching up to do when we get there, and I'm not just talking about chatting and sleeping.

I'm talking about lots of hot sex.

Just in case that wasn't clear.

It feels like we're in the middle of nowhere. Perhaps because we are. Not that Bodmin Moor is nowhere – I really like Cornwall and its pasties and beaches and clement climate – but we can walk for two hours in any direction before we stumble across anything remotely civilised, like a small farm selling eggs. I'm hoping – and praying – even McNamara won't be able to track us down here.

My parents' comfy cottage is a remote, two-storey abode at the end of a long private road with grassy moors surrounding us. It's got a nice-sized lounge with a TV, a fair-sized dining area and a well-equipped kitchen. There are basic rations tidied away in cupboards and a small larder. Two bedrooms and a bathroom are upstairs. We take the bigger of the two double rooms and I try not to think about the fact we'll be sleeping in my parents' bed.

I wake up abruptly halfway through the night – McNamara nightmares again – but seeing Sophie's beautiful, peaceful face is all I need to relax and fall back into a deep slumber. It's so comforting to have her warm body back next to mine. We sleep soundly until mid-afternoon the next day.

Before I can slip properly into holiday mode I need to answer all of my messages I avoided yesterday. I'm so popular. When we finally get out of bed, I listen to my endless voicemails and make some phone calls. I tell Fat Pat that Sophie and I are safe, but I don't tell him where we're hiding. I don't plan to tell anyone about our secret holiday home. Gary's left me a total of thirteen messages, but first I need to sort things out with my favourite Detective Chief Inspector. Before I attempt to explain what the hell I've been up to over the last 48 hours, I listen to Johnson's stream of messages. They go a little something like this:

"Matthews, DCI Johnson. What are you doing on the front page of *The Sun* saying you're mates with the Hitman? Where are you? Call me back."

"Matthews, there seems to be two of you. On Sunday night you were in Exeter at a music festival with a 'Leggy Carly' according to *The Sun*. But Dragonfly's tour bus driver, a Mr Keith Smart, swears he spoke to you in Bournemouth on the same night, and later saw you get on their bus and drive away with Dragonfly and their manager."

Eh? But there's only one Hardy.

"DCI Johnson calling again. It's 1:30pm on Monday. Two hours ago Dragonfly's tour bus was found on its roof half submerged and half full of seawater at the bottom of a cliff just outside Bournemouth. It appears to have taken a nosedive off the edge. Diving teams recovered five dead bodies: they've been identified as the four members of Dragonfly and their manager. They'd each been shot twice, but from initial inspections the boys are likely to have drowned and not died from their bullet wounds. It seems the sick Hitman has struck again, unless there's something you know that we don't? Ring me back. I hope you're getting these bloody messages by the way."

It seems Dragonfly were Hit No.3.

"Matthews, DCI Johnson. Mr Keith Smart has given DS Denning a detailed description of the man in Bournemouth calling himself Hardy Matthews. It doesn't sound like you, especially the arms full of tattoos. We think the Hitman borrowed your identity for the night to get close to Dragonfly. Well done, Matthews. You seem to have stayed out of the way of the murders for once. Where are you? I would still like to talk to you."

"DCI Johnson here. It's 11:10am on Tuesday. Are you avoiding me? I thought you'd like to know DS Cheadle has spoken to Ms Carly Morgan from PR Power and she confirmed you were with her on Sunday night at the X-Festival in Exeter."

It's surprising what happens when you do nothing. Problems can sometimes solve themselves. If you're a jammy git like me.

"Matthews, where the hell you are? Okay, it's Tuesday and 1:04pm. Yesterday your VW Golf GTI was caught on camera speeding at six different times north and south bound on the M5 and M6. Your speeds were 123mph, 121mph, 119mph, 112mph, 103mph and 101mph. Being caught once at 30mph over the legal speed limit results in an instant ban. Six times means you may be sent to jail if you do not surrender your driving licence and yourself at the nearest police station as soon as possible. Would you like to tell me why you were in such a hurry yesterday? Thank you."

Bugger. Not so jammy after all. Maybe that means I'm just a git.

I call Johnson. He's excited to hear my voice. "Matthews, I was just about to release a missing persons report! Where the bloody hell are you?"

I don't tell him we're on Bodmin Moor. Instead, in as few words as possible, I explain that of course I was in Exeter on Sunday, and not on the Dragonfly death bus in Bournemouth, and that I was racing up to Liverpool to rescue Sophie who'd been kidnapped by the

Hitman. Johnson's reaction is to start shouting lots of long-winded questions at me. I give him short, unhelpful answers without shouting back. But I do tell him one piece of information he's been waiting to hear for months.

I tell him that McNamara's the Hitman.

He doesn't take it very well. He shouts about wanting to arrest me for "withholding crucial information relating to a mass murder case," and other serious-sounding charges, but I give him McNamara's address and it seems to shut him up... Until he starts shouting and demanding to know why I didn't give it to him sooner. I know I should've given it to him as soon as we'd escaped McNamara's clutches in Liverpool, but I was too busy racing down south with Sophie to think straight.

He shouts at several of his detectives to get the Liverpool armed response squad around to McNamara's place immediately, and to put out 'the Hitman's real name for the first time' along with a detailed description and his various disguises to the papers and TV news stations.

When Johnson comes back on the line I ask, "Why haven't you sent out a description to the press and TV before?"

"We have. Several times. But because of all his bloody disguises it's hopeless. All we have to go on are his tattoos and we can't arrest every man who's got similar tattoos otherwise we'll be overrun with angry, innocent, tattooed men."

"Glasgow would be very quiet for a while, though," I say.

Johnson comes back at me with more questions. I keep it short and tell him about breaking into the flat, our car chase, evading McNamara, and escaping back down south. I don't tell him where we're staying.

"Leave the heroics to the trained professionals next time you bloody idiot. You acted bravely, but you're still an idiot. You could've been killed," says Johnson.

"Yes, Mr Johnson," I say, feeling like I've just been told off by my physics teacher for messing about with the Bunsen burners.

"You sure you don't want to tell me where you're staying for the sake of your safety? I'm sure you realise Mr McNamara will be very keen to catch up with you and Sophie."

"We'll take our chances."

"We would obviously like to talk to Sophie about Mr McNamara as well."

"No way. She can't tell you anymore than I just have anyway."

I think he's going to flare-up again. But he simply says, "Okay."

Then he does something completely out of character. He says something kind.

"Look, I can't promise anything but I might be able to sort out your speeding tickets under your extenuating circumstances."

"Cheers," I say and hang up before he changes his mind.

I tell Sophie the good news and bad news from Johnson, and what McNamara was up to with my name in Bournemouth while she was tied to a bed and I was wasted at the X-Festival. Sophie's apathetic about the Dragonfly news. Me too. We're more interested in each other's safety now. She's wearing one of my T-shirts and nothing else. Her bare legs aren't as long as Carly's but they're ten times sexier because Sophie's attached to them. She reaches up and hugs me around my neck. I let my hand hang down and pinch her bare backside. All I want to do is go back to bed with her and to make everything go away.

I decide to call Gary and get him out of the way as well. I go through the same process of updating him but don't go into as much detail as I did with Johnson. But I do tell him about the Hitman on our tail.

"Jesus Christ, Hardy, I didn't realise you were up to your neck in it all," says Gary.

That's because I kept him on a need to know basis.

"I think we can forgive your front page indiscretion and if you need a break, take a break. God knows you deserve one," says Gary being unusually nice.

"Great. I want all of October off," I say.

Last year I had to beg just to get a week off. But now Gary knows I'm too valuable to *TOP 10 HITS* and our sales figures.

"Okay, sure. Take October off," says Gary a little reluctantly, "but can you just get two more Insider articles over to me before you start convalescing?"

I could tell him to piss right off but I don't want to burn any bridges just yet.

"Okay, and then that's it."

"Great, thanks Hardy." He's such a creep. "Where are you anyway?"

"I'm not telling anyone, it's better that way."

"Are you leaving *TOP 10 HITS* to go and work for *Q* or *Mojo* or someone?" I can hear the paranoia in his voice.

"No, and no."

"*Uncut*, or *Classic Rock*?"

"No, no." A while ago I would've liked to work for any of them, but for now I don't want to work for anyone.

"If money's the problem we can come to some arrangement. John has given me a bigger budget in light of our dramatically increased sales. I can guarantee you a ten grand pay rise if you promise to come back."

Might as well take advantage of his increasing dementia.

"Okay. I'll come back but…"

"Great, okay, anything," Gary says butting in, "you can do shorter hours…"

He shouldn't put such ideas in my head. "Okay, I want my salary doubled. I want it back-dated to when our sales figures rocketed thanks to my dedicated journalism, and I'll only come back if I can work part-time and remotely. I don't want to be in the office as much and I won't be coming to any more pointless meetings," I say.

"Okay, fine. We can do that. Consider it done."

After the call I stand in wonder at how I managed to negotiate such a sweet deal.

I'm about to switch my phone off when Johnson calls. I think about cancelling it, but I'm not worried about him anymore.

"Thought you'd like to know the house including Mr McNamara's first floor flat has been burned down to the ground. Luckily the flats above and below were vacant otherwise we would've had even more bodies on our hands. Fire engines finished putting out the blaze late last night and we don't hold out much hope of any clues or evidence left behind."

"I didn't think he'd still be at home watching TV," I say.

"By the way, we've checked McNamara's profile. He was a highly ranked and respected soldier and served extensively in The Gulf. He is a TK, Hardy."

"TK?"

"Trained killer," says Johnson. "You both need to be very, very careful."

"You never know, Johnson, you might actually catch him before he reaches us. Now there's something for you and your detectives to work on," I say. It feels better when we're bickering.

"Don't you start as well," says Johnson. "I've had Hoodwink and Kitty Bomb's ex-band managers on the phone demanding we bring in the Hitman."

"At least Dragonfly's manager won't be hassling you as well."

Johnson ignores me. "And I've just had a report from the Chief Super telling me thousands of teenage girls haven't been attending school as they're apparently too traumatised that Sean Bates or Dazza or whoever is dead. It's ridiculous. It's like the whole country's gone into mourning. I mean, I know it's terrible how these innocent celebrities have been killed, but everyone acts like it's their brother or sister who's just died."

"I think people like an excuse to cry. It's easy for people to feel like they've bonded with someone they've only actually ever seen on TV."

Johnson ignores my social commentary. I feel like I'm becoming pals with the police so I make my not-too-polite excuses and hang up.

With my explanations to the outside world sorted I hand Sophie the phone. "My turn," she says. Sophie makes a few quick calls and is very pragmatic considering what she's been through. It seems to take her half the time it took me to square everything with her photo agency and put her parents and friends at ease that she's safe.

"I'm all yours for a month, honey," she says, and does a sexy little dance for my delectation. As she twirls around the T-shirt rises up to give me a flash. She *is* flash dance. I grab hold of her and we do a quick two-step jig, and then I pull the T-shirt over her head. She tears at my clothes and we do some more catching up, utilising the dining room table.

Afterwards Sophie curls up on the two-seater sofa in a dressing gown she found in the bedroom. She stares at the not-yet-lit pile of logs. "Fancy starting up a fire?"

"Me man. Make fire," I say.

I use some kindling and a few logs, and after shoving some old newspaper in there and wafting the flames, I manage to create a fair-sized fire. I sit with Sophie and she cuddles up next to me as we stare silently into the shimmering flames. The logs crack and pop and I find my body and mind slowly relaxing. I try not to wonder if McNamara's outside waiting for us in his dented Astra with his gun ready to shoot us dead.

At 3am the following night we drive to the local 24-hour supermarket for some inconspicuous late-night shopping. I still twitch when I see a white car but we make it there without so much as a high-speed car chase. I wear Sophie's red cap, she wears her hair in a ponytail, and we play Stealth Supermarket Sweep. We buy three hundred and fifty pound's worth of food, drink, toiletries, some bleach, hair straighteners, a pair of scissors, some warm clothes for Sophie, and a new jacket for me. All in under twenty minutes. We don't buy any Dazza tribute CDs by who's left in West Side and we leave the Hoodwink T-shirts and Danny Stone mugs behind.

Back at the cottage, taking a leaf out of a certain Hitman's disguise book, Sophie and I get to work on a bit of home hairdressing. I chop her beautiful long dark locks and get them shoulder length and level-ish to give her a bob after a fashion. I'm not sure what fashion it's after, but after using some bleach and the hair straighteners, it does look exceedingly sexy.

"You look like the pretty blonde Bond girl who played the cello," I say.

"You think?" she says, "I thought perhaps I look more like a young Debbie Harry. It's fun having shorter, straighter hair."

"You look bloody sexy anyway."

"Are you saying I looked ugly before?"

Women!

To make things equal she cuts off my dark brown man-length tresses to leave about half an inch of hair that she bleaches blonde.

"You look a bit like Simon Pegg when he was in *Spaced*," says Sophie.

"I think I look more like Daniel Craig's 007, only sexier... and with a better body and more charisma," I say while pouting and puffing out my chest.

"You're so modest," she says sarcastically.

"This, Sophie my gorgeous blonde girlfriend, is another fundamental difference between men and women. You lot look in the mirror and see all your so-called bad bits. Us men look in the mirror and only see the good bits that make us hot studs," I say.

I pull Sophie around so she's next to me in front of the mirror. I gently hold her chin and make her look at her reflection.

"See you there?" I say, looking in the mirror with her, "you're gorgeous you are."

Sophie fights me off, twists around and starts getting passionate.

*   *

We've been hiding away in our remote slice of Bodmin for five days. We don't leave each other's sight the entire time and that's how we like it. I know Sophie's safe and she knows she's safe. The October weather has been predictably unpredictable as the leaves change colour and autumn makes its pretty mark in auburn and orange. When it's been sunny we've bravely ventured out and hiked across the moors, soaking up the views stretching all the way to the horizon, always looking out for a Hitman, perhaps with a Labrador in tow.

When it's been too cold and rainy we've been happily, unhurriedly making our way through the vast selection of tunes on my iPod rigged up to a pair of little white speakers. They're not very loud but they're perfect for filling the little cottage with sweet, sweet music. We've shuffled through the songs alphabetically and, today, we're up to the letter J. Sophie's been playing Jane's Addiction, I've been playing Johnny Cash, and we both did a silly over-the-top hip hop dance to some Jay-Z.

"Let's go for a spin somewhere. We could drive to Land's End for a fish supper," says Sophie.

Agreeing that a drive will do us good, we're out the door and on the road in ten minutes. I drive the Golf down our private road that picks up a minor road so narrow I've been wondering if it's classed as a D-road or E-road. Eventually it leads to the A-road we need.

A few miles down the road, Sophie says, "I've been naughty."

"You've fluffed?"

"No," she says and frowns. "I've brought this." She holds up my mobile phone. We haven't switched it on for five days. "Okay then. See what messages the world has left us," I say.

As I drive us towards the toe of the boot bit of Great Britain, Sophie listens to my voicemails for about five minutes, making happy and sad faces.

"Gary wants you to email over your second Insider article ASAP and your Mum rang to say hello."

"Good, good. That's it?"

"No. DCI Johnson called. He's checking to see if we're alive and if we've had any contact from McNamara. Since he left Liverpool without a trace Johnson said they don't even know if he's still in the country."

"Why haven't they caught the crazy psycho yet? He must've left a string of evidence behind somewhere. Or a shred of evidence at least."

"Is a string more than a shred?"

"I think a string's more. It sounds like more."

On the way to Land's End we drive through places with funny names like Indian Queens and Marazanvose. I still flinch whenever I see a white car in my mirror but relax each time when I discover it's not the Hitman. As we pass Angarrack, named after the Great Anorak Tribesmen who settled there in the rainy season, my mobile starts ringing.

"The constant calls are starting again," I say. Sophie picks my phone up, looks at the display, but doesn't say anything. It keeps ringing.

"Who is it?" I ask, smiling.

"It's me," says Sophie, not smiling.

"You?"

"Me."

It keeps ringing.

"But you're with me. You can just speak to me here and now."

"No, it's my mobile calling you."

"So who's got your phone?"

"I don't know. I think I lost it at Anfield. I'd forgotten all about."

"Give it here. Someone might be calling to return it to you." Sophie passes me the phone. "Hello?"

"Hello Hardy, it's McNamara."

Holy mother of Christ on a bike.

"Hello McNamara," I say as coolly as I can.

Sophie brings her feet up on to the seat and hugs her knees. I struggle to keep the car in a straight line and not just because I'm driving with one hand on the wheel.

"It seems you've taken something that was mine," says McNamara.

"Something?"

"Sophie."

"She wasn't yours. Sophie's mine. Well, she's not mine, she's not anyone's," I say looking over at her. Sophie's eyes look big and afraid but she manages a brave smile. "But if it's between you and me, she's mine."

"You were a very cheeky little bastard taking her from under my nose like that," he says.

"You were a very cheeky big bastard for taking her in the first place," I say. My hand's shaking and my foot's tapping on the accelerator. I grip the wheel and make sure I don't stray into the oncoming procession of traffic. "Anyway, I can't really talk now, I'm driving."

"Off anywhere nice?" asks McNamara.

"Just leaving the country. Quick holiday overseas," I say. "We're just driving to the airport now," I say. Sophie nods at me indicating that was a good thing to say.

"We? So you're with Sophie now. Say hello for me," he says and laughs a little.

"Sophie says shove your hello up your crazy arse." I don't like his friendly tone. It's unnerving. I spot Sophie's knuckles turning white as she grips her knees.

"That's not very nice," he says.

"Where are you?" I say casually.

"Look behind you," says McNamara.

I look in the mirror, then over my shoulder, practically expecting to see his white Astra and ugly face in a new disguise. But instead there's a metallic silver car. The driver and woman in the front look over fifty years old and they have three kids in the back.

"No you're not," I say.

"Okay, I'm not. But I made you look," he says. "Just remember that one day soon you will look over your shoulder and I'll be there. I'm never far away."

"You're still in the UK?" I say not so casually and a little shakily.

"You sound concerned that I might still be in the country. Why would that be if you're heading abroad? Is that because you're not leaving the country at all perhaps?"

"I hope you realise the police will be tracing this call," I blurt out, hoping it might scare him.

"Of course they are, Hardy," he says sounding not remotely bothered.

I'm not sure how to make small talk with a serial killer so I say, "How's your Top 10 Hit List going? Nice touch borrowing my name to get close to Dragonfly for your Hit No.3…"

"I didn't think you'd mind. Just my little joke. I quite enjoyed the journalism. I did a great interview and I've got some good material from Dragonfly's manager. I think me and you aren't so different, Hardy. I think in another land we'd be mates."

"In crazy land maybe," I say. He's clearly crackers. "I heard about your bus driving skills…"

"That was a lot of fun. You should've seen the bus flying off the edge of the cliff. It was quite a magnificent sight under the moonlight," he says.

I want to tell him how bonkers he sounds but I don't want to make the baboon angry. The road narrows through a village and I watch my speed as I pass tourists in colourful jumpers stepping off a coach.

"Two hits left now…" I say.

"Yeah, it's great isn't it? Who'd've thought it would all be so easy? I get more excited the closer I get to No.1. But I'm really looking forward to No.2. My disguise is first-rate."

"Want to tell me who's at No.2 on your list?" I say.

"Don't be daft. You'll find out very soon though," he says. "Now, enough of these pleasantries. I really just called to say that you and Sophie have made it onto my Hit List and I'll catch up with you both soon."

I want to say something smart back but can't. My mouth stops working.

"I'll find you both, Hardy, and when I do… I'll kill you both. I'll kill Sophie first and make you watch her die and then I'll kill you."

My mouth still won't work.

"Cheerio," says McNamara and hangs up.

"Cheerio you raging psycho pop star serial killer Hitman nutter bastard," I say as my mouth starts working again, if a little late.

I unsteadily hand the phone to Sophie and concentrate on staying on our side of the road. I nervously tap the steering wheel and my legs start twitching.

"We're on his Hit List," I say apprehensively. "He wants to kill us. You first, me second."

*   *

You've enjoyed having a week to settle into your hideaway. Your new base is up in the North Welsh Mountains. You knew there was a disused army hideaway tucked away deep in Gwydyr Forest. It was occasionally used for training missions but you know it hasn't been used for years. The door and windows were firmly padlocked shut, but by climbing up on to the flat roof you were able to get in through an unlocked access hatch.

You feel right at home and you're enjoying the silence and tranquillity to think about who's next on your Hit List. It's been two weeks since your last hit and you're quietly excited you're down to Hit No.2. Not that you need to be quiet in the middle of nowhere.

Purge the pop charts.

You could shout it from the roof and nobody would hear you.

The hideout is painted with green and brown camouflage shapes on the outside and the windows have netting over them. You wouldn't ever see it unless you were really looking for it through the dense rows of fir trees. Only seriously lost hikers or mountain bikers could get within five miles of the forest tracks that, a few miles later, eventually lead to your hideaway on the side of the mountain forest.

Nobody is going to be disturbing you up here. Now you can focus.

Purge the pop charts.

The hideaway is one big room about the size of a tennis court inside four walls and a flat roof. You put up a few foldable tables and chairs to lay out your plans and notes. Your sleeping bag lies on top of a single bed. There's running water and the gas stove works fine, as do the electric heaters dotted around on the walls. There's even a little portable TV that gets a fairly good reception with some creative positioning of the aerial.

The camo colours bring back happy memories of your army time and you find yourself wondering why you ever left. You've even been wearing your old fatigues this past week. You're glad you're back on your own again and that Sophie's not around. You didn't need the hassle of a hostage. You can concentrate on what you do best now: killing wannabe pop stars.

Purge the pop charts.

You make a brew and start preparing for Hit No.2. You hang up your black suit from the rafters and brush it down to get rid of any dust and dirt. You use the army issue iron stashed at the hideaway and flatten out the creases in your white shirt and black tie. You start going through your professional 'Actors Makeup' and the special black wig you ordered from Authentic Synthetics' website a while ago. Your next disguise is going to be your best yet. You lay out the colourful cosmetics in the order you'll need them and get an early night. You've got an early start and long drive in the morning. You need to be in Richmond at 10:15am to report for work.

You set your alarm, get comfortable in your sleeping bag and drift off, dreaming about murder.

Purge the pop charts.

If someone insists on being called 'The D-Cup Diva' you know she's going to be a silly bitch. It just goes without saying. If a woman actively seeks attention by using her big, brown breasts and big pop-bitch persona, she's going to be a silly bitch. If she tries to sell herself by using her mammaries instead of her melodies, she's always going to be a silly bitch.

The D-Cup Diva.

It's not even a name the press came up with for her. She calls *herself* The D-Cup Diva and wants to be affectionately referred to as The D-Cup Diva.

She's been known as a demanding diva since she popped onto the scene two years ago. Even back then she commanded an entourage. Apparently she had thirty-two of her people fussing over her when she arrived at *Top Of The Pops*, back when it was still going. Nowadays she still demands white sheets covering every surface in her dressing room, she needs two humidifiers to preserve her 'voice' and requests fresh green tea to be brewed only from boiled Evian water. She's also known to shout and complain if and it's not exactly eighteen degrees when she makes her grand entrance on stage. She's always hiring and firing staff. Nobody lasts with The D-Cup Diva.

Big breasts, big gob, big ego, big silly bitch.

But you know for a fact she's a silly bitch as you've had the pleasure of being one of the suited bodyguards working for her today.

Of course she doesn't need five trained bodyguards in sharp black suits and shades to protect her. She's using you to *promote* her. She's not in danger from the general public she encountered as she insisted on doing some serious shopping. They're in danger from her. She's dragged all of you in and out of every shop on Sloane Street and Bond Street as she looked at all the over-the-top and over-priced high-fashion clothing. She bought some ridiculously priced diamond earrings and put them in straight away. You think you might just help yourself to those later. Normally she'd have a manager and PR girl bowing to her every need but she fired them three days ago. Still, she loved the attention she got from the shoppers and public as she minced about with her bodyguards in tow.

But The D-Cup Diva wants it on her terms and that at least means at arm's length. When an eager, skinny young lad came close to dribble down her top, she was quick to put him in his place.

"A girl with boobs like these don't talk to a boy with a face like yours," she said bitchily before you bundled the humiliated lad out of her way.

Twice you had to steer the paparazzi away but not before The D-Cup Diva pouted and posed with her large, pendulous breasts in an offensively low-cut top. You didn't mind being given a licence to rough up some irritating snappers once they'd got a few shots. Gorilla-shaped, cockney rebel Jonny laughed as you walloped the porky paparazzi in the guts when he wouldn't back off. Essex boy-cum-bruiser TJ said it must've been a good punch because it lifted the guy clean off the ground.

The D-Cup Diva's name is actually Shaneequa, although you're pretty sure that's fake too. Whatever her bloody name is, she seems to switch personas when it suits her. When she was interviewed for MTV in a London studio earlier today she called herself The D-Cup Diva.

Impossibly glamorous female interviewer: "Shaneequa, do you mind being called The D-Cup Diva?"

Shaneequa with her shades on inside the studio: "Nah, The D-Cup Diva don't mind being called The D-Cup Diva one lil bit. In fact, The D-Cup Diva loves it. If you've got D-cups, flaunt 'em."

Interviewer trying to be cheeky: "Do you think having a big chest helps you sing R&B better?"

From the sidelines you wanted to shout, "No, it just means she can sing *louder*." But you kept quiet.

Shaneequa, smiling, leaning forward to reveal cleavage to camera: "You better believe it, girlfriend. The D-Cup Diva and her black ass is all woman. The D-Cup Diva ain't called The D-Cup Diva for nothing. These D-Cups help The Diva sing loud and proud. But I ain't into no lesbionics, you get me?"

But when she was being interviewed by a studious, bespectacled female DJ for an urban radio station in London, it was all about Shaneequa.

Radio interviewer being as polite as she can: "Your latest album, *Ghetto Girl*, has had a slow start in the R&B charts…"

Shaneequa with her shades off: "Shaneequa is still going to be huge. Shaneequa is still well famous. Shaneequa is gonna sell billions more records. Not just London and da UK, everyone all around da world is gonna know about Shaneequa. Big time."

Radio interviewer: "But you're Shaneequa, right?"

Shaneequa, putting her shades back on: "Of course I am Shaneequa."

Radio interviewer: "Why are you talking about yourself in the third person as though you're someone else?"

Shaneequa, taking her shades off again: "Because I am. Shaneequa is my alter ego. Shaneequa is the superstar that's within me. I mean, I'm Shaneequa. Shaneequa is me. But Shaneequa is also Shaneequa the superstar."

Radio interviewer: "I see."

But it's not London that has made her successful. Hollywood decided to do that after using two of her thunderous R&B songs on two big summer blockbusters last year. The global film promotion using her songs and the chart success that followed meant Shaneequa became a household name and very rich in a matter of months – even though the instant appeal of both of her songs was down to the heavily sampled James Brown horn loops. She hasn't released a decent song since. The only time you hear her tunes these days is as ring tones.

The D-Cup Diva has been demanding from the moment you started your bodyguard shift this morning. Jonny said you're not allowed to look at her directly and you must wear your shades at all times. You'd been warned before today of that rule. It suits you to hide behind dark glasses and it suits your undercover disguise dressed as a black man complete with afro. Jonny also said to speak only when spoken to and, "basically do what The D-Cup Diva fucking well says."

But you're not complaining. She's hired you as a bodyguard but she's effectively paying you to kill her.

Not that you need paying. You'd do The D-Cup Diva for free.

No. 1

When the music's over, turn out the lights
The Doors

It's been five days since McNamara called and we haven't been out much since. A death threat by a qualified Hitman can make one feel like one should stay in hiding. We're in our secluded cottage cuddled up on the sofa in front of the log fire and watching Wednesday evening's *Argyle Street* on telly. Sophie wanted to watch it. I'd rather watch the fire crackling away. I wonder how much worse it was when Danny Stone was in it. A stern-faced barwoman wearing too much makeup is about to serve two gormless mechanics – which always makes riveting television – when ITV cuts to an urgent newsflash.

"We interrupt your viewing tonight to bring you the shocking news that the Hitman has struck again. The UK R&B singer Shaneequa was found dead yesterday in a swimming pool at her home in Richmond, London. Police have not yet confirmed full details, but we believe Shaneequa drowned in suspicious circumstances late on Monday night after the notorious Hitman was able to get inside her house by posing as a personal bodyguard," says a slick-looking male newsreader in a slick-looking suit.

"The Top 10 Hitman has struck again and it seems Shaneequa – also known as The D-Cup Diva – was No.2 on his Top 10 Hit List. It seems The Hitman is still able to keep evading the long arm of the law.

For once, every pop band, talent show singer, and manufactured musician in Britain will be living in fear, terrified of reaching No.1, not in the music charts, but No.1 on the Hitman's Hit List. This is leaving the path clear for rock and indie bands and singer-songwriters to step up and fill the Top 20."

As I stare, engrossed in the news, I start to think that the Hitman's pop plan is actually working. I've not paid attention to the pop charts lately – hiding from McNamara has been more important – but I like what I'm hearing.

"I think McNamara is actually, finally eradicating the chaff from the charts," I say, standing up but staying transfixed by the television.

"Is this really happening?" says Sophie glued to the screen.

"Is the bad guy really doing some kind of good…?" I say.

"Is this really happening?" says Sophie again.

The slick reporter looks pensive and continues with his sensationalised news reading: *"Police believe the Hitman was again heavily in disguise, but they are still appealing for witnesses who saw a thirty-to-forty year old black man, around six foot tall, with neat afro hair. He was wearing a black suit, white shirt, black tie, and sunglasses, and walking around Richmond between 10-11:30pm on Monday night. Please contact the police via the freephone number at the bottom of the screen if you have any information about this incident or any of the previous Hitman murders.*

Details of the other Hitman disguises can be found on the website, also at the bottom of the screen, although police would like to remind viewers that he has tattoos down both of his arms, one of which is of a naked woman riding a camel.

DCI Johnson heading up the ongoing Top 10 Hitman investigation released a statement tonight."

ITV brings up a photo of Johnson and plays a recorded message: *"We're still doing all we can to put an end to these brutal murders. Police stations throughout the country are working hand in hand and I would like to personally reassure the people and the music industry of Great Britain that we will work day and night until we catch the Hitman."*

Johnson sounds so convincing I nearly believe him, although I still picture McNamara running rings around him before jogging back to kill us on his way home. The newsflash ends and ITV switches back to *Argyle Street*. I still can't believe McNamara's really purging the pop charts.

"That crazy psychopath's pop plan is really working isn't it?" I say walking around and around the sofa.

"It would seem the real musicians are beginning to outweigh the artificial artists," says Sophie.

"So, he placed Shaneequa at unlucky No.2 on his Hit List," I say, sitting back down.

"I photographed Shaneequa once. She was a total bitch. She played the diva card tenfold as she ordered her gaggle of assistants about while I attempted to get a few flattering shots without her tits getting in the way," says Sophie without remorse. "It was the ugly 'I'm more powerful than you' look in her eye that I really hated. Didn't like her at all."

"Seems McNamara agreed. At least we didn't have to witness this one being drowned," I say. Sophie hugs me tightly as *Argyle Street* flickers in the background. "His disguise as a fully blacked-up black man is a stroke of genius though."

"I'm intrigued to know what McNamara would've looked like as a black man," she says perking up.

"A bit like 50 Cent, only more mean looking?" I say.

"No way. 50 Cent is one cool looking dude. McNamara is not. He would've been more like Ice Cube."

"No way. Ice Cube's ultra cool. Cooler than 50 Cent."

"Okay, how about Michael Jackson?" suggests Sophie.

"He's not been black since the early '80s. Can't believe you even suggested him. What about Will Smith..."

"No way, too pretty. Goldie? He'd be perfect, without his golden teeth..."

Our pointless comparisons continue until bedtime but I think Sophie and I both know we're only using humour to defuse a terrifying reality that McNamara, whether he's black or white, is still on the rampage, and he's coming for us next.

*   *

You've drawn up a strict daily routine for yourself in your Welsh Forest hideaway and you're taking full advantage of having lots of land to train on. You know how important it is to stay in good physical shape, the mental sharpness follows easily after that. You've been very disciplined and getting up at 6am to go jogging for an hour before breakfast, afterwards using the mornings to draw up plans for your No.1 Hit. Before lunch you do 100 press-ups and 100 sit-ups. An hour for lunch, then afternoons are for more planning, paying extra attention to killing methods with and without weapons.

Before dinner you take Sadie for a good hour's walk. You always take your Glock 17 in case of intruders and check your traps you laid for rabbits on alternative nights. You occasionally see deer but as much as you love venison you don't want any forestry rangers snooping around your neck of the woods because they're missing a few. On top of the rabbit meat, you stock up every two weeks at 7:30am in the larger of the supermarkets in Betws-y-Coed. You're growing a beard so usually you just wear the slicked black hair wig as a safety disguise, sometimes with a woollen hat pulled right down.

Evenings are for reading one of several good war novels left in the hideout or relaxing in front of the idiot box.

You've been avidly watching the television coverage of your pop hits from the comfort of your hideout. The little portable TV makes the news seem unreal, like it's a bit of fun. Which it is for you, really. You've also seen your popularity grow on the Met Police's Most Wanted list throughout the year. At the start you were behind a couple of Asian shooters, a Brummie drug dealer and an Islamic terrorist, and only had a reward of fifty grand on your head. But since Hit No.4 you've been a clear winner. There's a £500,000 price on your head now. The image you saw on the Met website, when you were last in an internet café, was an artist's impression of when you were at Anfield. It looked nothing like you.

When you were online you came across your very own Hitman fan base: around seven sites have been started up. They've all got black backgrounds which you appreciate and one or two had all your media cuttings online. You knew people would eventually come round to your way of thinking.

On Wednesday evening you catch a newsflash on TV. The newsreader announces that Shaneequa's body has been found, although you're disappointed he doesn't mentioned her ears were missing. That reminds you, you've still got those jewel-encrusted earrings to flog to your contact in Liverpool. You should get a pretty packet for them. The newsreader goes on to tell you what you've been waiting for since you started your Hit List.

The manufactured music industry is afraid.

He announces that man-made bands are so terrified of becoming No.1 on your Top 10 Hit List that they're no longer releasing singles or albums. The music charts are slowly being taken over by the hard-working rock bands and intense indie acts you really admire. You're finally starting to see some results.

You're finally purging the pop charts.

You open a bottle of Jack Daniels and pour yourself a large one.

"To me," you say toasting yourself, "and to purging the pop charts." Sadie barks and with a little burst of energy she starts running around inside the hideaway. She really empathises with you sometimes.

The newsflash finishes by talking about your disguises and a statement from the ineffective DCI Johnson who hasn't got close to you since you started your Hit List. You've enjoyed all the various descriptions the police have been putting out, and their various inaccuracies. In fact, the only part of the Hitman TV coverage you haven't enjoyed is the talk of your tattoos. Your tattoos need to go.

You can't compromise your position. If you want to reach your No.1 Hit and go down in history as the man who changed music forever, you can't take any chances.

You book an appointment under a false name at a private health clinic in Shrewsbury to have your arm tattoos removed via the wonders of laser surgery. You arrive wearing the slick businessman wig and your naturally-grown beard – it's a new combination and a new disguise.

You check in and nobody pays you a second look, not the doctor, or nurses, not even the surgeon operating the laser machinery as he removes each of your arm tattoos.

Four hours later you're released and even allowed to drive home – well, you don't tell them you're driving back to north Wales, but you don't feel life threateningly dizzy. You pay in cash and walk out a different man.

The doctor said it will be one week before the swelling goes down, and four weeks for the skin pigmentation to return to its natural state. Unless you're really looking closely, the nurse said nobody would ever know you'd had tattoos. You'll be fully repaired before the end of November and you can still continue with your strict daily routine. This means you'll have some quality time over the next four weeks to meticulously plan the No.1 Hit.

Back in the hideaway you try not to scratch your arms as you think about ploughing some time and energy into hunting down Hardy and Sophie. You're sure a bit of investigative phone calling, or paying a polite visit to their parents, would soon reveal where they're both hiding, or at least set you off in the right direction.

*   *

We've been getting more and more reclusive in our cottage by staying in, cooking, pottering and reading books. It's been exactly what we've both needed, but on the morning of Halloween I wake up and start craving a busy, bustling, smoky, loud, chatty city full of busy, bustling, smoky, loud, chatty people. Perhaps it's because I don't want to spend the scariest night of the year in the middle of the moors wondering if McNamara is going to knock on our door and ask, "Trick or treat?"

After four weeks of lovely isolation, clean fresh air, the sea, sweet dreams, long lie-ins, mind-blowing sex marathons, and little contact with the outside world, I feel refreshed and recharged. I think it's time Sophie and I seek solace in a city. But not Bath, or Bristol, as it's too easy for *him*.

So where?

It's got to be London town. Big enough to stay anonymous but with lots of busy, bustling excitement. I run the idea past Sophie and she simply says, "It's about time we moved on. Let's go."

"You sure?" I say. "I mean, that's great..."

"Yep. Let's hit the city. We can lay low in London. Instead of grassy moors to hide behind we can use the people, the backstreets and the Underground to stay out of sight of Mr Hitman."

"Exactly. It'll be a doss hanging out there, too, leisurely checking out gigs – instead of rushing in and out for an evening like we usually have to do."

"I can get back to work when we're up there. I'll buy some new camera kit and lenses," says Sophie. "But where shall we stay?"

I call my man in the city and hope he's ready for a visit.

"Well if it isn't Hardy Matthews as I live and breathe," says Fat Pat as he answers his mobile.

"Fancy that beer then Pat?" I say.

"Thought you'd never ask. You'd better be bringing a big wallet," says Fat Pat.

"Of course," I say.

"When you in London?"

"Sophie and I were hoping you're free this evening?"

"Yeah. Sounds great. Be fun to see the pair of you. You can fill me in with all the juicy Hitman details. Do you want to stay in my spare room?"

"Yes please," I say. "How does two weeks suit you?"

Fat Pat laughs. "You need somewhere to hide for a bit do you?"

"Yeah, just a couple of weeks. It'll be a laugh with the three of us. Sophie and I are a nice couple – friendly, cultured, easy going, like a laugh, and we're clean. We're non-smokers, we're solvent, but we do have a mate who's a Hitman and he may want to pop round and kill us in our sleep."

"Apart from your mate, you both sound perfect. The only rule I have is that you keep my fridge full of tasty beverages throughout your stay."

"Deal."

Fat Pat lives in a second floor flat in Balham, and now so do we. For the next two weeks it shall be our home and hideout. I said two weeks, but I imagine it will be more like three, or four, or more. Fat Pat's well kitted-out two-bedroom flat has big bay windows, large-sized rooms, white walls, high ceilings, and beige carpets that feel nice as I walk around bare foot. It seems freelance music journalism for the tabloids pays quite well. For a fat bloke it's a surprisingly tidy place and the only clutter are the obligatory piles of CDs, DVDs and records balanced on top of speakers, mantelpieces and any spare floor space. CD racks and posters of bands hang on the wall in the lounge. Music magazines and newspapers are piled neatly in a corner at a dangerously high level like paper skyscrapers.

We're drinking beer and sat on sofas in his front room when Fat Pat says, "Well, it's great to see you both safe and in good health, but, in the name of all things holy, what the fuck have you two done to your hair?"

I'd pretty much forgotten about that.

"You look like Billy Idol's better behaved brother." He points to me. "And you remind me of one of the girls from Bananarama." He points at Sophie.

"Couldn't you come up with more contemporary comparisons?"

We chat bollocks over a few more beers in his flat then head out for the long night of pints I've been promising Fat Pat for far too long. We go to a few local haunts in Balham and Sophie and I lap up the rowdy pup atmosphere as multi-racial crowds in fashionable clothes rub shoulders, talk loudly at each other, and drink expensive beer. I make sure Fat Pat doesn't put his hand in his pocket all night and I keep the pints coming thick and fast. After a few rounds that changes to thick and slow, the pint buying, and us.

Sat at a table in The Bedford, Balham's pub-cum-comedy club, several sheets to the wind or sails or whatever, Fat Pat says, "I take it they've got televisions in Cornwall and you heard the Hitman's No.2 turned out to be Shaneequa aka The D-Cup Diva aka big-titted beeatch?"

"Yeah, he drowned her in her swimming pool as her giant tits deflated or something," I say. A few months ago we would've only discussed these serial killings in hushed tones in the corner of a darkened pub, but now everyone's talking about it as the nation follows the Hitman and Hit List stories in the press. Not that more people knowing about the Hitman makes it any more comforting.

"And the rest. Your Hitman was disguised as a black bodyguard – still can't believe he actually pulled off the blackness – and tied her to a big pink chair, sliced her ears off, then chucked her in the deep end. Needless to say she didn't float up to the surface, she sunk to the bottom and drowned," says Fat Pat.

"He cut her ears off?" asks Sophie looking more than a little shaken *and* stirred.

"Yep. When they found her dead body both of her ears were missing, according to my source," says Fat Pat.

"McNamara probably chopped them off to make a point about her being tone deaf," I add, not so helpfully.

"That is freaking sick. That could've been me with my ears missing." Sophie pulls a sad face and puts her hands over her ears.

"Apparently the bodyguards working with him at Shaneequa's place got a real roasting for leaving her alone with someone who wasn't from their regular crew."

"Quite right too," I say.

"You were very lucky. You both were. This McNamara is a very dangerous man," says Fat Pat. "My source said the police still haven't got much to go on, McNamara never leaves any evidence at a crime scene. He's always one step ahead and his disguises are so believable nobody ever spots him until it's too late. They're saying he's the most professional and ruthless serial killer the UK has ever seen."

"I'd feel proud to have fought with him if it wasn't for the fact that he may kill me one day soon."

"Don't say that. Don't even joke about it Hardy," says Sophie aggressively. I think the drink has given her some Dutch courage. "We'll be ready for him this time. I have no plans to die soon. McNamara's got some karma coming back his way and I plan to give it to him by any means necessary."

"You've got my support as well. I can bloody take him on I reckon," says Fat Pat flexing his bingo wings. "With the help of a cricket bat."

Sophie's drunken spirit warms me from my feet up to my forehead, and Fat Pat pledging his lardy allegiance is equally heart warming, but I can't help thinking the H&S Detective Agency might need some real back up this time.

We fall in and out of pubs for the rest of the night then finally head back to Fat Pat's flat in the early hours, full to the brim with booze. We round off the night by playing DJs with Fat Pat's colossal music collection. All sorts of cheese and classics get aired, prompting groans and cheers in equal measure. It soon leads to drunkenly surmising who we all think is going to be the No.1 Hit. Fat Pat comes up with a few terrible singers who should get it, and Sophie impresses me with her venomous suggestions. I pitch in with plenty I've had bottled up, but we all come to the conclusion that McNamara could still choose any number of wannabes who believe they're the biggest singing talent in the world, ever.

*   *

The month of November drifts by slowly without so much as a bang. Apart from earlier on in the month when there were continuous bangs, some very loud indeed, followed by bright flashes of pretty colours in the sky. There seemed to be bonfires going on all over the place as well. But there's not so much as a 'Bang! Bang! You're dead' from the Hitman.

McNamara's sitting back and letting the UK drive itself mad with anticipation.

The press and police have become more and more nervous, wondering when he's going to strike. Everybody and anybody is talking about who's going to be the Hitman's No.1, speculating if he really is going to pull it off. Newspapers, celebrity magazines and news channels are discussing the Hitman, and on every programme from Richard & Judy to Jonathan Ross he's the No.1 topic of conversation. Radio 1 even dedicates an entire night to the Hitman and lets the public speculate who they think will be his No.1.

Meanwhile, in a sinister twist, there's a TV talent show backlash as viewers start voting for the artists they hate rather than the ones they want to win, thinking they might go on to release a single and then get obliterated by the Hitman. Websites with tributes to the Hitman run blogs and rants about what a great job he's doing of cleaning up the music scene.

I have to remind myself to stop blindly slipping onto the Dark Side and supporting Darth McNamara.

To take our minds off it all, we act like tourists. Sophie and I visit London's fine museums and galleries and we go to see small, passionate little indie bands in dirty pubs we've been meaning to watch for months. Fat Pat joins us for gigs when he's not working at other concerts or schmoozing one of his tabloid contacts. But he sticks close by when he can: it's reassuring to know he'd put his jelly belly on the line for us.

Sophie buys new camera gear and a new mobile phone. She doesn't cancel the old number as McNamara might call and Johnson's been very insistent that I try to find out more information. Every day we try to call Sophie's old mobile to speak with McNamara but it's always switched off. It's strange hearing Sophie's voice on the answer message. It sounds like a different, younger, more innocent Sophie.

We stop in cafés for expensive lattés, pubs for overpriced pints and go to Chinatown for a reasonably priced 'Hitman Special' noodle supper. People walk around with T-shirts that say things like 'Do you wanna be on my Hit List?', 'Shaneequa: Rest In Peace, Bitch' and 'I'll be your Hitman'. Huge billboards are plastered with the web address and phone number to contact the police with any information on the Hitman. The web address letters are six feet high.

Spending so much time with Sophie becomes second nature. We don't go as far as finishing each other's sentences, but it's easy to be in each other's company 24-7. After being briefly separated by McNamara we're now stupidly happy to be with each other all the time. I find myself falling more in love with Sophie every day.

But it's not all play. I have to keep Gary off my back by emailing him the odd live review. I keep my name off the by-lines in the mag by using the pseudonym, Ryan Dodge, and keep my writing suitably anonymous so McNamara doesn't trace me to any London gigs. I actually enjoy the work now it's my choice because Gary's finally letting me report on the bands I want to see in *TOP 10 HITS*, rather than any plastic pop. Sophie and I produce an efficient words and photos package: she photographs any gigs I review and I interview any bands she photographs.

As we tramp around London's music venues, Sophie and I get to witness the live scene changing as rock bands and indie punks get promoted to the bigger venues vacated or cancelled by whatever manufactured band has run away into a small corner. It's almost too good to be true. Which means it probably is and that it won't last. But for now, the UK's live music scene is the best it's been in Britain since the late '60s and early '70s. We get to feel the excitement as the progressive underground bands get the plaudits they've long deserved. For now the raw talent and real, honest musicians and singer-songwriters move out of the shadows and into the limelight. Audiences that used to watch whatever man-made pop artists they were force-fed on TV and the radio, start actively seeking out the real bands for a change. Hopefully it won't be long before the music industry moneymen switch sides soon too.

One night near the end of November, I'm standing with Sophie in the press pit at the front of the Astoria taking pleasure in a young, half male, half female electro-rock act from Leeds called Giant. I've got goose pimples all over and I'm tingling with delight as they thrash through a set as pure, quirky and original as anything I've seen or heard in the last ten years. I get the feeling something special is happening. It's like we're witnessing Nirvana just before they released *Nevermind*. I look back at the shiny, sweaty faces in the crowd and almost expect to see McNamara there grinning and rocking along with the best of them.

In a cab on our way back to Fat Pat's, with eardrums humming and satisfied smiles, I look out of the window at London's bright lights. If it wasn't for the billboards asking who's going to be the No.1 Hit, and if I wasn't still looking over my shoulder to see if a white Astra is behind us, I'd almost feel like life couldn't get any better.

It's the first of December and all the shops, papers and TV news channels are telling us there are 'only 24 days' to go 'til Christmas. The media is starting to discuss who's going to be the Christmas No.1 single, and how exciting it will be that the No.1 will be announced on Christmas Eve as it falls on a Sunday this year. But it's still getting overshadowed by sensational media coverage on who's going to be the Hitman's No.1. A certain tabloid suggests isn't it about time he put us all out of our misery, or at least put that cocky singer from Swagger that nobody really likes out of his misery.

I'm walking down Clapham High Street, avoiding Christmas shoppers, Big Issue sellers, and anyone who might be McNamara. I'm wearing a grey woollen hat pulled over my ears, and wrapped up in a jacket and scarf so I feel warm as well as unassuming. I'm wandering around while Sophie takes portraits of a mopey-looking emo rock outfit in the SO.UK pub/bar near Clapham Common. There's a cold, bracing wind in the air which takes my breath away. It gives it back though, so I'm not totally breathless.

We're still alive, still avoiding McNamara, and still in London. Fat Pat has enjoyed having us stay so much that he said we could stay indefinitely. A foolish but generous offer that Sophie and I have gladly taken him up on.

It's exactly midday when my mobile rings. The screen says it's Sophie calling. Not her new number, her old number.

Which means it's McNamara calling. Yikes. I can't not answer it can I?

"Hello Hardy my man. Are you well?" he says chirpier than a serial killer really should.

"Very well, thanks," I say. I stop in the middle of the crowded high street and look all around to check if anyone on a mobile phone could be him deep in disguise. "Where are you?"

"That would be telling. You still in New York?" he says. Why does he think that? "Your Mum told me after I called her to see if she'd seen you recently. She's a lovely old dear isn't she?"

I feel queasy. He's a Hitman, he can't phone my Mum. I don't want to let him know it bothers me to my very core, so I keep cool by shouting, "Stay the fuck away from my Mum you bastard."

"Alright, don't get touchy," says McNamara. "I just wanted to check you were both safe. I know you're still in the UK really. In fact, I know which street you're walking down right now."

I canter across the road without looking properly. Cars beep as they skid and swerve around me. A cab driver hangs out of his window and shouts something as he misses me by inches. I just make it to the other side without being flattened. I walk and keep looking around and over my shoulder. A 30-year old man in a suit, a posh middle-aged woman in a chequered coat with a yellow handbag, a homeless man sat on the pavement drinking a can of Special Brew – they could all be him. But I'm hoping McNamara's bluffing again.

"You've know idea where I am, have you?" I say, timidly.

"That cab driver who just shouted at you sounded Cockney so I'd say you're hiding in London," he says confidently.

Oh, bollocks.

"That's where you're wrong." I sound like a petulant child. "Because there's lots of chubby London cabbies working in bright yellow taxis in New York these days. The money's better, the coffee's stronger, and the donuts are bigger."

McNamara laughs. I don't think he's buying it. "Anyway, you're not important right now, my No.1 Hit is. Have you seen the news? They're gagging more than ever to find out who the special someone is going to be. Taking a break off has really heightened the anticipation. Don't think I'm getting lazy. I've been in training, and putting lots of thought into who's going to get it."

"Would you like to tell me who's going to be your No.1 Hit?" Three attractive girls in short skirts and tights walk past but they're all too busy talking into their own mobiles to hear me. "I'm sure the weight of responsibility is becoming very heavy," I say provocatively.

"I would tell you, Hardy, honestly I would. But I can't. Because I don't know who it's going to be," says McNamara. "However, I do know how to work out who will be my No.1 Hit."

"And how's that?"

"I'm going to tie in my No.1 Hit with the UK's Christmas No.1."

My legs go weak and I almost collapse on the pavement. I grip my phone to my ear and start walking quickly in the opposite direction.

"Want to run that by me again?"

"Sure. I'm going to tie in my No.1 Hit with the UK's Christmas No.1."

"But... but... eh? You can't do that."

"I can and will, my friend," he says. "Fantastic idea isn't it, don't you think? The great British public get to decide who's going to be No.1 in the charts and my No.1 Hit all by simply buying their Christmas single of choice."

"You're going to let the UK's Christmas shoppers tell you who to murder without them having a clue that they're consigning someone to their death?" I say.

"I thought about leaving it like that, but I feel I should share the good news. It is Christmas and the season for sharing after all."

"You want to tell the British public it's their lucky day and that they get to choose who dies this Christmas?"

"Well, I'm not going to tell them." He pauses. "You are."

The wily bastard. I'm speechless.

"That's why I've called you. Can you spread the word for me, my man?"

"The country will be thrown into chaos. People won't know what to do, you sick freaking psycho," I say.

"I'm sure they'll work it out. It should be fun to see who buys what songs this Christmas. Let's see who releases songs and who doesn't. I can't wait."

"This is crazy. It'll never work," I say. "And why can't you do your own dirty work?"

"You're so much better at PR than me. The media won't believe me if I email them now. You're the one with all the police friends and press contacts. Get the big news out to the UK. You can tell the police now but I want the public to find out in a week's time when the Christmas single shopping sprees start. The song needs to be No.1 not in the first week of December, it needs to be No.1 on Sunday on Christmas Eve."

"Yeah, yeah, I know. So when do you plan to hit them? You'll never get close enough. The security will be treble the strength at least."

"It will be my proudest moment. On the night of Christmas Eve at the BBC's Christmas Chart Show live in Leicester Square I will be there – you won't see me – but I'll be there, and when the time's right my No.1 Hit will get it for all to see."

"That's a bit ambitious isn't it?"

"Lucky I'm feeling ambitious then," he says. "I'll deal with you and Sophie at the same time if you like?"

"It's a nice offer, but I think we'll pass." I was hoping he might just forgive and forget.

"Maybe I'll catch up with you two after." He lets out a little laugh.

"You'll never get away with it," I say.

"It's me, McNamara. Of course I'll get away with it." I can tell he's smiling. "Do you realise I haven't been this excited before Christmas since I was at school? It's going to be a very merry Christmas."

"That's one way of putting it."

"Right. Better go. Spread the word, Hardy."

With that he's gone.

I walk around the block several times in a daze and try to avoid getting run over whenever I cross the road. Why did McNamara have to call and tell me his cunning plan? I was looking forward to Christmas as well.

I meet Sophie as she's finishing the emo group photoshoot in SO.UK. She's in a roped-off section so I go to the bit of the bar that's open to the public and buy two pints of Guinness. I start greedily drinking one of them at the bar even though it's not even settled properly or anything.

"Is that one for me?" Sophie says when she walks over, pointing to the untouched pint.

"No, er, that's mine too. I'll order you one now," I say, asking the barman for one more pint. Sophie furrows her brow. "Sorry, you have that one, I'll have this one he's pouring now."

"You okay, baby?"

"I will be."

I neck the last of my first pint at the bar and drink the head off the second one. I lead Sophie to a quiet table in the window, take off my hat, and try to relax enough to tell Sophie what McNamara's unloaded on me.

"That crazy nut bag wants to do what this Christmas!?" says Sophie. "Jesus, Mary and Joseph, and jingle all the way, are you taking the piss?"

"No I am not." I'm still shell shocked.

"Are you going to tell Johnson and the press then?"

"I don't know yet," I say. "A few months ago I would've almost liked McNamara for his sterling work on making the pop charts and live scene a better place, but that all changed when he tried to take you away from me."

Sophie tilts her head and smiles at me.

"Now I want the bastard six feet under," I say. "He can't keep on plucking pop artists out of the charts and killing at will for Christ's sake. Enough's enough."

I swig my pint and get a bit of Guinness on my top lip. Sophie wipes it off for me.

"I can't not tell anyone. It's too much responsibility to worry about, but I don't want to be the one telling the whole country that they're all invited to a new game show called 'Kill A Pop Star Wannabe This Christmas!'"

"The country will go totally mental," says Sophie looking thoughtful. "Although Johnson might block the news going out. But then the public will be innocently condemning somebody to the slaughterhouse. Can they cancel the pop charts for Christmas?"

"No! We must have a Christmas No.1 single. It's a national tradition that's embedded in our culture. It won't be Christmas without a Christmas No.1," I say.

"If word got out, some people would boycott the charts anyway," says Sophie, "but others might buy CD singles to try and get certain artists killed."

"Oh Christ, you're right. Young goth girls will buy the James Blunts of this world to get them bumped off. Punk rock kids will buy the boy band Christmas single if there is one. Butch lesbians will be buying sexist male chauvinist cock rock bands' music. Twenty and thirty-something men will be buying Cliff Richard, and twenty and thirty-something women will buy..." I look to Sophie for answer.

"Cliff Richard," says Sophie. "Old punks will end up buying naff girl bands' pop CDs, and indie kids will buy whichever old crooner releases a single."

We sip our pints. "If that happens the Prime Minister will have to issue a pop chart embargo. There'll be riots in the high-street shops as people attempt to voice their music-buying rights," I say.

"The internet will fall over with all the online activity as people download their most-hated band's single," says Sophie. "Artists will stop releasing singles."

We pause briefly, then I say with a devilish smile, "It would make it a fun Christmas if I told the papers before telling Johnson. One of the tabloids would pay big money and gladly run an exclusive this big, even if they get smacked wrists and a hefty fine afterwards."

"Hardy, not even you're naughty enough to think it would be fun to see Britain go ballistic."

I stare out of the window as people walk past with their heads down, some are carrying shopping bags with images of gold Christmas trees on. A man with a scarf fashionably tied around his neck stops on the pavement and starts texting on his phone. He's stood next to a giant advert by one of the red-top tabloids, it's white with basic black lettering and simply says, 'Who's going to be No.1?'.

"I can't let this whopper get out," I say. "Besides, I don't think I could handle anymore media saturation."

Sophie nods and says, "I second that."

"Somehow we need to stop McNamara pulling off this crazy Top 10 Hits murder binge... and stop him before he starts on us."

Sophie looks at me and can see I'm putting on a brave face over a worried one. "You're just a journalist, Hardy. You should tell Johnson and let him do his job and deal with it. This isn't your responsibility."

"I am just a journalist, but if there's one thing we're good at, it's building people up, and then bringing them crashing back down. We make 'em and break 'em."

"What are you saying?" says Sophie.

"It's time to break McNamara."

We leave SO.UK and walk across Clapham Common. The drone of mid-afternoon traffic quietens a little as we get further away from the road. I pull my mobile out and call Johnson.

"Hello Matthews. I'm kind of busy, what's troubling you?"

"McNamara just called."

I let it hang in the air to see if he's really listening.

"Really!? Excellent, excellent. What did he say?"

"He's told me who his No.1 Hit is going to be."

"Excellent! Really? Excellent. Who?"

"He's going to kill the singer of the UK's Christmas No.1."

"I'm sorry!?"

"His No.1 Hit is going to be whoever is at No.1 this Christmas."

"That's not so excellent."

"No. Not excellent at all. He was quite excited about the prospect though. He's asked me to tell you and wants me to spread the word to the all the UK press and media in a week's time in order to hit the peak Christmas single shopping period. He wants to cause even more mass hysteria."

"We can't let him do this."

"I know we can't," I say. "I have a better idea. Can you come up to London tonight with Detective Sergeant Cheadle?"

*   *

I've been in a fair few radio studios over the years to interview DJs, meet bands at press junkets, and go on air to talk about the pop industry in an informal yet informative way. But I've never been invited to talk live on Chris Grant's Radio 1 Breakfast Show that's broadcasted to eight million UK listeners. It's 8:15am and my stomach's filled with nervous excitement. Sophie's waiting outside the studio in the Radio 1 offices next door. Two detective sergeants are sitting with her. There are eighteen days to go until Christmas and it's been six days since McNamara called.

I've never met Chris Grant before. I wasn't sure what he'd be like. Most of the time he's quite witty and good at waking me up in the mornings, and he seems to play a fair bit of indie and rock music, but Grant's sycophantic Breakfast Show Crew can climb too far up his arse when laughing loudly at another riotous tale of his socialising with Z-list celebrities.

However he seems decent enough as I sit across from him with a microphone poised in front of me. He's got a good face for radio and a stocky build. Various fashionably-dressed Breakfast Show Crew sit around at desks, some have microphones in front of them. The one who I think is Jack The Joker is tapping away on a keyboard. I'm not sure what they all do. They're all thumbing through paper work. A script? Surely not.

The music fades and we're 'Live On Air' according to a sign and a red light.

"Okay, in the studio with us right now we've got Hardy Matthews from the pop magazine, *TOP 10 HITS*. Unless you've been living in space you'll know that earlier this year Hardy was getting a little too close for comfort with the still-at-large Hitman," says Grant. "How you doing Hardy?" His radio voice is more upbeat and polished compared to his off-air voice.

"Cool, thanks mate!" I say into the microphone wanting to sound cool and matey, but probably just sounding over excited. It's funny to think I'll be coming out of everyone's radio speakers as they drive to work and eat their cereal at home. "Can I just say that I'm bored of the Hitman. He's old news. I'm much more interesting than him," I say.

"Er... okay. We've been following your progress this year with your magazine Insider articles, and we saw you on the front page of *The Sun*," says Grant. "Who was that fit chick with the really, really long legs you were with then? Eh?"

"She was a PR girl working at the X-Festival. We were just drinking mates for the day, nothing more than that. I've got a beautiful girlfriend anyway..." I say.

"...the foxy babe waiting outside the studio?" says Grant as his eyes light up.

"Yeah, that's her," I say. "Her name's Sophie, and she's great."

"Well Sophie seems very nice, and may I say, very saucy," says Grant doing a Barry White impression into the mic.

"She is... Yes... Thank you," I say, not knowing quite how to respond.

"So, what with all the Hitman stuff, it's been quite a year for you."

"It certainly has. I didn't exactly plan to get close to the Hitman – who I'm so over by the way – but it's been a rollercoaster ride and I've had to hold on for grim death," I say, and instantly regret it.

"But, like the Hitman himself, you seem to have gone quiet lately, what've you been up to?" says Grant looking at some questions on a sheet on his desk.

"I've still been really busy. I've just been keeping my head down, and avidly following the evolving music scene."

"Yeah, it's been interesting – in a perverse way – to see the rock and indie lot climbing up the ranks," says Grant. He looks at me and gives me the thumbs up. "I'd like to play more rock but we've got a

319

play list of mainstream music to stick to on Radio 1." He gives me the thumbs down. "So what else have you been doing?"

"I've been going to lots of gigs. I saw a wicked new, half-boy, half-girl electro-rock group called Giant the other night," I say. I never say wicked, but I figure the kids listening will be down with that, yeah dudes?

"What? The band was a half-girl/half-boy monster?" says Jack The Joker not quite living up to his name.

Grant ignores him so I do as well. "They're like Electric Six crossed with Elastica," I say

"They sound electronica rocktastica. Rocktastica? That's a great name for a new band," says Grant excitedly. His various crew laugh loudly into their microphones. I'm not sure what to do but not wanting to feel left out I laugh along too.

"And of course I've been wondering who the Hitman's No.1's going to be," I say.

Jack The Joker pushes a button and a fanfare goes off. Grant gives me the thumbs up.

"We can't get enough of talking about who's going to be the No.1 Hit can we gang?"

"We can't get enough!" Say all of the Breakfast Show Crew eagerly in unison.

"But we're banned from talking about it on air," says Grant flatly.

"Boooo," says Jack The Joker.

There's now a blanket ban on discussing the Hitman's No.1 on the radio and TV, and it's all because of me. It's part of my plan to bring McNamara down a peg or two and to reduce his media exposure. I got Johnson to flex his police-sized muscles over the media, so now nobody's allowed to talk about the Hitman's No.1 unless they want to get arrested.

"But he's dull now anyway and the Christmas No.1 single is much more exciting," I say, and give Chris the thumbs up. "We can speculate about who's going to be No.1 this Christmas can't we?"

"Yes! The biggest song of the year," says Grant. The biggest serial killing moment of the year as well if McNamara has his way.

"It's like a British institution," I say.

"My money's on Cliff Richard again," says Jack The Joker.

"I reckon the Scissor Sisters are going to bring out a stomping camp anthem for the dance floors this Christmas," says the young, slim Welsh boy member of the Breakfast Crew.

"I know who I'd like to be at the top of the tree come Christmas Eve," I say loudly to make sure they all hear me.

"And who's that?" says Grant.

"I don't want to bring the mood down, but it's a bit of a sad story."

Looking at Grant, I lean closer to the mic and put on my practiced slightly-sad-I-could-almost-cry face.

"A week ago I met a little known new singer calling himself Jack Frost and he's releasing a brilliant new version of Wham's *Last Christmas*, but it's more of a ballad now with big beats, sleigh bells and slightly different vocals. MC Whitey from the Nuff Respect Crew does a mellow little rap for him in the middle."

"Sounds almost cool," says Grant. "So what's so sad about that?"

"Jack Frost has cancer. Liver cancer. It's terminal. He's only thirty two, and he's just been told he's only got three months to live," I say with my sad face.

"Are you serious? That's terrible," says Grant.

"Poor bloke," says the pretty, brown haired girl in the crew.

"Oh God that's so sad," says the Welsh boy. He looks ready to cry.

"That's awful," says Jack The Joker, not even sarcastically.

"The *Last Christmas* title means something completely different this time then eh?" says Grant softly.

"It's very, very sad. He always wanted to be a pop star and his last wish is to release a Christmas single. With a little help from me and my contacts, he now has the backing of a record label to release the song. He's got a great voice and the song deserves to be No.1 for that reason alone. But as Jack Frost's only got three months to live I hope the UK public can find it within themselves to buy a copy, and buy one for their Mum or mates or whoever, as Jack Frost will be very thankful. All the money from sales will be going to Cancer Research UK." I'm addressing the nation now.

"Nicely put Hardy, and all for a good cause. Well, I for one will be buying Jack Frost's single this Christmas," says Grant. He does look genuinely touched. His pale skin seems to have turned even paler.

"Me too," say all of the Breakfast Show Crew in turn.

"When's it out, Hardy? I haven't seen it in the charts or heard it yet," says Grant.

I hold up a copy of the new *Last Christmas* single that was pressed yesterday. "It's out in the shops tomorrow. I know you can't normally just play any song on Radio 1, but do you think you could make an exception for Jack Frost?" I say, passing the CD to Grant. I'm hoping by asking him on air he won't be able to say no. He doesn't look happy as he takes the CD off me. I think he's going to tell me to piss off.

"Is it any good?" he says.

"It's a good, honest Christmas pop song," I say ruefully.

Grant slots it in a CD player on his desk and says, "Let's play it right now then. You've already given it a good introduction, so ladies and gentlemen, for the first time on national radio, this is Jack Frost with his version of *Last Christmas*."

Grant pushes a button and sleigh bells followed by a bass-heavy, thumping drumbeat start to kick out of the speakers in the studio. The soulful voice of Jack Frost starts singing about giving someone his heart. He's not exactly George Michael. But then again he's not Jack Frost either. It's Detective Sergeant Cheadle singing in Abbey Road Studios three days ago.

"Mate, what the fuck were you thinking springing that on me?" says Grant off air.

"I'm really sorry. It was the only way I knew you'd play it." I show him my sad face one more time.

"Can't blame you really…" Grant says, easing back, pausing to listen to the single.

"It sounds quite good. As you know we can't just play anything because of boring legal reasons and in case of profanities… There's no swearing by MC Whitey or anything is there?"

"No, it's clean," I say. Jack The Joker bobs his head to the beat and the little Welsh boy taps his hands on the desk.

"Good, good. I was worried it was going to be terrible, just some cancer victim croaking out an old Wham number. I was hoping it wouldn't be, but…" Grant listens to the revamped chorus, "it sounds pretty damn good. I'm loving the sleigh bells."

Grant's influence will be a massive boost. If he backs our song to be the Christmas No.1, Cheadle may well end up at the top of the charts. Which is exactly what we need to set a trap for McNamara come Christmas Eve.

MC Whitey's smooth rhymes flow over the drumbeat as the sleigh bells ring out. It's the first time I've enjoyed listening to him rap. "So, this is a wind up, yeah? This Jack Frost bloke hasn't really got cancer has he?" says Grant.

"I wish it was." I really need Grant to believe me now. I look him straight in the eye. "If I hadn't met him I'd think it's a hoax. Sadly for Jack Frost, it's not. He really does only have three months to live."

"That's rough bloody luck."

"Do him a favour and plug it once each morning would you? Only subtly."

"Subtly? I'll bloody shout about it every other hour, mate. Don't you worry about that," he says. "Although the song will probably sell itself all the way to No.1 if Jack Frost has got a good video to go with it."

"He's releasing one in a couple of days to go with the single. There's sexy Mary Christmas dancers in it."

"Sounds fantastic," says Grant.

"I'll leave the CD with you."

"Yeah, nice one."

As *Last Christmas* comes to an end, Grant fades out the beats and bells and goes back on air. "That right there was the new single from the unknown quantity that is Jack Frost. And we really liked it didn't we gang?"

"Yeah!" shout the crew in unison.

"You heard it on Radio 1 first. The sad fact is, Jack's got cancer and the shockingly bad news is he's only got three months to live. If you buy one song this Christmas, buy Jack Frost's and make his last Christmas one to remember," says Grant like a true pro. "Watch out for the video – it's got sexy Mary Christmas girls dancing in it. Log on to the Radio 1 website for details."

Someone puts on a jingle then Grant says, "Right, Hardy, thanks for coming on the Breakfast Show, and thanks for bringing that wicked exclusive single from Jack Frost. Nice one, mate." Grant hints that it's time for me to leave.

"No worries, thanks for having me. Er, Merry Christmas everyone," I say.

"Bit early for that, mate, now clear off..." says Grant half-joking. He pushes another button and an old Embrace song starts up.

"Cheers for coming in," says Grant off air. He puts his hand across the desk and we shake. Not all over, just with our hands. I wave to the Breakfast Show Crew as I leave and they nod, trying to look busy at their desks.

I find Sophie waiting for me in the office next door. The detectives are sat on top of some empty desks nearby.

"It was so weird listening to you coming out of the radio!" says Sophie excitedly. "I couldn't stop giggling for some silly reason. The office manager must think I'm crazy. You went down really well. Nicely dismissive about the Hitman, and the Jack Frost single sounded great. We couldn't have hoped for a better response from Grant. Well done, honey." Sophie reaches up and kisses me on the lips.

"Cheers," I say.

Sophie leaves several copies of the *Last Christmas* CD with the nice female Radio 1 office manager and also asks her to pass copies to the Radio 2 and 6 Music DJs. We pop to see the Radio 1 website editors and give them the link where people can buy and download the song as well as Jack Frost's MySpace address.

The detectives escort us downstairs, past the BBC's security and out of Broadcasting House. One walks in front of us in case McNamara's heard me on the radio and is now somehow in the area. He's not. Sophie and I get in the back of the cop car and the detectives escort us to join DCI Johnson and DS Cheadle at New Scotland Yard in Westminster.

A few protesters with placards are walking around outside the New Scotland Yard main entrance on Broadway. They're chanting 'Hang The Hitman'. We drive around to the car park and walk in through a smaller entrance at the rear. Sophie and I flash our special Met ID we've been given and the uniformed policemen on the door let us through. The two detectives follow close behind.

New Scotland Yard is very officious, almost sterile, as formidable-looking policemen wander around the stark corridors. I wonder if the old Scotland Yard was more friendly. We keep walking until we reach the secure office unit that's on the Victoria Street side of Scotland Yard. We flash our ID again and the uniformed officers nod and let us through.

Inside, Johnson, a team of his detectives and more London detectives are making police plans for Operation: Mistletoe. As an experienced DCI, who started the Hitman case, Johnson is still in charge, even though the Met are now heavily involved.

"Good work, Matthews," says Johnson. A team of detectives smile and clap as I take a bow. A radio sat on a desk is playing Slade's Christmas classic.

"But I couldn't've done it if I didn't believe in Jack Frost himself!" I say pointing at Cheadle. He blushes and stands to take a bow as the office erupts.

"I sounded better than I thought," says Cheadle full of pride. "It's weird hearing yourself singing anyway, but hearing yourself on Radio 1 was really weird."

"MC Whitey's rapping is the best bit," says DS Denning mockingly.

"Shut it, Denning," says Cheadle playfully.

"Let's not get carried away, people. This is only the start," says Johnson. "We've still got a lot of work to do on Operation: Mistletoe. The song's not released in the shops until tomorrow, and reaching No.1 is a long way away. It's all well and good preparing Cheadle to sing in a recording studio but he's nowhere near ready to reproduce it live."

Cheadle looks sheepish and kicks a non-existent pebble off the office floor.

"We need this single promoted far and wide. Everyone in the UK needs to know about it," says Johnson.

"Already on it," says Sophie. "The pressed and printed CDs are going into distribution to reach UK shops tomorrow. I've got Shaneequa's ex-PR girl, Gill Roach, onboard promoting the song around the country. She's already prepared a press release following on from Hardy's interview with Chris Grant on Radio 1 this morning. That'll go with the copies of *Last Christmas* to all national and local newspapers, as well as every other publication that might run an article. Gill's also working her little arse off organising boxes of CDs to be sent to schools and universities. It won't be long before everyone will know about Jack Frost."

"Excellent, excellent," says Johnson.

"We're continuing to remind the press and media to lay off any 'Who's going to be the Hitman's No.1?' stories. Your enforced blanket ban has helped, but I've been steering my national newspaper and music mag contacts onto stories about Jack Frost instead. Fat Pat's been pestering his tabloid contacts into doing the same," I say.

"Excellent," says Johnson.

"And *TOP 10 HITS* mag is running with Jack Frost on the cover for our special Christmas edition out next week. Don't forget the photo shoot at 10am tomorrow in Kensington, Cheadle," I say. Cheadle nods and jots it down in his notebook. "I'll write up a suitably heart-wrenching yet heart-warming story to go with it inside the mag."

"Will you be interviewing me at some point then?" asks Cheadle hopefully.

"Nah, I'll just make it up," I say.

"You can make him sound interesting then," says Denning.

"We all still good for the music video shoot this afternoon?" I say looking at Sophie and Cheadle.

"Yeah, we're due at Pinewood at 1:30pm," says Sophie. "We've got the huge Stage R booked and we've got a great, frosty set sorted so Jack Frost will be right at home. We've got an ice cool outfit for you, and MC Whitey will be there dressed in white. I just hope the reindeer and half-dressed dancing Mary Christmas girls show up."

"The dancing girls sound like fun. I'm glad the wife's still back in Bristol," says Cheadle giving Sophie a cheeky wink. She doesn't wink back. "You know I'm only joking don't you? I love my wife very much really."

"Remember we will have to transfer the video shoot set to the BBC for Christmas Eve when – note I said when, not if – we reach No.1. But watch the costs. The Chief Super is already doing his nut because we haven't caught the bloody Hitman. I really had to go out on a limb to convince him the only way to catch the Hitman was to set an elaborate trap within the music industry."

Sophie and I nod and Cheadle goes very quiet. I think the enormity of his task hits him every now and then. I'm just excited that we might finally nail McNamara.

"Don't fret. We're pulling in favours from all over to keep costs down. There are a lot of pop industry players eager to get back in the game and they're happy to work at reduced rates for charity.

Hoodwink's old singing coach is training Cheadle, Shaneequa's ex-DJ helped in the studio, and MC Whitey was surprisingly keen to help out," I say.

"Excellent," says Johnson.

"Kitty Bomb's ex-make up artist is on her way to give Cheadle a makeover so good he'll think he's Robbie Williams when recording the video. Although not too good as he'll need to look a little peaky and ill," says Sophie.

"That won't be hard then," says Cheadle rubbing his oafish chin.

"Okay. Good job. I know you've all been working hard, but we can't assume we're going to get Cheadle to No.1. We need to do all we can so the only way Jack Frost is going is up."

I resist the urge to start singing that Yazz song.

"If we don't deliver the Hitman, it won't just be me lining up against the wall," says Johnson, ominously. "We'll all be for it."

*   *

Rewind back to the first night of December. When Johnson and Cheadle met Sophie and me in The Bedford in Balham, they were more than sceptical about my plan. I was stubbornly reluctant to join forces too, and I still hadn't forgiven them for arresting me in Anfield. But I knew we now had to work together if we were going to stop McNamara. With our music industry and media knowledge, and their murder investigation and undercover experience, we could make a good team.

Initially they both dismissed my plan as impossible and ridiculous. They dismissed our new blonde haircuts as ridiculous as well so at least they were being consistent. But after we discussed every other option, including closing the charts for Christmas, Johnson and Cheadle finally came around to the idea. Mainly because they were desperate.

After a couple more pints, and the more we discussed undercover options, the more Cheadle liked my idea. It soon became apparent that he always wanted to sing live on national television.

"We need to hear you sing first, of course," I said.

Fifteen minutes later we were back at Fat Pat's flat. I dug out the copy of Wham's *Last Christmas* from Fat Pat's CD collection and put it on the stereo. I gave Cheadle the CD case with the lyrics inside. Sophie, Johnson and I sat on the three-seater sofa like a panel of *Pop Factory* judges and Cheadle assumed the singer's position in the middle of the large lounge. He was bashful at first, but after a few beers from the fridge, and after Sophie and I sang a couple of verses with him, he loosened up. The next time Cheadle restarted the song he used his beer bottle as a microphone and belted it out like a karaoke king, drowning out George Michael's softer tones. Two drinks later and we couldn't shut him up. He sang other Christmas crackers without provocation, but his voice was certainly easy on the ear and it was quite nice to see the slightly stocky, slightly loutish policeman sing with such enthusiasm and control.

"I think we've got our Jack Frost," I said.

"I agree," said Johnson, nodding approvingly.

"Sophie?" I said.

"Your voice betrays your appearance, but in a good way. A very good way," she said. "I was quite moved by your final rendition, Cheadle. Or should I call you Jack?"

Cheadle got called Jack after that, so he got to know his name in case anyone addressed him in an interview or anywhere else. Apart from me and Sophie and the police working on the Operation: Mistletoe, nobody else was to know that Jack Frost didn't have cancer. Everyone externally who came onto the team knew him as Jack Frost. Cheadle took to the role like a trained actor and, apart from actually doing the whole method acting thing and developing liver cancer, he started to become Jack Frost.

With only twenty-three days to go until Christmas at that point, we had to act fast.

If life was like the movies, the following week would've been a cheesy montage like when Rocky trains to get in shape for the big fight, but instead of running and boxing, Cheadle was training and singing. But this wasn't the movies. Instead we had Hoodwink's ex-singing coach putting Cheadle and his voice through some intensive training. He had a good, solid vocal range so within two days it had improved enough to get Cheadle in the Abbey Road Studios. Along with Danny Stone's ex-songwriter (a surprisingly talented man), Sophie and I re-wrote the lyrics of *Last Christmas*. Shaneequa's ex-DJ then came in and pulled some amazingly complex yet cool drumbeats and sleigh bell samples out of his colourful hat. Cheadle impressively laid down his vocals, and MC Whitey's chilled hip hop 'Christmas Carol from the crib' was recorded too. Hoodwink's producer and mixing engineer boosted the vocals in all the right places and added layers and depth.

We all sat back and listened to the finished product in the studio, collectively grinning because we'd managed to record a Christmas single in less than a week.

The morning I went on Chris Grant's Breakfast Show, the CD manufacturers had only just started pressing the finished copies. I had some early samples of the CD biked over as a cab waited to take me to the BBC. I hoped to hell it was up to scratch. In the cab on the way, I got the driver to put the single in his stereo.

I knew everything was going to be alright when halfway through the song the cab driver said, "This is like that old Wham song, only not as shit."

*   *

It's been four days since you heard Hardy on the Radio 1 Breakfast Show on your little portable radio while sat drinking black coffee in the hideaway. You knew he was in London and not New York. Stupid boy. You nearly drove down to London there and then. But you resisted, relaxed, and decided to give Hardy a few more days to tell the press.

But all has been quiet on the media front – strangely you haven't been in the headlines or on the news for a few days now – so on Saturday at 2:12pm you call Hardy on his mobile from a pay phone just south of Liverpool. You had returned to collect a package you had delivered to your secure PO Box. You have a dark fleece hat on and your beard's coming along nicely. A sign in a shoe shop window says there are fourteen days until Christmas. He answers after six rings.

"Hardy, it's your mate McNamara," you say.

"I know it's you," says Hardy cockily.

"I heard you on Radio 1 the other morning. It was a nice surprise to hear your voice and I thought you'd done me proud getting on national radio to tell the UK about my plans for Christmas," you say. "But I couldn't help noticing you were less than complimentary about me and missed out a certain little announcement about my No.1 Hit as we'd agreed."

"You didn't expect me to go through with it did you?" says Hardy.

"Yes. I did. You have disappointed me," you say. He has. You really thought you could count on him to deliver the good news. "Instead you were banging on about some Christmas cover version of a Wham song. Who is this Jack Frost fucker? What kind of name is that anyway? I've never heard of him."

"He's never released a single before that's why."

"Who's ever heard of a cancer victim releasing a Christmas single anyway?" you say. You've smelled a rat ever since you heard Hardy on the radio.

"That's not very charitable of you."

"I know you're trying to get me to do a bit of public euthanasia by killing this Jack Frost who's going to die soon anyway. So it's not like I'm murdering someone, just bringing death to their door a smidgen early," you say.

"I don't know what you're getting at, Mac me old mate."

He never calls you Mac or mate. He's up to something. Perhaps he's trying to impress someone. Sophie, probably.

"Don't get smart. It doesn't suit you," you say. A lorry rumbles past the phone box followed by a police car. The car doesn't stop.

"I'm already smart, and I don't condone any sort of murdering, euthanasia or not," says Hardy.

He's definitely up to something. Is he trying to set a trap?

"Well, from what I've seen already Jack Frost could well be the Christmas No.1. His *Last Christmas* song has only been on sale for three days but it's nearly in the Top 10 already."

"Thanks to the Radio 1 listeners – it's all about downloads these days," says Hardy.

"So it seems," you say. "Shop sales are high too," you say. You know this after you had a look in HMV in Liverpool and checked out the chart listings stuck on the wall. "So if Jack Frost does become the Christmas No.1 I should, technically, pick him as my No.1 Hit…"

Hardy doesn't say anything. He's playing games. He probably thinks you'll be too scared to play. Well you can play games too. Big boy's games. He probably thinks you'll back down because Jack Frost has cancer. Well, that's where he's wrong. You're a man of your word. You're up for it. If Jack Frost is No.1 at Christmas, then he becomes your No.1 Hit.

You must purge the pop charts.

Hardy still doesn't say anything. He's not normally this cool… suddenly your instincts kick in. The police could be with him right now. Better make this quick before they trace your call.

"You don't think I'll do it, do you Hardy?"

"You'd kill a man who only has three months to live?" he says.

"If he reaches No.1 at Christmas then he's on the top of my Hit List. End of story."

"You're sicker than I thought, Mac."

"See you on Christmas Eve," you say. "You might want to be there to get the biggest exclusive of the year. But don't forget, once I'm done, I'll be coming for you and Sophie."

You put the receiver down calmly. You pick it back up. Hardy's gone. You slam it back down repeatedly and kick the inside of the phone box. A middle-aged lady walking past gives you a funny look.

"Get fucked," you say.

The lady trundles away and you kick the phone booth door open, stomp to your car and angrily drive back to your hideaway. You know the police will be expecting you come Christmas Eve.

But you'll be expecting them. You look at the box on the passenger seat. There's black and yellow tape around it that says, 'Danger: Explosives'.

You will make this a Christmas to remember.

*   *

I pass my mobile phone to the detective sitting next to me. Lady Luck seems to be on our side as Sophie and I were inside the secure unit in Scotland Yard when McNamara called. My phone's sitting inside a tiny plastic case with a series of wires coming out of it, one wire leads to a detective's headphones and another leads straight into a large computer on the desk next to me.

I'd been shown what to do by the police if McNamara rang me.

"Plug your phone in here before answering then casually keep him talking. We'll do the rest," said the fair-haired policeman.

The same policeman is now tapping away on the computer, clicking the mouse and looking closely at the screen. He stops suddenly and says firmly, "He's in a phone box on Jubilee Street, south-west of Liverpool."

"Lazy bastard staying around there," shouts Johnson from on a desk to my left. "Right Denning, chop chop, get Armed Response around there immediately!"

Denning's straight on the phone as Johnson looks across to me. He seems lost in thought. After a while he says, "Is he going to show on Christmas Eve?"

"He'll be there. He can't resist the challenge to try and turn you lot over for one last finale," I say. Sophie's sitting next to me. She nods in agreement.

"He seemed agitated Hardy didn't announce his plans on Radio 1 but I think he'll show, sir," says the detective.

"But what if he bottles it?" Johnson sounds worried. Why wouldn't he be worried? Johnson knows everything's riding on McNamara showing up. All our weeks of preparation and turning Cheadle the cop star into Jack the pop star will be a complete waste of time.

"He'll be there. I know he will. He wants to finish his Top 10 Hits off in style, and he'll be there because Sophie and I will be. He plans to kills us both on Christmas Eve too remember."

"He will come, and let him come. He won't get us this time: we're going to get him," says Sophie resolutely.

She's not even pissed this time.

Blimey.

When you get back to base you skip your exercises and slump in front of the TV. You woke up in a bad mood, you've had a piercing headache all day, and now fucking Hardy has pissed you off because you know you're not the one totally in command anymore.

You should've killed him in Liverpool when you had the chance.

You pour yourself a big JD and coke and sit back to watch Saturday night TV. A talent show is on BBC1 and a 'Boy bands vs Girl bands' programme is on ITV. BBC2 is showing a reality show set in a zoo. Channel 4 is doing a *'Top 100 Big Brother Moments'* countdown. Everyone wants to be on TV and to become instantly famous these days. Now you're infamous.

You must purge the pop charts.

You can't find any coverage about you and your pop project on TV, so you grudgingly turn back to ITV to see what embarrassment of talent is singing tonight. What really sets you off is that the whole country seems so asleep. So accepting of the wank choice of pop music on offer. All these TV shows with their weak, fake, and passionless pop singers, all desperate for any attention they can get. People don't question why there's so much sugar-coated dross, they just lap up whatever's put out, instead of searching for real music.

You sometimes wish you'd done a Top 20 Hit List.

You could really purge the pop charts then.

You switch off the TV. You need to get out. You ignore Sadie and her wagging tail, and quickly glue on a light brown, fairly long haired wig and pull a cap over the top. You put on your dark green jacket, pick up a book you're reading about a war veteran's trip back to Vietnam, and drive to a pub on the coast in Llandudno. It's 8:20pm and the wintry air gets more blustery against your car the closer you get to the sea. You park on the outside of town and walk about a mile and a half to a pub that looks empty enough for you to have a drink in without being recognised or drawn into conversation.

You don't want to talk. You're still in a mood. You just want to drink. Heavily.

You've been drinking pints of strong lager and JD chasers steadily for two and half hours. The pub has pale, yellow lighting and dull decoration to match. The carpet is worn through in various places on the floor around the bar and wallpaper hangs off the damp walls in the toilets. Old men have come and gone, and now they've mostly gone as you're sitting on a wobbly stool at the end of the bar drinking and reading. The stool wasn't wobbly when you first sat down.

You've been looking at your book for the last half hour, but you haven't been reading it properly. You've been thinking.

You must purge the pop charts.

You will not let Hardy the fucking journalist stop you now. You don't care if Jack Frost has cancer or if the police are using Hardy to set a trap. You can handle them. You can deal with them. You'll rise up and beat them all to reach your No.1. You must stay focused. If you can't be a rock star, you can clear the way for rock stars. Purge the pop charts. Make way for the real musicians. The great guitarists.

Purge the pop charts.

"Purge the pop charts... Kill the fuckers."

A man sitting at a table to the right of the bar stops talking Welsh to his mate and turns round to look at you. He's thick-set and thick-necked.

"You say something?" he says in English.

Did you? Say something? You're not sure. You're not sure how many pints and chasers you've had either. What time is it anyway?

"Did you say something?" he says, louder this time. He thinks you didn't hear the first time. You sip your pint.

"Purge the pop charts," you say, spitting at him. You didn't mean to spit. But you still had some lager in your mouth you'd forgotten about.

"What's your pissing problem, mate?" says thick head, wiping his face dry with the back of his hand.

"I don't have one, mate, it's all those bastards that do."

Those bastards. Those bitches. The ones with the record contracts.

Thick head stands up. You fall off your wobbly stool and stand in front of him. You seem to be looking down at him. It seems he's thick-set *and* set short.

"What bastards?" he says.

"They're everywhere... Well, they were. There's a few less around now, and a few others have gone into hiding..." You stumble into him, knocking him backwards so he ends up sitting back in his chair. "Oops a daisy." You laugh loudly.

He doesn't try to stand back up, but he does say, "Well, yeah, watch what you're saying next time eh?" It's almost an apology. He probably wasn't counting on you being taller than him. Stupid, edgy short bastard. Like that pissing poppy singer Danny Stone. He was a short, edgy bastard too. Lived a short, edgy life as well.

Purge the pop charts.

The barman starts collecting glasses from tables. You grab your coat and book, neck the last of your drinks, and walk out of the pub, bumping into the doorframe as you leave.

Purge the pop charts.

You stagger towards your car on the outskirts of the village. You don't bother putting your jacket on. You've got your beer coat on to keep away the chills. You eventually fall into your car and drive back to your forest hideaway.

Purge the pop charts.

Purge the pop.

One of your eyes wants to sleep so you drive half the way home with one eye closed. Your headache appears again.

Purge pop.

Purge pop.

Purge.

Purge.

Purge.

*   *

Nine days to go before Christmas. It seems like there's only nine hours to go judging by the way everyone in London is rushing from shop to shop panic-buying bag after bag of presents.

Needless to say the Scouse squad cars didn't catch McNamara in a phone box south of their city. They have since increased police units in Liverpool and have brought in extra bobbies from Manchester and Birmingham to walk the beat and make door-to-door enquiries. Undercover detectives in Liverpool are still trying to infiltrate criminal gangs to find out if anyone has got anything on McNamara. Johnson predicts they'll uncover precisely bugger all and it's a big waste of manpower.

Meanwhile, I'm sticking with Jack/Cheadle as we do the media circuit of interviews. Two-to-four detectives are always close by our side. Some interviews I've arranged. For others, the publishers have contacted me. All help towards promoting Jack Frost and the Christmas single.

I'm gagging to tell the journalists he's really a cop – the headlines have such potential: *'Cop Idol'* or the sublime *'The Singing Detective'*. But I keep my mouth shut and instead embellish Cheadle's clunkier answers or reword any journalists' questions to help Cheadle along. I'm a media mediator.

At the end of each interview I ask journalists to lay off the 'tired Hitman coverage' in their publications and replace it with more Christmas No.1 stories instead. Not necessarily Jack Frost biased, just not Hitman biased. I need to continue to bring McNamara down the pecking order in the press.

Thanks to his daily voice coaching, Cheadle's singing gets stronger every day. He focuses on his breathing techniques and note control and, sitting in on a coaching session one afternoon, I feel confident Cheadle will make everyone believe he is Jack Frost when he sings live on the BBC on Christmas Eve. Not if, when.

I keep tabs on the online activity as well, which appears to have gone berserk. The Jack Frost MySpace site is overloaded with support and by now Jack's officially got 718,496 friends, most of which have gone on to buy the single. Chris Grant's public displays of affection help to drive further download sales, and people clamber over themselves to buy the CD in shops. Everyone seems more charitable around the festive season and the sympathy vote to make Jack Frost's last Christmas a special one reels in even more shoppers.

I'm missing our quality time, but Sophie's busy working flat out with Gill Roach to ensure the entertaining music video gets played regularly on the satellite music channels and terrestrial music shows in the run up to Christmas. Nobody cares that it's low budget and a bit shit, as it's the tradition for Christmas music videos.

After a while *Last Christmas* takes on a life of its own and the publicity becomes self-perpetuating throughout the UK.

Sometimes the plans I make in life turn to shit. But sometimes the plans I make can come up smelling of roses. This is how I feel when I learn that Jack Frost's *Last Christmas* is at No.1 with three days to go until the BBC's Christmas Chart Show.

Everyone involved in Operation: Mistletoe gathers for a meeting of ego-massaging and backslapping. I'm so happy we've got Jack Frost to No.1, I insist on taking Sophie out for champagne and dinner at an expensive London restaurant. I half-heartedly invite Johnson, Cheadle and the other detectives, but they make up excuses so we can have a night off on our own. It's a thoughtful gesture that doesn't go unnoticed.

After a satisfying supper and one bottle of bubbly too many, I make one final toast.

"To my number one... you, my loverly Sophie," I say.

We clink glasses, and stretch across the table to meet in the middle for a kiss.

"You're my number one as well," mumbles Sophie as we kiss.

"Get a room," says one of the plain-clothed policemen sitting at the table next to ours.

I'll be honest. It spoils the mood.

I tried to convince our police bodyguards to let us have a romantic meal for two on our own, but they only had to mention

'McNamara' and 'murder' for us to concede that it's best if they stick by our sides.

The Christmas No.1 juggernaut keeps on trucking. We're at No.1, but we need to stay on top until Christmas Eve on Sunday.

With Jack Frost at No.1, chasing behind at No.2 is mock rock group Rockford who wear spandex and sing in high pitched voices. They look like they're from the '70s and their music sounds like it too. Rockford rule. Jack Frost's sales keep them at bay by selling three singles to their every one. At No.3, just trailing behind Rockford, is the oldest young man in pop, Cliff Richard. But even with God on his side, he can't catch Jack Frost now. Famous last words, so I haven't been saying them out loud in case I make God angry and he curses Operation: Mistletoe with the plague.

Chris Grant, true to his silver-tongued word, continues to promote the song every morning on his show, as does the dear Terry Wogan on Radio 2. Jonathan Ross happily plugs it on his Friday night TV show and Saturday morning radio show, as do many other mainstream radio DJs. Every TV channel from breakfast news to daytime TV get behind Jack Frost, and he gets regular support and coverage from the national newspapers as the Hitman headlines get sidelined.

Online downloads still make up most of the sales, but as every shop from book stores to supermarkets sell the single, people are picking up the £2.99 CD when they're out Christmas shopping.

I begin to feel slightly guilty about duping the British public with Jack Frost, but not as guilty as if I'd thrown the country into turmoil as McNamara had requested. Besides, we're making lots of cash for charity so it's not all immoral.

Time flies when you're telling lies and it's soon Sunday morning and Christmas Eve. After Sophie and I and a few detectives from the Operation: Mistletoe unit devour a heart-bothering full English breakfast with 'festive sausages' in the police canteen, we head up to the secure unit in Scotland Yard to make final preparations, and to wait by the phone.

It's mid-morning when we get the call from The Official UK Charts Company. The figures are in and they tell us... Jack Frost's *Last Christmas* is officially the Christmas No.1 single. I'm standing next to Sophie and Cheadle and we all do a group hug and give each other a round of applause. Policemen and detectives start singing the song and Cheadle has to resist correcting their vocal mistakes. Champagne corks pop and we all toast and drink. Although it's mostly me and Sophie tucking into our second and third glass.

We're told Jack Frost's *Last Christmas* has sold 4.35 million copies. That's three quarters of a million more than Band Aid's seminal *Do They Know It's Christmas?* charity single, and only half a million behind the best selling No.1 single ever, Elton John's *Candle In The Wind* re-released as a tribute to Princess Diana. Over four million singles means a hell of a lot of money. Cancer Research UK will be pleased. Johnson looks on proudly like our Dad as we jump around and slap each other's backs.

As the mood in the secure unit settles, there's overwhelming relief that we've actually done it: No.1 at Christmas. But the room soon falls silent and everyone involved with Operation: Mistletoe realises the fun is over and now the real work begins. It's time to launch Phase II. The preliminary plans are already in place, but now it's all systems go to get Leicester Square and the entire Metropolitan police force ready.

We've got a Hitman to catch.

The night before Christmas. Normally I'd be about ten pints in by now as Good Publishing Network shuts up shop early and we head to the pub to celebrate finishing work for the year, all secretly excited tomorrow's Christmas Day. But this evening, on a chilly Christmas Eve night, I'm wearing a bullet-proof vest and stood backstage at the BBC Christmas Chart Show outdoor extravaganza in Leicester Square. The atmosphere is fizzing with a mixture of excitement, from the crowd, and trepidation, from the Operation: Mistletoe police units.

It's 8:25pm and there are 35 minutes to go before Jack Frost appears to sing live for the first time in front of the entire country. Not appears, as in, he *seems* to be singing live. He will actually go on stage and sing live. Unless you count karaoke, Jack Frost has never sung live before, let alone sing a Christmas No.1 song in front of an entire expectant nation.

Slightly more concerning, Jack Frost is No.1 on a determined Hitman's Hit List.

Perhaps it's really the *nightmare* before Christmas.

Sophie's also wearing a bullet-proof vest over her knee-length red dress, with a very thick, long, black padded jacket over the top. She's got a small yet powerful digital camera draped around her neck, and always has one hand cupping the camera, protecting it. She's had her hair freshly bleached blonde, cut and straightened so hopefully McNamara won't instantly recognise her. I'm wearing a smart, padded black jacket over my bullet-proof vest, and have a woollen hat pulled down over my blonde hair.

"Well, I didn't expect our first Christmas Eve together to be like this," says Sophie.

"Me neither," I say, my breath visible in the cold, still air.

"But I wouldn't want to be anywhere else, but here tonight with you." Sophie slips her gloved hand inside mine and squeezes. In my other hand I've got a police radio like the other heads of Operation: Mistletoe.

"Me neither. I wouldn't miss tonight for the world."

Uniformed officers are everywhere. I spot an officer walking past with a large gun: normally I don't think it suits a British bobby to carry a firearm, but tonight it suits them just fine.

"Whatever happens tonight," I say, "thank you for the best year of my life."

"So far. You mean, best year of my life, so far," says Sophie.

She's right, of course. But I haven't even thought about what we're doing tomorrow, on Christmas Day, let alone thinking about next year. For the past month all I've focused on is tonight. On making sure Jack Frost gets to No.1. On luring McNamara out into the open so Johnson and his men can finally catch him, and on protecting Sophie and simply surviving through the night.

I look around at the teams of police and try to reassure myself we're safe. Two hours earlier, and throughout the evening, Sophie and I have assisted the police as they carry out body searches of everybody coming in. Based in a large – and, thankfully, heated – white and red stripy search tent, the BBC crew were thoroughly checked before the public started to come in. We don't do the searching, the officers do that, they also check everyone's arms for tattoos, while we check if we recognise McNamara under any old or new disguise. I always look into their eyes, Sophie seems to look at the shoes and work her way up, taking a photo of everyone on her camera.

Other uniformed police units line the front, back, and sides of the main stage, facing out towards the crowds. Twenty foot high temporary metal fencing has been erected in a giant square around the perimeter, as people outside go to the cinema or fall out of bars and restaurants, full of Christmas cheer. Tall metal gates are on every corner with uniformed police and security guards checking people and tickets as they come in. Johnson has briefed units to be subtle as he doesn't want to take the emphasis away from the Christmas Chart Show or scare the general public by drawing attention to the fact they've got the entire Metropolitan Police Force down there to catch the dastardly and elusive Hitman.

The great DCI Johnson and a team of detectives from the Met are stood up high on a temporary lookout tower that stares down across the stage. They've currently got an excellent view of Rockford doing fun things with double-necked guitars and spandex outfits while belting out their single which slipped down to No.3 in the charts. Some of the crowd are singing along to their cheesy, racy lyrics that have somehow slipped under the censors' pre-watershed noses.

I survey the crowd. I know there are plain-clothed detectives dotted regularly throughout and they'll be standing by the trees in the central Leicester Square gardens, politely pulling people out at random to search them.

Tickets for tonight's BBC Christmas Chart Show were as rare as rocking horse shit. Only exclusive tickets were available with two levels of security to pass on a police-run BBC website in case McNamara somehow tried to obtain a ticket. If people were lucky enough to get through, they'd be paying £55 for near the back and sides, £75 for the central section covered in pretty lights, and £105 for the VIP area at the front.

Huge Christmas lights hang from the trees inside the square along with red carpets laid around the edges to give it a regal and traditional Christmas feel. The vast stage and tall LCD screens down either side are decorated with giant red and silver tinsel and wrapping paper to make it look like the stage is an enormous present that's been half opened. Icicles of various sizes hang off the gantries and sides of the stage to make Jack Frost feel at home.

We take a minute to go backstage to witness DS Cheadle attempting to take his cop head off and put his pop star head on. His Jack Frost outfit consists of a white suit, white shirt, white tie, white shoes, dyed white hair, with pasty skin makeup and red eyes. The ex-Kitty Bomb makeup girl has done a great job of making him look ill but not so he'll scare the kids in the crowd or viewers watching on television at home.

"I always go down well at the police Christmas karaoke night," says Cheadle nervously as he fiddles with his tie.

"That's what they always say, you massive homo," says Denning, ever present, trying to lighten the mood with his gutter-level humour.

Cheadle's wife is at the front of the VIP crowd ready to cheer her husband on. She's had to sign the official secrets act like all the Operation: Mistletoe team. MC Whitey has shown up backstage dressed head-to-toe in an excessively baggy white denim outfit. Even his cap perched on top of his shaven head is white denim. I say hello and he says something incomprehensible in a fake Jamaican accent he found in the Midlands, so I leave him to it.

Sophie drags me around the side so we can safely see over the VIP area as Cliff Richard takes to the stage to sing his single that, any other year, would've been a clear Christmas No.1. He sings a moderately updated version of one of his previous Christmas songs I can't remember the name of but it's not important as all his songs are rubbish anyway. Old ladies in the crowd swoon and cream their undergarments.

My radio suddenly crackles into life. A voice says, "Hardy, can you and Sophie come to the security tent to check over the final batch of punters coming in?"

We hurry back to the security tent as the last members of the public make their way through. There's a mixture of ages including babies in prams, middle-aged mums, and ancient, half-blind granddads. But the police, Sophie and I diligently check them over and make sure there aren't any concealed arm tattoos or crazy Hitmen in disguise. It's getting close to show time for Jack Frost and we've not even discovered anyone with a wig, concealed weapons or even a cross-dresser yet.

Has the Hitman really stayed at home tonight?

*   *

You roll your shirt and jumper sleeves back down to cover up your bare arms. The laser surgery was even better than you'd hoped but what scars are left make your skin look wrinkly and that only adds to your disguise tonight. You slowly bend down like an old man should and pull your outfit back on, careful to keep your face and grey hair intact. You do one leg at a time, making a meal of it, and groan and stretch as you reach back and slowly slide your arms back in the armholes of your outfit.

You watch Hardy and Sophie, now at the far end of the line of people being searched. You didn't notice them at first but it will take more than blonde hair and a hat to throw you off their scent. But you're not ready for them yet. You're saving them for later. You nearly laughed when Hardy checked you over and looked you in the eye earlier. You knew he couldn't see past the green-grey contact lenses you're wearing, partly because they have cataracts blended in for that OAP touch. You didn't keep a straight face when Sophie took your picture but she said, "Say cheese, Granddad" so you went with it. You put the small, silver rimmed glasses with clear lenses back on. You pull on your white wig and beard. They're big and bushy and nothing like your normal slick disguises such as the one underneath.

You leave Hardy and Sophie and the search crew to it and slowly slip outside the small tent to head to the stage with the help of a policewoman whose perfume smells of sweet honey. She guides you through to the backstage. It's bitterly cold outside. You think of the old man you knocked unconscious, tied up and gagged and put in the boot of his car. He might not make it through the night. You're very proud of your research and preparation, finding out from your security contact that the old man would be part of the show. From there you were able to find out where he lived, what he looked like so you could match his old man's ID you've faked, then you simply followed him here in a hire car, parked at the same multi-story and jumped him as he got out of his car. You're now using his identity and staff pass, and will replace him on stage tonight. He was only partially sighted but you've embellished the blindness and added Sadie to help authenticate your disguise.

You nod and smile at the policewoman as she holds your arm and gives you back Sadie's lead. She was made to wait outside the search area. You could've smuggled some sort of concealed weapon in Sadie's special harness you've put on her this evening, but thought better of it. The police won't find any concealed weapons on you, though: you're not carrying any. You've got your backpack stashed in a dumpster two streets away with your guns and a second disguise. But for Hit No.1 you will mostly be using your bare hands, or anything you can lay your hands on. You're looking forward to improvising. The policewoman helps you up some stairs to the backstage area.

After a brief bit of small talk with the BBC stage manager, you're on. You put your hood up and shuffle past the reindeer. They smell earthy but seem very tame compared to the ones roaming wild back in the forests in North Wales. You take your position on stage and wave at the crowd cheering at you and the Mary Christmas dancing girls dressed up in sexy Christmas outfits. You take in the stage with its extravagant Christmas decorations and rows and rows of huge, bright lights. You like the massive tinsel, and the icicles look very realistic.

A long line of policemen are positioned below and around the stage. Half are facing the stage, half are facing the crowd. They're all wearing bullet-proof vests and you spot a few holding semi-automatic weapons.

*   *

In what feels like seconds, it's time for Jack Frost to make his grand entrance. The BBC compère gives him a heart-warming introduction and there are united sighs from the crowd when he mentions the cancer and ETA of Jack Frost's death. Backstage Denning is rubbing Cheadle's shoulders and giving him a final pep talk like he's a fighter. I know he's shitting himself about singing live, yet he's twice as concerned about the Hitman. But Cheadle is a policeman at heart and is staying focused and prepared for any attack. Sophie wishes him luck and pecks him on the cheek. I grit my teeth, clench my fist, and clench my buttocks although I don't think he notices, and say, "Do it for Great Britain, Jack."

Jack Frost seems to gain a few inches and his shoulders widen as he walks onto the stage, controlling his breathing, while the crowd greet him with rousing applause. Before the music begins there's an air of sadness and respectful silence from the crowd. They know – or think they know – this is his last Christmas. It will be for Jack Frost, hopefully not for Cheadle.

"Everybody stand by. Eyes open. The Hitman may strike at any moment," says Johnson over the police radio.

The sound of sleigh bells starts ringing out of the forty-foot high speakers. A white-haired, fully-bearded, red suited Father Christmas in little glasses is sat on a sleigh with seven very well-trained reindeer attached. The one on its own at the front is wearing a red plastic nose. As the drumbeats start rolling, the twelve Mary Christmases in red lipstick, white tops, red mini skirts and white tights start energetically dancing on stage. Fake snow begins to fall on stage from the makeshift rafters above and the crowd start cheering and clapping.

The trap is set. Cheadle's the cheese. Too bad McNamara's not a mouse. Sophie and I watch avidly from the side of the stage and hope to hell that when – not if – McNamara shows up, Cheadle and the Met police force will be ready.

Television cameras swing around on long mechanical arms high up in the gantry and in front of the crowds, filming anything that moves. MC Whitey is poised the other side of the stage ready to jump on and off for his rap. Denning and other detectives watch from the same side. Uniformed officers have alternated in front of the stage so half are watching over Jack Frost with the other half watching the crowds.

As Jack Frost starts singing the song he's been practicing over the past month, I do a little prayer inside to hope this won't be mine and Sophie's last Christmas. I make a conscious effort to not stick my head out so if McNamara's hiding up a tree or in a third floor window, he won't be able to blow our brains out. I pull Sophie back a little so we're hidden from view.

Cheadle sounds like he's been singing live to millions for years. I look at him on stage and for a moment, I forget it's Cheadle, as Jack Frost comes to life. He's really doing it. I think of Fat Pat who would've enjoyed the show if he hadn't decided to go to New York for Christmas. Every note sounds pitch perfect as Cheadle relaxes into his routine and starts enjoying himself, warming up the crowds of Leicester Square.

I eagerly scan the crowds for any sign of McNamara. The tempo and drumbeats change and MC Whitey joins Jack Frost on stage to cheers from youths in the crowd. He raps and swaggers and bounces and bobs. Jack Frost isn't quite sure what to do so he does a bit of bad-yet-endearing man dancing. MC Whitey runs off stage, as the chav contingent chant his name, leaving Jack Frost to sing the last verse beautifully.

My last Christmas but I give you my heart,
My last Christmas but I give you my heart

The crowd joins in, singing along. It's more than moving, but I can't help thinking McNamara's going to jump out from inside one of the reindeer at any moment and eat Cheadle's face off or something. But he doesn't, and Jack Frost continues to sing the final lines of our reworked masterpiece.

I'll give it to someone special,
I'll give it to someone special

As the sleigh bells and drums fade the crowd all stomp their feet and cheer louder and longer than they have done the whole evening. Jack Frost stays on stage and bows, waves and smiles as the crowd continue to cheer and clap. I'm sure I see a tear run down his cheek. Completely unscripted Jack Frost shouts into his microphone, "Thanks a lot London! I can't thank everyone enough! You've made my pop star dreams come true and you've made my last Christmas very special!"

Jack Frost exits stage left. The crowd goes spastic as some people cheer, others clap and clap and clap, some hug each other, and others break down and openly weep. Sophie rests her head on my shoulder.

I'll almost miss the singing oaf now his fifteen minutes of fame are over.

Backstage the Mary Christmases are jumping with joy and relief. Denning's hugging Cheadle in a relatively manly way by lifting him off the ground. The old man in his Father Christmas suit ambles by slowly with his guide dog. BBC crew in black coats unplug things, looking important with their clipboards and headphones. Police keep an eye on everyone as the BBC compère out front thanks the crowd for coming and hopes they'll have a very Merry Christmas and safe journey home. Carols start playing out of the huge speakers. The crowds start gradually, slowly filing out of the exits in the four corners of Leicester Square. Large groups of people remain, some still crying, others still hugging and a few couples are kissing. Jack Frost wasn't that good was he? Perhaps they're just all drunk.

But back to Operation: Mistletoe.

What an anticlimax. Where is he? Is he here?

I feel I can sense his presence.

But I could just be thinking of *presents*. The Christmas presents Sophie and I will open tomorrow.

Sophie is with me backstage talking to Gill Roach. Johnson calls me on the radio. "Matthews, can you see anyone down there? None of the Met have spotted anyone suspicious or anyone fitting any of the Hitman's previous disguises. I don't like it. I bloody well know he's here. I can feel his presence," says Johnson. He's at it too.

"It all seems under control," I say into the radio. "Cheadle looks relieved that he didn't cock up the song and that he's still alive. Denning's here, and there are only the Christmas lot from the stage, BBC staff and lots of Met police here. Over." I notice MC Whitey in the background hanging about and sleazing over one of the dancers.

"Okay, keep your eyes peeled down there. We'll keep watch from the tower up here," he says.

"Okay. Roger that. Over," I say.

Is it bad that all I really fancy now is a drink?

A BBC crew girl with impeccable timing brings round a tray of champagne and mulled wine and I grab two glasses of the warm stuff. I pass Sophie a glass and we chink and drink. It heats up my mouth and the warm glass soothes my frozen fingers. I hold Sophie's hand to make sure she stays with me, and to keep my other hand warm.

*   *

You hobble past the BBC crew in the sheltered backstage area and resist the urge to scratch the flaky, old-looking skin on your face or rub the itchy contacts in your eyes. You make your breathing appear laboured as you walk, stooped over, holding the handle attached to Sadie's harness and pretending she's your guide. Walking like this means you can hide the fact you've got a long fake icicle hidden up your big red sleeve. It's made of plastic, but feels real judging by how cold it is in your hand.

BBC crew hand round drinks and look set to wind down now the show's over. You spot Hardy talking with Sophie and another woman. You don't bother to say hello as you can see your target down the other end. He's hugging a man who's wearing a bullet-proof vest over a jacket. A policeman. They seem close. That's strange.

You slowly make your way towards him acting like there's no hurry. Nobody's paying you any attention. Nobody wants to talk to the old blind man. The other man leaves your target alone for a minute so you seize your opportunity.

"Jack Frost, dear boy?" you say in a croaky voice. Jack Frost looks across and you beckon him over to where you're standing hunched old man-like near an exit. You can feel the cold draft from the doorway.

"Father Christmas! Did you enjoy that?" says Jack Frost animatedly, and loudly, probably because he thinks you're deaf as well as blind. "Wasn't it a totally amazing atmosphere!? I'll never experience that again."

You pull your big, bushy white Father Christmas beard down slowly to reveal an old man's grey beard underneath.

"I guess you won't, you poor, poor boy," you say. He doesn't seem that terminally ill apart from some pale skin and bloodshot eyes. Maybe they've pumped him full of drugs. You slowly say, "It's been a wonderful evening, so not wanting to piss on your fire, so to speak…"

Jack Frost lets out a raucous laugh, and you smile revealing your old man's dirty dentures. You rest your arm on a large black amp, still hiding the icicle from view with your big sleeve. A group of policemen are chatting to the dancing girls. You edge around so their view of Jack Frost is blocked by the amp. There aren't any TV cameras, and you can't see Sophie from here so that means her camera can't see you.

"I just want to say I'm so sorry to learn of your very sad situation," you say. "At least you can go out on a high."

"That's why I did it. I always wanted to be a pop star. I love karaoke!" says Jack Frost. "Getting the chance to sing a version of Wham's classic song live on stage, in front of millions of people on TV, was a dream come true."

There's something you don't like about his spiel, and not just because he likes karaoke. It's like he's reading it off a cue sheet. Maybe he's been saying the same thing to the papers all week. You let go of Sadie's lead and she wanders outside for a sniff. You pretend you want to give Jack Frost your condolences and reach up to give him a big hug, but as he bends down you act as if you've stumbled and grab his right shoulder with your left hand.

"Easy there, Father Christmas," says Jack Frost.

You can feel the edge of a bullet-proof vest hidden under his white suit and shirt. The texture is unmistakable. That's not good. The police have obviously given him one to wear as protection from you.

You hold on to him with your left hand and let your right arm hang straight down, hiding the icicle in your hand with the large sleeve. Jack Frost thinks you're grabbing him to stop wobbling and stays crouched over to hold you up, helpfully exposing his left side. In one swift move you feed the icicle down into your right hand, hold it up and drive down hard and fast under his armpit and vest to penetrate

344

his heart. You push it all the way in as Jack Frost gasps silently. You've hit the spot because he goes quiet and limp and loosens his grip on you. You support him and let him flop on to you so it looks like you're hugging, making sure the wound is out of view from everyone backstage. His breathing becomes erratic as he gasps for air.

"Merry bloody Christmas," you whisper in his ear.

You quickly glance over his shoulder while you pat his back. You're still partly hidden by the amp, but you can see all the crew are drinking and joking, and the handful of police are still chatting to the dancers. You can't see Hardy from where you're standing, you can just see the side of Sophie's face. She looks pretty with her shorter, blonde hair.

Pushing up with your legs you quickly stand up straight and lean Jack Frost's considerable dead weight softly against the amp, making sure he's not going to fall over. His mouth is partly open, his eyes look like they want to blink and blood is starting to stain his white suit. You duck out the door before his body has a chance to hit the ground.

Instead of the old man's hobble, you walk quickly away from the backstage area. Sadie runs to catch you up. You pick up her lead and, checking no police are looking, you run behind a line of double-stacked portacabins. You check your watch. 9:24pm. You pull your Father Christmas beard back in place, reposition your wig and glasses, and walk around the cabins until you find a big BBC lorry. You tie Sadie's lead underneath so she's sitting in the darkness and out of sight.

"You've been a good dog," you say as you rub her soft, furry ears.

You hate to do this, but you don't need her anymore now, and you will not compromise your position. You feed Sadie a Mars Bar from your pocket that you've injected with poison. She gobbles down the chocolate in one.

"Goodbye girl," you say as you put the Mars wrapper in your Father Christmas suit pocket.

You walk out from behind the cabins and join the crowds still streaming out of one of the exits. You walk past a bank of armed police staring over the departing mob as the BBC plays Christmas carols to send everyone on their way. You walk quickly but inconspicuously and fall in behind a group of smartly dressed men so you're out of sight of any police near the BBC stage. You try to ignore the shouts of "Santa, I've been a good boy this Christmas!" as you walk past them but give them a "Ho! Ho! Ho!" to shut them up.

There are no security or police checking the general public on the way out so you drift off into the night, walking less like a hunched old man, and more like the broad shouldered, confident Hitman with each stride.

Hit No.1. Done and bloody dusted.

You feel euphoric. You can't help grinning and giving a few more merrymakers a "Ho! Ho! Ho!" as you glide away from Leicester Square.

*   *

Hark The Herald Angels Sing is streaming out of the speakers all around backstage and I hear someone's high-pitched voice singing along. It's so high it sounds as if someone's messing about. It's not until more high-pitched singers join in that I realise it's not people singing, it's people screaming. Denning runs over to the screams like a shot. Sophie drops her wine and runs towards the noise which seems to be coming from several female BBC crew. Like human homing missiles police officers and crew are drawn towards the commotion. I hurry past people to reach Sophie's side.

It's Cheadle. Blood has turned his white Jack Frost suit dark red. The tip of something is sticking out of his chest near his armpit. It looks like the end of a white plastic stake. His eyes are open but he doesn't blink. He looks like he's concentrating.

Women continue to scream and others hold their hands over their mouths. Uniformed policemen stare in disbelief. BBC crew and roadies appear, have a look and turn away unsure what to do.

Nobody knows what to say.

Denning quickly squats down and checks for a pulse. He holds his fingers to Cheadle's neck, getting some blood on his hands in the process. After an age he removes his fingers and slowly shakes his head.

"What's going on down there? Somebody's said they heard women screaming." Johnson's voice crackles out of the radio in my pocket and Denning's radio strapped to his chest. Still nobody knows what to say, including me.

Denning reaches for his radio, takes a deep breath, stares directly at his best mate dead on the floor and says, "Denning here, sir. It's Cheadle. The bastard's got him."

"What the... Jesus bloody Christ no! How... what...?" says Johnson.

"He was only chatting to the old blind man two minutes ago, the one dressed as Father Christmas... wherever he's gone with his dog..." I stop mid-sentence.

McNamara and his dog.

They've just played blind man's bluff.

"McNamara is the old blind man dressed as Father Christmas, his guide dog is his Labrador Sadie," I say in a strange monotone.

It's terrifying to think he's been here all along, taking the piss out of the entire Metropolitan police force. So conspicuous he became inconspicuous.

Denning looks up at me then starts shouting into his radio. "Sir, he's the old blind man in the Father Christmas outfit. He has a Labrador guide dog with him."

"Father Christmas!? The one who was on the sleigh?" shouts Johnson.

"I'm afraid so, sir," says Denning still looking at Cheadle's motionless face.

"And where is he now!?"

"Disappeared, sir," says Denning apologetically.

"Jesus Christ, Denning," shouts Johnson. There's a hint of a pause, then Johnson's back on the radio. "Right, all units, all units, everybody listen up. This is now a Red Alert. Everyone be on their guard, we all know how dangerous the Hitman can be – with or without weapons. I want every man looking high and low for a blind Father Christmas, possibly with a Labrador guide dog. I want every armed and unarmed officer hunting inside and outside Leicester Square. I want the Met squads to split into groups of threes searching the surrounding two mile radius using their local knowledge of every goddamn back street and hiding hole, up past Charing Cross Road, across Shaftsbury Avenue, past Trafalgar Square and across Haymarket. Hunt that bastard down. Put armed police on all the exits here in Leicester Square. Anybody who's still here doesn't leave without being searched for a Father Christmas outfit or old man's disguise."

I'm amazed Johnson can function so professionally when one of his closest colleagues is lying dead at our feet.

"I'll spread the word up here to the rest of the Met. I want men on the entrance and exits to the Underground stations checking everyone and every Father Christmas in the area," Johnson says shouting even louder. "I want him found. Nobody gets away with killing one of our own men. I don't care if he's dead or alive. If you find him, shoot the bastard..."

The armed policemen surrounding us dart off in all directions. A uniformed officer calls an ambulance on his radio.

"DS Price and DS Carson, you two stick with Hardy and Sophie. The Hitman may well come back for them next," says Johnson over the radio.

DS Price and DS Carson appear by our side and look alert, while we look scared.

"I thought I recognised Sadie earlier, but I saw the guide dog harness and figured she was just another Labrador, and that I was being paranoid," says Sophie quietly, holding her forehead.

"The crafty bastard was even on stage as Cheadle was singing…" I shut my big mouth as Cheadle's wife pushes through the gathered crowds. I stand aside as she walks past to be greeted by the sight of her husband's lifeless body covered in blood, sprawled out on the floor. Denning looks up at her but he doesn't need to say anything. She knows from the crestfallen look in Denning's eyes that it's the terrible, terrible news every policeman's wife fears.

She screams so loudly I'm scared the stage will fall down on top of us.

*   *

You walk around the block from Leicester Square, weaving around the hordes swaggering and swaying from pub to pub. You slip down a narrow, dead-end side street that leads to a dumpster, you reach in and rummage through the pungent rubbish to retrieve your black backpack. There are no streetlights down here to illuminate your position as you see three policemen run past the top of the street.

Crouching down behind the dumpster you quickly take off your Father Christmas glasses, wig, beard, boots and suit, carefully pull the old man's skin off your face, and pluck out the contact lenses. You take off the old man's jumper, shirt and chino trousers and put on a T-shirt, some dark jeans and a pair of black boots from your backpack. You put the sealed polythene bag from your pack safely in your jeans pocket. You put on your old army bullet-proof vest that you've decorated with your home-made squibs and make sure the small liquid sacks are in place before you carefully pull a black jumper over the top. You pull out a black cap from your pack and pull it down firmly on your head. You yank out the black BBC Crew jacket you procured from the corporation last year when you did some security work for them, and clip on the fake BBC ID. It says Andrew Scott, BBC Christmas Chart Show, Assistant Production Manager. Above it is a mug shot of you in your cap from your trip to a photo booth last week. You put a remote control detonator safely in your jacket pocket.

You shove the Father Christmas and old man disguises into the middle of the dumpster and squeeze some lighter fluid all over them, then use a match to light it. You put the fluid and matches back in your pack, wipe off any rubbish hanging off your backpack and walk away as flames start to leap up out of the dumpster.

You hustle through the crowded streets and dive into a pub that's heaving with revellers. It's hot and steamy inside. Police inside have handcuffed a confused-looking man in a Father Christmas suit and are marching him outside. You head straight for the toilets. You wait until two men have finished, then shove a wedge from your backpack under the door to stop anyone coming in. You check yourself in the mirror and pull off any Father Christmas hairs and old man skin left on your face. You've still got the old man's teeth in so you put those in your backpack. You wash the grey from your beard until it's all black again. You quickly splash some water on your face and gargle a bit. You can feel a headache coming on but you refuse to let it bother you.

You look at your reflection.

You've given yourself a short crew cut when at the hideaway and you're not wearing a fake beard this time – you've got your real one instead. You feel naked yet you've never felt more invisible. You are yourself. The police have been so busy circulating all your various disguises they've assumed you wouldn't ever return to your real hair-colour and natural look.

You slip out of the toilet, and out of the pub, and hastily walk past the crowds and bars, cafés and cinemas, and past three armed policemen. Two of them are trying to arrest an old, bearded homeless man. He's pleading for them not to shoot. Three other uniformed policemen march past with another man in a Father Christmas suit. Your plan is working even better than expected. You reach what's left of the BBC Chart Show and from outside the temporary fencing you can see the main stage lights are off now. However the streetlights and lights from the cinema façades mean it's far from dark. You walk against the flow of the last of the crowds filtering slowly out from Leicester Square.

On a gate in the corner a young, armed policeman is trying to keep control of the impatient queue of people trying to leave.

"I'm really sorry officer," you say. He spins round and looks at you with an eye still on the queue of people. "I'm such an idiot. I was so keen to get to the pub I left my wallet in Portacabin No.5. Mind if I pop back in quickly?"

The queues of people are shouting about it being Christmas Eve and shouldn't they have checked people going in, not going out. The young policeman tries to remain unflustered as he clocks the BBC jacket and ID badge you're wearing. "You got any more ID?" he says officiously.

"It's in my wallet," you give him a smile. He's not looking for you, he's only interested in an old, blind man in a Father Christmas suit.

"Go on then, be quick," says the policeman and lets you through. He doesn't notice your black backpack. You squeeze past the queue of people and back to scene of the crime.

You've made it back in fourteen minutes. You don't retrace your steps behind the cabins, instead you walk directly towards the stage as police walk in all directions except yours. All that's left on the otherwise empty stage is the sleigh you'd sat on earlier. Roadies are starting to take down gantries and moving the soundstage equipment. You think back to Cardiff to Hit No.10 and how your ambitious pop project all started. Was that really nine months ago? You walk around the backstage but the party's over. An ambulance is parked up with its rear doors open. A woman is sobbing uncontrollably as two paramedics slowly wheel out a man strapped to a stretcher.

Jack Frost.

It was his last Christmas but at least he gave you his heart.

You smile but not too openly as you walk past policemen helping the woman climb into the back of the ambulance. Jack Frost's eyes are closed. You can still see the tip of the icicle sticking out of his chest. A blanket covers the rest of his body with his shoes poking out at the bottom. He doesn't have any breathing equipment attached to his mouth.

You didn't need clarification that your Top 10 Hits were a resounding success, but it's nice to get some stone, cold, dead evidence.

Your No.1 Hit.

Gone, and now forgotten. You need to move on. You've got two more of Santa's little helpers to deal with before you can celebrate Christmas.

It's 9:41pm as you walk towards the tent that was used for the security checks earlier. You find a few BBC staff milling about and one or two are crying. None of them look twice at you. You keep walking and head around the front of the stage, passing uniformed policemen talking into radios and mobile phones. Only plastic glasses and programmes are left where the crowds stood earlier.

In the far corner of the square, uniformed officers frisk people. You head back to the banks of portacabins. You're about to look elsewhere when you catch sight of a man and woman in black jackets stood near one of the cabins, the former pacing around, the latter biting her fingernails. They're not BBC as they don't have the logo on their backs. You're about to dismiss them when you catch a glimpse of blonde hair. The man turns around and even with his hat on you recognise him.

Hardy and Sophie.

They look a little lost.

A couple of policemen are stood with them.

You slide your backpack off your back and squat down. You quickly dip inside your pack and put your hand on your Glock 17 that's strapped to the lining. Checking nobody can see you, and bending over to hide your pack, you pull out your gun and put it swiftly in your jacket pocket. You slip your pack on your back, put your hand in your pocket, your finger on the trigger, and pop over to say good evening.

Or should that be good night.

"Hello you two," you say, making sure the two policeman are out of earshot.

Hardy turns around but doesn't acknowledge you. Sophie looks confused and reads your Andrew Scott BBC ID. Both of their eyes are red and Sophie still looks teary. Hardy looks you up and down and politely says, "Hello?"

"Hello," says Sophie.

"Hello," you say and smile.

"Hardy, you remember? This is Andrew. Andrew Scott? He's from the BBC," says Sophie. Bless her, trying to cover for him by pretending to know who you are. Not realising you're a threat, the two armed policeman walk off to check something by the side of the square.

"Of course," says Hardy. "I knew I recognised your face from somewhere. I wasn't sure because of the cap, and the beard…"

Hardy stops talking and stares at you, his mouth hangs open slightly.

"Hardy? You alright?" says Sophie looking at him. "Sorry Andrew, we're both still in shock after Chea… I mean, poor Jack Frost was…" Sophie grips hold of Hardy's arm and sniffs back some tears. "Sorry, did you hear what happened backstage? It's very, very sad news I'm afraid."

Hardy looks like he's seen a ghost.

"Of course I bloody heard about it. I did it!" you say brightly.

"Oh fuck… it's you," says Hardy quietly.

Now Sophie stares at you too.

"It's me, McNamara," you say and smile cheerfully. " Now, don't say a fucking word. Either of you." You flash them a shufti of your Glock.

"You wouldn't dare shoot me. Not here," says Hardy. His jaw and neck muscles visibly tense up.

"Don't be daft, not you. I'm going to shoot Sophie," you say, and grab Sophie's right arm with your left, pulling her in close. With your right arm across your front you push the gun into her rib cage through her jacket and dress, hiding it under your left elbow so the gun's out of sight. "Wrap your arm around mine," you say.

Sophie does as she's told. Hardy's not sure what to do.

351

"I'm wearing a bullet-proof vest so why shouldn't I scream for help right now?" says Sophie, in a burst of flippancy.

"I'm using armour piercing bullets. Want to see if they work?" you say.

Sophie's legs give way and you pull her up and dig the gun back into her side.

"What happened to old Father Christmas and his guide dog?" says Hardy.

"I had to dump them," you say.

"Very clever cover, Mac," says Hardy.

"No more talking please children," you say sternly, while jabbing the gun into Sophie's ribs. "Not another a word. Don't make me shoot you in the legs like a Dragonfly. Such nice legs. I'm sure you'd like to keep using them, if only for the rest of the night," you say. "You know I'll do it. I'm chicken oriental, me. Now nod if you understand."

Sophie nods. Her face looks timid. Hardy nods, and looks livid.

"Great. Let's go for a little walk," you say

You lead them away from the stage and towards the quietest corner and exit. Hardy walks by your side as you walk with Sophie with her arm linked through yours and the gun nuzzled into her ribs. Policemen rush all around. Two more walk past with a blind man and his dog. You're getting a great buzz from outsmarting them for a second time tonight when you notice Hardy staring wildly at a pair of policeman.

"Take that look out of your eyes Hardy." His eyes are full of fury and frustration. You steer them both behind a line of trees and up to a pair of policewomen guarding the exit gate. The queues have almost disappeared now.

"Sorry folks just need to check your ID please," says the policewoman.

"No problem," you say. You look down indicating the BBC ID on your jacket.

"That's fine, thank you Andrew," says the policewoman.

"Cheers," you say. Her radio attached to her chest buzzes, then a crackly voice says, "We've found the dog under the lorry... It's dead."

You don't let it show, but inside your heart skips a beat. You keep hold of Sophie's arm as she slowly pulls out some sort of Met ID. Hardy flashes the same.

The policewoman smiles as she looks at Hardy and Sophie. "Won't keep you a moment longer folks. Have a good night."

"Good night," you say. You walk off, still prodding the gun into Sophie's ribs. Outside of the square, a man in a suit throws up against a wall. You pass people semi-dancing in the street as cars drive by and beep their horns. Corny Christmas songs blare out of a big, brash bar across the road. You notice CCTV cameras attached to walls and a bank of cameras further down at a crossroads. They won't be able to see anything more than three people among hundreds out enjoying Christmas Eve. You look at Hardy and Sophie's long faces.

You shuffle down to Charing Cross Road. Sophie makes a fuss of walking in her heels as Hardy walks stiff and tense next to you. The traffic is busy but flowing. You hear a voice through some sort of shortwave radio and Hardy instinctively pats his pocket. You stop and say, "Show me." He begrudgingly pulls out a police radio from his pocket and hands it over. "And your mobile phones," you say.

Hardy passes you his from his pocket and Sophie plucks hers from her purse and gives it to you.

"You won't be needing them now," you say and drop them all into a nearby bin. "Right, let's get a taxi," you announce. Hardy looks at Sophie. She looks at him.

"Where are you taking us, Liverpool?" says Hardy sarcastically.

"Shut it!" you shout, "I said no talking."

"Ow!" says Sophie. You must've pushed the gun into her ribs.

"Flag a taxi down, Hardy my man," you say.

He hesitates but puts his arm up and seconds later a black cab pulls over. You shove the gun in your jacket pocket but keep your finger on the trigger, and slip off your backpack. You sit on the back seat with Sophie to your left, and prod the gun into her hip, hiding it from view under left forearm. Hardy sits opposite you with his back to the driver.

"Where you wanna go?" says the taxi driver in an Eastern European accent.

"Docklands," you say.

"No problem," he says.

"Got a boat to catch?" says Hardy.

You ignore him.

"You taking us swimming?" says Sophie.

"I'd rather not talk if it's all the same to you two. Let's be quiet and enjoy the drive," you say, cocking the hammer back with a satisfying click.

They don't need telling twice.

Compared to central London, the Docklands feel like a ghost town. The streets throughout the office blocks are empty, only the odd light is on at a seventh or fifteenth floor. There are no pubs or restaurants around here, no Christmas carols and no drunken singing, just the occasional sound of an airplane flying into London City Airport and the hum of traffic on the dual carriageways in the distance. The wind blows pieces of litter up in the air as the wintry weather chills your bones.

You show Hardy and Sophie the way through some empty car parks and down flights of steps to a wide concrete path leading along the side of the Thames. Streetlights are positioned every fifty metres. Not even a lone drunk or beggar ventures around here at night. Apart from the wind whipping off the top of the river, it's quiet and peaceful.

Hardy's the first to break the silence. "You do realise your No.1 Hit this evening wasn't a real pop star don't you?"

"Of course. I knew he wasn't a cancer victim," you say.

"But did you know Jack Frost was an undercover detective?" says Hardy firmly.

"An undercover cop? Oh dear. Now they'll really be after me," you say mischievously.

"You don't care you've killed an innocent policeman?" says Sophie still tight to your side. Your finger twitches on the trigger.

You think for a second, then say, "In one way it was really important who my No.1 Hit was tonight. But on another level it didn't matter who, it mattered when. I needed to make a big impact with my final hit. It's all about the pop project as a whole – not the people," you say.

Neither of them respond.

"Isn't that right Sophie?" you say. You keep the gun stuck in her ribs and slip your arm around her neck to get her in a playful headlock. Her breathing quickens, but she doesn't say anything. You'd like to snap her neck. You've been thinking about it for long enough.

Hardy looks at you like he wants to kill you.

Everything's going according to plan.

"Now, no more stupid fucking questions," you say. "Or I'll shoot your faces off and shove them up each other's arses."

You release the grip around Sophie's neck but keep your arm around her, and walk along the side of the Thames until you're behind the gigantic ExCel buildings that cover an area the size of Wales. The exhibitions and trade shows have long been closed for the night and there won't be any security knocking about anymore. You can only hear the faint sound of traffic now.

It's a perfect place for a perfect double murder.

You stop and let go of Sophie so you're standing equal distance from her and Hardy. You wave the gun around, pointing it up at the sky.

"Right, I'm going to let you keep your vests on. My bullets will pierce them anyway, but just so you know, I'll be aiming at your heads," you say.

You start tossing the gun from hand to hand, watching them closely, never taking your eyes off them.

"Okay who wants to be first?"

*   *

Whenever I've seen an upset in a rugby game and the underdog has managed to overpower the bigger, better players, it's always been down to sheer hunger and self belief. As I look at McNamara under the streetlight playing with a gun in his lump hammer fists, I remind myself over and over that this is one fight I will not lose. So what if he's a trained killer and he's got a gun. I've got a score to settle. I've got an arse to kick. Bring it on.

"I'm first," I say. I move in front of Sophie to act as a shield.

"Oh God, oh God. Be careful Hardy," Sophie says. I was born to be careful. Or careless. That's not important right now.

McNamara circles around. So do we. He circles around again so his back's facing the river.

"But I wanted to do Sophie first," he whimpers.

I think of his threat on the phone to kill Sophie and make me watch. I cannot let that happen. I clench my fists like I'm crushing cashew nuts. I squeeze them tighter and move towards McNamara. We're really close now. He's still chucking the gun from hand to hand.

I briefly wonder if there's someway Johnson will find us in time and save us. He would probably say clichéd things like, "Can't we work this out?" But I don't want to. I want to annihilate the bastard.

"Come 'n' 'ave a go if you think you're 'ard enough," he says.

Alright then.

I move towards him and feign to crack him with my left but quickly catch him hard and square on the jaw with my right. His eyes roll back in their sockets and McNamara goes down for the count.

Well, he would have if he hadn't deftly dipped out of the way to leave me wildly swinging at thin air.

McNamara grins, inviting me to move in again. He takes his eyes off me for a split second to catch the gun. I lamp him good and proper around side of the skull putting my full body weight behind the punch. McNamara thinks he's invincible. I don't think he ever considered I'd land one on him. I knew I would. It's enough to knock him off balance and drop the gun. It rattles across the concrete floor and is now nearer to me than him. The silver glints under the streetlight. I throw myself onto the gun, and manage to grab it and roll over on my shoulder. I quickly get back up with the gun in my hand, pointing it up at him.

I'm in control now. I've got the gun.

But in the time I've taken to dive and get the gun, he's got Sophie.

"Careful. You might shoot the wrong one," says McNamara as he puts his arms around her neck once again. He's got a thing about her neck.

I will not let him take away the woman I love this time. I stand up without taking my aim off him as he backs towards the waist-high metal railings by the side of the river. The gun feels heavy but nicely weighted. The metal handle is still warm from being in McNamara's hands.

"Let her go, McNamara," I say trying to sound like I'm the one in charge.

"Make me," he says like an insolent brat.

He hides partly behind Sophie. I move my aim across to his shoulder and he moves Sophie around to block my shot. I raise my aim up to his head and he ducks behind Sophie.

"Who's head are you aiming at?" he laughs.

I can't get a clear shot. Even if I was a good shot I could easily shoot Sophie by mistake. I suddenly realise that I may be a very bad shot.

"Heads up!" he laughs.

I keep my gun on them as McNamara continues to hold Sophie's neck in his vice-like grip.

"Heads or tails?" he says bobbing out from behind Sophie.

Unexpectedly Sophie wriggles and lashes out with her elbow into his stomach. McNamara flinches but doesn't let go. Instead he grips her neck even tighter.

"Get off me you bloody bastard," says Sophie.

"Make me," he says.

Sophie manages to make him by stamping down hard on his foot with one of her heels. Even through his boots she makes fleshy contact. McNamara lets go and hops back on one foot. High heels do have a purpose after all. Sophie runs to me, puts her hand on my shoulder and hides behind me. McNamara bends over and his backpack slides off his shoulder and onto the floor with a clunk. I hope he's not got a bomb in there.

I keep pointing the gun at him. It starts feeling heavy but there's no way I'm dropping my guard now. He's had a hold over our lives for too long. Now I hold a gun over his.

Sophie is screaming. "Don't do it Hardy! Don't do it! Don't do it!"

I partly hear her but it's muffled by a noisy jet flying overhead.

McNamara starts to pull something from his backpack. It's another gun. Can Sophie see it? I don't know. He stands up and looks at me. He holds the gun in his hand but doesn't raise it. He looks too casual because his other hand's in his jacket pocket.

"Well, this isn't exactly going to plan," he says flatly.

"Oh Christ, he's got another gun!"

I can't let him kills us. Not now. Not after everything.

"Don't let him kill us Hardy! Don't let him!" she screams.

I keep the gun trained on him, holding it in two hands to keep it steady. I have to concentrate to stop my hands shaking. I aim at his heart. I know he hasn't got one but I can't bring myself to shoot him in the head – or take the chance of missing him.

"Okay. I'm going to raise my gun, Hardy, and I'm going to shoot you between the eyes. The blood from your brains will probably spray over Sophie to match her nice red dress," he says. "Then I will shoot Sophie in the face."

He stops talking. I will not let him kill us.

I keep my gun on him. My heart's going like a piston.

I stare into his cold, empty eyes.

It doesn't all happen in slow motion, like they say, it happens on fast-forward. McNamara raises his gun. Before he's got it high enough, I squeeze my trigger. The noise is deafening, smoke fills the cold Christmas air. I squint as I pull the trigger again and again. I think I fire three shots into his torso as thick blood sprays from his chest after each impact. McNamara's body judders backwards. He's still holding the gun as he tumbles over the railings and disappears into the Thames.

I drop the gun to the ground as the realisation that I've just shot a man hits me. I feel like I've taken a bullet myself. Although I'm not the one who's been blasted into the fast flowing, icy river. My ears are ringing. I can't bring myself to look over the railings. My body starts shaking.

"Oh my God, Hardy."

"Cripes, that was bloody loud wasn't it?" But I can't hear myself or Sophie.

"Oh my God, Hardy. Oh my God."

"I can't hear you," I say.

I pick the gun backup and walk slowly over to the railings. I look over the edge, but there's no sign of McNamara's body. I walk back and forth along the edge with one hand on the cold metal railings while pointing the gun down towards the water. The Thames looks black under the weak streetlight as the powerful current moves downstream. McNamara is swimming with the fishes now.

Or maybe he's taking a shortcut straight down to hell.

"I can't believe I shot... a fellow man."

"A Hitman."

"But still, a man."

"It was self-defence. You had no choice."

The ringing in my ears fades slightly.

"He was going to shoot you and then he was going to shoot me. It was self-defence. You had no choice, self-defence…" Sophie's gabbling. She grips my hand and I can feel her shaking as we stare down at the surging river. "It was self defence. It was you and me or him. Self defence…" Sophie squeezes my hand even tighter.

"It's okay, it's over now," I say.

"You've just killed the Hitman… you're a Hitman killer…"

I can't really hear, and I'm not really listening.

"I need to get rid of this thing," I say, holding the gun up in disgust. I hurl the gun into the middle of the river. A few seconds later there's a small splash.

"I need a big drink," I say.

I put my arm around Sophie and we start walking back along the Thames. Every few steps I look over my shoulder half expecting to see McNamara, with seaweed hanging off his face, about to lunge at us. But not even he can survive bullets and sub-zero waters. We keep walking as Sophie holds me tightly. I check my watch. It tells me it's past midnight.

Which also means it's tomorrow.

"Happy Christmas, Sophie."

Sophie looks up at me. She smiles and pulls me close to give me the best kiss of my life.

"Happy Christmas, Hardy."

Christ, why would anyone ever want to go swimming on Christmas Day? The water's literally freezing. It's even worse with the dragging current of the Thames. Even so, you keep swimming for a hundred metres, out of the glare of streetlights on the river's edge. Your head aches and you're struggling to breath as your body tries to shut down because of the ice-cold water. You quickly swim to the side and drag yourself up the long metal ladder bolted to the riverside wall. You start shivering as your water-soaked clothing turns brittle with the cold.

You peer up and down the pavement to check they've gone. They're gone. Long gone. Which means they bought it.

You've bloody done it.

You look down at the gun in your hand. Don't need it anymore. Better lose it now. You toss it into the river, and wonder if Hardy enjoyed the kill as much as you do. Probably not. He's too soft. You enjoyed acting out the fall into the Thames. You've seen many a body reel backwards after being shot so you knew how to make it look believable. You knew how much of a fight to put up beforehand too, and which buttons to press to make them want to kill you. You smile as you think of the blanks you'd put in the other gun, using the magazine you'd taken from the Nuff Respect Crew hit all those months ago.

You run back to where you left your backpack. You're so, so cold. You frantically tear off your wet clothes and jog on the spot as you rip off what's left of the fake blood soaked-squibs and bullet-proof vest. You rub your bare chest. A few scorch marks from the explosive, and some of your own blood, but nothing that won't heal. You pull on a thin Merino wool base layer and another wool layer from your pack. You're still shivering as you pull on a thick roll-neck jumper that reminds you of Sadie as she always got excited when you wore it as it meant time for her walk. You'll miss the daft old girl.

You hear the distant sound of fireworks. You keep checking left and right to make sure you're alone. With numb hands you rub the water out of your hair and put a wool hat on. You quickly pull on a fresh pair of pants, trousers and some socks from your pack, and pull your wet boots back on. You reach inside the wet pocket of your jeans to find the sealed polythene bag, you take out a thick roll of notes and a fake passport, and tuck them into your trouser pocket.

You sling the wet clothes and backpack into the river and break into a jog along the Thames, heading in the opposite direction you came from. After half a mile you jog past the large Sunborn Yacht

Hotel that's moored against the dockside. As you run you can feel the warmth coming back to your legs and chest. You keep jogging. Only a few more miles to go until London City Airport.

Beyond The Charts

The times they are a-changing
Bob Dylan

It makes a refreshing change to be stood by the side of the Barrowlands stage in Glasgow and not have to think about how you're going to kill the band that are singing in front of an adoring crowd. You drink your beer, smile with pride and pat your leg along to the melody. You haven't had a headache since you were in London over eighteen months ago. Your dark hair has turned slightly grey but that hasn't stopped you growing it down to your shoulders. Your trimmed beard has turned ever so slightly ginger. You've got used to wearing the dark brown contact lenses everyday now.

Your tight-knit rock band are called Boxer and they are four twenty-somethings from Glasgow. Larry the lead guitarist is a singer-songwriter, the rhythm guitarist and bass player have written four of the twelve songs on their album, and the drummer just loves to sit at the back and play his drums. You've seen them cook up a storm many times when playing their confident, tuneful songs. Larry has an impressive vocal range, a voice with a lot of heart, and he leads well from the front.

But what made you want to become their manager was that they didn't create Boxer to become rich and famous. They just love music. They just want to hang out, write some great songs and play on stage when they can get gigs. They want to make enough to get by and perhaps enough to buy a minibus to go on a UK tour next year. You've already said you'd drive it. You won't be going near any cliffs this time though.

With your backing and guidance, and a few suggestions on chord changes, Boxer released their first single three weeks ago. It's a beautifully melodic, guitar-led rock song that's starting to get a respectable amount of radio time. It's already proving a popular download thanks to Boxer's MySpace site activity. It went straight into the charts at No.43 in its first week and now it's up to No.14. You may break the Top 10 if this continues.

You like to think you've helped make this happen. Not just by being Boxer's manager, but by changing the music industry for the greater good. Money-hungry A&R men and pop band managers now think twice before creating a manufactured band.

You sip your beer and enjoy the sound of the guitar solo. Half the Scottish crowd already know the words, the others are content to pogo along.

And what's the single called?

I Always Wanted To Be A Rock Star

You knew you'd make it.

The End